D0210720

THE SHIELD OF TIME

ALSO BY POUL ANDERSON
Published by Tor Books

*Alight in the Void**
A Midsummer Tempest
The Boat of a Million Years
No Truce with Kings
The Saturn Game
Tales of the Flying Mountains
Hoka! (with Gordon R. Dickson)
*The Longest Voyage**
*The Queen of Air and Darkness**
*Tales of the Time Patrol**

The Psychotechnic Saga:
The Psychotechnic League
Starship
Cold Victory

(*forthcoming)

THE SHIELD OF TIME

POUL ANDERSON

A TOM DOHERTY ASSOCIATES BOOK
NEW YORK

Designed by Diane Stevenson/SNAP-HAUS GRAPHICS

THE SHIELD OF TIME

A Tor Book
Published by Tom Doherty Associates, Inc.
49 West 24th Street
New York, N.Y. 10010

Printed in the United States of America

Quality Printing and Binding by:
Berryville Graphics
P.O. Box 272
Berryville, VA 22611 U.S.A.

TO FELICE AND BLAKE

CONTENTS

CONTENTS

THE SHIELD OF TIME

PART ONE

THE STRANGER THAT IS WITHIN THY GATES

1987 A.D.

Maybe returning to New York on the day after he left it had been a mistake. Even here, just now, the springtime was too beautiful. A dusk like this was not one in which to sit alone, remembering. Rain had cleared the air for a while, so that through open windows drifted a ghost of blossoms and green. Lights and noises from the streets below were somehow softened, turned riverlike. Manse Everard wanted out.

He might have gone for a walk in Central Park, pocketing a stun gun in case of trouble. No policeman of this century would know it for a weapon. Better, when he had lately seen too much violence—any amount was too much—he could have strolled downtown along a route till he ended in one or another of the little taverns he knew, for beer and homely companionship. If he chose to get away altogether, he could requisition a timecycle at Patrol headquarters and seek whatever era he chose, anyplace on Earth. An Unattached agent needn't give reasons.

A phone call had trapped him. He prowled the darkening apartment, pipe a-fume between teeth, and occasionally swore at himself. Ridiculous, this mood. Sure, a letdown after action was natural; but he'd already enjoyed two easy weeks back in Hiram's Tyre, taking care of leftover details after his mission was done. As for Bronwen, he'd provided for her, rejoining her could only destroy the measure of contentment she'd found, the calendar said that tonight she lay twenty-nine hundred years dust, and there should be an end of the matter.

The doorbell relieved him. He snapped on the lights, blinked in the sudden harshness, and admitted his visitor. "Good evening, Agent Everard," greeted the man in subtly accented English. "I am Guion. I hope this is in fact not an inconvenient hour for you."

"No, no. I agreed to it when you rang, didn't I?" They shook hands. Everard doubted that the gesture occurred in Guion's native milieu, whenever and wherever that was. "Come in."

"You see, I thought you would wish to dispose of mundane business today, and then perhaps depart tomorrow for a holiday—ah, vacation, you Americans say, don't you?—at some restful spot. I could have interviewed you when you got back, of course, but your memories would be less fresh. Also, frankly, I would like to get acquainted. May I invite you to dinner at a restaurant of your choice?"

While speaking, Guion had entered and taken an armchair. He was of undistinguished appearance, on the short and slender side, dressed in a plain gray suit. His head was big, though, and when you looked closely you saw that the thinly carved face wasn't really a dark white man's—didn't quite belong to any race presently living on the planet. Everard wondered what powers lay behind its smile.

"Thanks," he replied. Superficially the offer meant little. An Unattached agent of the Time Patrol drew on unlimited funds. Actually it meant a great deal. Guion wanted to spend lifespan on him. "Suppose we get the basic talking out of the way first. Care for a drink?"

The request given, he went to the bar and mixed Scotch and soda for both. Guion didn't object to his pipe. He settled down.

"Let me repeat my congratulations on your accomplishments in Phoenicia," his caller said. "Extraordinary."

"I had a good team."

"True. But it had first-class leadership. And you did the preliminary work solo, at considerable risk."

"Is that what you're here about?" Everard demanded. "My debriefing was pretty damn thorough. You must have seen the records. I don't know what further I can tell."

Guion stared into his lifted glass, as if the ice cubes were Delphic dice. "Possibly you omitted a few details you assumed are irrelevant," he murmured. The scowl opposite him was fleeting but did not escape notice. He raised his free hand. "Don't worry. I've no intention of intruding on your privacy. An operative who had no emotions about the human beings encountered on a mission would be . . . defective. Worthless, or downright dangerous. As long as we don't let our feelings compromise our duties, they are, ah, nobody else's affair."

How much does he know, or suspect? wondered Everard. A sad little romance with a Celtic slave girl, foredoomed by the abyss between their birthtimes if by nothing else; his arranging at last for her manumission and marriage; farewell— *I'm not about to inquire. I might learn more than I want to.*

He hadn't been informed what Guion was after, or why, or anything except that this person was at least of his own rank. Probably higher. Above its lowest echelons, the Patrol didn't go in for organizational charts and formal hierarchies of command. By its nature, it couldn't. The structure was much subtler and stronger than that. Quite likely none but the Danellians fully understood it.

Nevertheless Everard's tone harshened. When he said, "We Unattached have broad discretion," he was not merely rehashing the obvious.

"Of course, of course," Guion responded with feline mildness. "I only hope to squeeze a few more drops of information out of what you experienced and observed. Then by all means enjoy your well-earned leisure." Softer yet: "May I ask if your plans include Miss Wanda Tamberly?"

Everard started. He nearly slopped his drink. "Huh?" Recovery. Grab the initiative. "Is that what you're here for, to talk about her?"

"Well, you recommended her recruitment."

"And she's passed the preliminary tests, hasn't she?"

"Certainly. But you met her when she was caught up in that Peruvian episode. A brief but strenuous and revealing acquaintance." Guion chuckled. "Since then, you have cultivated the relationship. That is no secret."

"Not heavily," Everard snapped. "She's very young. But, yeah, I consider her a friend." He paused. "A protégée of sorts, if you like."

We've had a couple of dates. Then I went off to Phoenicia, and on my time line it's been weeks . . . and I've returned to the same spring when the two of us were first together in San Francisco.

"Yes, I'll doubtless be seeing her again," he added. "But she has plenty else to keep her busy. Doubling back up to September in the Galápagos Islands, that she was snatched out of, and home in the usual fashion, and several months to arrange twentieth-century appearances so she can leave without raising questions in people's minds— Arh! Why the devil am I repeating what you perfectly well know?"

Thinking aloud, I suppose. Wanda's no Bronwen, but she may well, all unawares, help me put Bronwen behind me, as I've got to do. As I've had to do now and then before. . . . Everard wasn't given to self-analysis. The realization jolted him that what he needed to regain inner peace was not another love affair but a few more times in the presence of innocence. Like a thirsty man finding a spring to drink from, high on a mountainside— Afterward, let him get on with his life, and she with her new one in the Patrol.

Chill: *Unless they don't accept her, in spite of everything*. "And why are you interested, anyway? Are you concerned with personnel? Has anybody expressed doubts about her?"

Guion shook his head. "On the contrary. The psychoprobe gave her an excellent profile. Later examinations will be mainly for the usual purposes, to help guide her training and her earlier field assignments."

"Good." A glow kindled in Everard and eased him. He'd been smoking too hard. The tart coolness of a draught eased his tongue.

"I mentioned her simply because the events that caused your world line to intersect hers involved Exaltationists," Guion said. The voice was most quiet, considering what it bore. "Earlier along yours, you had thwarted their effort to subvert Simón Bolívar's career. In the course of aiding Miss Tamberly—who defended herself so ably—you kept them from hijacking Atahuallpa's ransom and changing the history of the Spanish Conquest. Now you have rescued ancient Tyre from them, and captured most of those who remained at large, including Merau Varagan. Wonderfully done. However, the task is not finished."

"True," Everard agreed as low.

"I am here to . . . feel out the situation," Guion told him. "I cannot express precisely what I seek, even if I use Temporal." His speech continued level, but he smiled no longer and something terrible stood behind the slanted eyes. "What is involved is no more amenable to symbolic logic than is the concept of mutable reality. 'Intuition' or 'revelation' are words equally inadequate. I seek . . . whatever measure of comprehension is possible." After a silence in which the city noises seemed muted by remoteness: "We shall talk, in an informal fashion. I will try to get some sense of how your experiences *felt* to you. That is all. A reminiscent conversation, after which you will be free to go where you like.

"Yet think. Can it be entirely coincidental that you, Manson Everard, have thrice been in action against the Exaltationists? Only once did you set forth with any idea that they might be responsible for certain disturbances. Despite this, you became the nemesis of Merau Varagan, who—I can now admit—roused fear in the Middle Command. Was this happenstance? Was it accidental, too, that Wanda Tamberly got drawn into the vortex—when she already, unbeknownst to herself, had a kinsman in the Patrol?"

"He was the reason that she—" Everard's protest trailed off. Within him shivered: *Who is this, really? What is he?*

"Therefore we wish to know more about you," Guion said. "Not prying into your personal lives, but hoping for a clue to what I can only, misleadingly, call the hypermatrix of the continuum. Such knowledge may help us plan how to track down the last Exaltationists. They are desperate and revengeful, you know. We must."

"I see," Everard breathed.

A pulse beat through him. He scarcely heard Guion's coda, "And beyond that necessity, perhaps, a larger meaning, a direction and an ending—" nor how Guion chopped it short, as though he had let slip out what should not. Everard was harking back, gazing forward, abruptly hound-eager, aware that what he needed was not surcease but the completion of the hunt.

PART TWO

WOMEN AND HORSES AND POWER AND WAR

1985 A.D.

Here, where the Bear stars wheeled too low, night struck cold into blood and bone. By day, mountains closed off every horizon with stone, snow, glaciers, clouds. A man's mouth dried as he gasped his way over the ridges, rocks rattling from beneath his boots, for he could never draw one honest breath of air. And then there was fear of the rifle bullet or the knife after dark that would spill his bit of life out on this empty land.

To Yuri Alexeievitch Garshin, the captain appeared as an angel from his grandmother's Heaven. It was on the third day since the ambush. He had tried to head northeast, generally down though it always seemed most of his steps were upward, the weight of the earth upon them. Somewhere yonder lay the camp. His sleeping bag gave him small rest; again and again terror snatched him back to a loneliness just as cruel. Careful with what field rations were in his kit, he took few bites at a time, and hunger pangs had now dulled. Nevertheless, little remained to him. He found plenty of water for his canteen, springs or the melt of remnant snowbanks, but had nothing to heat it. The samovar in his parents' cottage was a half-remembered dream—the whole collective farm, larksong above ryefields, wildflowers to the world's edge, he walking hand in hand with Yelena Borisovna. Here grew only lichen on rock, thinly strewn thorn scrub, pale clumps of grass. The one sound other than his footfalls, breath, pulsebeat was the wind. A large bird rode it, well aloft. Garshin didn't know what kind it was. A vulture, waiting for him to die? No, surely the vultures feasted on his comrades—

A crag jutted from the slope ahead. He changed course to round it, wondering how much more that threw him off the proper track to his company. All at once he saw the man who stood beneath the mass.

Enemy! He grabbed for the Kalashnikov slung at his shoulder. Then: *No. That's a Soviet outfit*. A warm blind wave poured through him. His knees went soft.

When he could see again, the man had come close. His garb was clean, fresh-looking. Officer's insignia glittered in the hard upland sunlight, yet a pack and bedroll rode on his back. He carried merely a sidearm, yet he strode unafraid and unwearied. Clearly he was no Afghan government soldier, wearing issue supplied by the ally. His body was stocky, muscular, the face beneath the helmet fair-skinned but broad in the cheekbones and a bit slanty in the eyes—*from somewhere around Lake Ladoga, perhaps,* Garshin thought weakly.

And I, I'm just serving out my hitch, just waiting out this miserable war till I can go home, if I live. He made a shaken salute.

The officer halted a meter or so off. He was a captain. "Well," he asked, "what are you doing, private?" The Finnish eyes probed like a sunset wind. However, the tone was not unkindly and the Russian was Moscow's, the dialect you oftenest heard after they drafted you, except that his was better educated than usual.

"P-p-please, sir—" Sudden, helpless trembling and stammering. "Yu. A. Garshin, private—" Somehow he identified his unit.

"So?"

"We were . . . a squad, sir—reconnaissance up the pass—Blasts, gunfire, men killed right and left—" Sergei's skull a horrible spatter and his body flung bonelessly aside, then a crash, smoke and dust, you sprawled with ears ringing so loud that you couldn't hear anything else and a medicine taste in your mouth. "I saw . . . the guerrillas . . . no, I saw, one man, a beard and turban, he laughed. They d-didn't see me. I was behind a bush, I think, or they were too busy—bayoneting?"

Garshin had nothing to vomit but bile. It hurt his throat.

The captain stood over him till he was done and the headache that followed had lessened. "Take some water," the captain advised. "Swish it around. Gargle. Spit. Then swallow, not too much."

"Yes, sir." Garshin obeyed. It helped. He tried to get up.

"Sit for a while," said the captain. "You've been through a bad time. The *mujahedin* had rocket launchers as well as rapid-fire weapons. You crept away when they'd gone, eh?"

"Y-yes, sir. Not to desert or, or anything, but—"

"I know. There was nothing you could do on the spot. Rather, your duty was to return to base and report what had happened. You didn't dare go straight back down the pass. That would have been reckless anyway. You slipped uphill. You were still dazed. When you recovered, you realized you were lost. Correct?"

"I think so." Garshin raised his glance toward the form above him. It reared dark against the sky, as alien as the crag. He was regaining his wits. "What about you, sir?"

"I am on a special mission. You are not to mention me except as I order. Understood?"

"Yes, sir. But—" Garshin sat straighter. "Sir, you talk as if you know . . . a good deal about my squad."

The captain nodded. "I came by a while afterward, and reconstructed what must have occurred. The rebels were gone but the bodies were left, stripped of everything useful. I couldn't bury them."

He refrained from speaking of honored heroes. Garshin wasn't sure whether he was grateful for that or not. It was amazing that an officer explained anything to an enlisted man.

"We can send a party to retrieve them," Garshin said. "If my unit gets the news."

"Of course. I will help. Do you feel better?" The captain offered his hand. Clinging to its strength, Garshin rose. He found himself reasonably steady on his feet.

The foreigner eyes searched him. Words hit slow, like the hammer of a careful workman. "As a matter of fact, Private Garshin, this is a fortunate encounter for both of us, and others besides. I can direct you to your base. You can take something along that badly needs taking, but which my mission doesn't allow me time to deal with."

Angel from Heaven indeed. Garshin snapped to attention. "Yes, sir!"

"Excellent." Still the captain looked at him. Afar, clouds eddied around two peaks, now hiding them, now baring their fangs. Underfoot, twigs snickered in the wind. "Tell me about yourself, boy. How old are you? Where from?"

"N-nineteen, sir. A kolkhoz near Shatsk." Emboldened: "If that means anything to you, sir. The closest real city is Ryazan."

Once more the captain nodded. "I see. Well, you seem both intelligent and faithful. I believe you will appreciate what I want of you. It is simply to deliver an object I discovered. But it may be quite an important object." He hooked thumbs in his pack straps. "Here, help me with this."

They got it off, set it on the ground, and hunkered above. He opened it and took forth a box. Meanwhile his unofficerlike talkativeness continued, though almost as if to himself, peering beyond anything Garshin could see:

"This is a very ancient land. History has forgotten all the peoples who held it, came and went, fought and died, to and fro, century after century. We today are but the latest. Ours is not a popular war, at home or in the world at large. Never mind the rights or wrongs, it is hurting us in the same way their war in Vietnam hurt the Americans, when you were a kid. If we can retrieve a little honor out of it, a little credit, is that not good for the motherland? Is that not a patriotic service?"

The wind walked along Garshin's backbone. "You talk like a professor, sir," he whispered.

The other man shrugged. His tone flattened. "What I am in civilian life doesn't matter. Let's say I have an eye for certain things. I came on the scene of the ambush, and among the . . . objects that lay there, I saw this. The Afghans must not have noticed. They were in a hurry, and are primitive tribesmen. It must have lain a long time buried, till a rocket shellburst tossed it up. Some fragments were with it—pieces of metal and bone—but I couldn't stop to do anything about those. Here. Take it."

He laid the box in Garshin's hands. It was about thirty centimeters long by ten square, gray-green with corrosion (bronze?) but preserved by the highland dryness for (how many?) centuries. The lid was wired shut and sealed by a blob of pitchy material that had formerly borne some kind of stamp. Traces of figures cast in the metal were visible.

"Careful!" the captain warned. "It's fragile. Don't tamper with it, whatever you do. The contents—documents, I suspect—might well crumble away, unless this is opened under strict controls by the proper scientists. Is that clear, Private Garshin?"

"Yes . . . yes, sir."

"Tell your sergeant, immediately when you get back, that you must see the colonel, that it's vital, that you have information for no ears less than his."

Dismay. "But, sir, all I have to say is—"

"You have this to deliver, so it doesn't get lost in the bureaucracy. Colonel Koltukhov isn't a brainless regulation machine, like too many of his kind. He'll understand, and do what is right. Simply tell him the truth and give him the casket. You won't suffer for it, I promise you. He'll want my name and more. Tell him I never told you because my own mission is so secret that anything I said would necessarily be a lie, but of course he is welcome to notify GRU or KGB and let them trace me. As for you, Private Garshin, you convey nothing except a little casket, of purely archaeological interest, which you might have stumbled upon as easily as I." The captain laughed, though his eyes stayed altogether level.

Garshin swallowed. "I see. That's an order, sir?"

"It is. And we'd better both get on with our business." The captain reached into his pocket. "Take this compass. I have another. I'll explain how to find your unit." He pointed. "From here, bear north by northeast . . . so—

"—and when that peak *there* is exactly south-southwest—

"—and—

"Is this clear? I have a notepad, I will write it for you.

"—Good luck, boy."

Garshin groped down the mountainside. He had wrapped the box in his bedroll. However slight the weight, he imagined he felt it on his back, like the weight of boots on his feet, the drag of the earth upon all. Behind and above, the captain stood, arms folded, watching him go. When Garshin glanced rearward, a last time, he saw sunlight from behind the helmet make a kind of halo, as if on an angel who guarded some place mysterious and forbidden.

209 B.C.

The highway followed the right bank of the River Bactrus. Travelers were glad of that. Breezes off the water, shade cast by wayside mulberry or willow, every fleeting relief came as an event when summer's heat lay over the land. Fields of wheat and barley, orchards and vineyards in among them, even the wild poppies and purple thistles seemed bleached by the light from a sky burned empty of clouds. Nonetheless it was a rich land, the stone houses small but many, clumped in villages or strewn on farmsteads. It had been long at peace. Manse Everard wished he didn't know that that was about to change.

The caravan plodded doggedly south. Dust puffed up around the feet of the camels. Hipponicus had shifted his wares from mules to them after he left the mountains. Ill-smelling and foul-tempered, they did carry more per animal and fared better in those arid regions that his route would traverse. They were a breed adapted to Central Asia, scruffy now that their winter coats were shed, but one-humped. The two-humped species had not yet reached this country, from which it would take its later name. Harness creaked, metal jingled. No harness bells rang; they too were of the future.

Cheered by nearing the end of their weeks-long trek, the caravaneers chattered, japed, sang, waved at people they passed, sometimes shouted and whistled if a pretty girl was among them—or, for several, a pretty boy. They were mainly of Iranian stock, dark, slender, bearded, clad in flowing trousers, loose blouses or long coats, tall brimless hats. A couple of them were Levantine, with tunics, short hair, and shaven chins.

Hipponicus himself was a Hellene, like most present-day Bactrian aristocrats and bourgeoisie: a burly, middle-aged man with freckled face and thinning reddish hair under a flat cap. His forebears came from the Peloponnesus, where today was little of that Anatolian strain which would be prominent in the Greece of Everard's time. On horseback, in front of the train, still he was hardly less grimy and sweaty than the rest. "No, Meander, I insist, you must stay with me," he said. "I've already sent Clytius ahead, you know, and part of the word he carried is that my wife should prepare for a house guest. You wouldn't make a liar of me, would you? She's got a sharp enough tongue as is, Nanno does."

"You're too kind," Everard demurred. "Really. You'll be seeing important men in town, rich, educated, and I'm just a rough old soldier of fortune. I wouldn't want to, uh, embarrass you."

Hipponicus scanned his companion sideways. It had surely been difficult and expensive, finding a mount big enough for such a fellow. Otherwise Meander's outfit was coarse and plain, apart from the sword at his hip. Nobody else bore arms any longer; the merchant had dismissed his hired guards when he reached territory reckoned safe. Meander was special.

"Listen," Hipponicus said, "in my line of work it's needful to be a pretty sharp judge of people. You're bound to have learned a fair bit, knocking around the world. More than you let on. I expect you'll interest my associates too. Frankly, that won't hurt me any when it comes to making some deals I have in mind."

Everard grinned. It lightened the massive features, pale blue eyes beneath brown locks, nose dented in a long-ago fight about which he had said as little as he told of his past in general. "Well, I can give them plenty of whoppers," he drawled.

Hipponicus grew earnest. "I don't want you for a performing bear, Meander. Please don't believe that. We're friends. Aren't we? After what we've been through together? A man gives hospitality to his friends."

Slowly, Everard nodded. "All right. Thanks."

I've gotten fond of you in my turn, he thought. *Not that we've shared many desperate adventures. One set-to, and then the flooding ford where we barely saved three mules, and . . . a few similar incidents. But it was the kind of trip that shows what your travel mates are made of—*

—from Alexandria Eschates on the River Jaxartes, last and loneliest of those cities the Conqueror founded and named for himself, where Everard signed on. It lay in the realm of the Bactrian king, but on its very edge, and the nomads beyond the stream had taken to raiding across it this year, when garrisons were depleted to reinforce a threatened southwestern frontier. Hipponicus had been glad to acquire an extra guard, footloose free-lance though the newcomer be. And indeed there had been a bandit attack to beat off. Afterward the way south through Sogdiana threaded regions rugged, desolate, wild, as well as land irrigated and cultivated. Now they had crossed the Oxus and were in Bactria proper, arriving home—

—as the survey ascertained we would be. For a minute this morning, opticals aboard an unmanned spacecraft tracked us, before its orbit swung it out to a far rendezvous. That's why I was on hand to meet you in Alexandria, Hipponicus. I'd been informed that your caravan would reach Bactra on a day that seemed right for my purposes. But, yes, I like you, you rascal, and hope to God you survive what's ahead for your nation.

"Excellent," the merchant said. "You weren't anxious to spend your pay at some fleabag of an inn, were you? Take your time, look around, enjoy yourself. Quite likely you'll find a better new job that way than through an agent." He sighed. "I wish I could offer you a permanent billet, but Hermes knows when I'll travel again, what with this war situation."

Such news as they had gathered in the last few days was confused but ugly. Antiochus, king of Seleucid Syria, was invading. Euthydemus of Bactria had taken the army to meet him. Rumor said Euthydemus was now in retreat.

Hipponicus regained cheerfulness. "Ha, I know why you hung back!" he exclaimed. "Afraid you wouldn't get a chance at our Bactran fleshpots, staying with a respectable family, weren't you? Didn't that little flute girl two nights ago satisfy you for a while?" He reached out to dig a thumb into Everard's ribs. "You had her walking bowlegged next morning, you did."

Everard stiffened. "Why are you so interested?" he snapped. "Wasn't yours any good?"

"Ai, don't get mad." Hipponicus squinted at him. "You almost seem regretful. Did you wish for a boy instead? I didn't think that was your style."

"It isn't."—which was true, but also fitted Everard's persona of a semi-barbarian adventurer, half Hellenized, from the Balkans north of Macedonia. "I just don't care to talk about my private life."

"No, you don't, do you?" Hipponicus murmured. Abundance of colorful anecdotes; nothing personal.

Actually, Everard admitted, *it doesn't make sense for me to bristle at his wisecrack. Why did I? It didn't mean a thing. After long abstinence, we were in civilized parts again, and stopped at a caravanserai where girls were available. I had a hell of a fine time with Atossa. That's all.*

Maybe that's what's wrong, he reflected, *that that was all. She's a sweet lass. She deserves better than the life she's got.* Big eyes, small breasts, slim hips, knowing hands, yet toward dawn the wistfulness in her voice when she asked if he'd ever be back. And what he'd given her, apart from a modest fee and afterward a tip, was merely the consideration that most twentieth-century American men ordinarily tried to show a woman. Of course, hereabouts that was not ordinary.

I keep wondering what'll become of her. She could well be gang-raped, maybe killed, maybe hauled off to slavery abroad, when Antiochus' troops overrun the area. At best, she'll be faded by the time she's thirty, doing whatever drudge work she can find; worn out and toothless by forty; dead before fifty. I'll never know.

Everard shook himself. *Stop that gush!* He was no fresh recruit, tenderhearted and appalled. He was a veteran, an Unattached operative of the Time Patrol, who understood full well that history is what humans endure.

Or maybe I feel the least bit guilty. Why? That makes still less sense. Who's been hurt? Certainly not he, even potentially. The artificial viruses implanted in him destroyed any and every germ that sickened people anytime throughout the ages. So he couldn't have passed anything on to Atossa either, besides memories. *And it would not have been natural for Meander the Illyrian to forgo such an opportunity. I've taken more of them along my lifeline than I remember, and not always because I needed to stay in character on a mission.*

Okay, okay, shortly before starting out on this one I had a date with Wanda Tamberly. So what? None of her business either, was it?

He grew aware that Hipponicus was talking: "Very well. No offense. Don't worry, you'll be quite free to wander around most of the time. I'll be busy. I'll tell you the best places to go, and maybe once in a while I can join you, but mostly you'll be on your own. And at my house, no questions."

"Thanks," Everard replied. "Sorry if I was gruff. Tired, hot, thirsty."

Good, he thought. *It turns out I'm in luck. I can look up Chandrakumar without any problems, and in addition, I may well learn something useful from Hipponicus' acquaintances.* Admittedly, he'd be a trifle more conspicuous than he had planned on. However, in cosmopolitan Bactra he'd cause no sensation. He needn't seriously fear alerting his quarry.

"We'll soon take care of that," the merchant promised.

As if to bear him out, the road swung sharply around a stand of cedar trees and the city which they had been glimpsing sprang into full view. Massive, turreted, tawny, its walls reared above riverside docks. From within their seven-mile perimeter lifted the smoke of hearths and workshops, drifted the noise of wheels and hoofs, while traffic flowed in and out the great gates, walking, riding, driving. Settlements clustered close around a strip kept clear for defense: houses, inns, industries, gardens.

Like the caravaneers, the dwellers were predominantly Iranian. Their ancestors founded the town, naming it Zariaspa, the City of the Horse. To the Greeks it was Bactra, and the nearer to it you came, the more Greeks you saw. Some of their kind had entered this country when the Persian Empire held it. Often that movement was involuntary, the Achaemenid shahs deporting troublesome Ionians. After Alexander took it, immigration increased, for Bactria had turned into a land of opportunity, which finally made itself an independent kingdom ruled by Hellenes. The large majority of them were in the cities, or in the military, or plying trade routes that reached west to the Mediterranean, south to India, east to China.

Everard recalled hovels, medieval ruins, impoverished farmers and herders, mostly Turkic-Mongolian Uzbegs. But that was in Afghanistan, 1970, not far below the Soviet border. A lot of change and chance would blow from the steppes in the millennia to come. Too damn much.

He clucked at his mount. Hipponicus' had broken into a trot. The camel drivers made their own beasts shamble faster, and the men afoot happily kept pace. They were almost home.

Home to war, Everard knew.

They entered by the Scythian Gate. It stood open, but a squad of soldiers kept watch, helmets, shields, cuirasses, greaves, pikeheads ablaze in the sunlight. They turned a wary eye on everybody who passed. The bustle also seemed rather subdued, folk speaking less loudly and more curtly than was usual in the East. Pulled by oxen or donkeys, quite a few wooden carts were laden with family goods, the peasants who drove them accompanied by wives and children—seeking refuge behind the walls, if they could afford it.

Hipponicus noticed. His mouth tightened. "Bad news has come," he opined to Everard. "Only rumors, I'm sure, but truth hard on their heels. Hermes rates a sacrifice from me, that we arrived no later than now."

Yet everyday life went on. It always does, somehow, till the jaws close shut upon it. Between buildings generally blank-fronted but often vividly painted, people thronged the streets. Wagons, beasts of burden, porters, women balancing water jugs or market baskets on their heads, maneuvered among artisans, laborers, household slaves. A wealthy man in a litter, an officer on horseback, once a war elephant and its mahout, thrust straight through, leaving bow waves and wakes of human turbulence. Wheels groaned, hoofs clopped, sandals slapped cobblestones. Gabbling, laughter, anger, a snatch of song, a flute-lilt or drum-thump, roiled odors of sweat, dung, smoke, cookery, incense. In the shade of foodstalls, men sat cross-legged, sipping wine, playing board games, watching the world brawl past.

Along the Sacred Way were a library, an odeon, a gymnasium, marble-faced, stately with pillars and friezes. At intervals rose those ithyphallic stone posts, topped by bearded heads, known as herms. Elsewhere, Everard knew, were schools, public baths, a stadium, a hippodrome, and a royal palace modeled on the one in Seleucid Antioch. This main thoroughfare boasted sidewalks, elevated above manure and garbage, with stepping stones at the crossings. Thus far had the seeds of Greek civilization spread.

Yet it mattered not that the Greeks identified Anaitis with Aphrodite Ourania and built her a fane in their own style. She remained an Asian goddess, her cult the largest; and west of Bactria the upstart kingdom of Parthia would presently create a new Persian Empire.

The temple of Anaitis loomed beside the Stoa of Nicanor, principal marketplace in town. Booths crowded the square: silk, linens, woolens, wine, spices, sweetmeats, drugs, gems, brasswork, silverwork, goldwork, ironwork, talismans— with the sellers crying their wares and the shoppers haggling over prices mingled vendors, dancers, musicians, soothsayers, wizards, prostitutes, beggars, idlers, the faces, the many-hued and many-formed garments had come from China, India, Persia, Arabia, Syria, Anatolia, Europe, the wild highlands and the savage northern plains . . .

To Everard the scene was eerily half-familiar. He had witnessed its like in a score of different lands, in as many different centuries. Each was unique, but a prehistorically ancient kinship vibrated in them all. He had never been here before. The Balkh of his own birthtime held scarcely a ghost of Hellenic Bactra. But he knew his way around. A subtle electronics had printed into his brain the map, the history, the chief languages, and information that was never chronicled but that Chandrakumar's patience had gleaned.

So much preparation, so long and risky an effort, to clap hands on four fugitives.

They threatened his world's existence.

"This way!" yelled Hipponicus, gesturing from the saddle. His caravan struggled on, into a less crowded district, to stop at a warehouse. There a couple of hours went by while the goods were unloaded, inventoried, and stored. Hipponicus gave his men five drachmas apiece on account and instructions about the stabling and care of the animals. He would meet them tomorrow at the bank where he kept most of his money and pay them off. Right now, everybody wanted to go home, hear what had been happening, celebrate as merrily as that news would allow.

Everard waited. He missed his pipe, and a cold beer would have been overwhelmingly welcome. But a Time Patrolman learned how to outlast tedium. He half observed what went on, half daydreamed. After a while, he noticed he was remembering an afternoon two thousand years and more beyond this moment.

1987 A.D.

Sunshine, soft air, and city murmur passed through an open window. Beyond it, Everard saw Palo Alto going about a holiday weekend. The apartment he sat in was a Stanford student's, comfortably shabby furniture, cluttered desk, bookcase crowded with miscellany, a National Wildlife Federation poster thumbtacked to the opposite wall. No trace remained of last night's violence. Wanda Tamberly had seen to the fine details of cleanup. She must not suspect anything amiss when she returned from her family outing—she, four months younger in lifespan than Wanda who sat here now, a space-time universe younger in knowledge.

Everard looked out no oftener than habitual alertness compelled. He much preferred to keep his attention on the comely California blonde. Light glowed in her hair and on the blue bathrobe that matched her eyes. Even granted that she'd slept the clock around, she'd bounced back from her experience astoundingly fast. A girl, or a boy for that matter, who'd been kidnapped by one of Pizarro's Conquistadores and rescued in a teeth-skinning maneuver would have had every excuse for spending the next few days stupefied. Wanda had shared a large steak in her kitchen while asking intelligent questions. Here in the living room, she was still at it.

"How does time travel work, anyway? Impossible and absurd, I've read."

He nodded. "According to today's physics and logic, that's true. They'll learn better in the future."

"All the same— Okay, I'm into biology, but I've had some physics courses and I try to keep up, sort of. *Science News*, *Analog*—" She smiled. "I'm being honest, you see. *Scientific American*, when the style doesn't make me doze off. Real honest!" Her humor faded.

It had been defensive, he guessed. The situation remained critical, perhaps desperate. "You jump onto something sort of like a Buck Rogers motorcycle without wheels, work the controls, rise in the air, hover, fly, then push another control and you're instantly someplace else, anywhere, anywhen. Regardless of altitude differences or— Where does the energy come from? And the earth spins, it goes around the sun, the sun orbits through the galaxy. How about that?"

He shrugged, with a smile of his own. *"E pur si muove."*

"Huh? Oh. Oh, yeah. What Galileo muttered, after they made him agree the earth sits still. 'Nevertheless, it moves.' Right?"

"Right. I'm surprised a, uh, a person of your generation knows the story."

"I don't only skindive and backpack for recreation, Mr. Everard." He heard a tinge of resentment. "I take a book along."

"Sure. Sorry. Uh—"

"Frankly, I'm a little surprised you'd know."

Sure, he thought, *no matter how wild the circumstances, you couldn't mistake what I am, a plain Midwesterner who's never quite gotten the mud off his boots.*

Her voice softened. "But of course you live history." The honey-colored head shook. "I can't yet get a handle on it. Time travel. It won't come real for me, in spite of everything that's happened. Too fabulous. Am I being slow on the uptake, Mr. Everard?"

"I thought we were using first names." *The norm of this period in America. Which, damn it, is not so alien to me. I base myself in it. I belong here too. I'm not really old. Born sixty-three years ago. Run up a lot more lifespan than that, traipsing around through time. But biologically I'm in my thirties,* he wanted to tell her and mustn't. *Antisenescence treatment, preventive medicine future to this century. We Patrol agents have our perks. We need them, to carry us through some of the things we see.* He wrenched his mind into an attempt at lightness. "Actually, Galileo never said what I quoted, under his breath or aloud. It's a myth." *The kind of myth humans live by, more than they do by facts.*

"Too bad." She leaned back on the sofa and, in her turn, smiled again. "Manse. Okay, then, those timecycles or hoppers or whatever you call them, they are what they are, and if you tried to explain, scientists today wouldn't understand."

"They've got a glimmering already. Non-inertial reference frames. Quantum gravity. Energy from the vacuum. Bell's theorem was lately violated in the laboratory, wasn't it? Or won't that happen for another year or two? Stuff about wormholes in the continuum, Kerr metrics, Tipler machines— Not that I understand it myself. Physics was not my best subject at the Patrol Academy, by a long shot. It'll be many thousands of years from now when the last discoveries are made and the first working space-time vehicle is built."

She frowned, concentrating. "And . . . expeditions begin. Scientific, historical, cultural—commercial, I suppose? Even military? I hope not that. But I can see where they'd soon need police, a Time Patrol, to help and advise and rescue and . . . keep travelers in line, so you don't get robberies or swindles or"—she grimaced—"taking advantage of people in the past. They'd be helpless against knowledge and apparatus from the future, wouldn't they?"

"Not always. As you can testify."

She started, then uttered a shaky laugh. "Hoo boy, can I ever! Are there many guys in history as tough and smart as Luis Castelar?"

"Enough. Our ancestors didn't know everything we do, but they did know things we don't, stuff we've forgotten or leave moldering in our libraries. And they averaged the same brains." Everard sat forward in his chair. "Yes, mainly we in the Patrol are cops, doing the work you mentioned, plus conducting research of our own. You see, we can't protect the pattern of events unless we know it well. That's our basic job, protection. That's the reason the Danellians founded our corps."

She lifted her brows. "Danellians?"

"English version of their name in Temporal. Temporal's our mutual language, artificial, developed to deal with the twists and turns of time travel. The Danellians— Some of them appeared, will appear, when chronokinesis was newly developed."

He paused. His words turned low and slow. "That must have been . . . awesome. I met one once, for a few minutes. Didn't get over it for weeks. Of course, no doubt they can disguise themselves when they want to, go among us in the form of human beings, *if* they ever want to. I'm not sure they do. They're what comes after us in evolution, a million or more years uptime. The way we come after apes. At least that's what most us suppose. Nobody knows for certain."

Her eyes went large, staring past him. "How much could Australopithecus know for certain about us?" she whispered.

"Yeah." Everard forced prosiness back into his tone. "They appeared, and commanded the founding of the Patrol. Otherwise the world, theirs and everybody's, was doomed. It would not simply be wrecked, it would never have existed. On purpose or by accident, time travelers would change the past so much that everything futureward of them would be something else; and this would happen again and again till—I don't know. Till complete chaos, or the extinction of the human race, or something like that brought a halt, and time travel had never occurred in the first place."

She had gone pale. "But that doesn't make sense."

"By ordinary logic, it doesn't. Think, though. If you go into the past, you're as free an agent as you ever were. What mystical powers has it got to constrain your actions that the present doesn't have? None. You, Wanda Tamberly, could kill your father before he married. Not that you'd want to. But suppose, innocently bumbling around in a year when your parents were young, you did something that kept them from ever meeting each other."

"Would I . . . stop existing?"

"No. You'd still be there in that year. You've mentioned a sister, though. *She* would never be born."

"Then where would I have come from?" Impishness flickered: "Hardly from under a cabbage leaf!" and died away.

"From nowhere. From nothing. Cause-and-effect doesn't apply. It's sort of like quantum mechanics, scaled up from the subatomic to the human level."

Almost audibly, tension crackled. Everard sought to bleed it off. "Don't worry," he said. "Things aren't that delicately balanced in practice. The continuum is seldom easy to distort. For instance, in the case of you and your parents, your common sense would be a protective factor. Prospective time travelers are pretty carefully screened before they're allowed to take off unsupervised. And most of what they do makes no long-range difference. Does it matter whether you or I did or did not attend a play at the Globe Theater one of the times when Shakespeare was on stage? Even if, oh, if you did cancel your parents' marriage and your sister's life—with all due respect, I don't think world history would notice. Her husband-who-would-have-been would marry somebody else, and the somebody else would . . . happen . . . to be such a person that after a few generations the gene pool would be the same as it would have been anyway. The same famous descendant would be born, several hundred years from now. And so on. Do you follow?"

"You're throwing me curve balls till it's my head that's spinning. But, oh, I did learn a little about relativity. World lines, our tracks through space-time. They're like a mesh of tough rubber bands, right? Pull on them, and they'll try to spring back to their proper, uh, configuration."

He whistled softly. "You do catch on fast."

She wasn't relieved in the least. "However, there are events, people, situations where the balance is . . . unstable. Aren't there? Like if some well-meaning idiot kept Booth from shooting Lincoln, maybe that'd change everything afterward?"

He nodded.

She sat straight, shivering, and gripped her knees. "Don Luis wanted—he wants to get hold of modern weapons—go back to Perú in the sixteenth century and . . . take charge of the Conquest, then stamp out the Protestants in Europe and drive the Muslims out of Palestine—"

"You've got the idea."

Everard leaned farther forward and caught her hands in his. She clung. Hers were cold. "Don't be afraid, Wanda," he urged. "Yes, it is terrifying. It could turn out that you and I never had this talk today, that we and our whole world never were, not even a dream in somebody's sleep. It's harder to imagine and harder to take than the idea of personal annihilation when we die. How well I know. But it isn't going to be, Wanda. Castelar is a fluke. By a freak of chance, he got hold of a timecycle and learned how to operate it. Well, he's one man alone, otherwise ignorant; he barely escaped from here last night; the Patrol is on his trail. We'll nail him, Wanda, and repair any damage he may have done. That's what we're for. Our record is pretty damn good, if I do say so myself. And I do."

She gulped. "Okay, I believe you, Manse." He felt warmth begin returning to the fingers between his.

"Good girl. You're helping us a lot, you know. Your account of your experience was excellent, full of clues to what he'll try next. I expect to gather more hints as new questions occur to me. Quite likely you'll have suggestions of your own."

Further reassurance: "That's why I'm being this open with you. As I told you earlier, ordinarily it's forbidden to reveal to outsiders that time travel goes on. More than forbidden; we're conditioned against it, we're unable to. But these are rather special circumstances, and I'm what they call an Unattached agent, with authority to waive the rules."

She withdrew her hands, gently but firmly. *Cool customer,* he thought. *I don't mean frigid. Independent. Guts, backbone, brains. At twenty-one years of age.* Her look upon him cleared, and the slightly husky voice was again steady, unstrained. "Thanks. Thanks more than I can say. You're rather special yourself, you know?"

"Naw. I simply happen to be the operative working on this case." He smiled. "Too bad you didn't draw a hotshot glamour boy, like maybe from the Planetary Engineers milieu."

"The what?" She didn't wait for a reply. "I gather the Patrol recruits in all periods."

"Well, not exactly. Prior to the scientific revolution around 1600 A.D., persons capable of imagining the idea are few and far between. Castelar's an extraordinary guy."

"How did they find you?"

"I answered an ad and took some tests, back in—well, it was a while ago." *Not to say "1957" flat out. Why not? Because she doesn't have the whole background. She'd think of me as ancient. . . . And why should that matter, Everard, you old goat?* "Recruits are found in many different ways." He stirred. "Look, I realize you have ten million questions, and I'd like to answer them for you, and maybe later I can. But right now, could we get on with business? I want more details of what happened. Time is short."

"Really?" she murmured. "I thought you could double back to a split second before or after any moment."

Shrewd, shrewd. "Sure we can. But—well, we in the corps have only so much lifespan to give. Sooner or later the Old Man is bound to catch up with each of us. And the Patrol has too much history to guard; we're badly understaffed. And, okay, I personally have trouble sitting still like this when action is pending. I want to . . . to work my way to that point on my personal world line where the case is closed and I know we're safe."

"I see," she said quickly. Then: "It doesn't begin or end with Don Luis, does it?"

"No," Everard admitted. "He acquired a timecycle because some bandits out of the distant future tried to hijack Atahuallpa's ransom on a night when he was there. Those bandits are the really dangerous characters. For the present, though, let's track down our Conquistador."

209 B.C.

Like most well-to-do Hellenistic houses this far east, that of Hipponicus mingled Classical simplicity with Oriental lavishness. In the dining room, gilt molding framed walls on which frescoes depicted fanciful birds, beasts, and plants, gaudily hued. The same flowing lines graced the bronze candelabra whose tapers took over as daylight faded. Incense sweetened the air. Now in summer, a door stood open on the roses and fishpond of the inner court. However, the company reclined in Attic fashion, two on a couch, at a pair of small tables, wearing white tunics with little ornament. They watered their wine and ate food that was good but not elaborate, soup and soft bread followed by a dish of lamb, barley, and vegetables, lightly seasoned. The presence of any meat was somewhat special. Dessert was fresh fruit.

Normally the merchant would have made his first supper at home a family occasion, the only guest his friend Meander. The next evening would have seen a stag party complete with girls engaged to play music, dance, and otherwise entertain. This time circumstances were different. He needed an early and accurate briefing on them. The message he sent ahead bade his wife invite certain men at once. Male slaves waited on them.

He counted for enough in city affairs that the two who were able to come on such short notice did. Besides, what he had to tell from the northern frontier might be useful. They lay opposite him and Everard and, after the amenities, got directly to the way things were. It was not pleasant.

"—the latest courier," growled Creon. "The army should get here day after tomorrow." He was a burly, scar-faced man, second in command of the garrison left behind when King Euthydemus departed.

Hipponicus blinked. "The whole expeditionary force?"

"Minus the dead," said Creon grimly.

"But what about the rest of the country?" asked Hipponicus, shaken. He had hinterland properties. "If most of our men are bottled in this one city, Antiochus' troops can plunder and burn everywhere else, unhindered."

"*First plunder*, then *burn!*" Everard recalled. The twentieth-century joke, which doubtless had a hoary lineage, was not very funny when the reality drew nigh, but a man was apt to grab at any straw of humor.

"Fear not," soothed Zoilus. Hipponicus had explained to Everard that this minister of the treasury had connections throughout the realm. Beneath the big nose, gaunt features creased in a pursy little smile. "Our king knows well what he does. With his forces concentrated here, the enemy must stay close by. Else we could send detachments out to take them from behind, piecemeal. Isn't that right, Creon?"

"Not quite that simple, especially over the long haul." The officer's glance at his couchmate added, *You civilians always fancy yourselves strategists, don't you?* "But, true, Antiochus is playing it cautious. That's plain to see. After all, our army is still in working order, and he's far from home."

Everard, who had kept a respectful silence in the presence of the dignitaries, decided he could venture a query. "Just what did happen, sir? Can you tell us, from the dispatches you've gotten?"

Creon's reply was slightly condescending, but amicable, as one fighting man to another. "The Syrians marched along the southern bank of the River Arius." On the maps of Everard's milieu, that was the Hari Rud. "Else they'd have had desert to cross. Euthydemus knew Antiochus was coming, of course. He'd expected him for a long time."

Naturally, Everard thought. This war had been brewing six decades, since the satrap of Bactria revolted against the Seleucid monarchy and proclaimed his province independent, himself its king. The Parthians had taken fire about the same time and done likewise. They were more nearly pure Iranian—Aryan, in the true meaning of that term—and considered themselves the heirs of the Persian Empire which Alexander had conquered and Alexander's generals divided among each other. Long at strife with rivals in the West, the descendants of General Seleucus suddenly found an added menace at their backs.

At present, they ruled over Cilicia (south central Turkey, in Everard's era) and Latakia along the Mediterranean seaboard. Thence their domain sprawled across most of Syria, Mesopotamia (Iraq), and Persia (Iran), holding much directly, some in vassalage. Therefore language commonly lumped it under the name "Syria," although its lords were Graeco-Macedonian with Near Eastern admixture and their subjects wildly diverse. King Antiochus III had drawn it back together after civil and foreign wars nearly shattered it. He went on to Parthia (northeastern Iran) and chastened that new power—for the time being. Now he was come to reclaim Bactria and Sogdiana. His ambitions reached southward from them, into India. . . .

"—and kept his spies and scouts busy. He took position at the ford he knew the Syrians would use." Creon sighed. "But I must say Antiochus is a wily one, and as daring as he's tough. Shortly before dawn, he sent a picked force across—"

The Bactrian troops, like the Parthian, were principally cavalry. That suited Asian traditions and, most places, the Asian land; but it left them terribly handicapped at night, when they always withdrew to what they hoped was a safe distance from the enemy.

"—and drove our pickets back on our main body. His own main body followed. Euthydemus deemed it wisest to give ground, regroup, and make for here. He's been collecting reinforcements along the way. Antiochus has pursued, but not closely. Fighting has amounted to skirmishes."

Hipponicus frowned. "That isn't like Antiochus, from what I've heard of him," he said.

Creon shrugged, emptied his cup, held it out to a slave for a refill.

"Our intelligence is that he was wounded at the ford. Not enough to disable, obviously, but maybe enough to slow him down."

"Still," declared Zoilus, "he's been unwise not to follow up his advantage immediately. Bactra is well supplied. These walls are impregnable. Once behind them, King Euthydemus—"

"Can sit and let Antiochus blockade us into starvation?" Hipponicus interrupted. "I hope not!"

Foreknowledge gave confidence for Everard to say, "That may not be what he intends. If I were your king, I'd make myself secure here, then sally forth for a pitched battle, with the city to return to in case I lost it."

Creon nodded.

"The Trojan War over again?" Hipponicus protested. "May the gods grant a different outcome for us." He tipped his cup and sprinkled some drops on the floor.

"Fear not," said Zoilus. "Our king has better sense than Priam. And his eldest son, Demetrius, bids fair to become a new Alexander." Evidently he remained a courtier wherever he went.

Yet he was not merely a sycophant, or Hipponicus would not have wanted him present. In this matter he spoke truth. Euthydemus was a self-made man, adventurer from Magnesia, usurper who seized the crown of Bactria; but he governed ably and fought cannily. In years to come, Demetrius would cross the Hindu Kush and grab off a goodly chunk of the decaying Mauryan Empire for himself.

Unless the Exaltationists prevailed in spite of everything, and that whole future from which Everard sprang was annulled.

"Well, I'd better see to my own arms," Hipponicus said heavily. "I have . . . three men of fighting age in this household, besides myself. My sons—" He did not quite suppress a wince.

"Good," rumbled Creon. "We've reorganized things somewhat. You'll report to Philip, son of Xanthus, at the Orion Tower."

Hipponicus cast Everard a look. Their forearms were in contact. The Patrolman felt a slight quiver.

Zoilus took the word, a bit maliciously: "If you don't care for a part in our war, Meander, leave at once."

"Not so fast, I hope, sir," Everard answered.

"You'll fight on our side?" Hipponicus breathed.

"Well, this takes me by surprise—" *I lie like a wet rag*.

Creon chuckled. "Oh, you'd been looking forward to some fun? Spend your pay on the best, then. Drink good wine while it's to be had, and do your whoring before the army drives every street slut's price as high as Theonis' is now."

"Whose?" asked Everard.

Hipponicus' grin was sour. "Never mind. She's out of your class and mine."

Zoilus flushed. "She's not for any oaf who brings a bag of gold," he snapped. "She chooses the lovers she desires."

Oh-ho! Everard thought. *The great official has his human side, does he? But let's avoid embarrassing him. It'll be tricky as is, steering this conversation the way I want even for a minute or two.* Kipling's lines passed wryly through his mind:

> *"Four things greater than all things are,—*
> *Women and Horses and Power and War.*
> *We spake of them all, but the last the most. . . ."*

He turned to Hipponicus. "Forgive me," he said. "I'd like to stand with you, but by the time I could be enlisted, me, a foreigner, the battle that decides the victory might well be finished. In any case, I couldn't do much. I'm not trained to fight on horseback."

The merchant nodded. "Nor is it your fight," he replied, more pragmatic than disappointed. "I'm sorry your welcome to my city is so poor. You'd better leave tomorrow or the day after."

"I'll go around town among the metics and transients," Everard said. "Somebody may want to hire an extra guard for his trip home. Half the world passes through Bactra, doesn't it? If I can find somebody returning to some place I've never been before, that would be perfect." He had been at pains with Hipponicus to build the persona of a man who tramped around not simply because of having gotten into trouble with his tribe, but out of curiosity. Such were not uncommon in this milieu.

"You'll meet none from the Far East," Zoilus warned. "That trade has shriveled."

I know, Everard recollected. *China's been under the rule of Shi Huang-Ti, the Mao of his day. Totally xenophobic. And now at his death, it'll be turmoil till the Han Dynasty gets established. Mean-*

while the Hiung-nu and other nomad gangsters prowl freely beyond the Great Wall. He shrugged. "Well, what about India, Arabia, Africa, or in Europe Rome, Areconia, or even Gaul?"

The others showed surprise. "Areconia?" Hipponicus asked.

Everard's pulse thuttered. He kept his manner as casual as it had been when he planted the word. "You haven't heard? Maybe you know the Areconians under a different name. I heard mention in Parthia when I passed through there, and that was second or third hand. I got the impression of occasional traders from pretty far northwest. Sounded interesting."

"What are they like?" Creon inquired, still fairly genial toward him.

"Unusual-looking, I was told. Tall, slim, handsome as gods, black hair but skin like alabaster and eyes light; and the men don't grow beards, their cheeks are as smooth as a girl's."

Hipponicus wrinkled brows, then shook his head. Zoilus tautened. Creon rubbed his own bristly chin and murmured, "I seem to have heard talk, these past months— Wait!" he exclaimed. "That sounds like Theonis. Not that she'd have a beard, whatever she is, but hasn't she got men like that with her? Does anybody really know where she's from?"

Hipponicus went thoughtful. "I gather she set up in business about a year ago, very quietly," he said. "She'd have needed permits and so forth. There was no fuss about them, no, nor any gossip to speak of. All at once, here she was." He laughed. "A powerful protector, I suppose, who takes it out in trade."

A chill tingle passed along Everard's scalp. *Topflight courtesan, yeah, that's how a woman could get full freedom of action in these surroundings. I sort of expected it.* He bent his mouth upward. "Think she'd at least talk to a homely vagabond?" he asked. "If she does have kinfolk here, or if she herself thinks best to leave, well, my sword is for hire."

Zoilus' palm cracked onto his couch. "No!" he yelled. The rest stared. He collected himself and challenged Everard, raggedly: "Why are you so interested, if you know so little about these . . . Areconians, did you call them? I didn't think a hardheaded mercenary would chase after . . . a fairy tale."

Hoy, I've touched a nerve, haven't I? Back off! Everard raised a hand. "Please, it was just a notion of mine. Not worth making a fuss about. I'll inquire around town in a general way tomorrow, if I may. Meanwhile, you gentlemen have more important things to talk about, don't you?"

Creon's lips thinned. "We do," he said.

Nonetheless, throughout that evening Zoilus' glance kept straying toward Meander the Illyrian.

976 B.C.

After their attack on the Exaltationists, the Patrol squadron flitted to an uninhabited island in the Aegean to rest, care for the wounded, and assess the operation. It had gone as well as Everard dared hope: four bandit timecycles shot down, seven prisoners taken off the foundering ship on which they had left Phoenicia. True, three riders had flashed away into space-time before an energy beam could strike. His heart would have no real ease until the last of their breed was captured or slain. Still, there could be very few remaining at large, and today he had—finally, finally—nabbed the ringleader.

Merau Varagan walked some yards off from the group, to a cliff edge, where he stood looking out over the sea. The Patrolmen on guard let him. They had snapped a neuroinduction collar around the neck of each prisoner. At the first sign of any suspicious move, a remote-control switch would activate it and the wearer would collapse paralyzed. On impulse, Everard went to join him.

Water sparkled blue, flecked with white, dusted with radiance. Sunlight called pungencies out of dittany underfoot. A breeze ruffled Varagan's hair, which sheened obsidian black. He had shed his drenched robe and stood like a marble statue newly from the hand of Phidias. His face might also have been the ideal of a Hellas not yet born, except that it was too fine-chiseled and nothing Apollonian dwelt in the great green eyes or on the blood-red mouth. Dionysian, perhaps. . . .

He nodded at Everard. "A lovely vista," he said in American

English, which his voice turned into music. The tone was calm, almost nonchalant. "May I savor it while we are here?"

"Sure," agreed the Patrolman, "though we'll leave pretty soon."

"Does the exile planet offer anything comparable?"

"I don't know. They don't tell us."

"To make it more feared, I daresay. 'That undiscover'd country from whose bourn No traveler returns.'" Sardonically: "You needn't persuade me not to escape it by leaping off this verge, no matter how relieved some of your companions might feel."

"As a matter of fact, we'd cuss. It wouldn't be nice of you, putting us to all the trouble of fishing out your carcass and reviving it."

"In order to subject me to the kyradex."

"Yeah. You've got a headful of information we want."

"I fear you will be disappointed. We have taken care that none of us shall know much about any other's resources, capabilities, or contingency plans."

"Uh-huh. Natural-born loners, the bunch of you."

"And the genetic engineers of the thirty-first millennium set themselves to bring forth a race of supermen, bred to adventure on the cosmic frontier," Shalten said once, "and lo, they found they had begotten Lucifer." He sometimes talks in that vaguely Biblical style. Otherwise nothing about him is vague.

"Well, I will preserve what dignity I can," Varagan said. "Once on the planet"—he smiled—"who knows what may be possible?"

Physical weariness and letdown after excitement left Everard vulnerable to emotion. "Why do you do it?" he blurted. "You lived like gods—"

Varagan nodded. "Very much like gods. Have you ever considered the fact that that includes changelessness, trapped in a myth, ultimate meaninglessness? Our civilization was older to us than the Stone Age was to yours. In the end, that made it unendurable."

So you tried to overthrow it, and failed, but some of you had managed to seize timecycles, and fled back into the past. "You could have left it peacefully. The Patrol, for instance, would've been overjoyed to have people with your abilities as recruits; and for your part, I swear you'd never have been bored."

"We would have been what is worse, perverting our innermost natures. The Patrol exists to conserve one version of history."

"And you've kept trying to destroy it! In God's name, why?"

"So stupid a question is unworthy of you. You know quite well why. We have tried to remake time in order that we may rule it; and we have desired to rule in order that our wills may be wholly free. Enough."

Haughtiness departed, lightness returned. Varagan trilled a laugh. "The stodgy have triumphed again, it seems. Congratulations. You've done a remarkable piece of detective work, tracking us. Would you tell me how? I'll be most interested."

"Ah, it'd take too long," *and parts of it would hurt too much.*

The arched brows lifted higher. "Your mood has shifted, has it? You seemed amiable a minute ago. I still feel thus. You've been a rather exciting enemy, Everard. In Colombia-to-be," where Varagan came close to taking over Simón Bolívar's government, "in Perú," where his gang tried to steal Atahuallpa's ransom from Pizarro and change the course of the Spanish Conquest, "and now in Tyre," which they had threatened to blow up, were they not given an instrumentality that could have made them nearly omnipotent, "we have played our game, you and I. Where-when else, less directly?"

A dull anger had in fact come upon Everard. "It was no game to me, buster," he snapped, "and you're well out of it."

Irritation flicked back at him: "As you wish. Then kindly leave me to my thoughts. Among them is the reflection that you have not caught the last Exaltationist yet. In a certain sense, you have not caught me."

Everard bunched his fists. "Huh?"

Varagan regained self-possession, the will to cruelty. "I may as well explain. The interrogation machine will bring it out. Among the remnants of us is Raor. She was not on this expedition, because women are hampered in the Phoenician milieu, but she has taken part in others. My clone mate, Everard. She has her ways of finding out what went wrong here. She will be as vengeful as she always was ambitious. Pleasant dreams." He smiled and turned his back, again gazing out at sea and sky.

The Patrolman left him but, for a while, sought solitude also. He walked to the other side of the islet, sat down on a rock, brought out pipe and tobacco, got a smoke started.

Staircase wit, he thought. *I should've retorted, "Suppose she succeeds. Suppose she does blot out the future. You'll be in it, remember? You'll stop ever having existed."*

Except, of course, in those bits of space-time pastward of that change moment, in which he was engaged on his pranks. He'd've pointed that out with some glee, maybe. Or maybe not. In any case, I doubt he fears obliteration. The ultimate nihilist.

To hell with it. Repartee never was my long suit. Let me just go back to Tyre, tie up the loose ends there—

Bronwen. No. I've got to make provision for her, but that's a matter of common decency, nothing more. After that, we'd better both start learning how to stop missing each other. For me the best place will be my familiar old twentieth-century USA, where I can put my feet up for a while.

He often felt that the privilege of an Unattached agent, essentially to make his or her own assignments, was worth the risks and responsibilities that the status entailed. *I might want to pursue this Exaltationist business further, once I've had a good rest. I might.*

He shifted about on his rock. *Not too good a rest! Some activity, some fun.*

That girl who got caught in the Peruvian events, Wanda Tamberly— Across months of his personal lifespan and three millennia of history, memory rose bright. *Why, sure. No problem. She accepted the Patrol's invitation to join. If I can catch her between that dinner I took her to and the day she leaves for the Academy— Cradle robbing? No, damn it. Just to enjoy myself, giving her a cheerful send-off, and then I'll get on with the raunchy part of my furlough.*

209 B.C.

At last the teaching of Gautama Buddha would ebb from his native India until there it was all but forgotten. Today it still flourished, and the tide of it flowed strongly outward. Thus far, converts in

Bactria were scarce. The topes and stupas whose ruins Everard saw in twentieth-century Afghanistan would not be built for generations. However, Bactra city numbered sufficient believers to maintain a vihara, at which visiting coreligionists usually called and sometimes stayed; and those merchants, caravaneers, guards, mendicants, monks, and other travelers were numerous, hailing from a wide range of territories. Hence it made a superb listening post, a principal reliance of the historical study project.

Everard sought it the morning after his arrival. The sanctuary-*cum*-hostel was a modest adobe building, a former tenement, in Ion's Lane off the Street of the Weavers, distinguished from the neighbors crammed wall to wall against it largely by motifs painted on the whitewash, lotus, jewel, flame. When he knocked, a brown man in a yellow robe opened the door and gave benign greeting. Everard inquired about Chandrakumar of Pataliputra. He learned that the esteemed philosopher did indeed live here, but was off on his accustomed Socratic argufying, unless he had settled down someplace to meditate. He should return by evening.

"Thank you," said Everard aloud, and *Damn!* to himself. Not that the news ought to surprise him. He'd had no way to make an advance appointment. Chandrakumar's job was to learn what the meager chronicles that survived had omitted, not only details of politics but economics, social structure, cultural activity, multifarious and ever-mutable everyday life. You did that largely by mingling.

Everard wandered away. Maybe he'd come upon his man. Or he might find some clues on his own. Partly he wished he weren't so conspicuous, towering above the average of this time and place, with features more suggestive of a barbarian Gaul than of a Greek or even an Illyrian. (A German would have been closer still, but nobody in Asia had ever heard of Angles, Saxons, or any of that lot.) A detective did best when he could fade into his background. On the other hand, curiosity about him should make it easy to strike up conversations; and the Exaltationists should have no reason to suspect the Patrol was on their trail.

If the Exaltationists were here. Quite possibly they had never winded the bait set out for them, or had been too wary to go after it.

Anyway, as for his appearance, no one else with equivalent ability and experience had been available for the groundside part of the operation. The joke was well-worn among English-speaking members of the Patrol, that their corps was chronically overextended. You used whomever and whatever came to hand.

The streets seethed. Beneath its permanent reeks, the air stank of anxiety-sweat. Criers were going about, announcing the imminent return of glorious King Euthydemus and his army. They did not say it was in defeat, but the populace already had a good idea.

Nobody panicked. Men and women continued their ordinary work or their emergency preparations. They spoke little or not at all about the thoughts that crawled in them, siege, hunger, epidemic, sack. That would have been like clawing at one's flesh. Besides, most people in the ancient world were more or less fatalistic. Events to come might work out for the better instead of the worst. Undoubtedly many a mind was occupied with schemes to make an extra profit from the situation.

Still, talk was apt to be loud, gestures jerky, laughter shrill. Foodstuffs disappeared from the bazaars as hoarders grabbed what had not gone into the royal storehouses. Fortune-tellers, charm vendors, and shrines did land-office business. Everard had no difficulty making acquaintances. On the contrary, he never bought a drink for himself. Men panted for any fresh word from outside.

In streets, marketplace arcades, wineshops, foodshops, a public bath where he took refuge for a while, he fielded questions as noncommittally and kindly as he was able. What he got in exchange was scant. Nobody knew anything about "Areconians." That was to be expected; but only three or four said they had seen a person of such appearance, and they were vague about it. Maybe someone was correct, but it had been an individual belonging in this milieu, a stray tribesman from afar who happened to fit an imperfectly understood description. Maybe memory was at fault. Maybe the respondent simply told Meander what he supposed Meander wanted to hear; that was an immemorial Oriental custom.

So much for the dash and derring-do of the Time Patrol, Everard said dryly to his recollection of Wanda. *Ninety-nine percent of our efforts are slogwork, same as for any other police force.*

He did finally luck out, to the extent of gaining information marginally more definite. In the bath he met one Timotheus, a dealer in slaves, plump, hairy, quick to set his worries aside and discuss lechery when Meander offered that gambit. Theonis' name entered readily. "I've heard tell about her. I'm not sure what to believe."

"So am I. So are most of us. Seems too good to be true, what gossip says." Timotheus wiped his brow and stared before him into the gloom, as if to conjure her from the steam-clouds. "An avatar of Anaitis." Hastily, he sketched a symbol with his forefinger. "No disrespect to the goddess. What I know is only what filters forth to the world, by way of friends and servants and such. Her lovers are few, and higher-ups, every one of them. They don't say much about her. I guess she doesn't want them to. Else she'd be as widely spoke of as Phryne or Aspasia or Lais. But her men do let words slip now and then, and those words pass on. Maybe growing in the telling. I don't know."

"Face and form like Aphrodite's, voice like song, skin like snow, gait like a panther's. Midnight hair. Eyes the green of a fire where copper is about to melt. That's what they say."

"I've never seen her. Few have. She seldom leaves her house, and then it's in a curtained litter. But, yes, so the song goes. A tavern song. Unfortunately, we can't do more than sing about her, we commoners. And it could well be exaggerated." Timotheus sniggered. "Maybe the bard was just wet-dreaming in public."

If she is Raor, it is not exaggerated. For Everard, the room suddenly lost its heat. He forced his tone to stay casual. "Where's she from? Any kin here with her?"

Timotheus turned his face to the big man. "Why so inquisitive? She's not for you, my friend, no, not if you offered a thousand staters. For one thing, the patrons she's got would be jealous. That could get unhealthy."

Everard shrugged. "I'm only curious. Somebody out of nowhere, almost overnight fascinating ministers of the king—"

Timotheus looked uneasy. "They do whisper she's a sorceress." Fast: "I'm not backbiting her, mind you. Listen, she's endowed a small temple of Poseidon outside town. A pious work." He couldn't resist cynicism. "It gives employment to her kinsman Nicomachus, its priest. But then, he was here before her, I don't know what he was doing, and maybe he prepared her way." Quickly again: "No disrespect. For all I know, she is a godess among us. Let's change the subject."

Poseidon? wondered Everard. *This far inland? . . . Oh, yes. As well as the sea, he's god of horses and earthquakes, and this is a country of both.*

Toward evening, he figured Chandrakumar would be back. First he stilled hunger at a vendor's brazier, with lentils and onions dished into a folded chapatti. Tomatoes, green pepper, and a roast ear of corn on the side were for the future. He would have liked coffee, too, but must settle for diluted sour wine. Another need he took care of in an alley that happened to be unoccupied. That amenity of civilization, the French pissoir, stood equally far uptime, and all too briefly.

The sun was under the ramparts and streets were cooling off in shadow when he reached the vihara. This time the monk led him to a room inside. Rather, it was a cell, tiny, windowless, a thin curtain across the doorway for privacy. A clay lamp on a shelf gave barely enough flickery, odorous light for Everard to pick his way over a floor whose sole furniture was a straw tick and a bit of rug on which a man sat cross-legged.

Eyeballs gleamed through murk as Chandrakumar looked up. He was small, thin, chocolate-skinned, with the delicate features and full lips of a Hindu—born in the late nineteenth century, Everard knew, a university graduate whose thesis on Indo-Bactrian society had led to the Patrol seeking him out with an offer to conduct his further studies in person. Here his garb was a white dhoti, his hair hung long, and he was holding near his mouth an object that Everard deduced was not really an amulet.

"Rejoice," he said uncertainly.

Everard returned the greeting in the same Greek. "Rejoice." The monk's footfalls dwindled away. Everard spoke softly, in Temporal: "Can we talk without anybody trying to listen?"

"You are an agent?" The question trembled. Chandrakumar made to rise. Everard waved him back and lowered his own bulk to the clay.

"Correct," he said. "Things are getting urgent."

"I should hope so." Chandrakumar had recovered equilibrium. Though he was a researcher, not a constable, field specialists too must need to be tough and quick-witted. His voice held an edge. "I have spent this past year wondering when somebody would arrive.

We are now at the very crisis point." Pause. "Are we not?" A spectacular episode in history was not necessarily one on which the whole future hinged.

Everard gestured at the disc on its chain. "Best turn that off. We don't want to risk our conversation falling into the wrong hands." It doubtless contained a molecular-level recorder, into which Chandrakumar had been whispering notes on this day's observations. His communicator and other, similarly disguised equipment were stowed somewhere else.

When the medallion dangled loose, Everard proceeded: "I'm passing for Meander, an Illyrian soldier of fortune. What I am is Specialist Jack Holbrook, born 1975, Toronto." On a mission as damnable as his, you didn't tell even an ally more than he had to know. Everard shook hands, the polite thing for men of their natal backgrounds to do. "And you are . . . Benegal Dass?"

"At home. Chandrakumar is the name I currently use here. You caused me a bit of trouble about that, you know. Before, I was 'Rajneesh.' Wasn't reasonable he should pop up so soon after he left for home, so I had to concoct a jolly good kinship story to explain why I look just like him."

They had slipped into English, almost unconsciously, a breath of the commonplace in this darkness. Perhaps for the same reason, they did not go immediately to the point.

"I was surprised to learn you hadn't meant to be present," Everard said. "Famous siege. You could fill in all the lacunae and correct the errors in Polybius, and whatever other fragments of chronicle will survive."

Chandrakumar spread his palms. "Given my limited resources and finite lifespan, I did not care to squander any of it on a war. Bloodshed, waste, misery, and after two years, what result? Antiochus can't take the city and doesn't wish or dare to stay bogged down before it any longer. He makes a peace that is sealed by betrothing a daughter of his to Prince Demetrius, and proceeds on south to India. The evolution of a society is what matters. Wars are nothing but its pathologies."

Everard refrained from expressing disagreement. Not that he liked wars; he had seen too many. By the same token, though, they must be as much a norm of history as blizzards were of Arctic weather; and all too often, their outcomes did make a difference.

"Well, I'm sorry," he said, "but we required an expert observer on the spot, and you're it. Uh, as Chandrakumar, you're a Buddhist pilgrim, am I right?"

"Not precisely. The vihara does possess a few holy objects, but nothing extraordinary. However, Chandrakumar seeks enlightenment, and the letters that his cousin Rajneesh sent from the silk dealership where he worked in Bactra, those decided Chandrakumar on studying the wisdom of the West as well as the East. For example, Heraclitus was approximately contemporary with the Buddha, and some of his thought shows close parallels. This is a good place for an Indian to learn about the Hellenes."

Everard nodded. In one identity after another, normally separated by timespans of a length to preclude recognition, Benegal Dass spent years adding up into decades among the Bactrians. Each arrival and departure was by the slow, difficult, dangerous means of the era; a hopper, anything that might seem strange, would have destroyed his usefulness and run afoul of the Patrol's prime directive. He had watched this city grow great, and he would watch it die. The end product of his labors was the story of it, deep and wide-ranging but never seen except by a handful of interested individuals within the corps or up in the far distant future. When he took furlough in his native country and century, he must lie to family and friends about what he did for a living. Surely no monk had ever accepted an existence harder, lonelier, or more devoted. *I don't have that kind of fortitude*, Everard confessed.

Chandrakumar laughed nervously. "Pardon me," he said. "I delay matters. Long-windedness, the scholar's disease. And of course I'm rather in suspense myself, don't you know. What *is* afoot?" After a moment: "Well?"

"I'm afraid you won't like this," Everard answered heavily. "You've been put to a lot of trouble for what's just a sideshow, if it's that much. But the main event is so important that every bit of information counts, including negative information."

It was hard to see whether Chandrakumar bit his lip. His voice went cold. "Oh, really? What is this main event, may I ask?"

"Take too long to explain in detail. Not that I know a lot myself.

I'm only acting as a liaison with you, a messenger boy. What the Patrol has to prevent is several years uptime. A sort of . . . equivalent of the Sassanian dynasty . . . rising and taking over Persia. Soon."

The little man stiffened where he sat. "What? Impossible!"

Everard's grin was skewed. "That's what we have to make it. I repeat, I can't say much. In intelligence work, operatives don't get told anything they don't need to know. But, roughly, as I understand it, the plot they've uncovered is for King Arsaces of Parthia to be overthrown by a usurper who denounces the peace treaty with Antiochus, attacks the Seleucid army when it's on its way back from India, routs it and kills Antiochus himself."

"The consequences—" Chandrakumar susurrated.

"Yeah. The Seleucid realm would very likely fall apart. It's always on the brink of civil war. That should give the Romans a leg up in the eastern Mediterranean, unless Parthians eager to avenge the humiliation Antiochus handed them sweep east through the power vacuum, restoring the Persian Empire three and a half centuries before the Sassanians are scheduled to do so. What could come of that is anybody's guess, but it won't be the history you and I studied."

"This usurper . . . a time traveler?"

Everard nodded. "We think so. Again, I've been told hardly anything. I get the impression the Patrol has clues to a small band of fanatics who've somehow obtained two or three vehicles and want to—I don't know what. Lay a groundwork for Mohammed and the ayatollahs to take over the world? That's probably farfetched; though the truth may be farther fetched yet. At any rate, an operation is under way to forestall them, without tearing up the continuum ourselves in the process."

"Caution, yes. . . . Of course I am ready to do whatever I can. Your role, sir?"

"Well, as I told you, I'm a field researcher too, though my area is military, Hellenistic warfare to be exact. I'd intended to observe this siege anyway. It is more interesting than you care to admit. The Patrol ordered me to change my plans slightly, same as it did you. I was to come into town, contact you, and take whatever relevant information you've gathered during this past year. Tomorrow I'll leave, make my way to the invaders, and enlist with them. I'm too big for a cavalryman on present-day horses, but the Syrians make heavy use of infantry still—the good old Macedonian phalanx—and a pikeman my size will be welcome. In due course a Patrolman will contact me and I'll pass your data on. After the peace with Euthydemus, I'll accompany the Syrian army to India and then back west. A Patrol agent will have slipped me an energy weapon, and I'll try to protect Antiochus' life if things look desperate. Naturally, we hope it won't come to that. We hope the usurpation can be smoothly aborted, and all I need do is collect details about how the Syrians manage a campaign."

"I see." Everard heard the reluctance. Waging war against Chandrakumar's beloved Bactrians? However, he could accept a necessity and inquire: "But I say, why so roundabout? This kingdom doesn't seem involved. In any case, someone could simply arrive on a hopper in a discreet location and get in touch with me."

"Precaution. The enemy may have a watchman here, who'd probably be able to detect an arrival or departure nearby. We don't want to risk alerting anybody like that. If they don't know we're aware of their existence, we can more handily bag them. And Bactria does have its role in history. While it exists as a military power, it helps keep the Parthians more cautious than they might otherwise be." *That much, at least, is true. Now for more mendacity.* "Maybe, as part of the plot, the gang wants to undermine Bactria somehow. Or maybe not—they can only be a few individuals—but we're coppering every bet we can. Before you left base, you were told to keep an eye out for any visitors who seemed peculiar. I'm here to get that information from you."

"I see," Chandrakumar repeated, but in friendly wise, now eager to help. The vision Everard presented terrified him, as it certainly should. He stayed calm, though, tugged his chin, stared into the dimness around them. "Hard to tell. This city is such a potpourri of races. I'd be sorry if I cause the corps to waste effort on quite harmless persons."

"Never mind. Tell me everything. They'll evaluate it uptime."

"If you could give me some notion—"

"For openers: who stopped by this house, paid his respects, and in the course of chitchat found out what's been going on—whether any *other* oddball strangers were in town, for instance?"

"Several, off and on. An establishment like this is a sort of verbal bulletin board, you know, and not only for Buddhists."

Right. That's why the Patrol quietly helped found it, half a century ago. In medieval Europe we do the same for certain monasteries. "Go on. Get specific. Please."

"Well, as per instructions, I have maintained myself here, not moved to more comfortable quarters, so I have been in a position to pay heed. Generally, I would call them unsuspicious, those who dropped in. I do wish you could indicate a little better what you have in mind."

"Individuals who don't seem to belong anywhere in this milieu, whether racially or culturally or . . . any hallmark that struck your notice. I was told the gang may be a mixed bunch."

Lamplight flickered over a bleak smile. "You, coming from when you do, think of Arab terrorists? No, there were a pair of Arabs, but I have no reason to believe they were anything but the spice dealers they said they were. Irishmen, however— Yes, conceivably two Irishmen. Black hair, marble-white skin as if this Asian sun had never touched it, fine features. If they are of that stock, they cannot well be contemporary, can they? The Irish at present are barbarian headhunters."

Everard must struggle to show no more interest than Holbrook would in any other potential suspects. He trusted the Indian, but when you stalked such an enemy as his, you didn't willingly add the slightest hazard to those you already confronted. The Exaltationists surely realized that at least one historical worker was intermittently in town. If they decided there was reason to take the trouble, they might well manage to identify him. Cover your own trail!

"What did they themselves claim to be, do you know?" he asked.

"I didn't listen to their talk with Zenodotus. He's a Greek convert, the most active mundanely of these monks. I tried to pump him afterward, but of course I was under orders never to show excessive curiosity. He did tell me that they had told him they were Gauls—civilized Gauls, from the neighborhood of Marseilles."

"Could be. A long ways from home, but wanderings like that aren't unheard of. Like this persona of mine."

"True. It was mainly their appearance that set me wondering. Shouldn't southern Gauls more or less resemble southern Frenchmen of our time? Well, perhaps their family immigrated from the North. They told Zenodotus they liked this city and inquired about the prospects of starting a horse-breeding farm in the hinterland. I haven't heard that anything came of the idea. Since then I have glimpsed them, or persons remarkably like them, in the streets a time or two. Judging by gossip, a courtesan who has recently gained notoriety may have been of their party. That is all I can say about them. Is it of any use?"

"I dunno," Everard grunted. "My job is only to pass whatever you tell me on to the real operatives." *Cover up, cover up.* "What more? Any strangers who called themselves Libyans, Egyptians, Jews, Armenians, Scythians—any kind of exotic—but didn't seem quite to fit the nationality?"

"I have paid close attention, round about in the city as well as at this house. Mind you, I am scarcely qualified to identify anomalies in most persons. Greeks and Iranians have ample ethnic complexities for me to cope with. However, there was a man from Jerusalem, let me think, about three months ago. I'll give you my recorded notes. Palestine is under Ptolemy of Egypt, you know, with whom Antiochus has been at loggerheads. This man said nothing about difficulties in traversing Syrian territory—"

Everard half listened. He felt sure the "Gauls" and Theonis were the objects of his hunt. But he didn't want to give Chandrakumar that impression.

"—a half-dozen Tocharian tribesmen from beyond the Jaxartes, who'd come down through Sogdiana with furs to trade. How they got permission to enter—"

Somebody cried out. Feet fled down the corridor. Behind them, hobnails thudded and metal rattled.

"What the devil!" Everard surged to his feet. He'd come forth weaponless, as a civilian must, and his secret gear also rested in the house of Hipponicus, lest somehow it give him away. *It's for you, Manse,* he cried to himself, crazily, foreknowing.

A hand ripped the curtain aside. Vague light shimmered on a

helmet, breastplate, greaves, drawn sword. Two other men hulked shadowy at the back of the first. Maybe more were in the hallway. "City guard," rapped the leader in Greek. "Meander of Illyria, you're under arrest."

They'd've learned at the front door what room I'm in, but how do they know what name to call me by? "Great Heracles!" Everard yelped. "Whatever for? I haven't done anything." Chandrakumar crouched into a corner.

"You're charged with being a spy for the Syrians." Law did not require the squad chief to tell, but the unease that harshened his voice made him talkative. "Step out." His blade gestured. He'd need a single stride and a thrust to put it in the belly of a resister.

Exaltationists behind this, got to be, but how'd they know, how'd they arrange, and so fast?

He who hesitates is bossed. Everard flung an arm around and knocked the lamp from its shelf. Oil blazed for half a second and went out. Everard had already shifted his weight the opposite way and dropped to a squat. Suddenly blind, the Macedonian roared and lunged. Everard's eyes, adapted to gloom, found shapes in this deeper dark. He rose with the upward-rocketing heel of his hand. It crashed into bone. The other man's head snapped back. His blade clattered free. He lurched against his followers and collapsed in a tangle among them.

A fist would have meant broken knuckles if it had connected wrongly, when Everard had only the barest vision and neither time nor room to maneuver. Across his mind flitted a hope that he hadn't killed a man who was merely doing his duty, who doubtless had wife and kids— It was gone. His mass smote the confusion at the entrance. Seizing and twisting with his hands, levering with a shin, he got past them. Ahead of him a fourth guard yelled and flailed about, bare-handed, afraid his steel might strike a comrade but able to delay escape long enough for them to act. Light-colored, his kilt was a visible mark. Everard gave him the knee. His shouts became screams. Everard heard another soldier stumble over him where he writhed.

By then the Patrolman was in a common room. Three monks scrambled aside, aghast. He charged by, through the front door, out.

The map in his head told him what he should do—turn left at the first corner, take the third lane beyond because it met an alley which joined a jumble of similar crooked paths— Distant halloos. A lean-to, booth for cheap wares during business hours, that looked fairly sturdy. Chin yourself up and lie flat on top, in case a pursuer comes past.

None did. After a while Everard descended.

Twilight was thickening into night. One by one, more and more, stars glimmered forth above shadow-cliff walls. Quiet had fallen; before streetlights, most people were indoors by dark. The air had cooled. He snatched it into his lungs and started off. . . .

The Street of the Gemini stretched satisfactorily gloomy, well-nigh deserted. Once he passed a boy with a torch, once a man with a horn-paned lantern. He himself now went at the pace of a reputable citizen, belated unexpectedly and thus forced to walk by star-glow, trying not to step in too much muck. He did carry a flashlight, his sole anachronism. It lay among the coins in the purse at his waist, disguised as a religious charm. But it was for extreme emergency. Did somebody see it shine, he couldn't explain that away as he could the rankness of sweat in his tunic.

Occasional windows faced the street, mostly in upper stories. They were shuttered, but light leaked yellow through cracks. Behind them the dwellers would be eating a light cold supper, drinking a nightcap, swapping news of the day, playing a game, telling a bedtime story to a child, making love. A harp twanged. A snatch of minor-key song drifted like a breeze. All seemed more remote than the stars.

Everard's heart slugged at its wonted beat. He had willed the tension out of his muscles. Reaction wouldn't set in till he allowed it to. He could think.

Why the trumped-up charge and the attempt to haul him off? Mistaken identity? That was implausible at best, and the fact that the squad knew his name denied it altogether. Somebody had told them it in connection with giving the orders, along with a physical description. Obviously the idea was to avoid possible foulups which could alert him or any companions he might have. The Exaltationists were as anxious to stay undercover as he was.

Exaltationists—yeah, who else? But they scarcely had secret control of the government . . . yet. They could not dispatch bullyboys disguised as garrison troops; too risky. Nor could they personally send legitimate soldiers. No, they worked through somebody who did have the power, or at least the political influence, to make such arrangements.

Who? Well, that led back to the question of who had fingered Everard.

Zoilus. I see it now, with the dazzling clarity of hindsight. A big wheel, and an infatuated customer of Theonis. She must've given him a song and dance about enemies who'd seek her out even in this distant refuge. He was to tell her if any newcomer started inquiring after foreigners of her peculiar type. With a wide acquaintance among a gossipy people, he had a good chance of hearing about that.

By sheer bad luck, Zoilus was one of Hipponicus' guests yesterday and heard personally, immediately. Everard muttered lurid phrases. *So today, I guess, he informed her. Though he probably didn't think Meander had been anything but idly curious, she—suspecting otherwise—talked him into sending the squad after me. That'd take some hours. He isn't in the army himself; he'd have to scare up an officer he can control. Especially since everything must be kept very discreet.*

My size and looks make me noticeable enough that the men could eventually track me down.

Everard sighed. *They'll bring Chandrakumar in. Possible accessory; and they've got to show some result, if they don't want to suffer worse than five or six lashes with a weighted whip for letting me skite off. Poor little guy.*

He hardened his feelings. *Once the Exaltationists have established that he's conditioned to silence, they'll know there's no point in torture, unless for fun. Of course, the fact of the conditioning will prove he's from uptime. If they have a kyradex to break it—well, the beans he spills will be fake. My good luck is that Shalten coached me before I left, gave me a supply of red herrings to strew around.*

His other assets—training, knowledge, strength, agility, mother wit, a well-stocked purse of money—were also on hand, for whatever they were worth. He had more, but aside from the flashlight, they lay in Hipponicus' house. A finger ring held a transmitter for brief messages. The wattage was proportionately minuscule, but Patrol receivers could handle individual photons, and no manmade interference existed today. A medallion of Athena's owl was a more powerful, two-way communicator. In the hilt of a knife rested a stun beam projector with charges for twenty shots. The haft of his sword doubled as an energy gun.

He was not alone on Earth. Historical investigators like Chandrakumar, other kinds of scientists, entrepreneurs, esthetes, esoterics numbered in the hundreds around the globe. More to the point, the Patrol kept stations in Rome, Egyptian Alexandria, Syrian Antioch, Hecatompylos, Patalipushtra, Hien-yang, Cuicuilco . . . and regional posts in between. They were aware of this operation. A distress call would bring help on the instant.

If he could recover the means to make it.

At best that would be a desperation move. The Exaltationists must be taking every precaution available to them. Everard didn't know what they had in the way of detectors, but at the minimum they could surely monitor local electronics for nearby transmissions and tell when a timecycle appeared in this vicinity. They'd keep ready to scramble, flee into tracklessness, at the first sign that the Patrol might be after them.

Probably not every one of them at every instant could skip on half a minute's notice. Their activities were often bound to take them, individually, away from their vehicles. But probably, too, they were never all of them gone at any given moment. A single one who escaped would be too many, an ongoing mortal danger.

Mental map or no, it wasn't easy finding your way with neither lamps nor signs. Everard lost his a couple of times, and cursed. He was in a hurry. When the Exaltationists learned the arrest had failed, they'd surely, through Zoilus, send the men on to Hipponicus' place to confiscate Meander's belongings and lie in wait for him. Everard had to get there ahead of them, feed the merchant some story, gather his gear, and clear out.

He didn't think a second group had gone there separately. Zoilus would have had problems aplenty, cashing in favors, obtaining the services of four guards. Moreover, two bands would double the risk of an uncorrupted officer finding out and demanding to know what the hell went on—which would compromise Theonis.

Regardless, I'd better be careful. Good thing the telephone hasn't been invented yet.

He slammed to a halt. His guts contracted. "Oh, heavens to Betsy," he groaned, for no swear word sufficed. *Where was my brain? On vacation in Bermuda?*

At least it didn't return absolutely too late. He stepped aside, into the darkness under a wall, pressed himself against rough stucco, gnawed his lip and beat fist in palm.

The night had grown coldly brilliant with stars and a gibbous moon had risen over the Eagle Tower. The street where Hipponicus dwelt would be equally illuminated. He would be clearly visible as he arrived, knocked on the door, waited for a slave porter to come unbar it and admit him.

He glanced up. Vega glinted in Lyra. Nothing stirred but the trembling of the stars. A timecycle could hang unseeably high while its opticals brought the ground close and day-clear to the rider. A touch on a control, and it would instantly be down there. No lethal shot; a stun beam, the fallen man slung over a saddle, and off to interrogation with him.

Sure. When she learned what had happened at the vihara, which she soon would, Raor could dispatch a comrade of hers downtime to lurk above the merchant's dwelling until the fugitive showed up or the troopers came in ordinary wise. The Patrol had no vehicle anywhere close, and Everard had no way to call one in. Not that he would. Nabbing the rider wasn't worth alarming the rest into flight.

Maybe she won't think of it. I almost didn't.

Everard gusted a sigh. *Too dicey. The Exaltationists may be crazy, but they aren't stupid. If anything, their weakness is oversubtlety. I'm just going to have to let my outfit fall into their hands.*

What would they make of it? They might or might not have the equipment to probe its secrets. If they did, well, they wouldn't discover anything they didn't know already, except that Jack Holbrook was not a complete fool.

Small consolation, when Manse Everard was completely disarmed.

What to do? Depart the city before the Syrians reached it, strike out for the nearest Patrol station? Hundreds of miles, and he'd likeliest leave his bones along them, the scraps of knowledge he had gained blown away on a desert wind. If he did survive the journey, the corps couldn't well hop him back to carry on where he'd left off. Nor could it spend more man-years on insinuating a different agent by the same kind of tortuous devices as for him. He'd used up all the good opportunities.

That wouldn't matter to Raor, if she faced this dilemma. She'd double through time, annul her original attempt, and start on a fresh one. To hell with the possibility of generating a causal vortex, unforeseeable and uncontrollable consequences to the course of events. Chaos is what the Exaltationists want. Out of it they'll make their kingdom.

If I quit here, and somehow convey a warning to the Patrol, it can only come in force, an escadrille of timecycles swooping secretly into this night. Probably it can rescue Chandrakumar. Certainly it can put a stop to Raor's plot. But she and her buddies will escape, to try again at a place and year we'll know nothing about.

Everard shrugged. *Not much choice for me, is there?*

He changed direction, toward the waterfront. According to his neural briefing, yonder lay several low-life taverns, any of which could provide a doss, a hidey-hole, and perhaps some more palaver about Theonis. Tomorrow— Tomorrow the king came home, the enemy at his heels.

I suppose I shouldn't be too surprised at how things have worked out. Shalten and company crafted a fine scheme. But every officer knows, or should know, that in every action, the first casualty is your own battle plan.

1987 A.D.

The house was in a bedroom community outside Oakland, where you encountered your neighbors as little as you chose. It was small, screened by pines and live oaks at the end of an uphill driveway. Entering, Everard found the interior cool, dim, anachronistic. Mahogany, marble, embroidered upholstery, deep carpet, maroon hangings, leather-bound books with gold-stamped French titles, molecularly perfect copies from Toulouse-Lautrec and Seurat, hadn't much business nowabouts, did they?

Shalten noticed him noticing. "Ah, yes," he said in English whose accent Everard couldn't identify, "my preferred *pied-à-terre* is Paris of the *Belle Époque*. Refinement that will turn into revulsion, innovation that will turn into insanity, and thus, for the foreknowledgeable observer, piquancy becoming poignancy. When required to work away from it, I take souvenirs along. Welcome. Have a seat while I fetch refreshment."

He offered his hand, which Everard clasped. It felt bony and dry, like a bird's foot. Unattached agent Shalten was a wisp of a man, features wizened on a huge bald head. He wore pajamas, slippers, a faded dressing gown, and, though he was presumably not Jewish, a skullcap. When the arrangements for this meeting were being made at milieu HQ, Everard asked where-when his host-to-be originated. "You don't need to know" was the answer.

Still, Shalten bustled about hospitably enough. Everard took an overstuffed armchair, declined Scotch because later he must drive back to his hotel but accepted a Nevada Pale. Shalten's tea with Amaretto and Triple Sec didn't fit his French affection; he seemed uninterested in personal consistency. "I will remain standing, if you do not mind," said his rusty voice. A churchwarden lay beside a humidor on a bureau. He filled it and kindled a rather nauseatingly perfumed tobacco. Partly in self-defense, Everard stoked his briar. Nevertheless the atmosphere was companionable.

Well, they shared a purpose, and belike Shalten was wise to tone grimness down.

Gab about weather, traffic strangulation, and the food at Tadich's in San Francisco occupied the first minutes. Then he turned oddly luminous yellow-green eyes on his visitor and said, tone unchanged, "So. You have thwarted the Exaltationists in Perú and disposed of several. You have captured your runaway Spanish Conquistador and put him back in his proper setting. You have thwarted the Exaltationists again in Phoenicia and, again, disposed of several." Lifting a hand: "No, please, no modesty. It required well-coordinated teams, yes. Yet though the cells of the body be many, the works of the body are naught save that the spirit order them. Not only did you lead these undertakings, when necessary you worked solo. My compliments. The question is simply, have you since had sufficient free time, on your world line, to recuperate?"

Everard nodded.

"Are you certain?" Shalten persisted. "We can allow you more. The stress was undoubtedly considerable. The next stage that we contemplate is likely to be still more dangerous and taxing." He sketched a smile. "Or, on the basis of what I have heard about your political views, perhaps I should say 'dangerous and demanding.'"

Everard laughed. "Thanks! No, really, I'm raring to go. Why else should I claim privilege? It bothers me that Exaltationists are still running loose." In English, his remark was ridiculous; but Temporal, alone among languages, had the grammatical structure to handle chronokinesis. Unless precision was essential, Everard favored his mother tongue. Both men knew what he meant. "Let's finish this job before they finish us."

"You need not have insisted on taking a key part, you know," Shalten said. "Your qualifications for it made the Middle Command hope very much you would volunteer, but it was not required of you."

"I wanted," Everard growled. He gripped his pipe bowl tightly, warm between his fingers. "Okay, what is your plan and how do I fit in?"

Shalten blew smoke of his own. "Background first. We know the Exaltationists were in northern California on the thirteenth of June 1980. At any rate, one of them was, in connection with their Phoenician devilry. They took adequate precautions, used legitimate crosstemporal activity to help camouflage theirs, et cetera. We have no prospect of finding them. The fact of their presence might give us a way of playing some kind of trick, except that, in the nature of the case, they know that we know. That day they were certainly on the *qui vive*, avoiding everything of which they were not absolutely assured."

"Uh-huh. Obvious."

"Well, upon studying the matter, I realized that there is another little space-time region in which one or more Exaltationists probably lurk. It is not guaranteed, and the precise dates are unknowable, but it is well worth considering." The long pipestem jabbed in Everard's direction. "Can you guess what?"

"Why, m-m . . . why, here and now, because you are."

"Correct." Shalten grimaced. "Wherefore I pass weeks in this abominable milieu, nursing the development of my trap along, detail by daily detail. And perhaps all for naught. How often does man, vain of his intellect, find that the harvest of his efforts is vanity! Whether mine bear fruit shall be for you to discover." He sent another leisurely stream of smoke from his lips. "Can you guess how I concluded this miniperiod might have potentialities for us?"

Everard stared as if the gnome standing before him had turned into a rattlesnake. "My God," he whispered. "Wanda Tamberly."

"The young contemporary lady caught up in the Peruvian case, yes, indeed." Shalten nodded and went on, maddeningly deliberate: "Let me spell out my reasoning, although given this hint, you can doubtless reconstruct it unaided. You will recall that, when their attempt to commandeer Atahuallpa's ransom failed, the Exaltationists bore off as captives the two men whose presence had—momentarily, they hoped—frustrated them, Don Luis Castelar and our disguised Specialist Stephen Tamberly. They identified the latter as a Patrolman and, in their hiding place, interrogated him at great length under kyradex. When Castelar broke free and escaped on a timecycle, bearing Tamberly with him, the Exaltationists had gained considerable detailed information about our man and his background. Your team struck at them immediately afterward, and killed or captured most."

Of course I recall, God damn it! Everard snarled in his head.

"Now consider the situation from the viewpoint of those who got away, or who had not been there at the instant of your raid," Shalten went on. "Something had gone hideously wrong. They must most passionately have desired to know what. Was the scent onto which the Patrol had gotten now cold, or might it lead the Patrol onward to the rest of them?

"They are bold and all too intelligent. They would follow every clue of their own that they dared. We have no way to prevent it. We cannot mount guard over every moment of the rest of the lives of the persons concerned. They could come back to Perú years after 1533 and, making veiled inquiries, learn the later biography of Castelar. Likewise, to a lesser extent, for Agent Tamberly. Granted, they could not acquire a full account of the merry chase that Castelar led us, or how we recovered Tamberly, or how his niece was swept along by events. Their data would be fragmentary, their deductions correspondingly incomplete and ambiguous. However, it is clear that they decided they were in no further proximate danger—as witness the fact that they went on to the Phoenician escapade.

"First, I am sure, they carried out some investigation of everybody Tamberly had spoken of during that skilled, ruthless interrogation. Associates, acquaintances, relatives. Looking in on years subsequent to this one, they may well have found reason to suspect his niece Wanda became involved, and as a consequence was invited to join the Patrol. They could have traced the date of that involvement to sometime in May 1987—"

"And we sit here doing nothing?" Everard shouted.

Shalten lifted a hand. "Compose yourself, my friend, I pray you. Why should they strike at her, or at anyone else? The damage is done. They are without conscience, cat-cruel, but not foolishly vindictive. The Tamberly family poses no further threat per se to them. On the contrary, they proceed very, very carefully—for they can well imagine the Patrol keeping surreptitious watch on, say, Miss Wanda (I will not employ that preposterous 'Ms.' appellation) in hopes that she will draw them to her. After all, they themselves would have no compunctions about setting out a human lure. No, they do nothing but nibble at the fringes of observation, gather what few data they can, and retreat elsewhen."

"Just the same—!"

"As a matter of fact, she is under our observation, against that contingency. I deem the contingency vanishingly improbable and the guarding to be a waste of precious lifespan. But headquarters insisted. Do set your mind at ease."

"All right, all right," Everard grumbled, though gladness welled up in him. *Why do I care so much? Oh, she's gallant and bright and good-looking, but still, a single girl, out of a million years of our species on earth—* "Is this enough preliminaries? Can we please get to the point?"

Shalten sipped his drink. "The end result of my reasoning," he said, "is what I told you at the outset. Quite likely one or more Exaltationists are in the San Francisco Bay area during some days of this month, May 1987. They are being so circumspect that we have no chance of finding them. What we can do instead, and are doing, is to bait our real trap."

Everard tossed off his ale and hunched forward, his tobacco fuming. "How?"

"Have you noticed the matter of the Bactrian letter?" Shalten responded.

"The what?" Everard considered. "No, I . . . don't think I have. Something in the news? I've only been around for a short timespan, and mighty busy."

The big skull nodded. "I understand. You have pursued the Peruvian affair to a conclusion, and paid attention to the charming young lady, and when one knows what lies ahead in history, one's incentive to follow the daily news is slight. I thought you might have caught mention nonetheless. It is no mere local sensation. It is, in a subdued, scholarly, but publicly interesting fashion, a small international nine days' wonder."

"Which you manage so it develops exactly as you want," Everard deduced. His heart knocked.

"I told you that was why I reside here."

How does he do it? A webwork of connections, operations, carefully engineered stories fed to carefully chosen journalists—and this shrimp shepherding it all? Even with the computer power he's got backing him up, it is to be awed. But don't ask him, my boy, don't ask him, or he'll talk through the middle of next week.

"Please fill me in,"Everard said.

"We might have chosen June 1980, when we know positively that Exaltationists are present," Shalten explained, "but I decided that, besides their wariness lest we play some trick then, that presence was probably too brief. The odds were that they would not notice our bait. This year is better, provided that they do also visit it. They must necessarily conduct their investigation of the Tamberly family piecemeal, making appearances through a period of several days at least. Disguised as ordinary twentieth-century individuals, they cannot avoid spending hours on end in lodgings, on omnibuses—tedium which they will naturally relieve with the help of newspapers, television, et cetera. Besides, theirs are lively intelligences. They will feel curiosity about their surroundings, which to them are immemorially ancient. And . . . as I said, the story that I hope will attract their attention is in the news. Only for a short while, of course; then the public forgets. But if they are intrigued, they can pursue it, obtaining scholarly publications and the like."

Everard sighed. "Could I ask you for another beer?"

"My pleasure."

When he was settled again, Shalten still standing with his churchwarden, grotesque in front of the beautiful old bureau, Everard heard: "What do you know about the Greek kingdom of Bactria?"

"Hm? Uh—let me think—" His historical information was intense concerning societies where he had worked, spotty about everything peripheral. "In what's now northern Afghanistan. Alexander the Great passed through and made it part of his empire. Greek colonists moved in. Later they declared themselves independent and conquered . . . m-m . . . most of the rest of Afghanistan and a chunk of northwestern India."

Shalten nodded. "Rather good, on no notice. You shall learn much more, of course. You should also reconnoiter the terrain—I suggest in 1970, before Afghanistan's current troubles, when you can pose as a tourist."

He drew air into his narrow chest and proceeded. "Two years ago, a Russian soldier in the mountains of the Hindu Kush came upon a box dating back to the Hellenistic era, evidently unearthed by guerrilla shellfire. That is a provocative story in its own right. The vagueness of official accounts, while attributable to habitual Soviet secretiveness, spices it. The point is, this man turned his find over to superior officers, and at length it reached an institute of Oriental studies in Moscow. Now one Professor L. P. Soloviev has published the result of his studies. He has no doubt that the object is genuine, and that it throws significant light on a period about which historians know little. Much of what information they do have is derived from nothing better than coins."

"What was in the box?"

"Pray let me outline the context first. Bactria occupied, approximately, the region between the Hindu Kush and the Amu Darya.

North of it lay Sogdiana, bounded by the Syr Darya—today in the Soviet Union—also under the suzerainty of the Bactrian kings.

"They had broken away from the Seleucid Empire. In the year 209 before Christian reckoning, Antiochus III marched east across Asia to regain this rich territory. He defeated his rival Euthydemus in battle and besieged him in his capital, Bactra, but failed to take the city. After two years he gave up, made peace, and departed southward, to assert his power in India—although there, again, he concluded with a treaty rather than a conquest. While the siege of Bactra became as famous in its day as the siege of Belfort did in my France, no details about it have come down to later times.

"Well, the casket that the Russian soldier brought in held a papyrus, most of the text still legible. Radiocarbon tests, et cetera, established authenticity. It grew clear that this was a letter from Antiochus to someone southwestward. The courier and his presumed escort must have come to grief, perhaps victims of mountaineer footpads. Drifting soil buried the box, which the killers tossed aside after realizing it contained no treasure, and the dry climate preserved the document fairly well."

Shalten finished his blueberry tea and pottered off to the kitchen and liquor cabinet to make another. Everard practiced patience.

"What did this dispatch say?"

"You shall have your opportunity to examine a copy. Briefly put, it describes how, soon after Antiochus arrived at the gates of Bactra, Euthydemus and his dashing son Demetrius led out a sally in force. It drove a deep salient into the Syrian ranks before it was beaten back and retreated behind the walls. Had it succeeded, the Bactrians might have ended the war then and there, victoriously. Yet it was a wild venture. The letter relates how Euthydemus and Demetrius themselves, in the vanguard of their army, were nearly killed when Antiochus counterattacked. A rousing story, which I imagine you will enjoy."

Everard, who had seen men scream on the ground as blood and bowels spilled from them, asked merely, "Who was Antiochus writing to?"

"That part is missing. It may have been to a general of his, stationed as an 'ally' in the puppet realm Gedrosia on the Persian Gulf, or it may have been to a satrap in his own easternmost province—Whatever, he explains that this clash has convinced him the Bactrian war cannot be won quickly, and therefore plans for an attack on India from the west must be shelved. In the event, they were discarded."

"I see." Everard's pipe had gone out. He tamped the bowl and struck a fresh match. "That sally, the fight that followed, was more than an incident, then."

"Precisely," Shalten said. "Professor Soloviev elaborates on the idea, in an article for the *Literaturnaya Gazeta,* and this is what has triggered general interest."

He puffed, sipped, and went on: "Antiochus III is known to history as Antiochus the Great. Inheriting an empire in collapse, he hammered it back together and recovered most of what had fallen away. At the battle of Raphia he lost Phoenicia and Palestine to Ptolemy of Egypt, but eventually he was to win them back. He put the Parthians in check. He campaigned as far as Greece. He gave refuge to Hannibal after the Second Punic War. At last the Romans trounced him, and he left to his son less than he himself had ruled, but it still was an enormous domain. His cultural and legal innovations were no less important. A seminal figure."

Everard suppressed a remark about Antiochus' love life. "You mean, if he'd gotten killed at Bactra—"

"The dispatch gives no indication that he was ever in danger. His enemies Euthydemus and Demetrius were. And, obscure though their country later became, their resistance changed the course of Antiochus' career."

Shalten knocked the dottle from his pipe, laid it aside, clasped hands behind back, continued his parched lecture; and chill went up and down Everard's spine.

"Professor Soloviev, in his article, speculates at some length, with the weight of authority. He has, for the moment, caught popular fancy around the globe. The thesis is intriguing. The circumstances of the discovery are romantic. And, to be sure, albeit subtly, the professor by implication questions Marxist determinism. He implies that sheer accident—whether a given man does or does not die in a battle—can decide the whole future. That this can be published, and prominently, is a minor sensation itself. It is an early example of the *glasnost* that M. Gorbachev is proclaiming. Widespread attention is very natural."

"Well, I look forward to reading it," Everard said, almost mechanically. Most of him stood in a wind down which blew the scent of tiger . . . man-eater. "Does the idea really stand up, though?"

"Imagine. Bactria falls to Antiochus, early on. That frees the resources he needs for an outright conquest in western India. This in turn strengthens him against Egypt and, more significantly, Rome. One can well visualize him retaining his gains north of the Taurus and assisting Carthage sufficiently that it survives the Third Punic War. Although he himself is tolerant, a descendant of his attempted to crush Judaism in Palestine, as you may read in First and Second Maccabees. Given total power in Asia Minor, that attempt may well succeed. If so, then Christianity never arises. Therefore the entire world that brought you and me into being is a phantom, a might-have-been, which, conceivably, an alternate Time Patrol keeps suppressed."

Everard whistled. "Yeah. And Exaltationists who got themselves an in with Antiochus—and showed up again among later generations of the Seleucids—they'd have a pretty good shot at creating a world to suit themselves, wouldn't they?"

"The thought should occur to them," Shalten said. "First, we know, they will make their Phoenician effort. When that too fails, the remnants of them may remember Bactria."

209 B.C.

With a roar and a rattle that clamored for hours, the army of King Euthydemus re-entered the City of the Horse. Dust smoked over the land to the south, cast up by hoofs and feet, swirled by wind and human tumult. A cloud of it hazed that horizon, where the Bactrian rear guard staved off the foremost Syrians. Trumpets rang, drums boomed, mounts and pack animals neighed, men's voices lifted raw.

Everard mingled with the throngs. He had bought a hooded cloak to obscure his features. In the heat and crowding, such a garment was as unusual as his size, but today nobody paid heed. He worked his way quietly through street and stoa, around the city—*casing the joint,* he told himself; shaping what plans he could, for every set of circumstances he could imagine, within the contraints of what he saw.

Whip-wielding riders cleared ways from gates to barracks. After them came the soldiers, gray with dust, slumped with weariness, mute with thirst. Nonetheless they moved smartly. Most went on horseback, in light armor, lanceheads nodding bright above pennons and regimental standards, ax or bow and quiver at the saddle. They were seldom used as shock troops, for the stirrup was unknown to them, but they sat like centaurs or Comanches, and their hit-run-hit tactics recalled an onslaught by wolves. The infantry that stiffened them was a mixed bag, mercenaries, no few from Ionia or Greece itself; a ripple went over their long, serried pikes, the cadence of their march. The officers riding in crested helmet and figured cuirass seemed mainly Greek or Macedonian.

Jammed against walls, leaning out of windows and over rooftops, folk watched them go past, waved, cheered, wept. Women held infants up, crying against all hope, "See! See your child,——" and a beloved name. Oldsters blinked, peered, shook their heads, more nearly resigned to the caprices of the gods. Boys shouted loudest, sure that the enemy's doom would soon be upon him.

The soldiers never stopped. They were bound for their quarters, a gulp of water, assignments, immediate duty for some on the ramparts. Later, if the foe did not try to storm the gates, they'd get brief leaves in rotation. Then wineshops and joyhouses would fill.

That wasn't going to last, Everard knew. If nothing else, the city could not long feed so many animals. Zoilus and Creon had declared that granaries were well-stocked. The siege would not be a total encirclement. Properly guarded, people could take water from the river. Antiochus might try interdicting traffic on the stream with catapults, but he couldn't stop many supply-laden barges. Under strong escort, an occasional caravan might actually make it overland from other parts of the kingdom. Still, there would only be fodder for a limited number of horses, mules, and camels. The rest must be slaughtered—unless Euthydemus used them in an early effort to break the Syrians.

Short commons for the next couple of years. I'm sure glad I won't be stuck here. Though how I'll get out is, um, problematical.

Once this operation was completed, whether or not it had caught any Exaltationists, the Patrol would come in surreptitious fashion to look for Everard, if he hadn't already called in; and, of course, they'd check to see whether Chandrakumar was okay, and remove their agent in Antiochus' army. Until then, however, all were expendable. It mattered not that Everard was Unattached, thus more valuable than the other two, who made their respective careers as scientist and constable in this milieu. Everard was inside Bactra precisely because his capabilities were equal to a wide variety of unforeseeable situations. Shalten judged it likeliest by far that Raor would base herself here. Unless something went wildly awry, the man who accompanied Antiochus was a backup, no more. But rank made no difference now. What counted was getting the job done. If that cost the life of an Unattached agent, the loss to the corps would be heavy; but the gain was a future saved, everybody who would ever be born and everything they would ever do, learn, create, become. Not a bad bargain. His friends could grieve at their leisure.

This is assuming we do block the bandits and, preferably, nail them.

Records uptime said that the Patrol did succeed, at least in the first objective. But if it should fail, then those records had never existed, the Patrol was never founded, Manse Everard never lived. . . . He pushed the thought off, as he always did when it came to haunt him, and concentrated on his work.

Rumor fanned agitation, Eastern excitability broke into flame, and turmoil filled the streets from gate to gate. It was camouflage for Everard as he went around and around, observing detail after detail, annotating the map in his head.

Repeatedly he passed the house he had ascertained was Theonis'. Two-storied, it obviously surrounded a courtyard like other dwellings of the well-to-do. Though rather small of its kind, much less than Hipponicus', it was faced with polished stone rather than stucco and boasted a porch, narrow but colonnaded beneath a bas-relief frieze. Alleys separated it from its neighbors. The street on which it fronted held the mixture of residences and shops common in an absence of zoning laws. None of the nearby businesses were of a sort to stay open after dark, unless you counted Theonis' own, and it did not advertise itself. That suited her purposes best. *Good. It suits me too.* His plan of action was taking shape.

The populace couldn't sit still. They sought friends, milled aimlessly about, consoled themselves at foodstalls and wineshops where prices had gone into orbit. Hookers, of either sex or none, and cutpurses did a booming trade. Everard had some trouble late in the day finding places open that would sell him what he wanted, mainly a knife and a long rope. He too paid more than he should; the sellers were in no mood to haggle much. The city was hysterical. In due course it would settle down to the long grind of beleaguerment.

Unless Euthydemus sallies and wins. No, no way can he do that. But if he dies trying, and Antiochus enters—the Syrians will doubtless sack Bactra. Poor Hipponicus and family. Poor city. Poor future.

When racket of battle surfed unmistakable over the walls, Everard saw panic erupt. He betook himself elsewhere, fast, but spied guardsmen making for the scene. They must have quelled the disturbance before it touched off a riot, for the swarms began ebbing out of the streets. People realized they'd best get home, or wherever they might find shelter, and stay put.

Presently the noise receded. Trumpets pealed triumph on the battlements. It wasn't really, he knew. The Syrians had merely harassed the Bactrian rear guard until the last of it went through and archers kept off further attack long enough for the gates to be shut. Thereupon the invaders withdrew to make camp. The sun was almost down, the pavements overshadowed. On that account, as well as being emotionally wrung dry, few inhabitants ventured back outside to celebrate.

Everard found a foodstall not yet closed, ate and drank sparingly, sat down on the plinth of a statue's base and rested. That was easier for his body than his mind. He sorely missed his pipe.

Dusk deepened until the city brimmed with night. Coolness descended from stars and Milky Way. Everard got moving. Though he went as unobtrusively as he was able, in the quiet his footfalls sounded loud to him.

Gandarian Street seemed empty of all but shadows. He slouched past Theonis' house to make sure, before he returned to take stance a short distance from one corner of the porch. Now it was to act fast.

He let the coiled fifty feet of hempen rope slither from his arm to the ground. In the end that he kept he had made a running noose. A cornice jutted from the entablature, wan against heaven. Adapted, his eyes saw it pretty clearly, though distances were tricky to gauge. The noose widened as he swung it around his head. At the right moment, he let fly.

Damn! Not quite the right moment. He tautened, ready to flee. Nothing happened. Nobody had heard the slight impact. He drew the lasso back. On his third try, he caught the cornice and gave a silent whoop when the cord snugged tight. *Not bad, considering.*

He wasn't a celebrity hound, but after he'd decided roping was an art that might come in handy, he'd gone to the trouble of making acquaintance with an expert in 1910, who agreed to teach him. His hours with Will Rogers were among the pleasantest of his life.

If he hadn't seen a projection on the house, he'd have used some other way to get up, such as a ladder. He figured this was the least unsafe. Once he'd made his entry—what he did next depended on what he found. His hope was to retrieve some or all of his Patrol gear. If perchance then the whole Exaltationist gang were together for him to gun down— Hardly.

He swarmed aloft and pulled the rope after him. Crouched on the tiles, he removed his sandals and tucked them into a fold of the cloak, which he rolled together and secured to his belt with a short length cut off the cord. The lariat itself he left fast, carrying a bight along as he padded to the ridge above the courtyard.

There he stopped short. He had expected a well of blackness. Instead, light reached yellow fingers from the opposite side. They touched shrubbery around a pool where starlight glimmered. *Oh, oh! Do I roost here till whoever that is has gone to bed, or what?*

After a moment: *No. This might be too good to pass up. If I'm caught*—he touched his sheathed knife—*I should manage not to get taken alive.* Bleakness blew away. *And if I can pull it off, what a stunt!* Toujours l'audace *and damn the torpedoes.*

Nevertheless he lowered the rope, and at last himself, inch by inch.

Jasmine kissed his face, night-fragrant. He used the hedge for cover while he wormed his way around. It was forever and it was an eyeblink before he hunched in a position to watch and listen.

The heat of the day must still be oppressive inside, for a window stood open, uncurtained. From his blind of leaves, he saw straight into the room beyond, and voices floated clear. *Luck, luck, luck!* Ungratefully: *About time I had some*. His efforts had left him sweaty, dry-mouthed, skinned on an ankle, and itching in a dozen places he dared not scratch.

He forgot that, observing.

Raor alone could make a man forget everything else.

The chamber was small, for intimate meetings. Wax tapers in gilt papyrus-shape candlesticks, extravagantly many, cast glow across a Persian rug; furnishings of ebony and rosewood inlaid with nacre; subtly erotic murals that would have done Alicia Austin proud. A man occupied a stool, the woman a couch. A girl was setting a tray of fruits and wine down on a table between them.

Everard barely noticed her. Theonis lounged before him. She wore little jewelry; perhaps what gleamed on fingers, wrist, and bosom held electronics. The gown that fitted the curves and litheness of her was simply cut, thinly woven. She herself was the female of Merau Varagan, his clone mate, his anima. Enough.

"You may go, Cassa," her low voice sang more than said. "You and the other slaves are not to leave your quarters before dawn tonight, unless I call." The eyes narrowed very slightly. It was as if their green shifted for a moment from the hue of malachite to that of seas breaking over a reef. "This is a strict command. Tell them."

Everard thought, though he wasn't sure, that the girl shuddered. "Very good, my lady." She backed out. He supposed the household staff lived dormitory style upstairs.

Raor took a goblet and sipped. The man stirred on his seat. Clad in a blue-bordered white robe, he resembled her sufficiently to identify his race. The gray in his hair was probably artificial. The personality that spoke was forceful, though without the Varagan vividness. "Isn't Sauvo back yet?"

He used his birthtime language, which Everard had long since gotten imprinted. When this hunt ended, if it ever did, the Patrolman would be almost sorry to have those trills and purrs scrubbed from his brain. Not only was the tongue euphonious, it was precise and concise, so much so that a sentence might require an English paragraph to translate it, as if the speakers actually were telling each other what they both knew quite well.

However, he couldn't retain everything he learned in the course of his job. Memory capacity is finite, and there would be other hunts to come. There always were.

"At any moment," Raor said easily. "You are too impatient, Draganizu."

"We have spent years of lifespan already—"

"Not much more than one."

"For you and Sauvo. For me, five, establishing this identity."

"Spend a few more days to protect the investment." Raor smiled, and Everard's heart missed a beat. "Fuming ill becomes a priest of Poseidon."

Oh-ho! Then that's his alias. Theonis' "kinsman." Everard laid hold on the fact, gripped hard, stopped his slide down into infatuation.

"And Buleni even longer, often in hardship and danger," Draganizu continued.

"The merrier for him," Raor jested.

"If Sauvo, then, can't be troubled to time his arrivals—"

Raor lifted a hand that Botticelli could have painted. Her dark-tressed head cocked. "Ah, I think that is he."

Another male Exaltationist entered. His beauty was harsher than Draganizu's. He wore an ordinary tunic and sandals. Raor leaned a little forward, mercurially intent. "Did you lock the door behind you?" she demanded. "I didn't hear."

"Of course," Sauvo answered. "I've never forgotten, have I?" Discomfort crossed Draganizu's visage. Maybe he had been absent-minded in that respect. Once. Raor would have seen to it that he never was afterward. "Especially when the Patrol is on the prowl," Sauvo added.

So, Everard thought, *their garage for timecycles is in a Bluebeard room on this floor . . . toward the rear, since that's where Sauvo came from. . . .*

Draganizu half rose, sat back down, and asked anxiously, "It is, then? You have established it is active here-now?"

Sauvo took another stool; in the ancient world, chairs with backs were rare, mostly for royalty. He helped himself to wine and a fig. "Not to fear, camarado. Whatever clues they came upon, they've misread. They think the trouble spot is elsewhere, years uptime. They sent a man to inquire here-now merely in the interests of thoroughness."

He related the story that Everard had told in the vihara. *He got to Chandrakumar in prison and used a kyradex on him,* the Patrolman realized. *No secrets any more. But most of what Sauvo learned ain't so. Thanks, Shalten.*

"Another change-scheme!" Draganizu exclaimed.

"Ours will nullify it and its operators," Raor murmured. "But first, yes, it would be interesting to learn more about them. Perhaps even to contact them—" Her words stole off into silence, like a snake after prey.

"First," Draganizu said sharply, "we have the fact that this . . . Holbrook . . . broke free and is running loose."

Raor recalled herself to immediacy. "At ease, at ease. We have his weapons and communication equipment."

"When he doesn't report in—"

"I doubt the Patrol expects to hear from him at once. Set him aside for the present, together with those conspirators. We have more urgent matters at hand."

Draganizu turned to Sauvo and asked, "How did you obtain privacy for interrogation?"

"You haven't heard?" His fellow was faintly surprised.

"I only got here a few minutes ago. I have been busy with affairs of my Nicomachus persona. Raor's note said nothing but 'Come.'"

Hand-delivered by a slave, Everard deduced. *No radio. Maybe she feels confident still, but the "Holbrook" business has made her ultra-cautious.*

Silken shoulders rose and fell. "I had persuaded Zoilus to arrange solitary detention for any prisoners taken in this matter," Raor said. "I told him that my connections led me to believe they are dangerous spies."

And when guards and prisoners at the hoosegow were mostly asleep, Sauvo used a timecycle to pop into the cell. Raor was willing to allow that much risk; she didn't figure it was likely the Patrol had anyone in Bactra besides Chandrakumar and Holbrook, one now locked away, the other deprived of his gear and on the lam. Sauvo gave Chandrakumar a stun beam, clapped the kyradex on his head, and when he came to, interviewed him. Thoroughly.

I hope he left the little guy alive. Yes, he doubtless did. Why make the jailers wonder? What could Chandrakumar tell them tomorrow that'd show them he was anything but a lunatic?

Draganizu stared at Raor. "You do have him besotted, do you not?" he said.

"Him and several more," Sauvo responded, while Raor demurely sipped her wine. He laughed. "The seething, jealous looks that Majordomo Xeniades gets! And I'm only supposed to be her employee, not her pimp."

Ah. Sauvo is Xeniades, chief of the household staff. Worth remembering. . . . I sympathize with Zoilus and company. Wouldn't I love to get milady in the sack myself? Everard's grin twisted. *Though I wouldn't dare fall asleep in her arms. She might have a hypo of cyanide tucked away in those raven locks.*

"The Greeks are holding Chandrakumar for us, then," Draganizu said. "But what of the equipment that Holbrook had?"

"He left it behind when he went out, at the house of the man in whose company he arrived," Raor explained. "That person is simply a local merchant. He was dismayed when the squad came to say his guest is a spy and confiscate the guest's baggage. We have no reason to make further trouble for this Hipponicus, and in fact, obviously, it would be unwise." *That's a relief!* "As for the baggage, it is here." Her smile curved feline. "That took a little persuasion too, but Zoilus obliged. He has his ways. I have passed instruments over the property. Most is of this era. Some contains Patrol apparatus."

I guess she stowed it with the timecycles.

Raor set her goblet down and sat straight. Metal rang in the liquid tones. "It shows we must be warier than ever. Overleaping spacetime to get access to the prisoner was taking a necessary chance."

"Not a substantial one." Sauvo presumably wanted to remind her, and perhaps inform Draganizu, that he had maintained this beforehand and that events had justified him. "Holbrook was no more than a courier, and of low grade. Physically formidable, but now his teeth are drawn, and it is clear that his intellect is limited."

Thanks, buddy.

"Still," Raor said, "we must track him down and dispose of him before he somehow gets in touch with others, or before the Patrol takes alarm and comes looking for him."

"They won't know where to look. They will need days merely to gather the first clues."

"We need not help them," Raor clipped. "If we can detect electronics, nucleonics, gravitronics, chronokinesis in action, so can they, and at much greater range. We must not give them any hint that any time travelers other than themselves are present. Between tonight and the climax, we use no more high technology. Is that understood?"

"Unless in emergency," Sauvo persisted. *Yeah, he's trying to assert himself, trying not to be overwhelmed by the Varagan.*

"That emergency would likely be so extreme that our only course is to abandon this whole effort and scuttle off." Raor's scorn softened. "Which would be a pity. It's gone gloriously thus far."

Draganizu had his own self-assertion to make, in his own more querulous style. "Glorious, pleasurable, for you."

He got a look that could have frozen helium. "If you think I enjoy the attentions of Zoilus and his kind, you are welcome to them."

Their nerves are wearing thin, after all the long underground toil. They're mortal too. It encouraged.

Raor relaxed again, took up her wine, crooned, "I admit the puppeting of them has its interest."

Evidently Draganizu reckoned it prudent to return to practicalities. "Do you even forbid radio? If we cannot call Buleni, how shall we coordinate action?"

Raor arched her brows. "Why, you shall carry our messages. Did we not make the arrangement precisely in order to have a communication line in reserve? Siege or no, the Bactrians will let the priest of Poseidon go out on business of his temple, and the Syrians will let him fare in peace. Buleni will see to it that they respect the temenos, whatever they do elsewhere."

Sauvo stroked his chin. "Ye-es," he mused aloud. The three must have been over this same ground and over it during the past year; but they weren't so inhuman that they didn't find comfort in repeating things to each other, and in their language it was quickly done. "An aide to King Antiochus can exert that sort of authority."

It jolted through Everard. *My God! Buleni sure worked his way up, didn't he? Our man among the Syrians hasn't got anything like that rank*. Slowly: *Well, Draganizu mentioned Buleni's been at it for more than five years. The Patrol didn't figure it could spend that much lifespan*.

"Indeed," Raor added, "it is natural that Polydorus come personally to the temple and make an offering."

Buleni's played his Polydorus role as a Poseidon devotee, Everard deduced.

"Ah-ha!" chuckled, quite humanly, Draganizu, otherwise known as Nicomachus, priest at the rural temple of the god.

Raor's words fell crisp. At last they were getting down to brass tacks. "He should be on the alert for your possible arrival. When his pickets inform him you are on your way out of the city, he will go there himself, and engage you in private conversation. This will be late tomorrow, I think, although first we must see how circumstances have evolved."

Draganizu turned uneasy. "Why so soon? Zoilus can't give you Euthydemus' battle plan before he knows it himself. At the moment, surely, Euthydemus has none."

"We must establish the liaison in local eyes," Raor told him. "Besides, you can inform Buleni of the situation here and he can give you the latest details about the Syrians." After a moment, carefully: "The two of you must make certain that King Antiochus is aware of your meeting."

Sauvo nodded. "Ah, yes. Confirming for him that Polydorus does have ties to persons within the city, yes, yes."

Comprehension shivered in Everard: *"Polydorus" has told Antiochus that he has kinfolk inside Bactra with such a grudge against Euthydemus—resulting, maybe, from the usurpation—that they are ready and eager to betray their king. Antiochus must be inclined to believe. After all, he has Polydorus there for a hostage, and Nicomachus will come out from behind the walls. If things go right, Nicomachus will presently give Polydorus the plans according to which Euthydemus means to sally forth. Tipped off, Antiochus stands to win a quick victory. He'll be impressed, and grateful, and ready to accept Polydorus' family into his court. I daresay the lovely Theonis has her intentions concerning him. Be that as it may, the Exaltationists will have their foothold . . . in a world without Danellians or anything but shards of a Time Patrol . . . and they can go on and try to mold it however they want.*

The rumors about Theonis' witchcraft won't hurt. Everard's skin crawled.

"You will have to meet him a second time at least, to convey what Euthydemus means to do, once Zoilus has told me," she was saying. "If nothing else, we want no significant doubts in the mind of Antiochus about the intelligence we supply.

"Of course, at the critical moment, it will again be electronic communications and timecycle surveillance for us. If necessary, energy weapons. I hope, though, that Antiochus will dispose of his rivals in a normal way." Laughter rippled. "We do not want *too* sorcerous a reputation."

"That would attract the Time Patrol," Draganizu agreed.

"No, the Patrol will be nothing, from the instant when Euthydemus dies," Sauvo replied.

"Its remnants downtime will not vanish, remember," Draganizu pointed out, needlessly except to emphasize what followed. "They will not be negligible. The fewer clues to ourselves we leave, the safer we will be, until we have grown too powerful for anything they might attempt. But that will be the work of centuries."

"And what centuries!" burst from Raor. "We four, the last four who are left, become creator gods!" After a moment, deep in her throat: "It is the challenge itself. If we fail and perish, we will still have lived in Exaltation." She sprang to her feet. "And we will pull the world down with us, aflame."

Everard clamped his teeth together till his jaws hurt.

The men in the room rose too. Abruptly Raor went fluid. Her lashes drooped, her lips curved upward and swelled, she beckoned. "Before the next hard and dangerous days begin," she sighed, "this night is ours. Shall we take it?"

The blood leaped and throbbed in Everard. He dug fingers into soil and hung on, as if to anchor himself before he splintered the door and seized her. When he could see clearly and the thunder had faded from his ears, she was departing, an arm around either companion's waist.

Each man carried a candle. They had blown out the rest. Raor left the room, and night possessed it.

Wait. Wait. Give them time to settle down to their fun. Those two lucky bastards— No, I'm not supposed to think like that, am I? Everard considered the stars above him.

What to do? He'd stumbled into a treasure hoard of information. Some repeated what he already knew, some merely satisfied curiosity, but some was beyond valuation. If he could communicate it to the Patrol. Which he could not. Unless he found a transmitter. Should he risk trying, or should he retreat pronto?

Slowly, as he squatted among the blossoms, doubt hardened into decision. He was on his own, isolated. Whatever he did was a gamble. Complete recklessness amounted to dereliction of duty, but he thought he dared raise the ante by a chip or two.

He judged that almost an hour had passed. Raor and her boys would be well engaged, their alertness to the outside world set aside. Alarms must be spotted throughout the house, but probably not against entry. Those would be too liable to go off unnecessarily, when slaves or visitors went in and out; and that incident would be hard to explain away to them.

He rose, flexed cramped muscles, approached the still open window. From his purse he took the flashlight. About four inches long, it bore the appearance of an Apollo figurine carved in ivory, such as people often carried. When he squeezed the ankles, a pencil beam sprang from the head. What he had heard tonight confirmed what he suspected, that detectors were set to register electric currents, or other anachronistic forces, in this vicinity. He assumed the Exaltationists bore signal receivers on their persons that would inform them. This little gadget, though, was a photonic fuel cell, its action no different in principle from his breathing.

Guided by brief flashes, he slipped over the sill, into the room, out to a corridor. Lynx-footed, he passed a pair of open entries and took glimpses. The chambers beyond were furnished with ordinary opulence. Two more had interior doors, shut. The panels of the first were wood sculpture; nymphs and satyrs seemed to leap when the light touched them. He doused it, and the muffled sounds he heard were like their gibing merriment. On the other side, clearly, was where Theonis entertained her gentlemen friends. Everard stood for a minute, shaken by desire, before he could move on.

What the hell is it about her? Looks, behavior, or does she give off something that works like a pheromone? He forced a smile. *That'd be an Exaltationist sort of trick, all right.*

The other door was plain and massive. The room it led to evidently occupied the whole rear of the house. *Yeah, this has got to be where their hoppers and other gadgets and weapons are.* He wasn't about to try picking the clumsy lock. It was for show. The real lock would sense him and scream.

He padded upstairs but stopped at the landing. A few flashes cast around sufficed to verify his guess that this level was everyday utilitarian. Theonis would quite naturally seal off one chamber, where she kept the costly gifts that a meretrix of her class received. Any other visible secrecy would have excited comment.

Everard returned to ground level. *I'd better steal away while I can. Too bad that "away" is all I'm managing to steal. However, a gun or a communicator lying loose was more than I had a right to expect. I've learned the layout here, which is pretty good booty.*

Not that such embryonic plans as he had involved it. But you never knew.

From the courtyard he climbed back onto the roof. At the cornice he drew his knife. With his light to see by, he carefully cut the noose until only a few fibers remained. Then he cast the rope's end to the street, took hold, and slid earthward.

If the line parted when he was halfway down, he shouldn't land too noisily. As was, it held, and he must give several fierce tugs before it broke. There had better be no trace of his visit. He withdrew to an alley, where he put sandals and cloak back on, recoiled the rope and again made a lariat of it.

Okay. Now to skip town. That may be less easy. The gates were barred and manned, the sentinels posted thickly on walls and turrets.

During the day he had marked the likeliest place. It was at the river, of course, the side that could not be attacked by surprise, therefore lightly held. Still, those men were nervous too, wide awake, suspicious of everything that moved, and well armed. What he had going for him was size, strength, combat skills undreamed of here, and desperation.

Plus bullheadedness. One reason I could do my caper at Raor's was that she never looked for anything so unsubtle.

Near the target site he chose a lane opening on the pomoerium, in the murk of which he could stand and wait for an opportunity. That was a long wait. The moon rose and climbed. Twice he almost acted when somebody passed by, but assessed the situation and decided against it. He didn't mind too much, or seethe. The patience of the tiger was upon him.

His chance arrived at last, a soldier walking along the pavement, alone, on his way to report for his watch, and nobody else in sight. Doubtless he'd sneaked from barracks to be with a girl or whomever till a clepsydra, or the stars, or an innate time sense that clockless folk sometimes developed, told him he'd better get going. His hobnails rang on the flags. Moonlight tinged helmet and mail. Everard surged forth after him.

The boy never saw or heard. From behind, great hands closed on his neck and fingers bore down on his carotids. For a moment he struggled, unable to cry out. His heels drummed. He slumped, and Everard dragged him back to the alley.

The Patrolman poised, tense for escape. Nobody came running, nobody shouted. He'd pulled it off. The boy stirred, moaned, sucked in air, groped back toward consciousness.

The sensible thing was to stick the knife in him. But moonlight fell on his face, and he was quite young, and whatever his age, Everard bore him no grudge. The blade gleamed before his eyes. "Behave yourself and you'll live," he heard.

Luckily for him and for Everard's conscience, he did. In the morning he'd be discovered, lying bound with pieces of rope and gagged with pieces of his kilt. He might be whipped, or might be given pack drill—no matter. As for the robbery, that was an incident his superiors would not want publicized.

Without its coif, his helmet went onto the robber's head, just barely. His mail would never fit, but Everard didn't intend getting near enough to anyone else for that to be noticed. If it happened anyway, come worst to worst, a sword was now at his hip.

In the event, he went unchallenged up the stairs to the top of the wall and along it till he reached a suitable spot. Others saw him glimpsewise by poor light, and he stepped briskly, a man on some special errand who should not be hindered. The point at which he stopped lay between two sentry posts, both sufficiently far off that he was a shadow which, maybe, neither guard observed. A patrol on its rounds was farther yet.

The lariat had been around his shoulder. In a single swift movement he secured it to a merlon and cast the end free. Plenty remained to reach the strip of ground between wall and wharf. Immediately he swung himself over the edge and went down. They'd find the rope and wonder whether it was a spy or a hunted criminal who'd exited, but the news was unlikely to reach Theonis.

On the way, he cast his glance about. Dwellings and countryside reached into night-gray that became black, save where houses that had been torched still smoldered red. Elsewhere were brighter points of light, enemy campfires. From the opposite side of the city he would have seen many, many, hemming Bactra in against its river.

His feet struck turf. It was steeply slanted, he nearly lost his balance. Somewhere a dog howled. He made haste, around the rampart, forth into the hinterland.

First let's find a haystack or something and grab a few hours' sleep. Christ, I'm tired! Tomorrow morning the order of business will be water, food if possible, and—whatever seems indicated. We know the song we want, but we're singing strictly by ear, and one sour note could get us booed off the stage. California of the late twentieth century seemed more distant than the stars.

Why the devil am I remembering California?

1988 A.D.

When the phone rang in his New York apartment, he muttered a curse and was tempted to let his answering machine handle it. The music was bearing him upward and up on its tide. But the matter could be important. He didn't unthinkingly give out his unlisted number. He left the armchair, put receiver to ear, and grunted, "Manse Everard speaking."

"Hello," said the slightly burred contralto, "this is Wanda Tamberly," and he was glad he had responded. "I, I hope I haven't . . . interrupted you."

"No, no," he told her, "a quiet evening at home alone. What can I do for you?"

Her words stumbled. "Manse, I feel awful about this, but—that date of ours—could we possibly change it?"

"Why, sure. What's the problem, may I ask?"

"It's, oh, my parents, they want to take me and my sister on a weekend excursion . . . a family farewell party, before I go off to m-my new job— Bad enough, lying to them," she blurted, "w-without hurting them. They wouldn't blame me or anything, but, but it would seem like I didn't care much. Wouldn't it?"

"Of course, of course. No difficulty at all." Everard laughed. "For a minute there, I was afraid you were going to stand me up."

"Huh? Me, turn you down, after everything you've done and—" She attempted humor. "A new recruitie, on the eve of entering the Academy of the Time Patrol, cancels her date with an Unattached agent who wants to give her a jolly send-off. It might earn me a certain amount of awe, but that kind I can do without." The jauntiness broke down. "Sir, you—Manse—you've been so kind. Could I ask one thing more? I don't want to be grabby or, or a wimp, but—could we talk when you get here, just talk, a couple of hours, maybe? Instead of going to dinner, if you're short on time or, well, growing bored. I can understand if you are, though you're too nice ever to say it. But I do need . . . advice, and I'll try real hard not to cry on your shoulder."

"You're welcome to. I'm sorry you're having trouble. I'll bring an extra big handkerchief. And I assure you, I am not bored. On the contrary, I insist we have dinner afterward."

"Oh, gosh, Manse, you— Well, it needn't be anything F and E. I mean, you've taken me to a couple of great places, but I don't *have* to drink Dom Perignon w-with my beluga caviar."

He chuckled. "Tell you what, you pick the spot . You're the San Franciscan. Surprise me."

"Why, I—"

"Which, makes no difference to me," he said. "I suspect, though, you'd prefer something small and relaxed this time. You see, I've got a notion of what your problem is. Anyway, I'm mostly a beer and clam chowder type myself. Or whatever you feel like."

"Manse, the truth is, uh—"

"No, please, the phone's no damn good for what I think you have on your mind. Which is normal and innocent and does you credit. I can meet you whenever you want. Perk of being a time traveler, you know. When suits? Meanwhile, cheer up."

"Thank you. Thank you very much." He appreciated the dignity of that, and the way she went straight on to consider arrangements. *A swell kid. An extremely swell kid, in the process of becoming one hell of a woman.* When they said goodnight, he found that the interruption had not broken his enjoyment of the music, complex though the counterpoint was in this section. Rather, he was borne into its majesty as never before. His dreams afterward were happy.

Next day, impatient, he checked out a vehicle and skipped directly to San Francisco on the date agreed, a few hours early. "I expect I'll return home tonight, but late, maybe well into the middle-sized hours," he informed the agent. "Don't worry if my hopper's gone when you come in in the morning." He obtained an alarm-nullifying key, which he would leave in a certain drawer, and caught a city bus to the nearest car rental open twenty-four hours. Then he went to Golden Gate Park and walked off some restlessness.

The early January dusk was falling when he called for Wanda at her parents' home. She met him at the door and continued out, a "'Bye" flung over her shoulder. Streetlight glowed on the blond hair. Her garb was sweater, jacket, tweed skirt, low shoes; evidently he had guessed right about the sort of restaurant she preferred this evening. She smiled, her handclasp was firm, but what he saw in her eyes made him escort her directly to the car. "Good to see you," he said.

He barely heard: "Oh, you don't know how good it is to see you."

Nevertheless, as they climbed in, he remarked, "I feel a little rude, not saying hello to your folks."

She bit her lip. "I rushed you. It's okay. They're glad to have me staying with them again, before I leave, but they wouldn't want to keep me waiting when I'm on a heavy date."

He started the motor. "I'd only have swapped a few words, in my old-fashioned way."

"I know, but— Well, I wasn't sure I could've stood it. They don't pry, but they are interested in this, uh, somewhat mysterious man I've met, even though they've only seen him twice before. I'd've had to . . . pretend—"

"Uh-huh. As a liar, you have neither talent, experience, nor desire."

"Right." Briefly, she touched his arm. "And I'm doing it to *them*."

"The price we pay. I should have put you in touch with your uncle Steve. He could make you feel better about it."

"I thought of that, but you—well—"

He smiled ruefully. "Father figure?"

"I don't know. I truly don't. I mean, well, yes, you're high in the Patrol and you rescued me and you've sponsored me and, and everything, but I— It's hard getting in touch with my feelings— Psychobabble! I think I want to think of you as a friend but don't quite dare."

"Let's see what we can do about that," he suggested, calmer on the outside than the inside. *Damn, but she's attractive.*

She looked around her. "Where are you headed?"

"I thought we could park on Twin Peaks and talk. The sky's clear, the view's superb, and nobody else who happens to be there will pay any attention to us."

She hesitated an instant. "Okay."

Could be preliminary to a seduction. Which'd be fine under different circumstances. However, as is— "When we're finished, I look forward to the beanery you've picked. Then, if you aren't too tired, I know an Irish pub off lower Clement Street where they blarney and sing and two or three middle-aged, gentlemanly working stiffs will doubtless ask you to dance."

He could hear that she understood what he was saying. "Sounds great. I never heard of it. You do get around, don't you?"

"In random fashion." He kept conversation easy while he drove, and sensed that already her spirits were lifting.

Magnificence spread below the mountain, city like a galaxy of million-hued stars, bridges a-soar over shimmering waters toward heights where homes gleamed beyond counting. Wind boomed, full of sea. It was too cold to stand in for long. While they did, her hand sought his. When they took shelter in the car, soon she leaned against him and he put an arm about her shoulder; and at last, gently, once, they kissed.

What she had to say was what he had awaited. Demons needed exorcising. Her guilt toward her family was genuine, yet also the mask of a hundred fears. The first excitement, that she—she!—could join the Time Patrol, had inevitably waned. Nobody was able to sustain such joy. There followed the interviews, tests, preliminary study material, and the thinking, the thinking.

All is flux. Reality eddies changeful upon ultimate quantum chaos. Not only is your life forever in danger, the fact of your ever having lived is, with the whole world and its history that you know.

You will be denied foreknowledge of your triumphs, because that would make more likely your disasters. As nearly as may be, you shall work from cause to effect, without turn or twist, like any other mortal. Paradox is the enemy.

You will have the capability of going back and visiting again your beloved dead, but you shall not, for you might feel temptation to fend off death from them, and you would surely feel your heart torn asunder.

Over and over, helpless to help, you will dwell amidst sorrow and horror.

We guard what is. We may not ask whether it should be. We had best not ask what "is" means.

"I don't know, Manse, I just don't know. Do I have the strength? The wisdom, the discipline, the . . . the hardness? Should I quit while I can, take silence conditioning, go back to the life . . . my folks hoped I'd have?"

"Aw, now, things aren't that bad, they just seem that way. And ought to, at this stage. If you didn't have the intelligence and sensitivity to wonder, worry, yes, fear—why, you wouldn't belong in the corps.

"—doing science, studying prehistoric life. I more'n half envy you. Earth was a planet fit for gods, unbelievable, before civilization mucked it up.

"—no harm to your parents or anybody. Just a secret you keep from them. Don't tell me you were always absolutely frank at home! And in fact, there'll be undercover helps you can give them that'd be impossible otherwise.

"—centuries of lifespan, and never sick a single day.

"—friendship. Some pretty splendid people in our ranks.

"—fun. Experiences. Living to the hilt. Come a furlough, how'd you like to see the Parthenon when it was new or Chrysopolis when it will be new, on Mars? Camp out in Yellowstone before Columbus sailed, then stand on the dock at Huelva and wave him bon voyage? Watch Nijinksy dance or Garrick play Lear or Michelangelo paint? You name it, and within reasonable limits, you've got an excellent chance it can be arranged. Not to mention parties we throw among ourselves. Imagine what a mixed gang!

"—you know damn well you won't back out. It's not in your nature. So go for broke."

—until she hugged him a final time and said shakily, between tears and laughter, "Yes. You're right. Oh, thank you, Manse, thank you. You've put my head straight, and in . . . in . . . why, less than two hours, hasn't it been?"

"Naw, I didn't do much, except nudge you toward the decision you were bound to reach." Everard shifted his legs, cramped after sitting. "It made me hungry, though. How about that dinner?"

"You know it!" she exclaimed, as eager as he for escape into lightness. "You mentioned clam chowder on the phone—"

"Doesn't have to be," he said, touched that she remembered. "Whatever you want. Name it."

"Well, we were talking small and unfancy, plus delicious, and I thought of Ernie's Neptune Fish Grotto on Irving Street."

"Tally-ho." He started the car.

As they wound downward, losing the galaxy and the wind that roared above it, she turned pensive. "Manse?"

"Yes?"

"When I called you in New York, some music was playing in the background. I suppose you were having yourself a concert." She smiled. "I can see you, shoes off, feet up, pipe in one hand and beer mug in the other. What was it? Something Baroque, sounded like, and I imagined I knew Baroque, sort of, but this was strange to me and . . . and beautiful, and I'd like to get a copy of that cassette."

He harked back. "Not exactly a cassette. I use equipment from uptime when I'm alone. But, sure, I'll be glad to transcribe for you. It's Bach. The *St. Mark Passion*."

"What? Wait a minute!"

Everard nodded. "Yeah. It doesn't exist today, apart from a few fragments. Never published. But on Good Friday, 1731, a time traveler brought disguised recording gear to the cathedral in Leipzig."

She shivered. "That makes goose bumps."

"Uh-huh. Another value of chronokinesis, and another perk of being in the Patrol."

She turned her head and considered him. "You aren't the simple Garrison Keillor farm boy you claim to be, are you?" she murmured. "No, not at all."

He shrugged. "Why can't a farm boy enjoy Bach along with his meat and potatoes?"

209 B.C.

About four miles northeast of Bactra, a spring rose in a grove of poplars, halfway up a low hill. It had long been sacred to the god of underground waters. Folk brought offerings there in hopes of protection from earthquake, drought, and murrain on their livestock. When Theonis endowed remodeling of the shrine and rededication to Poseidon, with a regular priest coming out of the city from time to time to conduct rites, no one objected. They simply identified this deity with theirs, continued using the old name if they wished, and felt they might well have gained some special benefits for their horses.

Approaching, Everard saw the trees first. Their leaves shivered silvery in the morning airs. They surrounded a low earthen wall with an entry but no gate. It simply defined the temenos, the holy ground. Uncounted generations of feet had beaten hard the path toward it.

Elsewhere stretched trampled fields where some farmsteads stood intact but abandoned; others had become smoldering ash and blackened adobe. The invaders hadn't begun systematically plundering, nor had they ventured against the settlements close to the city. That would soon happen.

Their camp stood two miles south, thence reaching in ordered ranks of tents within a ditch and embankment. The royal pavilion lifted gaudily hued above the plain leather that housed the grunts. Pennons fluttered and standards gleamed. Metal flashed too, on men at their posts. Smoke drifted from fires. A muted surf of noise came to Everard, tramping, shouting, neighing, clangor. Afar, several parties of mounted scouts raised dust clouds as they cantered about.

Nobody had molested him, but he had bided his time, watchful, till none were near his route. Else he might have gotten killed on general principles; he didn't think the Syrians were ready yet to take captives for the slave market. Nor were they prepared to hazard Poseidon's wrath—especially after the king's aide Polydorus issued orders to that effect. It was a relief to enter the grove. The shade against the rising heat of the day was like a benison itself.

It scarcely eased the grimness within him.

The temple occupied most of its unpaved court although it was not much bigger now than when it had been just a shrine. Three steps led to a portico supported by four Corinthian columns, before a windowless building. The pillars were stone, perhaps veneer, and the roof ruddy tile. Everything else was whitewashed mud brick. Nothing fancier was expected at such a minor halidom, and of course to Raor it would have served its entire purpose when it had been the scene of two or three meetings between Draganizu and Buleni.

Two women squatted in a corner of the temenos. The young one held a baby to her breast. The old one clutched a half-eaten round of chapatti that, with a clay water jug, must be the entire rations they had. Their peasant gowns were torn and dirtied. When Everard appeared, they huddled back against the wall and terror overrode the exhaustion in their faces.

A man emerged from the temple's single entrance. He wore a plain but decent white tunic. Shuffling bent, almost toothless, squinting and blinking, he could be as old as sixty or as young as forty. Before scientific medicine, unless you were upper class you needed a lot of luck to reach middle age still in good health, if you reached it at all. *Twentieth-century intellectuals call technofixes dehumanizing*, Everard recollected.

The man wasn't senile, however. "Rejoice, O stranger, if you come peacefully," he said in Greek. "Know that this precinct is sacred, and though the Kings Antiochus and Euthydemus be at war, both have declared it sanctuary."

Everard lifted his palm, saluting. "I am a pilgrim, reverend father," he averred.

"Eh? Not me, not me. I'm no priest, only the caretaker here, Dolon, slave to the priest Nicomachus," replied the other. Evidently he lived in a hut somewhere nearby and was present during the day. "Truly a pilgrim? How did you ever hear of our little naos? Are you sure you've not gone astray?" He drew close, stopped, peered dubiously. "Are you indeed a pilgrim? We can't let anybody in for warlike purposes."

"I am no soldier." Everard's cloak draped over his sword, not that a traveler could be blamed for going armed. "I've come a weary way to find the temple of Poseidon that stands outside the City of the Horse."

Dolon shook his head. "Have you food along? I can offer nothing. Supplies are cut off. I've no idea when anything will get through to sustain me, let alone anybody else." He glanced at the women. "I dreaded a pack of fugitives, but it seems most countryfolk got into town or elsewhere in time."

Everard's belly growled. He ignored it and the pang. A man in good shape and properly trained could go several days without eating before he weakened significantly. "I ask for no more than water."

"Holy water, from the god's own well, remember. What brings you here?" Suspicion sharpened. "How can you know about this temple when it's only been Poseidon's these past few months?"

Everard had his story prepared. "I am Androcles from Thrace," he said. That half-barbarian region, its interior little known to Greeks, could plausibly have bred a man his size. "An oracle there told me last year that if I came to Bactria, I'd find a temple of the god outside the royal city, and help for my trouble. I mustn't tell you about that trouble, except that I haven't sinned, I'm not impure."

"A prophecy, then, a foreseeing of the future," Dolon breathed. He wasn't awed into immediate acceptance. "Did you travel all that way alone? Hundreds of parasangs, wasn't it?"

"No, no, I paid to accompany caravans and the like. I was in one such, bound for Bactra at last, when news came of a hostile army moving in. The caravan master turned back. I couldn't bear to, but rode on, believing the god I seek would look after me. Yesterday a robber band—peasants made homeless and desperate, I think—waylaid me. They got my horse and baggage mule, but by the god's grace I escaped, and continued afoot. So here I am."

"You've suffered many woes indeed," said Dolon, turning sympathetic. "What must you do now?"

"Wait till the god gives me, uh, further instructions. I suppose that will be in a dream."

"Well, now—well—I don't know. This is, is irregular. Ask the priest. He's in the city, but they should let him come out to . . . see to things."

"No, please! I told you I'm vowed to silence. If the priest asks questions, and I refuse to answer, and he insists—wouldn't the Earthshaker be angered?"

"Well, but—"

"See here," Everard proposed, hoping he came across as both forceful and friendly, "I have a purse of money left. Once I've gotten my sign from the god, I mean to make a substantial donation. A gold stater." It was the rough equivalent of a thousand 1980's U.S. dollars, insofar as comparisons of purchasing power between different milieus meant anything. "I should think that would let you—the temple buy what you need from the Syrians for a long time to come."

Dolon hesitated.

"It's the god's will at work," Everard pursued. "You wouldn't thwart his will, I'm sure. He helps me, I help you. All I ask is to wait in peace till the miracle happens. Call me a fugitive. See." He reached down, opened the purse, took forth several drachmas. "Plenty of money, if nothing else. Let me give you this for yourself. You deserve it. For me, it's a deed of piety."

Dolon trembled a moment more, reached decision, and held out his hands. "Very well, very well, pilgrim. The gods do move in mysterious ways."

Everard paid him. "Let me go inside now, to pray and to drink of the god's bounty, become his guest in truth. Afterward I'll sit quietly out here and bother nobody."

The cool dimness kissed sweaty, dusty skin and dry lips. The spring bubbled up at the center, out of a slope on which the foundation rested. It partly filled a hole in the floor, then drained through a pipe inside the masonry, which must lead under the temenos wall to a rivulet in its natural channel. Behind was a rough stone block, the ancient altar. The image of Poseidon stood painted on the rear wall, barely discernible in this light. Elsewhere on the floor lay a clutter of offerings, mostly crude clay models of houses, beasts, or human organs that the god was thought to have aided. No doubt priest Nicomachus took whatever was perishable or valuable back with him when he returned to town from his visits.

Your simple faith hasn't availed you much, folks, has it? Everard thought sadly.

Dolon made reverence. Everard followed suit as best he was able, about as well as you would expect of a Thracian. Kneeling, the caretaker dipped a cup of water and gave it to the suppliant. In Everard's present state, the icy tang was more welcome than a beer. His prayer of thanks came close to sincerity.

"I will leave you alone with the god for a while," Dolon said. "You may fill yonder jug for yourself and, duly grateful, carry it out." Bowing to the icon, he left.

I'd better not take long, the Patrolman realized. *However, a little comfort and privacy, a chance to think—*

His plans were vague. The objective was to get into the Syrian camp and find the military surgeon Caletor of Oinoparas, known at home as Hyman Birnbaum and, like Everard, long since given a regenerative procedure enabling him to live among pagans without drawing comment. Maybe they could invent some excuse to go off together, maybe Birnbaum could arrange for Everard's unhindered departure. What counted was to take a transceiver sufficiently many miles away that the Exaltationist instruments wouldn't detect a call, above the faint intermittent background of communication between unheeding time travelers elsewhere in the world. Let the Patrol know what Everard had learned, so it could prepare a trap.

Though judging by what I've discovered about their precautions, the likelihood of our bagging all four is very small. Damn. God damn.

Never mind. The immediate need was to reach Birnbaum, with enemy troops apt to skewer a stranger on sight. He might deter them by shouting that he bore a vital message, but then he'd be haled before officers who'd want to know what it was, and if he named Caletor, the surgeon would surely be examined too—under torture, when it turned out neither man had anything convincing to say.

He'd come to the temple in hopes of finding somebody in charge with more authority than the slave, an underpriest or acolyte or whatever. From such a person he might have gotten religious tokens, an escort, or the like, passing him through the Syrian pickets tomorrow. If he demonstrated his flashlight and said Poseidon had personally given it to him in the night— Of course, that must wait till Nicomachus-Draganizu had met with Polydorus-Buleni and both had left again. Everard had considered not arriving here before then; but skulking about this countryside meanwhile was at least as dangerous as sitting unobtrusively in the court, and he just might observe something useful—

The scheme had been precarious at best. Now it looked ridiculous. *Well, maybe a fresh notion will occur*. He grinned, largely a snarl. *An action too unsubtle for them, same as yesterday only more so*.

He went out into sunlight that briefly overwhelmed vision. "I think already I felt the god's nearness, strengthening me," he said weightily. "I believe I am doing what he wants, and you are, Dolon. Let's not go astray."

"No, no." In a hasty mutter, the caretaker cautioned him against defiling the temenos—there was a privy on the far side of the grove—and hobbled back to shelter.

Everard sought the corner where the women sat. Fear no longer stared up at him. Instead he saw grief dulled by fatigue and despair. He couldn't bring himself to greet them with "Rejoice."

"May I join you?" he asked.

"We can't forbid you," mumbled the old woman (forty years of life behind her?).

He lowered himself to the ground beside the young one. She had been good-looking a day or two ago, before her spirit was shattered. "I too await the will of the god," he said.

"We only wait," she answered tonelessly.

"Uh, my name is Androcles, a pilgrim. You live hereabouts?"

"We did."

The crone stirred. For a minute, a bitter vitality flickered. "Our home was downstream, so far that we didn't get warning till late," she told him. "My son said we must load an oxcart full of what we could take off the farm, or we'd be beggars in the city. Horsemen caught us on the road. They killed him and the boys. They ravished his wife. At least they didn't kill us also. We found the gates shut. We thought the Earthshaker might give us refuge."

"I wish they had killed us," the young woman said in her dead voice. The infant began to cry. Mechanically, she bared a breast and gave suck. Her free hand stretched a fold of sleeve across to screen against the sun and the flies.

"I'm sorry" was all Everard could think of. *That's war for you, the thing that governments do best*. "I'll name you in my prayers to him."

They didn't reply. Well, numbness was a mercy of sorts. He raised his hood and leaned back. Poplars gave scant shade. The heat in the wall baked through his cloak.

Hours passed. As often before during a long and uncertain wait—though oftenest in future centuries—he withdrew into memories. Occasionally he drank some lukewarm water, occasionally he catnapped. The sun trudged up the sky and started down.

—clouds racing on the wind, light stabbing between them to blaze off the waves, cordage a-thrum, chill salt spray as the ship plunges through seas that thunder green, gray, white-maned, and "Ha!" Bjarni Herjulfsson shouts at the steering oar. "A gull," promise of the new land ahead—

The end came slowly at first, then in a rush. Everard heard noises grow, hoofbeats, voices, clatter. His flesh tingled. Instantly alert, he pulled the hood further forward to shadow his face, lifted his knees, and slumped his shoulders to look as apathetic as the women still were.

Respecting sanctity, the Syrians dismounted outside the grove. Six of them, armed and armored, followed a man into the temenos. Like them, he went in mail and greaves, sword at side, but a horsehair plume stood tall on his helmet, a red mantle hung from his shoulders, an ivory baton was in his hand, held like a swagger stick, and he overtopped his followers by inches. The features within the iron were as if carved by Praxiteles in alabaster.

Dolon hurried down the steps and prostrated himself. When Alexander prevailed over Asia, the Orient took Hellas over. Rome would have the same experience, unless the Exaltationists aborted its destiny. *They won't. One way or another, we'll stop them.* Energy blazed from Buleni-Polydorus. *But Christ, if they give us the slip again, with this experience for a lesson—*

"You may rise," said the aide of King Antiochus. He glanced at those who hunched in the angle of the wall. "Who are they?"

"Fugitives, master," Dolon quavered. "They claim sanctuary."

The splendid one shrugged. "Well, let the priest decide what to do about them. He's on his way. We require the temple for a private conference."

"Certainly, master, certainly."

Obedient to snapped orders, the soldiers took stance on either side of the entry and beneath the stairs. Buleni went inside. Dolon joined Everard and the women, keeping his feet, nervous, perhaps finding comfort in even such wretched company as was theirs.

Yeah. Nicomachus spoke to the authorities inside Bactra. He may or may not have needed a little help from Zoilus; Theonis would take care of that. The priest must go out and see to his temple. Best would be if a ranking enemy officer could meet him there and they discuss terms more precisely. Neither side in the war wants to offend the Earthshaker. Heralds negotiated. It went easily. Among other considerations, King Antiochus knows his ADC Polydorus is in league with a disaffected element inside the city, and this will establish the espionage link.

More noises, less arrogant. Again Dolon went flat. Dignified in a white robe that must have complicated his muleback ride from town, Nicomachus paced through the entrance. A slave boy trotted at his side, upholding a parasol. A soldier followed, obviously a Syrian assigned as escort. He and the boy halted while the priest went into the building, after which they hunkered down and relaxed.

Everard was barely aware of them. He sat as if blinded by sunblaze off the thing he had seen on Draganizu's breast. It wasn't big, a medallion hung on a chain, but he knew what was on the obverse, he'd have known that thing in a coal bin could he have touched it. Athene's owl. His own two-way communicator.

The world steadied around him. *Why not?* he thought. *Why sur-*

prised, even? They're maintaining radio silence for the time being, but they'll want to get in touch right away, should the need arise. Buleni's bound to have one on his person somewhere. Patrol issue is superior to anything they likely brought with them, and wearing this is typical Exaltationist swank, and there's no reason why a priest of Poseidon shouldn't pay Athene honor. In fact, it's a tactful gesture, considering how often those two are at loggerheads in the Odyssey. *Ecumenicism—* He strangled a laugh. *What startled me when I saw?*

The knowledge came forth. He understood he had seen what might be his death.

And yet—and yet, by God!

He'd have a fighting man's chance of pulling it off. His prospects of survival were poor in any event. This way, he stood to nail yonder bastards, and maybe, maybe—

I needn't commit right this minute. Let me think, let me marshal my memories elsewhere than in this oven of a courtyard.

Everard rose. He was stiff and he hurt after his long immobility. He started slowly toward the gateway.

A trooper drew blade. "Halt!" he barked. "Where are you going?"

Everard stopped. "Please, to the privy behind the temenos," he said.

"Now you just wait—"

Everard loomed at him. "You wouldn't make me befoul the holy ground, would you? I hate to think what the god would do to us both."

Dolon tottered over. "He's a victim of robbers, the Earthshaker's given him refuge, he's Poseidon's guest," the caretaker explained.

The soldier swapped looks with his mates and sheathed his sword. "All right," he agreed. Stepping to the entry, he called to the pair who watched the horses beyond that this fellow had leave to go. The women's gazes trailed the large man wistfully. He had given them a kind word.

Everard sauntered among the trees, savoring their shade. *Not too slow,* he reminded himself. *I don't imagine Buleni and Draganizu will be inside any longer than it takes them to update each other.* He didn't need the shack as such, but it screened him while he did a few exercises to limber his muscles and took sword in hand beneath his cloak. On the way back, he did drag his feet. That would seem natural enough to anyone who noticed. With his height, he could look over the wall into the temenos.

He was rounding the far corner when the two principals reappeared. Everard quickened his steps. The Exaltationists reached the ground as the Patrolman came through the opening. "Out o' the way, you," the nearest guardsman told him.

"Yes, sir." Everard made a production of clumsily salaaming and scuffing off at a slant that brought him closer to his prey. Those two walked on, side by side. Buleni noticed the loutish form ahead and scowled.

It was a small enclosure. When Everard sprang, he had just six feet to go.

Draganizu could touch a point on his medallion while he lifted it toward his mouth, and send an alarm. He must die first. Everard's leap was a lunge. His steel went in at the throat and out the nape. Blood spouted, sun-brilliant red. The corpse crashed backward.

Shifting weight as he pounced, Everard landed on his heel, pivoted, and brought his left fist in an uppercut to Buleni's chin. It was the only blow he could deliver quickly to a man in helmet and mail. The Exaltationist's weapon was already half free. He lurched, caught his balance, and completed the draw. A superman. But a little shaken, a tad slow. Everard closed. His left hand chopped edge on at the sword wrist. The blade of his right hand cracked into Buleni's larynx. He felt cartilage break. Buleni dropped on all fours and retched blood.

Dolon wailed. The soldiers dashed forward, armament aflash. Everard cast himself down beside Draganizu's gaping face. He snatched the wet medallion, thumbed it, and rasped in Temporal, "Unattached Everard. Come immediately. Combat."

That was what he had time for. The first Syrian was at him. He rolled over. Supine, he gave a two-footed kick. The man reeled from him. More arrived. They blotted out the sky.

One crumpled onto Everard. "O-oof-f-f!" A metal-clad body flopping bonelessly onto your stomach takes the wind out of you.

When Everard got it back again and sat up, the troopers lay around him where they had collapsed, an ungainly heap. Their breathing snored and wheezed. He knew those beyond the wall had likewise received stun beams and would be comatose for about a quarter hour. Otherwise they were unharmed. A timecycle had landed nearby. A Chinese-looking man and a black woman, hard and supple in skin-tight coveralls, helped him rise. Four more vehicles poised low above the temple; he spied energy projectors in taut hands. "Overkill," he croaked.

"What, sir?" asked the man.

"Never mind. Let's look this situation over, fast." Everard would not allow himself to think, yet, how nearly dead he was. He would not permit himself sentiment. That way lay the shakes, which he couldn't afford. Patrol training summoned the full reserves of mind and body. Later, at leisure, he would pay nature's debt.

When it got his call, the Patrol had mobilized a force, safely distant from here, and dispatched it to the instant of his need. Now he must use the resource given him with the same precision. However, he could spare a few minutes to plan his next move.

Buleni was still alive, barely. Everard pointed. "Bring him and the killed Exaltationist to operation headquarters," he ordered through an unsoiled transceiver given him. "They'll know there what they want to do with 'em." He walked around. Poor old Dolon sprawled in the dust at his feet. "Carry this man into the temple, out of the sun. Give him a medic check and whatever care he needs that you can administer on the spot. I suspect he'd benefit from a stimulant injection. The rest can lie where they are till they rouse."

The women had not been stunned, in the corner where they were. They cowered back, made alive again by terror, the grandmother embracing the mother, the mother clutching the child. Everard went over and stood above them. He knew he was a fearsome sight, bloodstained, sweat-dripping, begrimed, but he could fashion a smile.

"Listen," he said, as gently as his hoarsened voice was able, "listen well. You have seen the wrath of Poseidon. But it was not against you. I repeat, the Earthshaker is not angry at you. Men here have offended him. They shall be borne to Hades. You are innocent. The god blesses you. In token of that, I am to give you this." He had been unshipping his purse. He dropped it in front of them. "It is yours. Poseidon cast a slumber on these soldiers, lest they behold what they should not, but he will do them no further harm after they awaken, if they in their turn will see to the well-being of you, his wards. Tell them that. Do you understand me?"

The baby cried, the mother sobbed. The granny met Everard's eyes and said, with a steadiness that must be due in part to shock, "I who am old believe I dare understand you and remember."

"Good." He left them and resumed his Patrol business. He had done the best for them that he possibly could—bending rules well out of shape, but after all, he was an Unattached agent.

Anxiety touched his rescuers. "Sir," ventured the young woman, "excuse me for asking, but this thing we've done—"

She must be pretty new in the field, but she had handled her job smartly. He decided she and her fellows were worth a minute's field education. "Don't worry. We've not upset history. What's your birth milieu?"

"Jamaica, sir, 1950."

"Okay, to put it in terms of your era, imagine you see a brawl start. Suddenly several helicopters come down. They drop tear gas bombs that disable the crowd without seriously hurting anybody. Men climb out wearing masks. They lug two of the brawlers into a chopper. One man tells the witnesses that these are dangerous Communists and this squadron is from the CIA, seizing them at the request of the local government. The squadron flits away. Let's suppose this all happens in an isolated valley, the phone lines are cut, there's no immediate linkage with anywhere else.

"Well, locally it'd be a ninety days' wonder. By the time the story got to the rest of the world, though, it'd be stale and diluted, the news media would give it little or no play, most people who heard about it at all would guess it was a wild exaggeration and soon forget it. Even you folks who were on hand would stop talking much about it, and it'd fade in your recollections. You weren't really affected, and you have your lives to get on with. Besides, there's nothing inherently impossible. You know helicopters, tear gas, and the CIA exist. This was a weird sort of incident, but still, just an incident. You'd tell your children, but probably they wouldn't tell theirs.

"That's what a brief intervention by the gods is like, in the minds of people here-now. Of course, we only stage one when we absolutely must, and the sooner we scramble, the better."

Through his communicator Everard included the rest in his instructions. The slain and the live Exaltationist had been slung onto timecycles that blinked from the scene. An extra Patrolman had gone with them, leaving saddle and weapons for the Unattached. Everard's companion was a tough, stocky man from Europe of his own period, Imre Ruszek, who sat behind him while he piloted. He cast the women a last glance as he rose on antigrav, and saw bewilderment struggling with hope.

The three hoppers lifted high enough to be no more than glints to any eyes that might chance to catch them, and glided toward Bactra. Below them the land rolled vast from the mountains in the south, fields green and brown, spotted with trees and tiny buildings, the river mercury-bright, the city and the invader camp toylike. No hint of hatred and misery reached these clean cold winds, save what the riders bore with them.

"Now hear this," Everard intoned. "There are two bandits left, and if we go about it right, I think we may well take them. The operative phrase is 'go about it right.' We only get one shot. No fancy dodging around in time, trying to fix things, if this fails. It's all very well to show the locals a miracle, but we will *not* play games with causality and risk setting off a temporal vortex, even if the risk does seem small. Is that clear? You've had the doctrine drilled into you, I know, but Ruszek and I are going down, and if we come to grief, somebody could be tempted to rashness. Don't be."

He described Raor's house and its layout. Alarms were set to yell the moment a vehicle made a space-time jump, departing or arriving, anywhere in a radius of many miles. She and Sauvo would promptly dash for their own machine, or machines, and be off for parts unknown. To hell with the other two. Loyalty was a matter of expediency among those ultimate egoists.

That was the case *if* yonder alarms had been alert when Everard called and help for him appeared. The hoppers' computers knew to the microsecond when that was. He designated an instant sixty seconds earlier, when he was assaulting Draganizu and Buleni; they'd not been in a position to benefit from any warnings that were flashed them a minute later. "Call it Time Zero."

At hover, he used magnifying opticals and electronic range finders to determine within a few feet the spot at which he wanted to come into the house. He set the controls for that and Time Zero. The rest of the vehicles would return to then also, but remain aloft till it became clear what had happened on the ground.

"*Go!*" His finger stabbed the main control point.

He, his partner, his timecycle were in a corridor. A window on their right stood open to the light and fragrance of the garden court. The door on their left was massive, shut, and locked. They had cut off access to the enemy's transport.

Sauvo sped around the corner of the hall, deer-swift. His hand gripped an energy pistol. Ruszek shot first. A thin blue flame streaked past Everard. It pierced Sauvo's chest. The tunic around it scorched. For that eyeblink of time, the fury on his face became the pathetic surprise of a child suddenly struck. He fell. Scant blood ran from him, most was cooked, but otherwise he died in the usual human uncleanliness.

"A stunner might have been too slow," Ruszek said.

Everard nodded. "Okay," he answered. "Sit tight. I'll hunt for the last of 'em." Into his communicator: "Third down, one to go." The squad should catch his meaning. "We hold the depot. Watch the doors. If a woman comes out, nab her." As if from far away he heard terrified sobbing, a female slave, and wished that none of those innocents would suffer.

"That will not be necessary," sang coldly through the noise. "I will be no game for your curs to chase."

Raor walked toward them. A thin gown clung to every flowing stride. The ebon hair fell loose around beauty and scorn. Everard thought of Artemis the Huntress. His heart stumbled.

She halted a short way off. He dismounted and approached her. *My God*, he thought, filthy and stinking, *I feel like a naughty schoolboy called up by the teacher*. He straightened and stopped. His pulse throbbed, but he could meet the sea-green eyes.

She continued in Greek: "This is remarkable. I do believe you are that same agent my clone mate spoke of, who almost captured him in Colombia."

"And almost in Perú, and did it in Phoenicia," he replied, not as a boast but because it seemed she had the imperial right to know.

"You are no ordinary animal, then." Venom slid into the softness.

"Nevertheless, an animal. The apes have triumphed. The universe has lost any meaning it ever held."

"What . . . would you . . . have done with it?"

The glorious head lifted. Pride rang. "We would have made it what we chose, and unmade and remade it, and stormed the stars as we warred for possession, with an entire reality the funeral pyre of each who fell and entire histories the funeral games, until the last god reigned alone."

Desire blew out of him on a winter wind. Suddenly he wanted to be home, among homely things and old friends. "Secure her, Ruszek," he ordered. Through the transceiver: "Come join us and let's get this business finished."

1902 A.D.

Shalten's flat in Paris was large and luxurious, but on the Left Bank overlooking the Boulevard St. Germain. Had he chosen that street purposely? He did have a devious sense of humor. To Everard he remarked that he enjoyed the Bohemian life around him and his neighbors were used to eccentrics, paying him no special notice.

It was a warm fall afternoon. Windows admitted air that smelled slightly of smoke, richly of horse droppings. An occasional automobile stuttered among the wagons and carriages. Between soot-gray walls, under trees where green had begun turning yellow and brown, people thronged the sidewalks. Cafés, boutiques, boulangeries, patisseries did lively trade. The noise that rolled in was full of cheer. Everard tried not to remember that in a dozen years this world would crash to ruin.

The clutter around him, furniture, hangings, pictures, books, busts, bric-à-brac, declared a solidity that had endured and accumulated since the Congress of Vienna. But he recognized a few of the objects from California, 1987. That was quite another world, remote as a dream—a nightmare?

He leaned back in his armchair. Leather creaked, horsehair rustled. He puffed on his pipe. "We had a little trouble finding

Chandrakumar," he finished, "not knowing where in the jail he was. Prisoners in several cells got an astonishing vision. But we did locate him and take him out. He hadn't been harmed. I admit that added to the mess we'd already made, apparitions and vanishings and everything else. It might've caused a real sensation in peacetime. People then had too much else on their minds, though, and in crises, you always get a lot of hysterical stories flying about. They're soon forgotten. The field report I've seen says history is intact. But you've surely seen it too."

History. The stream of events, great and small, running from cavemen to the Danellians. But what about the eddies, the bubbles, the insignificant little individuals and happenings that are also soon forgotten, whose being or nonbeing makes no difference to the course of the stream? I'd like to go back and find out what became of my trekmates, Hipponicus, those two women and the baby. . . . No. I've only so much lifespan left me, whatever the length of it turns out to be, and it'll hold heartbreak enough. Maybe they survived okay.

Seated opposite, Shalten nodded above his churchwarden. "Naturally," he said. "Not that I ever feared. You might or might not have laid the Exaltationists by the heels—congratulations on your success—but you were certain to act in an informed and responsible manner. Besides, that is a particularly stable section of space-time."

"Huh?"

"Hellenistic Syria was important, but Bactria lay on the fringe of that civilization. Its influence was always marginal, at most. After Antiochus and Euthydemus made peace—"

Yeah, a nice reconciliation, the prince marrying the princess, everything lovey-dovey again, and who cares about a lot of killing, maiming, raping, looting, burning, famine, pestilence, impoverishment, enslavement, hopes crushed and lives broken? All in the day's work, if you're a government.

"—Antiochus, as you know, proceeded to India, but achieved nothing. His real interests lay in the West. When Demetrius succeeded to the Bactrian throne, he in his turn invaded India, but a fresh usurper rose behind his back and took Bactria itself from him. Civil strife followed." The big bald head shook. "I must admit that the genius of the Greeks never extended to statecraft."

"True," murmured Everard. "In, uh, 1981, I think it is, they'll take for their prime minister a professor from Berkeley."

Shalten blinked, shrugged the interruption off, and proceeded: "By 135 B.C., Bactria had fallen to the nomads. They were not inhumane, but under them civilization withered. The Hellenic dynasty in western India had meanwhile been absorbed culturally by its subjects, and it did not long outlive its northern cousin. It had had no lasting effect worth mention, and the memory of it faded fast."

"I know," said Everard, annoyed.

"I did not mean to patronize you," Shalten replied blandly, "only to make clear my point. Greek Bactria was as safe a piece of history as we could find to lure the Exaltationists to. It had never much mattered to the rest of the world, and an extraordinary concatenation of fantastically implausible occurrences, not just there but around the entire Hellenistic sphere, would have been required to change this. Therefore, by the law of action and reaction, its own mesh of world lines is especially stable, especially hard to distort. Of course, we were at pains to give the Exaltationists the opposite impression."

Everard sank back in his chair. "I'll . . . be . . . damned." *Probably*, gibed his mind.

Shalten's parched little smile twitched. "And now," he said, "we must terminate the deception. As I recall, the expression in your natal period is 'tie up the loose ends.' In your position among us, you need to know the whole truth. For you to learn it later in this century could poze a hazard. Causational loops can be very subtle. Your experiences and accomplishments in Bactria must continue to have happened. Therefore you must be informed well pastward of our preparations for them. I thought you would enjoy a visit to my *Belle Époque*."

"Uh, you mean, uh, that letter the Russian soldier found in Afghanistan, that became the bait in our trap—it was a fake?"

"Exactly. Did the thought never occur to you?"

"But—you had a million years or more to find some suitable incident—"

"Better to create one to specifications. Eh? Well, it has served its purpose. Prudence dictates that it be removed, annulled. There shall never have been a letter to find."

Everard sat straight. The stem of his pipe broke in his fist. He ignored the coals that fell onto the lush carpet. "Wait a minute!" he cried. "You've been tinkering with reality yourself?"

"Under authorization," he heard; and his jaws locked on silence.

1985 A.D.

Here, where the Bear stars wheeled too low, night struck cold into blood and bone. By day, mountains closed off every horizon with stone, snow, glaciers, clouds. A man's mouth dried as he gasped his way over the ridges, rocks rattling from beneath his boots, for he could never draw one honest breath of air. And then there was fear of the rifle bullet or the knife after dark that would spill his bit of life out on this empty land.

Yuri Alexeievitch Garshin stumbled lost and alone.

PART THREE

BEFORE THE GODS THAT MADE THE GODS

31,275,389 B.C.

"Oh!" Wanda Tamberly cried. "Oh, look!"

Her horse snorted and shied. Hands and knees worked for her, quieting it, while she herself leaned forward, sight grabbing what it could as the marvel passed by. Alarmed at the approach of the great beasts, a dozen animals had bolted from the underbrush on her left. Brightness flashed over mottled coats, bodies of wolfhound size, trifurcate hoofs, heads eerily equine. Then they were across the trail and lost again in wilderness.

Tu Sequeira laughed. "Ancestors?" He touched his mount and hers, as though to demonstrate he knew that man's forebears were snuffling and scuttling about in African jungles. On their way back, his fingers stroked across her thigh.

She hardly noticed. Happiness bubbled and danced. Earth of the Oligocene epoch was a paleontologist's paradise. "Mesohippus?" she wondered aloud. "I think not, not quite. Nor miohippus; too early for that, isn't it? But they know so little, really. Even with time machines, they've learned so little. An intermediate species? If only I'd brought a camera!"

"A what?" he asked. Unthinkingly, she had thrown the English word into the Temporal that was, thus far, their sole common language.

"An optical recording device." The act of explaining drew off most of her excitement. After all, today she had spied any number of creatures. Patrol folk could not avoid an impact on the surroundings of their Academy, a thinning out of nature. If nothing else, lionlike nimravus and saber-toothed eusmilus had long since been shot by holiday makers whom they attacked; and that affected the entire local ecology. However, when cadets had more than a single day free, they generally flitted to some distant region, a mountain to climb, a scenic path to hike, an idyllic island. On the whole, humankind touched very lightly the ages before humankind evolved. To Tamberly this region seemed still almost virginal, set against the Sierra or the Yellowstone of her birthtime.

"You'll have to learn about cameras," she said, "and a lot of other crude gadgets. Whew! Suddenly I get a notion of just how much you have got to learn."

"We all do," he replied. "I'd be hard put to master everything you must."

Modesty wasn't his usual style. The thought crossed her mind that maybe he was realizing that, although she enjoyed his flamboyancy, it wasn't the sort of thing that could hold her for long. Or—an inward shrug—maybe he'd decided to start practicing a more subdued manner. He'd need that capability in the career ahead of him.

Whichever, he spoke truth. The Patrol took education techniques from the far future of both their eras. In a couple of hours you could gain fluency in any language, directly imprinted in your memory; and that was a minor example. Nevertheless the intensity of training and education pushed the edge of human endurance. Any respite came, and went, like sunshine striking into a hurricane's eye. She had joined Sequeira on this excursion because she'd slightly rather do that than sleep.

"Well, but I'll be dealing with critters," she demurred. The Americanism dropped into her Temporal before she noticed. "People are what's complicated, and they'll be your problem."

Born on Mars in the Solar Commonwealth, after graduation he would be among those who studied and monitored the earliest stages of spacefaring. To work one's way into such places as Peenemünde, White Sands, and Tyuratam meant not only personal risk. It meant any sacrifice necessary to preserve the course of events heavy with consequences for history.

Sequeira's lips crinkled upward. "Speaking of people and complications, we don't have to report for class till 0800 tomorrow."

She felt the blood rise and beat in her face. What cadets did on their own scant time was their own business, provided it didn't make them unfit. *Temptation, oh, my. A fling before the next long grind—But do I want any such involvement?* "At the moment the mess hall calls," she said fast. They ate well there, often gloriously. The staff had the cuisines of the ages at their command.

He laughed again. "Far be it from me to stand in your way. I could get a Wanda-sized hole through me, couldn't I? Afterward—Let's go!" The trail was barely wide enough for them to sit side by side, knees touching. He put heels to his horse and set off at a brisk canter. Following, she thought that his litheness should not be clad in a plain issue coverall; a scarlet cloak ought to ripple from those shoulders. *Hey, gal, ease off.*

They left the woods and descended steeply out of the hills. An eastward view opened to her. For a moment she lost everything but the awe and the wonder of being here, now, she herself, thirty million years before she was born.

Light streamed golden across a prairie reaching beyond sight. Wildflower-starred, grass rippled and, she knew, rustled under the wind. In places, a grove or a thicket interrupted immensity, and in the distance trees lined a great brown river. She knew also how its water and its mud surged with life, larvae, insects, fish, frogs, snakes, waterfowl, herds of rooting merycoidodon like giant hogs or small slender hippopotami. Wings filled heaven.

The Academy stood closer, on an elevation which the builders had reinforced to keep it safe above the occasional floods. Through millennium after millennium, gardens, lawns, bowers, low-lying structures of subtle curves and shifty colors, remained inviolate. When the last graduate departed, the builders took it down, eliminating every trace of its existence. But that would not happen for another fifty thousand years.

Riding, Tamberly drank air that was mild, rich with odors of growth, soil, sulfury-sweet herbs. And yet the sun had barely passed through the vernal equinox. What was to be South Dakota lay about her like a dream of what was to be California. Not for geological epochs would the Ice come down from the north.

The trail broadened to a beaten path. A fork in it led around campus to stables at the rear. Sequeira and Tamberly stalled and cared for their horses themselves. Not all Patrol work, probably not most, required that kind of skills, but the Academy did—in case of need and, she suspected, to instill workmanship and responsibility. Banter flew back and forth across the chores. *He is a fetching rascal,* she thought.

They emerged hand in hand. Sunset rays fell hazily over the man who waited outside and cast his shadow gigantic behind him. "Good evening," he greeted. The voice was unemphatic, his garb resembled theirs, but somehow she got a sense of utter control. "Cadet Tamberly?" It was not actually a question. "My name is Guion. I would like a word with you."

Sequeira stiffened at her side. Her pulse jumped. "Is something wrong?" she asked.

"Nothing to cause you worry." Guion smiled. She couldn't tell how deep it went. Nor could she identify his race. The finely formed countenance hinted at—aristocracy?—but from what century beyond hers? "In fact, may I have the honor of your company at dinner? If you will pardon us, Cadet Sequeira."

How did he know I'd be here? Plenty of possible ways, of course, if you're high-ranking. Why, though? "Oh, gosh," she blurted, "I'm all dusty and sweaty and, and everything."

"You will have cleaned and changed in any case," Guion said dryly. "Would an hour hence suit you? Number 207, Faculty Lodge. Quite informal. Thank you. I look forward." He gave her a courtesy salute. Dazed, she returned it. He walked off toward officer country. His gait flowed.

"What's happening?" Sequeira whispered.

"I, I haven't the faintest idea. But I'd better go. Sorry, Tu. Another time." Maybe. She hastened from him. Soon she forgot about him.

Preparing herself helped clear away bewilderment. A cadet had a private room, plus a bath cubicle as exotically, efficiently equipped as Manse Everard had promised. Like most of her classmates, she'd brought along a few clothes from home. The mingling of costumes added color to social occasions. Not that those weren't amply romantic, give the diversity of origins. (At that, it was limited. She had had explained to her that people from really unlike civilizations would find one another too distracting—incomprehensible or downright repulsive. Most of her fellow recruits came from the years approximately between 1850 and 2000. Some, like Sequeira, originated farther uptime; their cultures were compatible with hers and exposure to her sort was a valuable part of their particular training.) After a while she chose a plain black dress, silver-and-turquoise Navaho pendant, low shoes, the least touch of makeup.

Neutral, she hoped, neither brash nor standoffish. Whatever Guion's agenda, she didn't imagine seduction was on it. *Nor on mine. God, no!* She must somehow be of some interest to him. At the same time, she was the merest rookie and he was . . . a big wheel. Unattached, almost certainly. Or more than that? She had been taught very little—hardly anything, she realized now that she examined it—about the upper hierarchy of the Patrol.

Maybe none existed. Maybe by Guion's era humankind had outgrown the necessity. Maybe tonight she'd learn a snippet about that. Eagerness tingled anxiety out of her.

Crossing the campus, where luminous paths shone softly beneath dusk, she hailed those of her fellows whom she met less warmly than they did her. Close friendships were developing, but her mind had gone elsewhere. Seeing how she was clad and where she was bound, they didn't try to detain her. Naturally, speculation would be thick in the dorms, and tomorrow she must be prepared with responses, if only "I'm afraid I can't tell you. Confidential. Excuse me, I've got a class."

Briefly, she wondered whether every lot of new recruits spent its year in the same collegiate format as hers. Probably not. Societies, ways of living and thinking and feeling, must vary too much through a million years of history. Indeed, a large part of what she did would look crazy to her professors at Stanford, utterly boggle them. She couldn't repress a giggle.

She had never been inside Faculty Lodge or seen any pictures from it, and a side entrance brought her into a small, bare chamber from which a gravity shaft bore her straight upward. The democratic atmosphere of the Academy was merely that, an atmosphere, useful for purposes of getting on with the job. She stepped into a corridor where the floor, uncarpeted, lay soft and warm underfoot, like live flesh, and light poured iridescent from all around. Door 207 vanished at her approach and reappeared when she had passed through. The rooms beyond were graciously furnished, in a style more nearly familiar—to put visitors such as she at their ease, she guessed. There was no window, but ceilings revealed the sky, the light of the stars enhanced so that she could see them blink forth, unblurred by the clean air, until the night was full of their majesty.

Guion welcomed her with a gentlemanly handshake and in the same wise conducted her to a seat. Frames on the walls enclosed moving, three-dimensional scenes, cliffs above surf and a mountain silhouetted against dawn. She didn't know whether they were recorded or live. She didn't recognize the background music either, but it could be Japanese, and again she suspected it had been carefully chosen for her.

"May I offer you an apéritif?" Guion invited. He used fluent, barely accented English.

"Well, a small dry sherry, if you please, sir," she ventured in the same language.

He chuckled and sat down across from her. "Yes, you shall keep a clear head for tomorrow morning. The dinner I have planned won't upset your Spartan routine too badly. How do you like our organization thus far?"

She spent several seconds arranging her words. "Very much, sir. Tough but fascinating. You knew I would."

He nodded. "The preliminary tests are reliable."

"And then you have reports on how I did—how I will do— No, let me try saying it in Temporal."

His gaze was steady upon her. "Don't. You should know better than that, Cadet Tamberly."

A machine glided in bearing her drink and something in a snifter glass for him. It gave her the chance to recover. "I'm sorry if I misspoke myself. The time travel paradoxes—" Mustering courage: "But honestly, sir, I can't believe you haven't looked."

He nodded. "Yes. That can be done with reasonable assurance and safety, in this protected environment. To no one's surprise, you will perform creditably."

"Which doesn't let me off the hook earlier, does it?"

"Of course not. You must do the work, gain the abilities. Some individuals, hearing that they will succeed, would be tempted to slack off on the grueling effort; but you have more sense."

"I know. Success isn't really guaranteed. I could change that bit of history by goofing; and I sure don't want to." Despite his low-key manner, tension was again gathering in her. She sipped fragrant pungency and tried to make muscles loosen, the way she was learning in phy ed. "Sir, why am I here? I didn't think I was anybody special."

"Every agent of the Time Patrol is," he answered.

"Well, uh, but me—I'm just going to be a field scientist. In the prehistoric, and not even anthropology. About as far from any causal nexus as you can get, I should think. What have I got that, uh, that interests you?"

"The circumstances that brought you to us are unusual."

"Isn't everything unusual?" she exclaimed. "How likely was it ever that I, this exact I with this exact combination of genes, would get born? My sister isn't a lot like me."

"Sensibly put." Guion leaned back and partook of his own drink. "Probability is relative. Granted, the events that caught you up were melodramatic; but in a way melodrama is the norm of reality. What could be more sensational than the fiery creation of the universe, of the galaxies and stars? What could have appeared amidst them more strange than life? Dire need, mortal conflict, desperation made it evolve. We survive by waging incessant warfare against invading microscopic hosts and betrayals within. Set beside this, clashes between humans seem ridiculously incidental. Yet they determine our fate."

His quiet tone and donnish diction calmed her more than did a little alcohol or relaxation technique. "Well, sir, what can I tell you?" she asked. "I'll do my best."

He sighed. "If I had definite questions, this session would doubtless not be necessary." Another smile. "Which would be my loss, true. I am not so alien to you that I don't expect to find pleasure in your company during these next few hours." On a level below words, she understood that his courtliness had no ulterior motive—except to soothe her till she could reveal the nuances he desired—and might be sincere.

"I search for clues to a certain matter," he went on. "You are analogous to a witness, an innocent bystander, who may or may not have noticed something at an accident or a crime, something helpful to the officer investigating the case. That is why I use your mother tongue. In any other, including Temporal, your expressiveness would be too limited. Your very body language would be poorly coordinated with what you are saying."

A crime? She shivered a bit. "Whatever I can do, sir."

"That will mainly be to talk freely, for the most part about yourself. People seldom object to doing that, eh?" He turned grave. "I repeat, you have done nothing wrong, and quite possibly have nothing to do with the business. But you understand I must find out."

"How?" she breathed. "What is this . . . business?"

"I cannot say." She wondered if that meant he was forbidden to. "But think of the countless world lines intermeshed throughout the continuum as a spiderweb. A touch on one strand trembles through many. A disruption somewhere changes the configuration of the whole. You have learned that causality does not work exclusively from past to future; it can double back on itself, can even annul itself. There are occasions when we know only that the web is troubled, not where or when the source of the disturbance lies; for that source perhaps does not exist in our yet, our reality. We can only try to trace it back up the threads—" He broke off. "Enough. I do not mean to frighten you."

"I don't scare easy, sir." *This could do it, though.*

"Consider my mission precautionary," he urged. "You, like Agent Everard, have been intimately"—sketched a grin—"if unwillingly associated with the Exaltationists, a major disruptive force."

"But they've all been, will be caught or killed," she protested. "Won't they?"

"Yes. However, they could be related to something larger." He raised a palm. "Not a larger organization or conspiracy, no. We have no reason to suspect that. But chaos itself has a certain basic coherence. Things have a way of recurring. People do.

"Therefore it is wise to study those who have been part of great events. They may again, whether or not our extant records know anything of it."

"But I was just, just borne along," she stammered. "Manse—Agent Everard, he was the one who counted."

"I want to make sure of that," Guion said.

He let her sit a span in silence, while the stars strengthened overhead and shaped constellations unknown to Galileo. When he spoke anew, she had come to terms with the situation.

She wasn't important, she decided. Impossible. This wasn't humility—she expected to do a topflight job in her coming line of work—but common sense. Enigmatic though he might be, this man was simply behaving like any conscientious detective, checking out every conceivable lead, aware that most led nowhere.

And, yes, he might well enjoy a meal and conversation with a young woman who wasn't bad-looking. Then why shouldn't she enjoy too? What might *she* learn about *him* and the world from which he hailed?

As it turned out, nothing.

Guion was affable. She could almost call him charming, in his detached scholastic fashion. He made no display of his authority, but left her in no doubt of it, much like her father during her childhood. *(Oh, Dad, who'll never know!)* Instead, he drew her out about herself, her life, Everard, asking for no confidences but nonetheless so deftly that only later did she realize she had told him more than she meant to. At first, after bidding him adieu, she knew simply that she had had an interesting dinner date. He didn't imply they would meet any more.

Walking back to her room on paths now deserted, among the night scents of ancient Earth, she found herself, oddly, thinking less about him, not to mention Sequeira, than about big, soft-spoken, and—she believed—rather lonely Manse Everard.

PART FOUR

BERINGIA

13,212 B.C.

She stopped when she reached her shelter and stood a moment, looking around her and back the way she had come. *Why?* she wondered. *As though this is the last time ever.* With an unawaited pang: *Well, maybe it is, almost.*

Southwesterly the sun hung low above the sea, but would not sink for hours yet, and then only briefly. Its rays washed chill gold over cumulus clouds towering in the east and set the waters agleam, half a mile away. Thence land rose steeply toward northern ridges. It was wan with summer's short grass, broken here and there by intense greens and browns of peat moss. Leaves shivered pale on stands of stunted aspen. Elsewhere grew thick patches of scrub willow, seldom more than ankle-high. Sedges rippled and rustled along a nearby brook. It tinkled down to a river not very wide either, sunken from her sight in a ravine. She could see the tops of dwarf alder clustered on the sides. Smoke tatters blew from the dens of Aryuk and his family.

A wind had risen off the sea. It made her face tingle. The boisterous damp quenched some of the weariness in her but roused hunger; she had tramped quite a ways today. Cries cut through, from birds aloft in their hundreds, gulls, ducks, geese, cranes, swans, plover, snipe, curlews, an eagle high at hover. After two years she still found marvel in the lavishness of life, at the very gates of the Ice. Not before leaving her home world had she really known how impoverished it was.

"Sorry, friends," she murmured. "My teapot and crackerbox are calling me." *After which I'd better do up my report. Dinner can wait.* She grimaced. *Reporting won't be the kind of fun it used to be.*

She stiffened. *Naw, why're you so spooky about what's happened?* she demanded. *A big event, sure, but not necessarily a big bad one. Premonitions? Scat! Listen, gal, it's natural to talk to yourself now and then, and okay to talk to the fauna just a bit, but when your bugaboos start talking to you, quite likely you have been in the field long enough.*

Unsealing the dome, she entered and closed it again. The interior was dim until she activated a transparency. (Nobody around to peep in it at her, not that the dear We ever would without her leave.) Warmth let her slip off her parka, sit down to remove boots and stockings, wiggle her toes.

There wasn't much else she could move freely, as cramped as the place was. Her timecycle occupied a large part of the floor, under a shelf on which she kept mattress pad and sleeping bag. The single chair stood at the single table, where a computer and auxiliary apparatus claimed half the top. Alongside was a unit for cooking, washing, et cetera. Miscellaneous boxes and cabinets completed the circle. Two held clothes and other personal possessions; the rest were full of stuff related to her mission. Policy required the dome be as small, as unobtrusive in the land and lives of the natives, as possible. Outdoors was plenty of space, elbows few and far between.

Having set water to boil, she undid her gun belt and put the pistols, stunner and killer, away beside the long weapons. For the first time, they felt ugly in her hands. She had seldom killed, just for meat and when she reluctantly deemed it necessary to take a specimen—and, once, a snow lion that Ulungu's family at Bubbling Springs told her had turned man-eater. *Humans? Nonsense! Judas priest, but you've gotten edgy all of a sudden.*

Recognizing the exclamation in her mind, she smiled. She'd picked it up from Manse Everard. He tried to keep his language polite in the presence of women, as he'd been taught. She'd noticed that he was more comfortable if she curbed hers likewise, and obliged him except when she forgot.

Some music ought to soothe. She touched the computer. "Mozart," she said. "Uh, *Eine Kleine Nachtmusik*." The strains lilted forth. Only then did she notice, with faint surprise, what she had ordered. Not that she didn't like Mozart, but she'd been remembering Manse and he detested rock. *Well, probably this'll work better anyway.*

A cup of Darjeeling and an oatmeal cookie wrought their own wonders. Presently she could settle down to record. Nevertheless, after speaking her preamble she played it back before going on, to find whether it was as unwontedly awkward as it had sounded to her.

From the screen, blue eyes under blond brows gazed out of a countenance blunt-nosed, strong of cheekbones and chin. Hair irregularly sun-bleached fell tousled to the jawline, past skin tanned darker than ever on a California beach. *Oh, dear, have I actually gotten to look like that? You'd think I was thirty, and I am only— I'm not born yet.* The thin-worn joke somehow heartened. *Once I'm back, beauty parlor, here I come.*

A slightly husky contralto said: "Wanda Tamberly, Specialist second class, scientific field agent, at—" Chronological and geographical identification followed, in the coordinates used by the Time Patrol. The spoken language was its Temporal.

"I suspect a crisis is in the making. As, uh, as reference to my previous reports shows, hitherto, throughout the duration in which I have made my visits—"

"Dry up!" she told the image, and blanked it. *Since when has the Patrol wanted academese? You're overwrought, girl. Reverting to the classroom. Don't. It's four whole years since you were an undergrad. Lifeline years, full of experience and history. Prehistory.* She took several deep breaths, consciously relaxed herself muscle by muscle, and thought about a certain koan. Though she wasn't into Zen or anything like that, some of the tricks were helpful. Starting over:

"I think they've got troubles ahead of them here. You remember how these people are the only ones in the world, as far as they are concerned. I'm the first outsider they've met." The explorers who learned how to talk with them and something of their ways had touched down three centuries ago and were totally forgotten, unless a wisp of folk memory had slipped into myth. "Well, today Aryuk and I found some newcomers.

"I'll take it from the beginning. Yesterday his son Dzuryan returned from a bachelor wandering. That was experimental, adolescent; the kid's no more than twelve or thirteen, I'd guess, not seriously looking for a mate. Never mind. Dzuryan returned and among other things told how he'd seen a herd of mammoth at Bison Swale."

The designation would suffice. She had already sent uptime the maps she sketched as she ranged around. Place names were her own. Those that the We bestowed often varied according to who was talking. They did tell the same stories about sites, over and over. ("In this hollow, in the spring after the Great Hard Winter, Khongan saw a pack of wolves bringing down a bison. He fetched men from two camps. With stones and torches they drove the wolves off. They carried the meat home and everybody feasted. They left the head for the spirits.")

"I got pretty excited." *Hoo boy, did I!* "Mammoth seldom come within twenty miles of the coast, never this close before. Why? When I said I'd go look, Aryuk insisted on accompanying me personally." *He's a darling, so concerned about his guest, his miracle-working, tale-telling, land-ignorant klutz.* "Well, I certainly didn't mind a partner. I'm not much acquainted with that area. We set off today at sunrise."

Tamberly reached up to remove her headband. She popped out the thumbnail-sized instrument that had captured everything she saw and heard, plugged it into the databox, ran fingers over keyboard. The whole contents would go into the record, but for this report she should enter only what was immediately relevant. However, as hours unreeled in minutes, she could not resist slowing down for an occasional scene.

A southern hillside gave shelter from wind. She and Aryuk had stopped to drink at a spring welling out of it. Watching, she remembered how cold the water was and how it tasted of earth and stone; she remembered sunlight on her back and the pungencies that it baked from small herbs. Soil lay soft underfoot, still wet from springtime's melt. Mosquitoes whined innumerable.

Aryuk filled his hands and slurped. Drops glistened in the black beard that fell to his breast. "You want to rest a while?" he asked.

"No, let's push on, I'm eager." That was approximately what Tamberly said. Still less than Temporal—which, being devised for time travelers, at least originated in a high-tech culture—did the Tula language have English equivalents. It was a trilling, clucking tongue, agglutinative, embodying concepts at whose subtleties she could only guess. For a single instance, the genders were seven, four pertaining to certain plants, weather phenomena, the heavenly bodies, and the dead.

Aryuk laughed, revealing the absence of various teeth. "Your strength is boundless. You wear an old man out."

The Tulat, a word that she rendered as "We," didn't keep track of days or years. She gauged him as being in his middle or late thirties. Few among his people got much past forty. Already he had two living grandchildren. His body, thin but whipcord tough, continued in good shape, aside from the scars left by injuries that got infected. He stood three inches shorter than she, but then, she was a fairly tall woman in the twentieth-century United States. All was plain to see, for he went quite nude. Ordinarily at this season he might have worn a grass poncho as protection against the mosquitoes. Today he traveled with Her Who Knows Strangeness. They never came near her. Tamberly hadn't tried to explain how a little gadget on her belt worked. She wasn't too sure herself; it was from the future of her birthtime. Supersonics?

Aryuk cocked his shock head and glanced at her from beneath heavy brow ridges. "You could wear me out in ways more fun than walking," he suggested.

When she waved dismissal, the weathered, big-nosed visage crinkled with more laughter. It had been evident that his proposition was mere teasing. Quick to realize that the foreigner meant them no harm, and indeed could occasionally use her powers to relieve distress, the We were soon joking and frolicking in her presence. She was mysterious, true, but so was well-nigh everything else in their world.

"We shall go on," she said.

Volatile, Aryuk sobered and agreed. "Wisest. If we make haste, we can be home before sundown." He flinched. "Yonder is not our territory. Perhaps you know what ghosts prowl it after dark. I do not." That mood also breezed away. "Perhaps I will knock down a rabbit. Tseshu"—his woman—"loves rabbit."

He picked up the rudely chipped, almond-shaped stone he carried along, missile and knife and bone-cracker. Other tools were as primitive and little more specialized. The style traced to the Mousterian or a similar tradition, Neanderthal man's. Of course, Aryuk was fully Homo sapiens, archaic Caucasoid; his ancestors had drifted here from western Asia. Tamberly had sometimes reflected on the irony that the very first Americans were closer to being white than anything else.

At a swinging, energy-conserving, mile-devouring pace, he and she had proceeded northwest. In the dome, she fast-forwarded. *Why'd I stop for that scene? Nothing significant. Unless it's the last of its kind for me, ever.*

She let herself relive two more. Once she saw a herd of wild ponies, shaggy and long-headed, gallop on a ridge against the sky. Once she saw, afar, a herd of Pleistocene bison, the lead bull eight feet at the hump. To those mighty ones Aryuk sang a song of awe.

His folk were not really hunters. They took fish from the rivers and lakes with their hands or in crude weirs. They collected shellfish, eggs, nestlings, grubs, roots, berries in season. They snared birds, rodents, other small game. Now and then they came upon a fawn, calf, whelp, or upon a large carcass still edible; in the latter case they took the hide too. It was no wonder they were scarce and had left hardly a trace of their presence, even in lands far south of the glacier.

A flicker in the screen caught Tamberly's eye. She stopped the playback, recognized the view, nodded. Restarting the record function, she moistened lips gone suddenly dry and said, "About noon, we reached what we were after." Distorted molecules held a notation of the precise local time. "I will enter this unedited." She could have done so in a fractional second, but decided to sit back and watch it through. Maybe she'd notice details that had escaped her before or think of a new interpretation. In any event, it was wise to refresh memory. At mission headquarters she was bound to get a skinningly intense debriefing.

Again she saw where she had been. The scattered woodlands of the seaboard were behind her. Watery though it was, this open country was better called steppe than tundra. Herbal growth spread like a carpet, dull greens occasionally interrupted by a few scrub willows or silvery patches of reindeer moss. In the offing were some birch, not much larger than the willows but densely clustered, vanguards of an invasion. Pools and sedgy marshes glinted manifold. Two hawks cruised the wind, theirs the only wings in sight; grouse, ptarmigan, and the rest must be lying as low as the muskrats and lemmings. The mammoths moved slowly, feeding, less than a mile away. Stomach rumbles rolled across the distance.

Aryuk heard her cry out. He tensed. "What is wrong?" he asked.

The screen showed her extended arm and the tiny figures at which her finger pointed. "There! Can you see them?"

Aryuk shaded his eyes, squinted, strained. "No, things blur away." That savages all have keen sight is a superstition on a par with their all enjoying robust health.

"*Men*. And—and—oh, come." The scene jounced. Tamberly had broken into a run. Aryuk tightened his grip on the hand ax and loped at her side, though fear stood naked on his face.

The strangers spied them, poised, briefly conferred, and sped likewise toward a meeting. Tamberly counted them: seven. That was as many adults as dwelt at Aryuk's place, if you included the half-grown, and these were entirely male.

They did not make straight for her and him, but at an angle. Soon she could see their leader beckon, and altered her course accordingly. She recalled thinking between breaths: *Yeah, they don't want to alarm the mammoths. Must've been trailing them for days, skillfully harassing, to bring them into parts where they wouldn't ordinarily go, an area poor in their kind of food but rich in mudholes and suchlike spots where hunters have a fair chance of trapping one and killing it.*

They were stocky, black-haired, attired in leather coats, trousers, boots. Each carried a spear with a head of bone slotted to hold a row of flint bladelets, a cutting edge long and keen. At his waist hung a pouch, which doubtless bore provisions and a sharpened stone that served as a knife. Under the belt was a hatchet. A roll of hide across the shoulders must be a blanket. It wrapped two or three more lances. Readily accessible beneath the lashings was tucked a spearthrower of the grooved type. Stone, wood, antler, bone, skin were beautifully worked. As Tamberly and Aryuk neared, the men halted. They took loose formation, ready to fight.

No band of Tulat would have done that. Personal violence, including homicide, was not unknown among them, though rare. Collective conflict did not exist, whether in action or imagination.

Both parties stopped. "What are they?" Aryuk gasped. Sweat shone on his sun-darkened skin and he breathed hard, not because of the sprint. To him the unknown was always supernatural, terrifying unless he could come to terms with it. Yet she had seen him venture out on broken ice floes in a storm, to club a seal pup that would feed his family.

"I will try to find out," she said, her voice not altogether steady. Palms raised, she walked toward the strangers; but first she had loosened her pistols in their holsters.

The peaceful approach eased them a trifle. Her vision flickered from one to the next. Beneath their individuality, she searched for underlying sameness, race. Twin braids framed broad countenances with naturally bronze complexions, almond eyes, strong noses, whiskers sparse or absent. Lines of paint patterned brows and cheeks. *I'm no anthropologist*, she had thought amidst her heartbeats, *but I'd guess these count as archaic or proto-Mongoloid. They have surely come from the west. . . .*

"Rich be your gathering," she greeted as she reached them. The Tula language had no word for welcome, which was taken for granted. "What do you find lucky to tell me?" Certain revelations might give an opening to evil spirits or hostile magic.

The tallest of the men, almost her height, young but hard-featured and bold-mannered, trod forth to confront her. What purred and growled from his lips was incomprehensible. She signed as much, smiling, shrugging, shaking her head.

He peered. She understood how weird she must be to him, size, coloring, clothes, accouterments. But he showed none of the initial timidity of the We. After a moment, inch by inch, his free hand crept forward until the fingertips touched her throat. They moved downward.

She had stiffened, then stifled a lunatic impulse to laugh. *Copping a feel, are you?* The exploration moved over her breasts, belly, crotch. It remained moth-gentle and, she saw, impersonal. He was simply verifying that she was the female she seemed to be. *What'd you do if I gave you a gotcha?* She had suppressed that too. Avoid conveying any wrong ideas. When he had finished, she stepped back a pace.

He snapped something to his fellows. They also scowled, first at her, next at Aryuk. Probably women in their tribe didn't go hunting. Probably they supposed she was his mate. Okay, why did he hang behind her?

The leader called to Aryuk. It sounded contemptuous. The Tula cowered the least bit before he braced himself. The leader raised his spear and moved as if to cast it. Aryuk threw himself to the ground. The newcomers barked laughter.

"Now hold on there. Just a minute, bo," Tamberly exclaimed in English.

In the shelter, she lost desire to watch further. She directed the capsule to transfer its remaining information immediately, sighed, and spoke: "As you've seen, we didn't stick around. Those were tough customers. Not stupid tough, though." Her show of indignation, as she brandished her steel sheath knife, had quieted them down. They couldn't decide what to make of her, but stayed put when she and Aryuk withdrew, staring after them until the horizon walled them off. "I'm glad I didn't have to shoot into the air or any such demonstration. Heaven knows what the consequences would have been."

A second later: "Heaven knows what they will be anyway. Those are surely Paleo-Indians out of Siberia. I'll sit tight and wait for further orders."

Removing her recording, she bore it over to one of the message capsules stored by her vehicle, inserted it, set the controls, activated. The cylindroid vanished in a *pop* of air. It wasn't bound for milieu headquarters, because none was maintained this far in the past. Its leap through space-time took it to the project office, which happened to be in her home country and century. All at once she felt very lonesome, very tired.

No prompt response came. They'd figure she needed a night's rest. And a square meal. Scrambling it together, eating, washing dishes relaxed her a lot. However, she wasn't sleepy. She sponge-bathed, donned night clothes, stretched out on her bunk shelf with a pillow against the dome side for a back rest. As the sun lowered more and the interior darkened, she turned on a light. For a while she hesitated over what show to screen or book to read. She'd brought *War and Peace* along, thinking that on this expedition she'd finally get around to it; but she never had, and after a day like today, she wasn't about to start. How about the Travis McGee novels she'd been saving, carried here from her last furlough? No, MacDonald cut too near the bone.

Ah, yes, good old Dick Francis.

II

Red Wolf and his men could not harry the mammoths much farther onto ground well suited for taking one. The beasts no longer gave way, almost carelessly, to their small pests. Oftener and oftener they stopped, stamped their feet, only moved on when they had eaten everything in reach. Yesterday a bull charged, forcing the hunters to scatter and wait till dawn to return. Clearly this herd had come about as far from its wonted range as it would endure.

"By now, hunger dwells in the camp," Horsecatcher said. "I think our undertaking was foredoomed. If the land-wights are angry, let us not offend them more, but go after other game instead, and give them our first kill."

"Not yet," Red Wolf replied. "You know how badly we need to bring down a mammoth. And we shall." More than the flesh and fat were the great bones, tusks, teeth, hide, hair, for making things grown scarce among the Cloud People. More even than that was the victory itself, luck reborn. The trek had been long and grim.

Fear fluttered in the eyes of Caribou Antler. "Has that witch whose hair is like straw said otherwise?" he mumbled. "Too many whispers blow on these winds."

"Why must you think she has powers?" Red Wolf challenged.

"She and the shaggy man went away from us. That was three days ago. Wait and hear what news Running Fox brings."

With such words he kept the band steady until their scout rejoined them. Running Fox told of a deep bog not far off. Thereupon Red Wolf harangued them and they agreed to try.

First everybody went about gathering twigs, dead reeds, and other dry stuff, which they bound into faggots. Red Wolf then took the fire drill. While he worked he sang the Raven Song, and his comrades danced the slow measures of it around him. Night had fallen, but it was the short light night of summer, a dusk through which ponds glimmered and earth reached gray to horizons still visible. The sky was like a shadow overhead, wherein a few stars dimly flickered. Cold deepened.

Red Wolf brought up the rear as they approached the mammoths, lest the burning torch he carried alarm the quarry too soon. Twigs crackled, herbs rustled, ground squelched underfoot. A breeze carried rankness and, he thought, a touch of warmth off the bulks ahead. It made him a little dizzy; he had eaten scantily of late. Noises from throats, trunks, shuffling huge feet quickened his heart and cleared his head. The animals were uneasy after being annoyed throughout these past days. They were ready to stampede.

When he deemed the moment ripe, he whistled. The men heard and dashed back to him. They kindled their brands at his. Now he took the lead. In a broad arc, his band leaped forward. They whirled their fires on high; flames flared, sparks streamed. They sounded forth the wolf's howl, the lion's roar, the bear's growl, and that terrible, sharp-edged, endlessly rising and falling scream which is man's alone.

A mammoth squealed. Another trumpeted. The herd fled. Earth quaked beneath. "Ya-a-ah, ya-a-ah!" Red Wolf shrieked. "This way! Yonder one—drive him— To me, brothers, to me, right and left, drive him! Yee-i-i-i-ya!"

The chosen prey was a young bull that happened to bolt straight toward the bog. Though his companions did not spread widely, they went separate ways, blundering and bleating through the dark. Men saw better than they did. Men overtook him, bounded along his flanks. As the faggots burned short, the hunters threw them. He bawled his terror. Red Wolf sprang close. The tail brushed his shoulders. He drove his spear in underneath, left it to waggle and rip, himself fell back. More weapons whirred from throwing-sticks. When they struck, they hurt almost as much. The mammoth pounded faster. His breath gusted hoarse.

Soil came apart, muck spurted and gulped, he sank to his belly and stood mired. His kin boomed past him, on into the night.

Left in peace, he could have worked free. The hunters gave him none. They darted yelping around the morass and cast spears. They waded out to thrust. Blood blackened starlit water. The bull bellowed in his agony. Trunk lashed, tusks swung to and fro, blindly, uselessly. The stars walked their silent paths above him.

His struggles weakened. His voice sank to a rasping pant. The men crowded close. Lighter in weight and helping each other, they did not sink deep in the mire. Their knives slashed, their axes chopped. Snowstrider lanced him in the eye. Even so, his other eye saw the sun rise, dulled and chilled by mist that had drifted in while he was being killed.

"Enough," said Red Wolf. The men withdrew to firm ground.

He led them in the Ghost Song. On behalf of everyone, he spoke aloud, northward, telling the Father of Mammoths why this deed was needful. Then: "Go, Running Fox, and fetch the people. Let the rest of us recover what spears we can." Though a point was easily made, nobody knew yet where the right kinds of stone were in these parts, and wooden shafts were always precious.

Having taken care of that, the band rested. They ate the last of the dried meat and berries in their pouches. Some spread blankets, which they had no reason to roll up in after air had warmed, and slept. Some talked, japed, watched the bull's death throes. Those went on until midmorning, when the vast body shuddered, filled the bog with dung, and slumped into stillness.

Thereupon the men stripped off their clothes and brought their knives to it. They sucked blood while it was fresh and hacked off pieces of tongue and hump fat such as were hunters' right. Afterward they washed themselves in a clean pool, to which they gave the unpierced eyeball as a thank offering. They hastened to get dressed again, for mosquitoes blackened the surroundings. Then they feasted. Shooing and throwing rocks, they defended the carcass against carrion birds. Drawn by the stenches, a wolf pack hovered in the offing but did not venture close.

"They know somewhat about men, these namesakes of mine do," Red Wolf said.

The tribe arrived late next day. They had had no great way to go after breaking camp, for the mammoth hunt went slowly and zigzag; but they were burdened with hides, tent poles, and other gear, as well as having small children and aged persons among them. Weariness weighted their cries of joy. Just the same, they were quickly settled; and Red Wolf went in that evening to Little Willow, his wife.

In the morning folk began butchering the catch, a task that would take days. Red Wolf sought Answerer in the shaman's tent. They sat silent while they breathed the smoke of a sacred peat fire into which herbs of power had been cast. It made the dimness stir with half-seen presences; noise outside reached them as if from across the world. Yet Red Wolf's thoughts flowed strong.

"We have come long and far," he said. "Enough?"

"The Horned Men walk no more in my dreams," replied the shaman cautiously.

Red Wolf moved a hand up and down, showing he understood. The folk who drove the Cloud People from their ancestral country had had no cause to pursue them, but the flight eastward had hitherto been through lands held by tribes much like their enemies, a threat that soon forced them onward. "Ill is homelessness," he said.

Answerer's face drew together till the wrinkles and furrows met the painted lines. He fingered his necklace of claws. "Often at night I hear those we buried as we traveled, wailing in the wind. If we could tend our dead as we ought, they would have the strength to help us, or even to go join the Winter Hunters."

"We seem at last to have reached territory where nobody else lives, save for a very few weaklings."

"Are you sure they lack might? Also, your followers complain of how hard the mammoth drive was."

"Will we ever find a place where it was easier? I wonder if we do not remember Skyhome as better than it truly was. Or else mammoth are everywhere becoming rare. Well, hereabouts I have found ample trace of bison, horse, caribou, and more. Also, when we were on this hunt we met something wonderful, and this is what I want to ask you about. Did it mean welcome or did it mean danger?"

Red Wolf told of the encounter with the strange pair. He went on to other things he and his fellows had noticed—stone chips, firesites, rabbit bones cracked for the marrow—that meant humans. Those must be feeble, unlike the tribes westward, for the big game of the region showed no special fear of man; and the one who accompanied the woman had been naked, carrying merely a rough-hewn rock for weapon. She was different, big, bright-pale of hair and eyes, peculiarly outfitted. She had shown anger when the hunters gibe-tested her companion. But she did nothing worse than depart. Might her kind be willing to deal with the Cloud People, with real men?

"Unless she is some sort of troll, and we should again move on," Red Wolf finished.

As he expected, the shaman gave him no answer to that, only: "Do you want to go find out?"

"I and a few bold friends," Red Wolf said. "If we have not come back when the carcass is ready, you will know this country is not for you. But we have been so long homeless."

"I will cast the bones." They fell in such a pattern that the shaman ordered, "Leave me by myself until dawn."

During the night Red Wolf and Little Willow heard him chant. His drum thuttered. Their children crept over to them and everybody clung together, yearning for sunlight.

At its first glow Red Wolf approached Answerer's tent. The shaman came out, haggard and trembling. "My spirit roved widely," he said low. "I walked in a meadow where the flowers were beautiful, but they forbade me to taste of them. I, an owl, hatched from the moon and in my talons caught the morning star. Snow fell in summer. Go if you dare."

Red Wolf drew a deep breath and straightened his shoulders.

Five men went at his side. Running Fox was no surprise to him, nor Snowstrider and Broken Blade. He decided that Horsecatcher and Caribou Antler had need to wrestle down their fears. The quest bore them south. In that direction the yellow-haired woman had gone; also, the signs of man were not quite so sparse there as everywhere else.

The land grew drier as it rolled downward. Grass and patches of woods took it over. Finally the travelers came to where the Great Water rolled gray beneath a smoky, flying, whistling sky. Surf brawled, ran up the sands, hissed back. Gulls soared on a sharp salt wind. Bones, shells, plants, and driftwood lay strewn. The Cloud People had only a slight knowledge of this; their usual prey kept inland. Mustering courage, Red Wolf and his men followed the shore east, for it seemed likeliest they would find somebody yonder.

As they fared, they became aware of riches. Stranded fish meant live ones in the water. Shells must have held flesh. Seal clamored and cormorants spread their wings on crowded skerries. Otter and sea cow rode the waves. "But we know not how to take this game," Broken Blade regretted.

"We might learn how," said Running Fox.

Red Wolf kept his own counsel. Within him stirred an idea, like a child stirring in its mother's womb.

Where a river flowed down a ravine and emptied across the beach, they suddenly spied two persons. Those saw them in turn and retreated up the stream. "Go easily," Red Wolf told his companions. "We would be unwise to scare them off."

He led the way, a spear in his right hand but the left palm held open before him. The strangers continued edging backward. They were young, boys rather than men, the beastlike whiskers of their breed still fuzzy. Hides, untanned but chewed to softness, were flung over their backs against the chill, fastened at the neck by thongs. The condition of the hides showed they must have been taken off carrion, not a kill. Pouches, not sewn but lashed together, hung over their loins. Footgear was of the same rough making. Each carried a shaped stone and a skin in which lay the mussels he had been gathering.

Snowstrider crowed laughter. "Why, they're brave as voles!"

Hope thumped in Red Wolf's temples. "They may be worth more than mammoths," he said. "Softly, now."

Alder grew on the slopes, man-high or less, seldom thickly enough to hinder movement or sight. A lad called out. His voice wavered. The wind bore it upward, through the rustling boughs. The Cloud People advanced. Others appeared from above the channel. They scrambled down to stand stiff. The boys turned and scampered to join them.

At the head of the forlorn group was a man whom Red Wolf recognized. Another, young but full-grown, was beside him. At their backs, two women and a girl entering upon womanhood, clad no better than the males, hushed several naked children. "Is this all?" Caribou Antler wondered.

"Some may be out searching for food," Red Wolf said, "but they cannot be many or we would have known of them earlier."

"Where is . . . she, the tall one with hair like sunshine?"

"Wherever she is. Do you fear a woman? Come." Red Wolf strode forward. His hunters took formation to right and left. Thus had the Cloud People warred against the Horned Men until numbers finally overcame them. This band were striplings then, but their fathers had later given them training. Someday they might have to fight again.

Red Wolf stopped three paces from the leader. Eyes stared into eyes. Silence stretched amidst the wind. "Greeting," Red Wolf said at last. "Who are you?'

The bearded lips moved. What came out sounded like birds twittering. "Can they not speak?" Horsecatcher grumbled. "Are they human?"

"They are certainly hideous," Caribou Antler said.

"Not the woman so much," Broken Blade murmured.

Red Wolf's gaze traveled across the maiden. Her tresses tumbled thick past a delicate face. She shivered and clutched the cape about her slight form. He pulled his attention back to the man, who he guessed was her father. Tapping his chest, he named himself. The third time he did so, the other seemed to understand, pointed at his own breast, and uttered, "Aryuk." Waving a hand: "Tulat."

"Well, we know what to call them," Red Wolf said.

"Real names?" wondered Running Fox. Among his folk, that was a secret between a man and his dream spirit.

"No matter," Red Wolf snapped. He saw, he could well-nigh smell, the strain in his company. It was in him too. What *of* that mysterious woman? They must not let fear suck away their courage. "Come, we will look about."

He stalked onward. Aryuk and the oldest youth moved to stand side by side, to hold him off. He grinned and jabbed air with his spear. They shrank, made way, whispered among themselves. "Where is your protector today?" Red Wolf jeered. Only the wind replied. Emboldened, his men pressed at his back. The dwellers trailed them, a disordered gaggle, half frightened, half sullen.

A little farther on, the Cloud People found their home. The gulch broadened and a bluff jutted into the river above high-water mark. From the brush-grown slope behind trickled a spring—surely fresh, for the stream was too salt to drink. Three tiny shelters huddled close together. For each, their makers had piled rocks in a circle about as high as a short man's shoulders, leaving a gap for entry, and rudely chinked them. Deadwood poles laid across the tops held slabs of peat for roofs. Sticks, lashed into bundles with gut, formed windbreaks to lean across the entrances. A banked fire, doubtless always kept burning, glowed red in the gloom of one den. Nearby was a rubbish midden, around which flies buzzed in swarthy clouds.

"Faugh, the stink!" Broken Blade snorted. "And a rabbit digs a better burrow than this." The sod huts his people would make against winter, until someday they could build real houses, would have more room and would be kept clean. Meanwhile, their leather tents were both snug and airy.

"See what is inside," Red Wolf ordered. "Snowstrider, stand guard by me."

The Tulat were plainly unhappy at having their places ransacked, though only Aryuk and the oldest son dared do so much as glower. The searchers found an abundance of meat and fish, dried or smoked, as well as fine pelts and birdskins. "They are clever trappers, at least," Red Wolf laughed. "Tulat, we will take hospitality of you."

His men brought out what they wanted and ate well. Presently Aryuk joined them, squatting on his haunches where they sat cross-legged. He gnawed a bit of salmon and often smiled, ingratiatingly.

Afterward Red Wolf's band explored the neighborhood above the riverbed. Their eye for tracks led them to a spot some distance off, at a brook. A patch of bare, packed soil showed that something round like a shelter, but far larger, had lately rested there. What was it? Who had made it, and why? Who had removed it, and how? From one another they hid the creeping in their flesh.

Red Wolf overcame his uneasiness first. "I think this was where the witch-woman stayed," he told them, "but she has left. Did she fear us or our help-spirits?"

"The dwellers can tell us," Running Fox said, "once we can talk with them."

"The dwellers can do much more than that," Red Wolf answered slowly. Exultance leaped. "We have nothing to dread, I believe. Nothing! The spirits have brought us to a better home than we dreamed of."

His men gaped. He did not explain at once. Entering the settlement again, he said thoughtfully, "Yes, we must learn their tongue, we must teach them . . . what we want them to know." His glance went ahead, to Aryuk's family. They stood bunched, waiting for whatever would happen. Hands gripped hands, arms lay around children. "We will begin on both these things by taking one of them along to our camp." He smiled at the girl. Terror stared back.

1965 A.D.

On this gentle April afternoon, across the Bay in San Francisco, Wanda Tamberly was being born. Time Patrol agent or no, she must stave off a certain eeriness. *Happy birthday, me.*

Coincidence. Ralph Corwin had requested she visit him then because it was the earliest afternoon on which his Berkeley house would not be a-bustle. As undermanned as it was, the outfit could spare but a handful of people to trace the migrations of man into the New World, no matter how important to the future those might be. Overwhelmed by the task, they were always coming and going at his administrative base.

Like many other special offices, this was a residential building, rented for several years by persons who did actually live there. Twentieth-century America was a logical locale. Most of the workers were native to it, blending easily in. They could not well use regional headquarters in San Francisco; too much activity would make it undesirably noticeable. Berkeley in the '60s came near being ideal. Nobody paid particular attention to an occasional oddity when everybody was being nonconformist. Eventually hysteria about drug abuse would make official surveillance too likely. However, by then the Patrol's group would have finished their job and quit the house.

Granted, it lacked a hidden space for timecycles to appear in. Tamberly took public transportation, got off on Telegraph Avenue, strolled north on it and across the campus. The day was gorgeous and she felt curious about the decade. It had been a legend of sorts while she was growing up.

Disappointment. Scruffiness, pretentiousness, self-righteousness. When a boy in dirt-stiffened jeans and what he probably imagined was an Indian blanket thrust a leaflet of pomposities about peace at her, she remembered ahead—Cambodia, boat people—and told him, with a sweet smile, "Sorry, I'm a fascist warmonger." Well, Manse had once reminisced about the Youth Revolution to her, in terms that she should have taken for a warning. Why care now, when cherry trees stood like sunlit snowstorms?

The address she sought was a few blocks west of the university on Grove Street (which would be solemnly renamed Martin Luther King Jr. Way, and referred to by her generation as Milky Way). The house was modest, well maintained. A satisfied landlord would not get inquisitive. She mounted its porch and rang the bell.

The door opened. "Miss Tamberly?" After she nodded: "How do you do. Please come in." She saw a man tall, slender, with a Roman profile and toothbrush mustache beneath sleek gray-shot hair. His tan shirt had shoulder straps and several pockets, his tan slacks were razor-creased, his feet bore Birkenstock sandals. He looked about forty, but lifeline age meant little if you had received the Patrol's longevity treatment.

He closed the door behind her and gave a firm handshake. "I am Corwin." He smiled. "Pardon the 'Miss.' I couldn't safely call you 'Agent Tamberly' when you might have been a solicitor for a worthy cause. Or do you prefer 'Ms'?"

"Whatever," she replied, carefully casual. "Manse Everard's explained to me how honorifics mutate." *Let him know I'm on friendship terms with an Unattached. In case he likes playing dominance games*. "Most recently—I suppose 'recently' is right, when I left Beringia less than a week ago, personal timespan—I was Khara-tse-tuntyn-bayuk, She Who Knows Strangeness." *Show the big anthropologist that a humble naturalist is not a complete naif in his field.*

She wondered if it was the British accent that put her off. Inquiring at HQ, she'd learned he was born in Detroit, 1895. He had, though, done good work on American Indians during the '20s and '30s, before he joined the Patrol.

"Indeed?" His smile broadened. *Actually kind of charming*, she admitted. "Brace yourself. I shall want every last drop of your information about that country. But first let's make you comfortable. What would you like in the way of refreshment? Coffee, tea, beer, wine, something a bit more authoritative?"

"Coffee, thanks. It's early yet." He guided her to the living room and an armchair. Furniture was well-worn. Full bookshelves lined the walls, holding mainly reference works. He excused himself, went kitchenward, soon came back bearing a tray of ware and morsels which she discovered were delicious. Having set things on a low table in front of her, he took a seat opposite and asked whether she minded if he smoked. That was quite considerate of a person from his birthtime; and he lit a cigarette, not a pipe like Manse.

"Are we alone here?" she wondered.

"For the nonce. I went to some trouble about that." Corwin laughed. "Have no fears. I simply thought we should get acquainted without distractions. I can better appreciate what I'm told when I know a bit about the teller. What's a nice girl like you doing in an organization like this?"

"Why, you know," she answered, surprised. "Zoology, ecology—what I think they called natural history when you were young."

Hey, that was tactless. To her relief, he showed no offense. "Yes, of course I've been informed." Soothingly: "You're a pure scientist, for the sake of the knowledge. I confess to a touch of envy."

She shook her head. "No, not really, or I wouldn't be in the Patrol. The pure scientists belong to civilian institutions uptime, don't they? My job, well, it's just that we, the Patrol, can't understand what goes on among people, especially people close to nature, unless we have some knowledge of their environments. That's why I was doing my Jane Goodall when and where I was, instead of elsewhere or earlier. The arrival of the Paleo-Indians was *expected* sometime about then. Not that I'd necessarily meet them personally—that just happened—but I'd've reported on the conditions they'd find, the resources available to them, and so on."

Concurrently, with dismay: *What a motormouth I'm being. He knows all this by heart. Nervousness. Pull yourself together, nit.*

Corwin had blinked. "I beg your pardon? Doing your, er, Jane Goodall?"

Tamberly relaxed a little. "Sorry, I forgot. She isn't famous yet. A breakthrough ethologist out in the wilds."

"Role model for you, eh? And a jolly good one, to judge by the result." He sipped from his cup. "I misspoke myself. Obviously I've been aware of your role, why you were where-when you were. What I'd like to know is more basic, why you enlisted, how you first learned about us."

To speak of that to an interested, interesting, handsome man quickly became more than pleasant—a release. How it hurt, up in 1987 and afterward, that she must lie to her parents, sister, old friends about her reasons for not going on to grad school and about the work that took her away from them. More than once, training at the Patrol Academy, she'd needed a sympathetic shoulder to cry on. She was past that now. Or was she entirely?

"Well, it's a long story, too long for details, I think. My uncle was already a Patrolman, unbeknownst to me or his other kin, when I was studying evolutionary biology at Stanford. He was, is, uh—oh, damn, shouldn't we speak Temporal? English ties itself in knots, trying to handle time travel."

"No, I'd prefer to hear this in your mother tongue. You reveal more of yourself. Which is delightful, if I may make bold to say so. Pray continue."

Good Lord, do I feel a blush? Tamberly hastened on: "Uncle Steve was in sixteenth-century Perú, with Pizarro, using the persona of a monk, to keep track of events."

(For surely that conquest was among the decisive episodes of history. Had matters gone otherwise than they did, all the future would have been different, more and more as time went on, until by the twentieth century, whatever there was on Earth, it would not have

included a United States of America or parents for one Wanda Tamberly. Beneath reality lies ultimate quantum indeterminacy. On the level of observable happenings it manifests itself as chaos in the physics sense of the word, the fact that often immeasurably small forces bring illimitably large consequences. If you go into the past, you can change it, you can annul the future that begot you. You will exist still, parentless, causeless, like an embodiment of universal meaninglessness; but the world from which you fared will exist—will have existed—only in your memories.

(When time travel became a fact, did altruism call the Danellian superhumans out of the remote future to ordain and establish the Patrol? It does help, succor, advise, adjudicate, the kind of work that mostly occupies any decent police force. But it also seeks to keep the foolish, the criminal, the mad from destroying that history which leads through the ages to the Danellians. For them this may be a matter of simple survival. They have never told us, we hardly ever see them, we do not know.)

"Bandits from far uptime, trying to hijack Atahuallpa's ransom—no, it *is* too complicated. We'd spend hours. What it came to was, one of Pizarro's men got hold of a timecycle, learned what it could do and how to operate it, also learned about me, where I was at a particular time. He kidnapped me with the idea of making me guide him around in the twentieth century, help him acquire modern weapons. He had grandiose plans."

Corwin whistled. "I can well imagine. Win or lose, yes, the mere attempt could have been disastrous. And I would never have known, because I would never have been born. Not that I matter, but that sort of thought drives the implications home, eh? What happened?"

"Unattached Agent Everard had already contacted me, investigating Uncle Steve's disappearance. He didn't let me in on the secret, of course, but he left me his phone number and I . . . I made a chance for myself to call him. He freed me." Tamberly must needs grin. "In the best marines-to-the-rescue style. Which blew his cover.

"Then he was duty-bound to make sure I kept my mouth shut. I could take conditioning against ever mentioning the subject to anybody not in the know, and pick up my life where I'd dropped it. Except he offered me another choice. I could enlist. He didn't think

I'd make a very good cop, and he was doubtless right, but the Patrol needs field scientists too.

"Well, when I got a chance to do my paleontology with live critters, did I agree? Does a bear—uh, is the Pope Catholic?"

"And so you went through the Academy," Corwin murmured. "I daresay the setting was especially wonderful to you. Afterward, I presume, you worked as part of a team until it was decided you were probably the best person to station in Beringia for conducting independent research."

Tamberly nodded.

"I must certainly hear the full story of your Spanish adventure," Corwin said. "Extraordinary. But you are right, duty first. Let us hope for leisure later."

"And let's not talk more about me," she suggested. "How did you come to join?"

"Nothing so sensational. Indeed, the most common way. A recruiter felt I might have potential, cultivated my acquaintance, got me to take certain tests, and when they confirmed his opinion, told me the truth and invited me in. He knew I would accept. To trace the unwritten ancient history of the New World—to help write it—you understand, my dear."

"Was it hard to cut your ties?" *I don't believe I ever will be able to, not really, before—before Dad and Mother and Susie have died—No, not to think about that, not now. Yonder window's too full of sunlight.*

"Not especially," Corwin said. "I was going through my second divorce, no children. I despised the petty infighting of academic life. Always have been rather a lone wolf. To be sure, I have led men, but field work and, yes, Patrol personnel are more congenial to me."

Better not let conversation get any more intimate than this, Wanda decided. "Okay, sir, you asked for me to come around and tell you about Beringia. I'll try, but I'm afraid my information is pretty limited. I generally stayed in the same area; the territory I have not seen is enormous. And I've spent only two personal years at it, including vacations back home or in some fun milieu. My presence there covers about five years, because naturally I spaced my visits months apart, according to what I hoped to observe at a particular season. It's an awfully small sample, though." *The best that could be managed,* she reminded herself.

"Even with your holidays, yours must have been a hard life. You're a brave young lady."

"No, no. It was utterly fascinating." Tamberly's pulse quickstepped. *Here's my chance.* "Both in its own right and because it matters to the Patrol, more than meets the eye. Dr. Corwin, they're doing wrong to stop it at this stage. I'm leaving some basic scientific problems half solved. Can't you make them see that, so they'll let me return?"

"Hm." He stroked his mustache. "I'm afraid other considerations override yours. I can inquire, but don't get your hopes up. Sorry." Chuckling: "Science aside, I gather you enjoyed yourself."

She nodded vigorously, though the sense of loss sharpened and sharpened in her. "I did, all in all. A stark land, but, oh, *alive*. And the We are sweethearts."

"The We? Ah, yes. That's how the aborigines referred to themselves, I presume. What the name 'Tulat' means. They had forgotten the preliminary expedition to their forebears, and had no clear concept of anyone else in the world until you appeared."

"Right. I can't see why there's no more interest in them. They were around for thousands of years. People like them got clear down into South America. But the Patrol sent only that one group. All it learned was their language and a vague notion of how they lived. When the machine had put the information into my head, I was, you know, appalled by how little it was. Why doesn't anybody care?"

His reply was measured, grave. "Surely you have been told. We lack the personnel, the resources, to study in depth what . . . will make no significant difference. Those first wanderers who trickled across the land bridge during an interstadial, some twenty thousand years ago, their descendants remained changelessly primitive. In fact, through almost the whole twentieth century, most archaeologists have doubted humans ever reached the New World that early. What scanty tools and firesites they left could well be due to natural causes. It is the High Stone Age people, the big game hunters, arriving between the Cary and Mankato substages of the Wisconsin glaciation, as the Ice Age itself drew toward a close, it is they who properly populated the two continents. The forerunner folk were killed off or crowded out. If some did interbreed—captive women, perhaps—that was seldom and their blood was swamped, lost."

"I know that! I know!" Her eyes stung. She barely kept from shouting, *You don't have to lecture me. I'm not some freshman class you used to teach. Old habits getting the upper hand?* "What I meant was, why doesn't anybody seem to give a damn?"

"A Patrol agent must become case-hardened, like a physician or a policeman. Otherwise what he witnesses will eventually break him." Corwin leaned forward. He put a hand over the fist that lay knotted in her lap. "But, yes, I care. I am more than interested. My duty lies with the Paleo-Indians. They bear the future. But I do want to learn everything you know about the old folk, and everything I can discover for myself. I want to love them too."

Tamberly gulped and straightened. She drew back from his touch, then said hastily, not wishing to seem as if she spurned his consolation: "Thanks. Thanks. What happens . . . at first . . . to the people I've known, the, the individuals . . . that doesn't have to be terrible. Does it?"

"Why, no. The newcomers you met probably belonged to a very small tribe. I rather imagine it was far in advance in the rest, and no more arrived for a generation or two. Besides, I've gathered your Tulat lived on or near the coast, and didn't go after big game. Hence no rivalry."

"If only that's true. If there is c-conflict, can't you help?"

"I'm sorry. The Patrol may not intervene."

Energy kindled anew. "Look," Tamberly argued, "time travelers are bound to intervene, interfere. I affected people in all sorts of ways, didn't I? Among other things, I saved several lives with antibiotics, shot a dangerous animal—and just my presence, the questions I asked and answered, everything I did had some effect. Nobody objected. I was up front about it, reported every incident, and nobody objected."

"You know why." Perhaps he realized that playing the professor had been a mistake, for now he spoke neither angrily nor patronizingly but mildly, as to a young person bewildered by pain. "The continuum does tend to maintain its structure. A radical change is only possible at certain critical points in history.

Elsewhen, compensations occur. From that standpoint, what you did was unimportant. In a sense, it was 'always' part of the past."

"Yes, yes, yes." She curbed the resentment she had felt in spite of his effort. "Sorry, sir. I keep sounding stupid and ignorant, don't I?"

"No. You are under stress. You are trying hard to make your intent clear." Corwin smiled. "You needn't. Relax."

"What I'm getting at," she persisted, "is why can't you take a hand? Nothing big, nothing that'll get into folk memory or anything like that. Just, oh, those hunters were . . . arrogant. If they start leaning too hard on the We, why can't you tell them to lay off, and back it up with a harmless demonstration, fireworks or something?"

"Because this is a different situation from yours," he replied. "Beringia is, was, no longer populated exclusively by a static society barely past the eolithic stage—if people that thinly scattered can even be called a society. An advanced, dynamic, progressive culture, or set of cultures, invaded. Let me remind you that in the course of mere generations they swept down the corridor between the Laurentide and Cordilleran ice, into the plains, where taiga was becoming fertile grassland as the glaciers dwindled. Their numbers exploded. Within two thousand years of the day you met them, they were making the superb flint points of the Clovis. Soon after, they finished off the mammoth, horse, camel, most of the large American beasts. They developed into the distinctive Amerindian races—but you know that story too, I'm sure.

"What it means is an unstable situation. True, the time is long ago. There will be no written record by which the dead can speak to the living. Nevertheless, the possibility of starting a causal vortex is no longer insignificant. We field researchers must henceforward keep our influence to an absolute minimum. No one less than an Unattached agent has competence to take decisive action; and such a man would only do it in extreme emergency."

Or woman, Tamberly thought. *But I should remember when he was born and raised, and make allowances. He means well. Though he does love to hear himself talk, doesn't he?*

Irritation somehow countered anxiety. When he added, "Remember, quite likely you are borrowing trouble and in fact nothing dreadful ever happened to your friends," she could accept it. Why had her moods been seesawing like this, anyway? Well, she was newly back from wilderness, tossed into a period whose likeness and unlikeness to home were equally disturbing. She was rebellious at having her work stopped uncompleted, concerned about the We, grieved that she might never see them again, skittish at meeting a man who had decades of Patrol experience under his belt against her paltry four. *High time you calmed down, gal.*

"Your coffee's gone cold," Corwin said. "Here, I'll see to that." He took her cup away, brought it back empty, gave it a partial refill from the pot, and held a flask of brandy above. "I prescribe a spot of additive for both of us."

"M-m, a . . . a microspot," she yielded.

It helped, more as a gesture and a taste than through the minute alcohol content. He didn't press more on her. Instead, he got to business. Intelligent queries and comments were the real medicine for strained nerves.

He fetched books, opened them to maps, showed her the geological ages of the land where she had camped. She had studied the history before, of course, but he recalled the larger context to her, vividly and with fresh details.

In the era she knew, Beringia had shrunk from its greatest extent. However, it was still a big territory, joining Siberia to Alaska, and its disappearance would take a long while if you reckoned in human lives. Finally the sea, rising as the ice melted, would drown it; but by then America would be well peopled from the Arctic Ocean to the Land of Fire.

She had much to tell about the wildlife, less about the wild folk, yet she had inevitably and happily come to know those in some degree. Already implanted in him was the knowledge acquired by the first expedition, the Tula language, something of the customs and beliefs. She found he had pondered it, compared it to what he knew of savages elsewhere and elsewhen, extrapolated from his own experience.

That had been among the Paleo-Indians as they drifted southward through Canada. His aim was to trace their migrations back to the sources. Only by knowing what had happened could the Patrol hope to know what the nexus points were over which it should keep special watch. Though skeletal at best, the data would be better than nothing. Besides, others uptime were intensely interested as well, anthropologists, folklorists, artists of every kind seeking fresh inspiration.

Under Corwin's guidance, Tamberly felt her recollections grow more fully fleshed than before—family groups dwelling apart, periodically gathering together, oftener linked by individual travelers, among whom young men in search of mates were commonest—simple rites, frequently grisly legends, pervasive fear of demons and ghosts, of storm and predator, of sickness and starvation—withal, merriment, much loving kindness, childlike joy whenever life offered pleasure—a special reverence for the bear, which might be older than the race itself—

"My goodness!" she exclaimed. Shadows stretched across the street outside. "I'd no idea we'd been at it this long."

"Nor I," Corwin said. "Time goes fast in company like yours. Best we call it a day, eh?"

"For sure. I can do horrid things to a hamburger and a beer."

"You are staying in San Francisco?"

"Yes, at a small hotel near HQ till I've finished this debriefing. No sense in commuting between now and 1990."

"Look here, you deserve better than a café meal. May I invite you to dinner? I know the worthwhile places in these years."

"Uh, m-m—"

"That dress of yours is perfectly fine. I'll make myself presentable. Half a tick." He rose and left the room before she could respond.

Whew! . . . Oh, why not? In fact—hm, easy there, gal. It has been a long while, but—

Corwin returned as fast as promised, sporting tweed jacket and bolo tie. He drove them across the bridge to a Japanese restaurant near Fisherman's Wharf. Over cocktails he suggested that perhaps, if she really wanted to continue in Beringia, he might just possibly arrange for a partnership. She decided on the spot that she'd better take that as a joke. When the cook came to prepare their sukiyaki at the table, Corwin told the man to stand aside and did the job himself, declaring, "Hokkaido style." He described his experiences among the Paleo-Indians of Canada at length, dwelling on the dangerous moments. "Admirable chaps, but ferocious, touchy, no inhibitions about violence." If any implications of that had crossed his mind, he didn't seem to think they might occur to Tamberly.

After they were done, he proposed a drink at the Top of the Mark. She pleaded tiredness. Outside her hotel she gave him a handshake. "We should finish tomorrow," she said, "and then I really must go straight uptime and see my folks."

13,212 B.C.

Every fall We met at Bubbling Springs. When weather grew daily more chill it was very good to wallow in warm mud and wash in the hot water that welled up thereabouts. Strong tastes and smells were defense against sickness; steam-wraiths kept unfriendly ghosts at a distance. We came from dwelling places along the whole coast, as far as the known world reached, for the jolliest of the year's festivities. They brought plenty of food, since no one family could feed such a crowd, and shared it around. Among the special delicacies were the tasty oysters of Walrus Bay, carried alive in water-filled skins; fish, fowl, animals freshly caught, stuffed with herbs; dried berries and flowers gathered on sunny slopes; blubber if someone had killed a seal ashore or, wonder of wonders, a whale had gone aground. They also brought things to trade, fine pelts, pretty feathers and stones. They gorged, sang, danced, jested, freely made love. They swapped news, dickered, laid plans, sighing recalled old days and smiling watched their little ones stump about. Sometimes they quarreled, but friends always composed that. When the food was gone, they thanked Ulungu for hosting them and went home, well provided with memories to brighten the dark months ahead.

came when a sorrow and a fear lay over Us. Talk was of the outsiders who, this summer, had arrived to live somewhere inland. Though few households had seen any, word had flitted on the lips of wandering youths and of fathers who sought their nearest neighbors. Unsightly, speaking with the tongues of wolves, wrapped in leather, fearsomely armed, the invaders went in small bands wherever they chose. When they came upon a homestead they helped themselves to whatever they wanted, food, goods, women, not like guests but like eagles robbing osprey. Men who tried to withstand them had been badly hurt, pierced or slashed. Orak's wound got inflamed and he died.

You Who Know Strangeness, why have you forsaken Us?

The celebration at Bubbling Springs went heavily, the laughter was often too loud. Perhaps the bad ones would go away, as bad years when snow lay well into summer finally did. Those left many dead behind them. What of this new evil? Folk drew aside and muttered to each other.

Suddenly a boy who had strolled a ways off sped back shouting. Fright went in a wave through the crowd, dashing bodies to and fro. Aryuk of Alder River seized the lead, shook or drubbed the panic-stricken, called the men to him, until everyone but the infants was quiet, shuddering only under the skin. He had grown broody and short-spoken in the past season. Now he stood before the men, outside the settlement. Each gripped a hand ax or a club. Their women and young huddled among the huts.

Behind them surf growled, above them birds shrilled, around them wind whistled emptily. It was a clear day, just a few rapid clouds. Westering, the sun cast heatless light over hills turning yellow-gray with autumn. A pool simmered nearby, its brown the deepest color in sight. Wind scattered its warmth, vapors, and magical smells into nothingness.

Other men walked toward Us. The pointed shafts that they carried swayed to their stride.

Aryuk shaded his eyes and peered. "Yes, the outsiders," he said, low in his gullet. "Fewer than Us, I think. Stand together. Stand fast."

As they drew near: "But what, who is that with them? A woman? Clad the same, but—her hair and—Daraku!" he screamed. "Daraku, my daughter they took!"

He started to run, halted, returned, stood atremble. Soon she reached him. Her face was thin, and something had departed from behind those hollow eyes. A hunter went beside her, the rest spread right and left. Eagerness shone and shivered in them.

"Daraku," Aryuk cried through tears, "what is this? Have you come back to your mother and me?"

"I am theirs," she answered dully. Pointing at the man next to her: "He, the Red Wolf, wants me to help speak. They have not yet learned much about our speaking. I know some of theirs."

"How . . . how have you been, my dear, oh, my dear?"

"Men use me. I work. Two of the women are kind when they meet me."

Aryuk wiped his eyes with the back of his free hand. He swallowed a lump of vomit. To the Red Wolf he said, "I know you. We met when you first came and I was with my powerful friend. Afterward, when she had gone away, you sought me out and took my girl. What wicked ghost is in you?"

The hunter made the motion of one who brushes off a fly. Had he understood? Did he care? "*Wanayimo*—Cloud People," he answered. Aryuk could barely follow the thick utterance. "Want wood, fish, *omulaiyeh*—" He looked at Daraku and snarled a string of sounds.

She talked in words, tonelessly, staring past her father and brothers. "I told them how you meet here. I had to. They said it is a good time to come to tell you. They want Us—they want you to bring them things. Always. They will tell you what and how much. You must."

"What do they mean?" cried Huyok of Otter Strand. "Are they hungry? We have little to spare, but—but—"

The Red Wolf ripped forth more noises. Daraku wet her lips. "Do what they say and they will not harm you. I am their mouth today."

"We can trade—" Huyok began.

A roar cut him off. Khongan of Curlew Marsh was the boldest among Us. He had raged when he heard what the invaders did. "They do not trade! They take! Does the mink trade his skin for the bait in the trap? Tell them no! Drive them out!"

The hunters scowled and hefted their weapons. Aryuk knew he should signal for calm. His hands were too heavy, his throat too tight. One by one, his men took up Khongan's shout. "No! No!"

Somebody threw a stone. Somebody else dashed forth and chopped at a hunter with a hand ax. Or so Aryuk afterward thought. He was never sure quite what happened. There was an uproar, a brawl, wildness, nightmare. Then We had fled. Scattered, they stared back and saw the invaders stand unharmed, blood dripping off edged stone.

Two men of Us sprawled dead. Guts spilled from a gashed belly, brains from a split skull. The less wounded had escaped, except for Khongan. Pierced again and again, he threshed on the earth and moaned a long while before he lay still. Daraku knelt at the Red Wolf's feet and wept.

1990 A.D.

"Hi," said Manse Everard's answering machine. "This is Wanda Tamberly in San Francisco. Remember?" The sprightliness faded. It must have been forced. "Of course you do. Been, oh, like three years, though, hasn't it? On my lifeline, anyway. I'm sorry. Time just slipped past and you— Never mind." *You didn't get in touch again. Why should you? An Unattached agent has important things to do.* "Manse, uh, sir, I feel bad about calling you, especially after so long. I oughtn't go asking for special privileges. But I don't know where else to turn. Could you possibly give me a ring, at least? Let me try to explain? If you then tell me I'm out of line, I'll shut up and not pester you again. Please. I think it's pretty big. Maybe you'll agree. Please. You can reach me at—" There followed a telephone number and a list of hours on successive days in this February. "Thanks ever so much for listening. That's all now. Thank you." Silence.

Having heard, he stopped the tape and stood for several minutes. It was as if his apartment had withdrawn from New York to a space of its own. At length he shrugged, grinned ruefully, but nodded to himself. The remaining messages had no urgency that he couldn't handle with a bit of time hopping. Nor did Wanda's, actually. However—

He went to the little bar across the room. The floor felt bare, merely carpeted. He'd removed his polar bear rug. Too many visitors had been reproaching him for it. He couldn't explain to them that it was from tenth-century Greenland, when, far from polar bears being an endangered species, things were oftenest the other way around.

And truth to tell, it had gotten rather scruffy. The helmet and crossed spears remained on their wall; nobody could see they were not replicas of Bronze Age work.

He prepared a stiffish Scotch and soda, charged and lighted his pipe, retired to his study. The armchair received him as an old shoe would. He didn't let many contemporary people in here. When it happened, they were apt to tell him how much better off he'd be with their brand of personal computer. He'd say, "I'll look into it," and change the subject. Most of what they saw on his desk was dummy.

"Give me the file to present date on Specialist Wanda May Tamberly," he ordered, adding sufficient information to identify. When he had studied what appeared before him, he pondered, then started a search through related matters. Presently he thought he was on the right track, and called up details. Dusk stole in to surround him. He realized, startled, that he'd been busy for hours and was hungry. Hadn't even unpacked from his latest trip.

Too restless to go out, he thawed some hamburger in the microwave, fried it, constructed a large sandwich, cracked a beer for accompaniment, and never noticed how anything tasted. A creative synthesizer could have whipped up a Cordon Bleu meal, but if you based yourself in a milieu before the technology to overleap spacetime was developed, you didn't keep any future stuff around that you didn't absolutely require, and you kept it hidden or well disguised. When he had finished, the time in California was the third of the hours she had named. He went back to the living room and picked up the phone. Ridiculous, how his heartbeat speeded.

A woman answered. He recognized her tones. "Mrs. Tamberly? Good evening. This is Manson Everard. Could I speak to Wanda, please?" He should have remembered her parents' number. It was no large span on his own time line since he'd last called there—though events had been tumultuous. *Good kid, comes back to her folks whenever she gets a chance, happy family, not too damn many like that these days*. The Midwest of his boyhood, before he went off to war in 1942, was like a dream, a world forever lost, already one with Troy and Carthage and the innocence of the Inuit. He had learned better than to return.

"Hello!" exclaimed the breathless young voice. "Oh, I'm so glad, this is so kind of you."

"Quite all right," Everard said. "I've got a notion of what you have in mind, and yes, it does need talking about. Can you meet me tomorrow afternoon?"

"Anytime, anywhere. I'm taking leave." She stopped. Others might overhear. "Vacation, I mean. Whatever's convenient for you, sir."

"The bookshop, then. Let's say three o'clock." While her parents weren't necessarily aware that he was not in the Bay Area at this moment, best was not to rush matters as perceived by them. "Can you save the evening for me too?" Everard blurted.

"Why, why, of course." Both abruptly shy, they exchanged only a few more words before hanging up.

He did need a night's sleep, and there was in fact considerable accumulated business to handle. Another twilight had fallen, cold and dun around hectic lights, when he entered city headquarters. In the secret room beneath, he checked out a hopper, mounted the saddle, set his destination, touched the controls. The cellar garage that blinked into existence for him was smaller. He went out the camouflaged door and upstairs. Daylight poured through windows.

This front was a high-class used bookstore. He saw her looking at a volume; she had arrived early. Her hair was sun-bright amidst the freighted shelves, and a dress the color of her eyes fitted close. He approached. "Hello," he said.

Almost, she gasped. "Oh! How d-do you do, Agent . . . Everard." Strain vibrated through the sounds.

"Sh," he cautioned. "Come on back where we can talk." Two or three customers watched them go down the aisle, but simply with a bit of envy; they were male. "Howdy, Nick," Everard said as he came to the proprietor. "Okay?" The little man smiled and nodded, though solemnity stared through thick lenses. Everard had sent a message in advance, commandeering his office.

It too held nothing overtly unusual. Along the walls, filing cabinets squeezed in between more bookcases. Boxes cluttered the floor, papers and tomes the table that acted as a desk. Nick was a genuine bibliophile; perhaps his main reason for serving the Patrol in this small but vital capacity was the ability he gained to go questing in other milieus. Some recent acquisitions, Victorian to judge by their appearance, lay next to the ostensible computer. Everard glanced over the titles. He made no pretense of being an intellectual, but he liked books. *The Origin of Tree Worship, British Birds, Catullus, The Holy War*—no doubt stuff that some collector would snap up, if the proprietor didn't decide to keep them for himself.

"Sit down," he invited, and pulled out a chair for Tamberly.

"Thank you." When she smiled she seemed all at once easier, more herself. *Not that anybody ever is, ever again. We can dance around in time all we want, but we don't escape duration.* "You still have your old-fashioned manners, I see."

"Country boy. I'm trying to unlearn. Ladies these days have snapped my head off for being condescending, when I thought I was just being polite." Everard went around the table and seated himself opposite her.

"Yes," she sighed, "I suppose it can be harder to keep track of your birth century than to learn your way around in a whole past civilization. I'm finding that out, a little."

"How've you been? Do you enjoy your work?"

Enthusiasm flashed. "Mostly super. Terrific. Splendiferous. No, language doesn't reach to it." A shadow fell. She looked away from him. "The drawbacks, well, you understand. I was getting toughened to them. Until now, this thing."

He delayed coming to the point. First let him work the worst tension out of her, if he could. "It's been a spell. I last saw you shortly after your graduation."—from the Academy; on her personal time line. They'd gone to dinner in Paris, 1925, and afterward wandered along the Seine and around in the Rive Gauche, through a spring evening, and when they stopped for a drink at the Deux Magots a couple of her literary idols were at the same sidewalk café, two tables over, and when he bade her goodnight and goodbye at her parents' door, 1988, she kissed him. "Nigh on three years since then, for you, hasn't it been?"

She nodded. "Busy years for us both, I guess."

"Well, the time for me wasn't that long. I've had only two missions worth mentioning."

"Really?" she asked, surprised. "Didn't you return to your place in New York in '88 when you were through? I mean, you didn't let it stand months vacant, did you?"

"I lent—officially, sublet—it to an operative who needed such a base for a task of her own. They've got rent control there in these decades, you know. Always guarantees slums, plus decent housing in such short supply that to become a new tenant you've got to show more money than is wise for a Patrol agent."

"I see."

Tamberly had stiffened a little. *"Her," she's thinking. It's also unwise for a Patrol agent to explain too much. Especially in a case like this.* "Messages to me from fellow members were robotically bucked on. If you'd called before yesterday—"

Whatever pique she felt had dissipated. Her gaze dropped to hands that caught each other in her lap. "I had no reason to, sir," she said low. "You'd been awfully kind, generous, but . . . I didn't want to get pushy."

"Nor did I." *The great Unattached overawing the new recruit. Unfair. Could be resented.* "Though if I'd known so much time was going by for *you*—"

Much time indeed, less in lifespan measured by pulsebeats than in life lived, newnesses, strangenesses, troubles, triumphs, gaieties, griefs. And loves? Her form had grown fuller, Everard saw, not in fat but muscle. The bones stood out more strongly than before in a face that weather had often savaged. The real change was subtler. She had been a girl—a young woman, if today's feminists insisted, but how very young. The girl in her had not died; he doubted she ever quite would. The person across from him remained youthful: yet wholly a woman. His own pulse stumbled.

He achieved a laugh. "Okay, let's drop the Alphonse-Gastonette act," he said. "And please remember, my name isn't 'sir.' Here, by ourselves, we can relax. Wanda."

She rallied fast. "Thanks, Manse. I kind of expected this."

He drew pipe and tobacco pouch out of his pockets. "And this? If you don't mind."

"No, go ahead." She smiled. "Since we are not in public." Unspoken: *Bad example, among people for whom smoking's lethal. Patrol medicine heads off or heals anything that doesn't kill us outright. You were born in 1924, Manse. You look about forty. But how much duration have you endured? What is your real age?*

He didn't wish to tell her. Not today. "I raised your file yesterday," he said. 'You've been doing a crackerjack job."

She grew sober. Her eyes took level aim at him. "And will I in my future?"

"I didn't ask for that information," he replied fast. "Discourteous, unethical, and it wouldn't have been given me unless I could show a damn valid reason. We don't look into our tomorrows, nor into our friends'."

"And nevertheless," she murmured, "the information is there. Everything you or I will ever do—everything I'll discover about the life of the past—is known to them uptime."

"Hey, we're talking English, not Temporal. The paradoxes—"

The tawny head nodded. "Oh, yes. The work has to *be* done. Has to *have been* done, somewhere along the line. No point in my doing it if I already knew; and the danger of setting up a cause-and-effect whirlpool—"

"Besides, neither the past nor the future is cast in concrete. That's why the Patrol exists. Have we repeated enough indoctrination lecture?"

"I'm sorry. It's still sometimes hard for me to, well, comprehend. I have to replay the basic principles in my mind. My work is . . . straightforward. Like going to an unexplored continent. Nothing to remind me of the problems you cope with."

"Sure. I understand." Everard tamped the pipe hard. "I have no doubt you'll continue doing first-class work. Your superiors are more than pleased with what you've accomplished in Ber—uh—Beringia. Not just the verbal reports and audiovisuals and such, but—well, it's out of my field, but they say you were finding the fundamental pattern of that natural history. You were making sense of it, in a way that contributes a lot to the total picture."

She tensed on her chair. The question rang. "Then why have they pulled me out?"

He busied himself before applying fire. "Um, as I understand it, you've done as much as necessary in Beringia. When you've had your well-earned furlough, they'll put you onto some other aspect of the Pleistocene."

"I have *not* done enough. A hundred solid man-years would be too few."

"I know, I know. But you know, or should, the outfit hasn't got them to spare. We, the scientists uptime and the Patrol itself, we have to settle for broad general outlines and forget about the nesting habits of the cootie-banded bandicoot."

She flushed. "You know, or should know, that isn't what I mean," she flung back. "I'm talking about the entire circumpolar migration of species, two-way traffic between Asia and America. It's a unique phenomenon, an ecology in time as well as space. If I can, at the bare least, learn why the mammoth population of Beringia is, was, shrinking that early, when it still flourished on either side— But my project's been terminated. And all I get is the same runaround you gave me. I'd hoped you wouldn't."

Spirit, Everard thought. *Reluctant to wheedle the Unattached man, but ready to tell him off when he seems to deserve it*. "I'm sorry, Wanda," he said. "That was not my intention." After a comforting draught of smoke: "The fact is, those human newcomers change everything. Wasn't that explained to you?"

"Yes. After a fashion." She spoke softly again. "But would my investigations really mess things up? One person, going quietly around on the steppe, in the hills and woods, along the beaches? When I stayed with the Tulat, you know, the aborigines, nobody worried about it."

Everard frowned at his pipe. "I'm not familiar with the details," he admitted. "I boned up yesterday as much as I could in a short time, but that wasn't a hell of a lot. However, it seems pretty clear, your Tulat aren't important to the long-range course of events. They vanish, leaving no record, not even as much of a clear-cut trace as the Vinland or Roanoke colonies. The Paleo-Indians become the real pre-Columbian Americans. And at this earliest entry of theirs, who can tell what might make a critical difference, might upset the entire future?" He raised a hand. "Sure, sure. It's extremely unlikely. Little waves and wrinkles in the continuum will almost certainly smooth out, get history back where it belongs. That's true of your . . . Tulat. But as for the Paleo-Indians, at this stage, who can guarantee the situation is stable? Also, the Ancient American office wants their history observed as their cultures develop uncontam—freely."

Tamberly clenched her fists. "Ralph Corwin is off to *live* among them!"

"Yeah. Well, he's a pro at that sort of thing, a high-rated anthropologist. I checked out his record too. He's got an excellent background, from his work with later generations. He'll minimize his own effect on these people, while he learns enough about them to give him a handle on what really happened—same as you've worked to find out what really happened among the animals and plants."

Everard roiled smoke around in his mouth, loosed it streaming from his lips. "That's the basic problem, Wanda. The newcomers are bound to interact with the aborigines. It may be slightly, it may be heavily, but it will happen and could well prove very complicated. We can't allow an extra anachronism on the scene. That could scramble events beyond any repair. Especially since you don't have Corwin's skills. Can't you see?

"The upshot is, your ecological studies are valuable, but the human studies now take absolute priority. No reflection on you, but it became necessary to end your project. You'll get another, and they'll try to make sure you can carry it to completion."

"Yes, I do see. This has all been explained to me." She sat mute for a space. When once more she looked squarely at him, her voice was calm.

"It's more than my science, Manse. I fear for the We—for my Tulat. They're dear people. Primitive, often childlike, but good. Boundlessly kind and hospitable to me, not because I was a wonder and powerful, but because that's their nature. What's going to become of them? What did? Their kind was lost, forgotten. How? I am afraid of the answer, Manse."

He nodded. "Corwin reported his opinion, confidentially, after he'd interviewed you. He seconded the recommendation that your assignment in Beringia be terminated, because he feared you might succumb to . . . temptation, the temptation to interfere. Or, at least, untrained, unsupervised, you might do so without knowing it. Don't think he's a bastard. He has his duty. He did suggest you could transfer to an earlier period."

Tamberly shook her head. "That's no use. As rapidly as conditions were changing in the interstadial, I'd essentially have to start over from scratch. And what I found out would not be much help in the era of human migration that the Patrol is interested in."

"Yeah. The suggestion was vetoed on those grounds. But give Corwin credit."

"As a matter of fact, I do." Her words quickened. "I've been thinking hard. And this is what I've come up with. My work is worth finishing—the rough sketch that's all we can ever hope for, but that will be mighty useful. And maybe I could help the Tulat, just a little, very carefully, under supervision, not to change their destiny or anything but just to take some pain out of those few insignificant individual lives. Dr. Corwin hinted—we went out to dinner— At the time, I dismissed the notion out of hand, but since then I've been thinking. What if I didn't go back to Aryuk, to the Tulat, but joined him among the newcomers?"

It thudded in Everard's head. He laid his pipe down and built his poker face. "Unconventional," his mouth said.

Tamberly laughed. "One thing I'll ask you to do is tip the word to the good doctor that he's not my type. I wouldn't want him disappointed. Besides, we'll both have a whopping lot of work to get done in a short time, or we really might affect those people too much."

She grew altogether serious. Did he see tears sparkle in her lashes? "Manse, that's what I need you for. Your advice, for openers, but then, if you decide I'm not totally out of my gourd, your influence. I asked my immediate superior what he thought, and he told me to get lost. As you say, unconventional; he's no prude, but in his mind the policy has been set and nobody should bother him about it. Ralph Corwin, too. He'll probably be taken aback when something he said over his second cocktail rises up and hollers, 'Boo!' You've got the authority, the prestige, the connections in this outfit. Please, won't you at least think about it?"

He did, stormily at first. They talked and talked. Before he agreed, the sun was down. When he had invited her into the Patrol, she whooped for joy. Now she was too tired for more than a whispered "Thank you, thank you."

They both revived, though, when they went out to dinner. He'd arrived sufficiently well dressed for the Empress of China, and she already was. Afterward they did some pub crawling. They talked and talked. When he bade her goodnight at her parents' door, she kissed him.

13,211 B.C.

I

Days dwindled away into winter, blizzards laid snow thick over earth frozen ringingly hard, the brown bear shared dreams with the dead but the white bear walked the sea ice. We spent most of the enormous nights in their shelters.

Step by step, slow at first but faster and faster, the sun returned. Winds mildened, drifts melted, streams brawled swollen, floes ground each other to bits, calves of horned beasts and mammoth tottered newborn over steppe where flowers burst forth as many as stars, the migratory birds were coming home. For Us it had always been the happiest of seasons, until now.

They dreaded the trackless interior, its wolves and ghosts, but cross it they must. In fall the hunters had come along to show the way and made them pile up cairns to mark it. Thereafter they went by themselves, bearing the gifts required of them. Once snow was on the ground they were free until spring. But during the warmer time, between every full moon and full moon, men from each family would make the journey. So did the hunters command.

Heavily burdened, Aryuk and his sons took three days. He knew the return would need less than two. Some homes were farther off than his, some not so far, but these absences weighed upon all, for while traveling you could not hunt, gather, or work for your household. Having come back, you would spend more days getting together the next load. Not much time or strength was left to take care of your own livelihood.

There had been talk of meeting so as to fare in a single band. Against the protection and consolation of that you must set the still more days it would cost most people. In the end, We decided groups should go by themselves. Perhaps they would do differently later, when they had learned more about this new order of things.

Thus Aryuk made the first springtime trek with his sons Barakyn, Oltas, and Dzuryan. Behind them they left Aryuk's and Barakyn's women and small children. They carried long, stout pieces of wood, such as they had been told to bring, and food to keep them going.

Wind and rainshowers harried them, often mud caught at their feet, always the loads bore downward. Howls and distant roars haunted their nights. By day they trudged on over the rising land. At last they reached the hunter camp.

From a height they looked across it. The site lay not far below them, a broad flat ground where soil was well-drained. From still higher hills northward, a brook ran through the middle of it.

Awe smote Us. On their last visit in fall, they had thought the steep-sided leather shelters were many, surely more than all the Tula dwellings put together. Aryuk had wondered if they would be warm enough for winter. Today he saw that the strangers had since made themselves great huts of stone, turf, and hides. Tiny at their distance, people moved among them. Smoke from fires rose into an afternoon gone calm and sunny.

"How did they do this?" marveled Oltas. "What powers are theirs?"

Aryuk remembered certain remarks of Her Who Knows Strangeness. "I think they have tools we do not," he answered slowly.

"Just the same," Barakyn said, "so much work! How could they find time for it?"

"They kill large beasts," Aryuk reminded him. "One of those will feed them for many days."

Tears of weariness and pain coursed down Dzuryan's cheeks. "Then why n-need they take from Us?" he stammered. To that his father had no reply.

He led the party downslope. On the way they passed a long, gravelly hillock. Beneath it, where a spring ran forth, hidden from the settlement and hitherto from them, stood something that brought them up short. For a moment darkness whirled through Aryuk's head.

"*She*," Barakyn croaked.

"No, no," wailed Oltas. "She is our friend, she would not move here."

Aryuk took hold of his spirit, lest it flutter from him. He might have cried out too, were he not so numbingly tired. Staring at the round gray shell, he said, "We do not know, but perhaps soon we shall. Come."

They plodded onward. Folk spied them. Children dashed out,

shouting, skipping, fearless. Several men followed at a lope. They carried spears and hatchets—Aryuk had learned those words—but smiled. He supposed the rest were off hunting. Women and more children seethed around as We reached the huts. Again he noticed persons who were wrinkled, toothless, bent, blind. Here the weak need not go off to die. The young and strong could feed them.

The guides brought Us to a dwelling larger than others. Before it, clad in fur-trimmed leather and a headband with three eagle feathers, waited the man who spoke for these folk. Aryuk had come to know him as Red Wolf. That was what the name meant in his speech. He would change it now and then during his life, therefore it had to mean something. To Aryuk, his own name was merely a sound that singled him out. If he had thought about it, he might have understood that it said "Northwest Breeze" with an accent different from his, but he never did think about it.

He forgot Red Wolf. He forgot all else. Another man was coming through the crowd. He loomed over them, even over their leader. They made way for him with much respect, yet also with smiles and greetings which showed he had been among them for some while. His face was thin and lacked beard, though a mustache grew beneath the curving nose. His hair was short. Skin and eyes, body and gait, recalled Her Who Knows Strangeness; his garments and the things hung at his waist were wholly like hers.

Dzuryan groaned aloud.

"Lay down loads," Red Wolf bade Us. He had gained some knowledge of their tongue. "Good. We feed you, you sleep here."

The one from beyond the world halted at his side. Unburdened, Aryuk ached but felt oddly light, as if about to fly off on the wind. Or was it only his head spinning? "Rich gathering be yours," the one hailed in Our words. "Be not afraid. Do you remember Kharatse-tuntyn-bayuk?"

"She . . . she lived near our dwelling," Aryuk said.

"You are that very family?" The one was plainly delighted. "You yourself are Aryuk? I have been waiting for this."

"Is she with you?"

"No. She is of my kindred, however, and asked me to give you her friendliest thoughts. My name is—the Cloud People call me Tall

Man. I have come to spend a few years among them and learn about them and their ways. I want to know you better too."

Red Wolf stirred, impatiently, and barked something in his own speech. Tall Man replied likewise. Words went between them, until Red Wolf made a chopping gesture, as if to say, "So be it." Tall Man looked back at Aryuk and his sons, who stood mute within the encirclement of hunters' eyes.

"Talk goes easiest when I help," Tall Man said, "though I have warned them they should take the trouble to learn your tongue better. In time I also will depart this country, and meanwhile I will not always be here. Red Wolf wants to talk with you when you have rested, about what you and your folk are to bring later."

"What have we to bring, other than driftwood and deadwood?" Aryuk asked, his voice gone as dull as his heart.

"They want more of that. But also they want good stone for their tools and weapons. They want peat and dung, dried for burning. They want pelts. They want dried fish, blubber, everything the sea gives."

"We cannot!" Aryuk cried. "They already crave so much that we can barely feed ourselves."

Tall Man looked unhappy. "This is hard for you," he said. "I cannot free you of it. But I can make it bearable, if you heed me. I will tell the Cloud People that they can get nothing from you if they cause you to die. I will have them give you and show you the use of things that make fishing and hunting easier. They fashion . . . points that fish bite on and then cannot escape, spearheads that go into an animal and stay fast. Clothes like theirs will keep you warm and dry—" His tone faltered. "I am sorry I may not do more for you than this. But we can try—"

He stopped, because Aryuk no longer heard him.

Red Wolf had shifted to the side of the entrance. Forth from it crept a woman. She was garbed like others, but the clothes were dirty, greasy, and stenchful. Her belly bulged them out. Hair hung lank past a face gone gaunt. When she rose to her feet, she wavered on them and her arms dangled slack.

"Daraku," Aryuk whispered. "Is it you?" He had not seen her here before, nor been able to ask what had become of her. He had wondered whether Red Wolf told her to stay out of sight, lest she bring on trouble, or whether she hid in fear and shame, or whether she was dead.

She stumbled to him. He embraced her and wept.

Red Wolf threw a command at her. She cowered against Aryuk. Tall Man frowned. He spoke harshly. Red Wolf and the hunters who were in earshot bristled. Tall Man lowered his voice. Bit by bit, Red Wolf eased. At last he spread his hands and turned his back, a sign that he was done with the matter.

Aryuk looked across Daraku's shoulder. How sharply her bones jutted under the buckskin coat. Hope flickered in him. Through a blur, through a surf he saw, he heard Tall Man:

"This girl that they took away is your daughter, is she not? I have spoken to her, a little, though she hardly ever answers. They wanted to learn your speech from her. They have done that now, as much as she was able to tell them before sadness grew too heavy in her. They still want the child she carries, to be another hunter or another mother for them, but I have gotten them to let her go. She may return with you."

Aryuk flattened himself and Daraku on the earth before Tall Man. Her brothers did the same.

Afterward it was to eat—the Cloud women were generous, though the food was so different that We could not swallow much—and sleep, together again, in a tent raised for them, and then talk at length, Tall Man explaining between Aryuk and Red Wolf. A great deal was said about what We must do henceforward and what would be done for them in exchange. Aryuk wondered how long it would take for him to discover the full meaning. Certain was that life had changed beyond his power to grasp.

He and his children set out for home on a morning when wind flung raw gusts of rain. They walked slowly and often stopped, for Daraku could only stumble along. She stared before her and seldom answered when spoken to, then in just two or three words. Yet when Aryuk stroked her cheek or took her hand, she smiled enough for him to see.

That night while they were camped, her pangs came upon her. Rain cut and torrented. Aryuk, Barakyn, Oltas, and Dzuryan clustered close around, trying to give shelter and warmth. She began screaming and did not stop. She was so young; her hips were still narrow. When morning sneaked gray from the unseen east, Aryuk saw that she bled heavily. Rain washed it off into the peat moss. Her face was stretched across the skull and her look was blind. She had scant voice left. The last noises rattled away into silence.

"The baby is dead too," Barakyn said.

"That is as well," Aryuk mumbled. "I do not know what I would have done about it."

Afar, a mammoth trumpeted. The wind loudened. This was going to be a cold summer.

II

The Patrol team came late on a moonless night, to do their work as fast and quietly as possible and then disappear. Local folk would soon know that another marvelous thing had happened, but best not have it occur in their sight. Always minimize impact.

However, Wanda Tamberly could arrive after sunrise. Her hopper brought her straight inside the shelter that had been erected for her. Heart thumping hard, she dismounted and looked around. The transparency was set at translucent and light was ample. Familiar stuff was arranged neatly enough. She'd need a while, though, to shift it around to the way she liked it. *First let's have a peek at the neighborhood*. Warmly clad in preparation, she added a mackinaw, unsealed the entrance, and stepped out.

The time was fall in the year after she last left Beringia (and she had spent only a few weeks in the twentieth century before this return). Astronomically, the season was not very far along, but snow could fly any day now, at a subarctic latitude in an ice age. Morning lay bright and bleak. Wind whistled over sere grass. Hills narrowed horizons north and south. A heap of till, left when the glacier retreated, bulked above her dome and Corwin's. A spring trickled from its foot. She missed the sea and dwarf trees at her earlier camp. What birds wheeled overhead were fewer, and inland species.

The domes were almost touching. Corwin emerged from his, immaculate in khaki, cardigan, and high boots. He beamed. "Welcome," he greeted, striding over to shake hands. "How are you?"

"Okay, thanks," Tamberly said. "How've you been getting along?"

He raised his brows. "What, you haven't played back my reports?" he asked playfully. "I am shocked and grieved. After all the trouble I went to, composing them."

"Composing" is right, she thought. *Not that they aren't scientific accounts. Elegant diction doesn't hurt them any. It's this sense I got of . . . glossing over, here and there. Maybe I'm prejudiced.* "Of course I did," she replied. Taking care to smile: "Including the objections you registered to my being reassigned here."

He stayed amicable. "No reflection on you, Agent Tamberly, as I hope you realized. I simply thought it would add an unnecessary complication and risk, including the risk to you. I was overruled. Quite possibly I was mistaken. Indeed, I'm sure we can work well together. From a personal standpoint, how can I be other than happy to have company like yours?"

Tamberly made haste to sidestep that question. "No hard feelings, sir. But we won't actually collaborate, you know. You study the, uh, Cloud People. I need to do a winter's worth of observations on the animals, to get a halfway complete picture of certain life cycles that seem to be critical to the ecology."

She had repeated the obvious as the most gracious way she could think of to say, "Let me go about my business in peace. I mean to keep out from under your feet, and from under you."

He took it in good part: "Certainly. With experience, we'll work out the practical details, of noninterference with one another's projects, cooperation and mutual assistance as called for. Meanwhile, may I invite you to breakfast? Since you've doubtless synchronized yourself with local time, I imagine you didn't eat before you left."

"Well, I figured—"

"Oh, do accept. We must have a serious discussion, and it may as well be in comfort. I assure you, I am not a bad cook."

Tamberly yielded. Corwin had arranged things inside his shelter more neatly and compactly than she had ever managed in hers, making it a trifle roomier. He insisted that she take the chair, and poured coffee from a pot already at work. "This is an upper-case Occasion," he declared. "Ordinarily in the field one merely refuels, eh? Today, what would you say to bacon, French toast, and maple syrup?"

"I'd say, 'Let me at 'em before I trample the fence down,'" she admitted.

"Splendid." He busied himself at the tiny electric stove. The nuclear miniunit that powered it also kept the dome warm. She shed her mackinaw, leaned back, sipped the excellent coffee, and let her gaze rove. Books—his tastes were more highbrow than hers, unless he'd gone for these when he knew she would join him; they didn't seem much handled. The two he had published while in academe stood among them. Some implements rested on a shelf, gifts or exchanges which he probably meant to take home for souvenirs. Among them were a lance with a composite head and a stone-bladed, antler-hafted hatchet, held together by thongs and glue. Even the handleless cutters, scrapers, burins, and other tools were finely made. Tamberly recalled the crude work of the We; tears stung her eyes.

"I trust you are aware," he said, keeping his look on the cookery, "the Wanayimo think you're my wife. That is, when I told them you were coming, they took it for granted. They haven't the free and easy sexual mores of the Tulat."

"Wanayimo? Oh, yes, the Cloud People. Uh—"

"Not to worry. They accept that you will have your own house, to work your own magic. You're safe among them, especially since they think of you as mine. Otherwise . . . fear of your powers might stay their hands, but scruples would not, and some young bucks could decide this was a test of their courage, their manhood. After all, I had to tell them beforehand what they were bound to find out, that you were earlier associated with the Tulat, whom they don't really consider human."

Grimness drew Tamberly's lips tight. "I've gathered that, from your accounts that I've seen. Frankly, I wish you'd paid more attention to it. The relationship between the two peoples, I mean."

"My dear, I can't cover everything. Not a fraction of what I should, if this were a proper anthropological undertaking. I've only been with them seven months or a bit less, their chronology." He'd gone uptime occasionally, to confer and take a rest, but unlike her among the We, always came back to a day soon after his departure. Continuity was important in human affairs, in ways that it was not when you studied wildlife.

I've got to admit he's done a remarkable job in so short a span, and under a lot of other handicaps as well, she thought. *He did have a head start on the language; it's close to that of tribes in eastern Siberia who'd been visited, and not terribly different from that of later generations migrating through Canada, whom he himself had worked with. But that was his solitary advantage at the beginning. It took nerve, too. He could've been killed. They're a fierce and touchy lot . . . he reports.*

"And I scarcely have more time ahead of me," Corwin continued. "Next year the tribe moves on eastward. I may or may not find it worthwhile to travel with them, or rejoin them wherever they resettle, but the interruption will be disruptive at best."

"What?" Tamberly exclaimed. "You haven't entered that!"

"No, not yet. It's such a new discovery for me. At present, they fully expect to stay, they believe they've reached their Promised Land. In order to get some idea of how they'd develop in it, the better to understand their interaction with the next immigrants, I jaunted several years uptime. The region is abandoned. I established that will happen this coming spring. No, I don't know why. Do they find certain resources insufficient? Perhaps you can solve the riddle. I doubt they will feel any threat from the west. I ascertained that no new Paleo-Indians will arrive in these parts for some fifty years, as slow and fitful as their migrations are."

Then my We will have that long a peace. The release within Tamberly lasted barely a second. She remembered what had been going on, and apparently would as long as the Cloud People remained. When they left, how many We would be alive?

She forced herself to tackle the matter. "You said a minute ago, they don't look on the Tulat as being quite human," she stated. "Your accounts say very little about how they actually treat them. You just mention 'tribute.' What is the truth?"

His tone grew slightly irritated. "I told you, I haven't had the chance to examine every detail, and I never shall." He broke eggs into a mixing bowl as if they were the heads of referees who had rejected an article. "I acquired the Tula language in advance. I spoke with some who came here bearing the levy; the season for that started shortly after my arrival. I mitigated the lot of two or three individuals. I paid a visit to one of their miserable little warrens on the coast. What more do you expect? Like it or not, my concern, my duty is with the peoples who will make the future. Aren't *you* supposed to concentrate on those things in nature that are important to them?"

His testiness evaporated. He offered her a smile. "I don't want to seem callous," he added. "You are new in the service, and from a country that had had a remarkably fortunate history. I don't want to seem condescending to you, either. But the fact is that throughout humanity's existence, till indefinitely far uptime of our birth period, clans, tribes, nations normally regard the rest of mankind as booty, potential or actual—unless somebody else is sufficiently strong to be an enemy, potential or actual.

"You'll find the Wanayimo aren't so bad. Not Nazis or, for that matter, Aztecs. War was thrust on them, because Siberia is becoming overpopulated for the resources available to Paleolithic technology. They keep memories of that defeat, but you can't call them warriors when they no longer have anyone to fight. They are bold, macho, yes. That's a requirement for the life they lead, hunting big, dangerous animals. It's as natural for them to exploit the Tulat as it is to exploit the caribou. They are not deliberately cruel. In fact, they have a certain reverence for all life. But they take from the world what they can, for their wives, children, old ones, and themselves. They must."

Reluctantly, Tamberly nodded. Corwin's reports had described what a stroke of fortune it was for the Cloud People to come upon the We. Yet it would not have been that had they failed to make use of it. He had not foreseen their doing so. Such a circumstance was unprecedented in their experience. Some genius among them had made an invention—taxation—that immensely benefited those folk to whom he owed his loyalty. It would be made again and again in the millennia ahead, around the world, usually with less justification.

The wandering had been as long as and far more desperate than the mythical forty years of the Hebrews in the wilderness. No manna fell from heaven, only snow, sleet, ice-cold rain. Others already occupied the good hunting grounds, and in a short time mustered themselves to drive the strangers onward. When at last they reached these parts, farther from the Asian motherland than men of their race had ventured before, their first winter was almost as cruel as the Pilgrims' first winter was to be in Massachusetts.

Now they flourished. Wood brought by the We enabled them to replace improvised shelters with real houses. The breaking of a spearshaft was no longer a calamity. Usable stone, fuel, fish, flesh, fat, skins—such things they could and did get for themselves. However, what the We added was priceless. It freed the energies of the Cloud People for bolder hunts, bigger constructions, craftsmanship ever more careful, art ever more beautiful, songs and dances, thoughts and dreams.

Corwin had pointed out that, for pragmatic reasons, they were following his advice and giving their subjects some recompense, fishhooks, harpoons, needles, knives, stoneworking techniques, ideas. It was progress, he said. "Yeah, and I'll bet the We sit happily around in the evenings singing spirituals," Tamberly had muttered.

Still, she knew the primordial Americans were doomed. Hard though the newcomers made a life that had been tough to begin with, at least these aborigines weren't being slaughtered like Tasmanians by nineteenth-century whites or pushed beyond their thin margin of survival like Ukrainians and Ethiopians by twentieth-century governments. Nor were alien diseases ravaging them; the bacteriological isolation of New World from Old would not start till Beringia drowned. As long as they brought their tribute and made no trouble, the We could live in their own ways. If occasionally a Wanayimo brave passing by forced himself upon a Tula girl, well, among her folk that wasn't the shattering disgrace it would have been among his; and wasn't it better the genes mingle than that one strain go entirely extinct? Wasn't it?

Tamberly noticed Corwin's regard. Time had passed. She shook herself. "Sorry," she said. "Woolgathering."

"Not overly pleasant, I suspect." His voice was sympathetic. "Really, matters could be far worse. They are far worse, in too much of history. Here we can even ameliorate things a bit. Oh, just a bit, and most cautiously. But, for example, I found that, early on, the Wanayimo had taken a daughter of your friend Aryuk—Daraku, her name is; you probably know her well—they'd brought her here. She wasn't purposely mistreated. Their idea was simply that they needed someone from whom to learn the rudiments of her language. But she'd fallen into deep depression—homesickness, culture shock, lack of companionship. I persuaded them to give her back to them."

Tamberly had jumped to her feet. "Huh?" She stood for a moment staring. The horror receded. A measure of warmth followed. "Why, that, that's wonderful of you. Thank you." She swallowed.

He smiled. "Now, now. Common decency, after all, when the opportunity presented itself. Don't get overwrought, especially not before breakfast. Which will be ready in the proverbial two lambshakes."

The smell of frying bacon restored her mood faster than she supposed was morally right. Over the meal he kept conversation light, often humorous; yes, he could talk about something besides himself, and give her a chance to speak too. "Delightful city, San Francisco, agreed, but someday you must explore her in the 1930s, before she professionalized her charm. Tell me, though, about that Exploratorium you mentioned. It sounds like a marvelous innovation, quite in the old and truly spirit. . . ."

When they were done and he had lighted what he called the virginal cigarette of the day, he got serious. "After I've washed the dishes—and no, you may not help, at any rate on this first morning—I had better take you to meet Worika-kuno." She recognized the name, Red Wolf, from frequent mention in his reports. "A courtesy rather than a requirement, but among themselves, the Wanayimo value courtesy as much as will the Japanese."

"He's the chief, right?" Tamberly asked. Her studies had not made his status perfectly clear to her.

"Not in the sense of being invested with any formal authority. Tribal decisions are a matter of consensus among the men and the old women, those who've survived past childbearing age. Outside of council, young women have a tacitly granted say in everyday affairs. However, by sheer ability and force of personality, someone is bound to dominate, to be the most respected, whose word usually settles things. That man is Worika-kuno. Get on the right side of him, and your path will be reasonably smooth."

"What about the, um, medicine man?"

"Yes, the shaman does have a unique and powerful position. My relationship with him is somewhat precarious. I have to go out of my way, over and over, to show that I have no intention of becoming his rival or stealing any of his prestige. So will you. Frankly, you were dispatched to this precise date on my recommendation, after it was determined that you would return, because he'll be preoccupied, mostly secluded, for the next several days. Give you time to learn the ropes before you come in contact with him."

"What's he busy at?"

"A death. Yesterday a band that had been out hunting brought home the body of a comrade. A bison gored him. That was more than a loss, it was an evil omen, because he was a skillful hunter, a good provider. Now the shaman must magic the bad luck away. Fortunately for everyone's morale, Worika-kuno played the animal till his followers got it killed."

Tamberly whistled softly. She knew the Pleistocene bison.

In due course she accompanied Corwin to the village. It was an impressive sight after they came around the concealing hillock. She had seen images, but they conveyed no sense of the human energy that had gone into this work. A dozen or so rectangular sod houses, timber-framed, bungalow-sized, stood on clay foundations along the banks of a shallow stream. Smoke rose from most of the turf roofs. Offside lay a ceremonial area, defined by a ring of stones, at its center a firepit and a cairn covered with the skulls of big animals. Some were from the steppe, some from the woods and vales south of it: caribou, moose, bison, horse, bear, lion, mammoth on top. At the opposite end of the settlement was a workplace. There a fire blazed and women in buckskin gowns or, for the youngest and hardiest, the lightly woven tunics of summer, prepared the latest kill. Despite the death of Snowstrider, talk and laughter blew on the wind. Prolonged grief was a luxury these people could not afford.

The chatter died away as they saw the pair approaching. Others came from the houses or ceased their amusements among them. Those were mainly men, off duty; they did the hunting and the brute-force heavy work while women handled the home chores. Children hung back. Corwin had related that they were greatly loved and generally brash, but were taught to defer when deference was due.

The scientists passed on through an obbligato of greetings and ritual gestures, which Corwin returned. Nobody tagged after them. Someone had apprised Red Wolf, for he waited at his dwelling. Two mammoth tusks flanked its doorway and he was better clad than average. Otherwise nothing marked him out but his presence, his panther assurance. He raised a hand. "Always are you welcome, Tall Man," he said gravely. "Always may you have good hunting and, in your home, contentment."

"May fair weather and kindly spirits ever walk with you, Red Wolf," Corwin responded. "Here I bring her of whom I told you, that we may pay our respects."

Tamberly followed the speeches. Corwin had downloaded his knowledge of the language, once he had a reasonable command of it, into a mnemonic unit uptime, and she had had it entered in her brain. Likewise had he painlessly acquired the additional vocabulary and nuances of Tula that she discovered for herself. (He "had!" No, he "would," some fifteen thousand years in the future.) Eventually, when they had no further use for the knowledge, it would be wiped from them to make room for something else. That was a rather sad thought.

She pulled her attention back to the Ice Age. Red Wolf's look lay keen upon her. "We have met before, Sun Hair," he murmured.

"W-we have." She rallied her wits. "I belong to no folk here, but go among the animals. I want to be friends with the Cloud People."

"From time to time you may wish a guide," he said shrewdly.

"Yes," she agreed. "Such a one will find me thankful." That was the closest this language could come to saying that he would be well rewarded. *Let's face it, with the kind of help available here, I can accomplish ten times what I was able to earlier.*

Red Wolf spread his arms. "Enter and be blessed. We shall talk undisturbed."

The interior was a single room. Flat stones at the middle made a hearth on which a fire smoldered; starting one afresh was toilsome, to be avoided as much as possible. Low clay platforms along the walls, richly provided with hides, could sleep about twenty adults and children. Hardly any of them were now on hand. Given daylight and reasonable weather, the outdoors had far more to offer. Red Wolf introduced his pretty wife, Little Willow. He went on to present another woman. Her eyes were red from weeping, her cheeks were gashed, and her hair hung unbraided, signs of mourning. She was Moonlight on the Water, Snowstrider's widow.

"We plan how to provide for her and her small ones," Red Wolf explained. "She does not wish to take a new man at once. Well, I think she can stay here until she feels ready to."

He gestured his guests to sit on skins spread near the fire. Little Willow brought a leather bottle, not unlike a Spanish bota, that held fermented cloudberry juice. Tamberly squirted a little into her mouth, just to be polite, and learned it wasn't bad. She was being treated more or less as a man, she knew, but then, her status was extraordinary. At that, Little Willow and Moonlight on the Water weren't kept in purdah, but listened. If either thought she had something important to say, she would speak.

"I heard how you slew the terrible bison," Tamberly told Red Wolf. "That was valiantly done."—the more so when, in his mind, it must have been possessed by a malignant spirit.

"I had help," he said, not modestly but matter-of-factly. He grinned. "By myself, I do not always win. Maybe you can teach me how to make a fox trap that works. Mine never do. I wonder if somehow I once offended the Father of Foxes. Toddling around as a baby, did I leave my sign on top of his?" The grin became a laugh.

He can joke about the unknown, Tamberly heard herself think. *Damn, I believe I'm going to like him. No doubt I shouldn't, but I believe I'll have to.*

III

She mounted her timecycle, projected a map with a coordinate grid, set her destination, touched the activator. Immediately the dome was gone from around her and she back at her old campsite. Locking the controls, though neither man nor beast would come so near so alien an object in the next few hours, she started off afoot.

Sky and sea reached steely gray, sunless. Even over distance and against the wind she could hear how surf crashed on Beringia and tore at it. The wind skirled across dead grass, dark moss, bare shrubs and trees, strewn boulders, out of a north where darkness had engulfed the horizon. Cold laved her face and searched for any opening in her clothes. The season's first blizzard was on its way southward.

Lifetimes of feet had beaten the path she found and took. It led her down into the gulch. Depth walled off most wind, but the river, engorged by high tide, foamed dirty white. She reached the bluff, now barely above that violence, where three stone huts huddled by a spring.

Somebody must have spied her through the dwarf alder, for as she arrived, Aryuk pulled aside the bundled wattles that served him for a door, crawled forth, and rose. He gripped a hand ax. His shoulders were stooped under a carrion skin. Between mane and beard she saw a haggardness that shocked her.

"Ar-Aryuk, my friend—" she stammered.

He stared at her a long time, as if trying to remember or understand what she was. When he spoke, she could hardly make out the mumble in the roar of river and surf. "We heard you have come back. Not to Us."

"No, I—" She reached toward him. He flinched before he stood his ground. She lowered her arm. "Aryuk, yes, I stay with the Mammoth Slayers, but only because I need to. I am not of them. I want to help you."

He eased a little—less in relief, she thought, than yielding to his weariness. "True, Ulungu said you were kind to him and his sons when they were there. You gave them the Lovely Sweet." He meant chocolate. In earlier days she had perforce handed it around very rarely. Else a van-sized Patrol vehicle couldn't have brought enough.

She recalled the dull gratitude of those who no longer hoped. *God damn it, I will* not *cry*. "I have Lovely Sweet for you and everybody here. First, though," since Aryuk had made no move to invite her in, not that she really wanted to enter the hovel, "why did you not come too, this moon?"

It had been the probable last month until spring for the We to bring tribute. After encountering the Bubbling Springs folk, she'd been glad she was away in the field when others appeared. What consolation she could offer was so tiny, and she hadn't slept that whole night. However, she had asked Corwin to inform her of Aryuk's advent. She couldn't forbear to meet him. If need be, she'd hop a few days downtime. But he never showed.

"The Mammoth Slayers are angry," she warned. "I told them I

would find out what the trouble is. Do you mean to go soon? I fear a storm is about to strike."

The shaggy head drooped. "We cannot go. We have nothing to bring."

She tautened. "Why?"

"At the fall gathering I told everybody that I did not think we would," Aryuk said in the rambling Tula fashion, but with none of the Tula liveliness. "Ulungu is a true friend. After he and his sons had made their own last trip, they came to see if they could help us. That was when I learned you had joined the Tall Man."

Oh, God, how betrayed you must have felt.

"They could do nothing, for we ourselves had done nothing," Aryuk went on. "I told them they should go home and care for their women and children. This has been a hard summer. Fish, shellfish, small game, everything was scant. We went hungry because we must spend time getting things and traveling for the Mammoth Slayers. Others suffered too, but the new hooks and spears helped. They are not much use here, where schools of fish and the seal that prey on them seldom pass by." *Shoal water in the estuary, currents, something like that,* Tamberly guessed. "We must make ready for winter. If we worked any more for the Mammoth Slayers, we would starve."

Aryuk raised his head. His eyes met hers. Dignity descended upon them. "Perhaps we can give them more next summer than we did in this," he finished. "Say to them that I alone decided."

"I will." She wet her lips. "No, I will do better than that. Fear not. They are not as—as—" Tula had no word meaning "cruel" or "merciless." It wouldn't be fair to the Cloud People anyway. "They are not as fierce as you think."

Knuckles whitened above the hand ax. "They take whatever they want. They kill whoever stands against them."

"There was a fight, true. Do the We never kill one another?"

His stare became wind-bleak. "Two more among Us have died at their hands since then." *I didn't know that! Corwin doesn't bother to inquire.* "And you speak for the Mammoth Slayers. Well, you have heard what I have to say."

"No, I, I only . . . . only am trying to . . . make you happier." *Give you heart to last out the winter. In spring, for whatever reason, the invaders will pull up stakes. But I'm not allowed to predict that. And you doubtless wouldn't believe me if I did.* "Aryuk, I will see to it that the Cloud People are content. They will want no more from Alder River before the snow is off the ground again."

He stayed wary. "Can you be sure? Even you?"

"I can. They will heed me. Did Tall Man not make them give you back Daraku?"

Abruptly an old man stood there under the darkening sky. "That was no use. She died on the way home. The child that so many of them put into her, it took her away with it."

"What? Oh, no, no." Tamberly realized she had moaned in English. "Why did you not let Tall Man know?"

"He was never there when I was, afterward," said the flat voice. "I saw him twice, but not nearby, and he did not seek me. Why should I go to him, then, if I dared? Can he call back the dead? Can you?"

She remembered her own father, whom she could gladden with a phone call and overjoy by stepping across his threshold. "I think you would like me to leave you alone," she said as emptily.

"No, come inside," where the rest crouch in murk, in fear and stifled, stifling rage. "I am ashamed at how little food we can offer, but come inside."

What can I do, what can I say? If I'd grown up alongside Manse, or in some earlier era, I'd have known what, young though I am. But where-when I hail from, they send printed sympathy cards and talk about the grief process. "I . . . I should not. I must not, today. You need . . . to think about me, till you understand I *am* your friend . . . always. Then we can be together. First think about me. I will watch over you. I will care for you."

Am I wise or weak?

"I love you," she blurted. "All of you. Here." She reached in her pocket and pulled out the chocolate bars. They fell at his feet. Somehow she smiled before she turned and left him. He didn't protest, merely stood where he was and looked after her. *I guess I am doing the right thing.*

A flaw of wind whirled down to rattle skinny boughs. She hastened her steps upward. Aryuk shouldn't see her cry.

IV

The council, the grown men and old women of the tribe, crowded the house where they met; but the sacred fire could not burn outdoors when a storm bade fair to blow for days. The booming and snarling of air came through thick walls as an undertone. Flames on the hearthstones guttered low. They picked out of darkness, waveringly, the crone who squatted to tend them. Otherwise the long room was filled with gloom and smoke and the smells of leather-clad bodies packed together. It was hot. When the fire jumped high for a second, sweat glistened on the faces of Red Wolf, Sun Hair, Answerer, and others in the innermost circle around it.

The same light shimmered along the steel that Tamberly drew and raised high. "You have heard, you have understood, you know," she intoned. On solemn occasions the Cloud People used a repetitive style that to her sounded almost Biblical. "For that which I ask, if you will grant me my wish, I give to you this knife. Take it of me, Red Wolf; try it; make known if it be good."

The man received it. The sternness of his features had melted away. She thought of a child on Christmas morning. Silence gripped the assembly until their breath seemed as loud as the gale, heavy as surf. Nonetheless he tested its heft and balance with skilled care. Stooping, he picked up a stick. His first attempt to slice it was awkward. Flint and obsidian take edges as keen as any metal, but they won't cut seasoned wood, being too fragile, and you can't properly whittle with them. He was also unaccustomed to the shape, the handle. With a little coaching, though, he got the knack fast.

"This comes alive as I hold it," he whispered raptly.

"It has many uses," Tamberly said. "I will show them to you, and the way of caring for the blade." When a stone grew blunt, you chipped it afresh, till it got too small. Sharpening steel properly is an art, but she felt sure he'd master it. "This is if you will grant me my wish, O People."

Red Wolf looked about. "Is such our will?" he inquired sonorously. "That I take the knife on behalf of us all, and for our return gift we forgive the tribute that the family of the Vole man Aryuk should have brought?"

A buzz of assent ran among shadows. Answerer's harsh voice cut through. "No, here is a bad thing."

Damn! Tamberly thought, dismayed. *I'd expected the whole business would be pro forma. What ails that wretch?*

The talk rose to a soft hubbub and died out. Eyeballs gleamed. Red Wolf gave the shaman a hard stare. "We have beheld what the Bright Stone can do," he said slowly. "You have beheld. Is this not worth many loads of wood or fish, many skins of otter and hare?"

The wrinkled countenance writhed. "Why do the tall pale strangers favor the Vole People? What secrets are between them?"

Anger flared in Tamberly. "All know that I dwelt with them before you entered this land," she snapped. "They are my friends. Do you not stand by your own friends, O Cloud People?"

"Then are you friends to us?" Answerer shrilled.

"If you will let me be!"

Red Wolf lowered his arm between the two. "Enough," he said. "Shall we squabble over a single moon's share from a single family, like gulls over a carcass? Do you fear the Vole folk, Answerer?"

Shrewd! Tamberly cheered. The shaman could only glare and reply sullenly, "We know not what witchcraft they command, what sly tricks are theirs." She remembered Manse Everard remarking once that societies frequently attribute abnormal powers to those whom they lord it over—early Scandinavians to the Finns, medieval Christians to the Jews, white Americans to the blacks. . . .

Red Wolf's tone went dry. "I have heard of none. Has anyone?" And he lifted the knife over his head. *A natural-born leader for sure. Standing there like that, Lordy, but he's handsome.*

Neither debate nor vote followed. That was not the way of the Wanayimo, and would have been unnecessary in any case. While they depended on their shaman for intercession with the supernatural and for spells against sickness, they gave him no more homage than was reasonable, and indeed looked somewhat askance at him: a man celibate, sedentary, peculiar. Tamberly sometimes recalled Catholic acquaintances, respectful toward their priests but not slavish and not uncommonly in disagreement.

Acceptance of her proposal went like a quiet billow, more felt than uttered. Answerer sat down cross-legged, drew a buckskin cloak over his head, and sulked. Men gathered around Red Wolf to marvel at the thing they had gotten. Tamberly was free to leave.

Corwin joined her at the exit. He had stood silent in the background, as beseemed an outsider present by courtesy. Dim though the light was, she saw the dourness upon him. "Come to my dome," he ordered. She bridled, then mentally shrugged. She'd rather expected something like this.

The door was hingeless but closely fitted into the entrance, a composite of sticks, withes, hide, and moss. Corwin freed it. Wind tried to snatch it from him. He wrestled it back into place when he and Tamberly had passed through. They raised their hoods, closed their jackets, and set off toward their camp. Air raved, bit, slammed, clawed. The snow that it drove was a white blindness. He needed a hand-held, compasslike direction indicator.

When they regained shelter, both were a little numb for a few minutes. The storm racketed, the dome fabric shivered. Objects clustered inside seemed fragile, weightless.

Neither sat down. When Corwin spoke, they stood as in confrontation. "Well," he said, "evidently I was right. The Patrol should have kept you home where you belong."

Tamberly had been preparing herself. *Not insolent, not insubordinate, but firm. He does rank me, but he is not my boss. And Manse has told me the Patrol values independence, provided it goes along with competence.* "What have I done wrong . . . sir?" she asked as gently as was possible in the noise.

"You know quite well," Corwin rapped. "Unwarrantable interference."

"I don't believe it was, sir. Nothing that could affect events any more than we already do by being here." *And that's taken care of. We have "always" been this small part of prehistory.*

"Then why didn't you confer with me in advance?"

Because you'd have forbidden it, of course, and I couldn't buck that. "I'm sorry if I've offended you. No such intention, honest." *Ha!* "I took for granted—well, what harm? We interact with these people. We talk, socialize, accompany them, use them for guides and reward them with little objects from uptime. Don't we? I did more among the Tulat than I did today, by a long shot, and headquarters never objected. What's a single knife? They can't make any like it. It'll break or wear out or rust away or be lost in a couple of generations at most, and nobody will remember it much longer."

"You, a new and junior agent—" Corwin drew breath. A touch less coldly, he proceeded: "Yes, you too are given considerable discretion. That can't be helped. But your motives. You had no sound reason for doing what you did, only a childish sentimentalism. We can't allow that sort of attitude, Tamberly. We dare not."

I couldn't stand by and let Aryuk, Tseshu, their kids and grandkids be brutalized or killed. I . . . didn't want Red Wolf involved in an atrocity. "I don't know of any regulation forbidding us to do a kindness when we safely can." She shaped a smile. "I can't believe you've never been kind to somebody you cared about."

He stood impassive for a space. It broke in a smile of his own. "*Touché!* I concede." Gravely: "You did take more upon yourself than you should have. I won't pursue the matter, but consider this a lesson, a warning."

Genial again: "And now that that's out of the way, let's re-establish diplomatic relations, shall we? Sit down. I'll make coffee, we'll have a spot of brandy on the side, and it's been far too long since we shared a meal."

"I've mostly been in the field," she reminded him.

"Yes, yes. However, we are weatherbound now, for days to come."

"I figure I'll skip uptime to when this has cleared."

"Hm, really, my dear, your zeal is admirable, but heed the voice of experience. Occasional rest, recreation, outright loafing is highly advisable. All work and no play, you know."

Yeah, she thought. *I know what kind of R & R you have in mind.* She didn't resent it. A natural notion under these circumstances; and probably he imagined it was a compliment. *No, thanks. What's the most tactful way out of here?*

V

The least of the houses, scarcely more than a hut, was Answerer's: for the shaman dwelt alone, save for whatever demons he kept at his beck. Often, though, a man or woman of the tribe sought to him.

He and Running Fox sat at the fire. More light than it gave straggled through the hole in the roof and the smoke swirling up. Clear weather, almost warm, had followed the great wind. Magical objects seemed to stir in shadows. They were few, a drum, a whistle, engraved bones, dried herbs. Everyday possessions were meager too. His strength and life lay mainly in the spirit world.

He squinted at his visitor. They had exchanged some careful, meaningful words. "You also have your reasons for unease," he said.

Running Fox's sharp visage drew into a scowl. "I have," he replied. "What quarry do the two tall strangers stalk among us?"

"Who knows?" Answerer breathed. "I have sought visions about them. None came."

"Have they cast spells against yours?"

"I fear that may be so."

"How could they?"

"We are far from the graves of our ancestors. Later we left our dead behind as we trekked onward. Thus far in this place there are very few to help us."

"Snowstrider's ghost is surely strong."

"One man's. Against how many of the Vole men's?"

Running Fox bit his lip. "True. A musk ox or bison is stronger than any wolf, but a wolf pack can bring down any bull." He pondered before he asked, "Yet—do the Vole People tend graves and stay friends with their dead, like us? Do their ghosts linger at all?"

"We do not know," Answerer said.

Both men shivered. A mystery is more daunting than the starkest truth.

"Tall Man and Sun Hair command mighty spells and powers," Running Fox said at last. "They call themselves our friends."

"How much longer will they abide here?" Answerer retorted. "And would they really help us in dire need? Might they even be lulling us while they prepare our destruction?"

Running Fox smiled sourly. "Just by being on hand, they threaten your standing."

"Enough!" snapped the shaman. "You feel yourself menaced."

The hunter looked downward. "Well . . . Red Wolf and most others . . . honor them more than I think is wise."

"And Red Wolf heeds you less than he did aforetime."

"Enough!" Running Fox barked a laugh. "What would you do about it if you could?"

"If we learned more, and got a hold on them—"

Running Fox signed for caution. "One would be crazy rash to go straight against them. But they do care about the Vole People. At least, Sun Hair does."

"So I was thinking. And what secrets, what powers, do she and they share?"

"By themselves the hairy ones are naught. They are indeed like voles, which a fox kills in a single bite. If we took them by surprise, unbeknownst to Tall Man and Sun Hair—"

"Can such a deed be hidden from those two?"

"I have seen both of them surprised when something unawaited happened, a ptarmigan breaking cover, river ice suddenly cracking underfoot, that kind of ordinary thing. They are not aware of all that is in the world . . . any more than you are."

"Still, you are a daring man."

"But not a stupid one," said Running Fox, turning impatient. "How many days have we been sounding each other out, you and I?"

"It is time we spoke openly," Answerer agreed. "You think to go there, I daresay to that very Aryuk whom she holds especially dear, and wring the truth out of him."

"I need a companion."

"I am not a man of weapons."

"I can do that work. You, for your part, understand spells, demons, ghosts." Running Fox peered at the shaman. "But can you make the journey?"

Answerer's response came stiff. "I am no weakling." He was in fact wiry and, while missing several teeth and seeing poorly, could walk long distances or run quite fast.

"I should have asked, do you wish to make the journey?" Running Fox amended.

Mollified, Answerer signed assent. "We will have a freeze in the next day or two," he forecast. "This softened snow will become like stone, easy to move upon."

Eagerness leaped behind Running Fox's eyes, but he kept his face blank and spoke thoughtfully. "Best we leave by dark. I will say I want to go scouting by myself for a while, to learn this territory better and to think." Folk would believe that of him.

"I will say I want to raise spirits in my house, and must not be disturbed for days and nights until I am ready to come forth," Answerer decided.

"At that time you may indeed have mighty tidings."

"And you may win much honor."

"I do this for the Cloud People."

"For all the Cloud People," Answerer said, "now and always."

VI

Like a hawk upon a lemming, there the invaders were. A shout pierced Aryuk's winter drowse. He groped through its heaviness. Another cry tore it from him. That was the call of a woman and small children in fear.

His own woman, Tseshu, clutched at him. "Wait here," he told her. Through the blindness of the den his hand found a weaponstone. He scrambled out of the skins, grass, and boughs in which they had rested, sharing warmth. Fear tore at him, but rage overwhelmed it. A beast, vexing his kin? On hands and knees, he shoved the windbreak aside and scuttled through the doorway. Rising to a crouch, he confronted what had come.

The courage spilled from him like water from a cupped hand flung open.

Cold seared his nakedness. Low in the south, the sun turned day to a blaze, hard blue sky, hard blue shadows, brilliant white over ground and alder branches. Ice gleamed duller on the stream, swept clean of snow by winds. Where the ravine ended, the stones of the beach lay rimed, and the sea itself had frozen a long ways out. Surf growled afar, as if the Bear Spirit spoke in anger.

Before him stood two men. Leather and fur covered them. One held a spear in his right hand, a hatchet in his left. Aryuk had met him before, yes, he knew that thin glittery-eyed face, they called him Running Fox in their tongue. The other was old, wrinkled, gaunt, though not much wearied by his traveling. He gripped a bone carved with signs. Both had painted their brows and cheeks, marks that must be powerful too. Tracks showed how they had come down the slope—quietly, so quietly, until they were here and yelled their summons.

Barakyn and Oltas had gone off to walk the trap lines. They would not return till tomorrow. *Did these two watch and wait for my strong helpers to leave me?* flashed through Aryuk. Barakyn's woman Seset huddled at the entrance of their dwelling. Aryuk's third living son, Dzuryan, hardly more than a boy, shuddered in front of the hut he shared with Oltas, where he had been tending the fire and otherwise dozing.

"What . . . what do you want?" faltered Aryuk. Though dread clogged his mouth, he could not bring himself to wish these newcomers well as one should for any visitor.

Running Fox replied, colder than the cloudlets that puffed from between his lips. He had learned Our speech better than any other Cloud man—in how many times with Daraku? "I talk to you. You talk to me."

That, yes, of course, Aryuk thought. *Talk. What else have we left? Unless they want to mount Seset. She is young and toothsome. No, I must not let myself know wrath. Besides, they do not look at her.* "Come inside," he said reluctantly.

"No," spat Running Fox—half in scorn, half in wariness, Aryuk guessed. Crammed into a Tula shelter, he would have no room to wield those beautiful, deathful weapons. "We talk here."

"Then I must cover me," Aryuk said. His feet and fingertips were already numb.

Running Fox made a brusque gesture of agreement. Tseshu crept forth. She had put on shoes and a skin cloak, which she held tight as if afraid or ashamed to have strangers behold sagging breasts and slack belly. She brought the same garb for her man. Dzuryan and Seset slipped back and outfitted themselves likewise. They returned to the entrances, very quiet. Meanwhile Tseshu helped Aryuk dress.

That comforted him mightily, as belittling as it was to do this while Running Fox flung his questions. "What walks . . . between you . . . and Sun Hair?"

Aryuk gaped. "Sun Hair? Who?"

"Woman. Tall. Hair like sun. Eyes like—" Running Fox pointed at the sky.

"She Who Knows— We, we were friends." *Are we yet? She abides in your place.*

"What else? Talk!"

"Nothing, nothing."

"Ho! Nothing? Why she give tribute for you?"

Aryuk stiffened. Tseshu finished tying on the moss-stuffed bags that were his shoes. "She did? What?" Joy rushed over him. "Yes, she promised she would save us!"

Tseshu straightened and took stance at his side. So had her way ever been.

His moment's happiness blew off across the ice. "What *kuyok* in knife?" Running Fox snarled.

"*Kuyok?* Knife? I do not understand." Was the man working a spell? Aryuk raised his free hand and made a sign against it.

The intruders tensed. Running Fox spoke to his companion. The elder man pointed his carven bone at Aryuk and uttered a short, shrill chant.

"No tricks," Running Fox rasped. His hatchet waved toward the elder. "Here is Aakinninen—you say 'Answerer.' He *kuyokolaia*. Got *kuyok* much more strong than yours."

The word must mean "magic," Aryuk knew. His heart shook his ribs. The cold slid through cloak and flesh. "I meant you no harm," he whispered.

Running Fox brought his spearhead near Aryuk's throat. "My strength much more strong than yours."

"It is, it is."

"You see Wanayimo strength at Bubbling Springs."

Aryuk clutched his hand ax tight, as if its weight could hold him from being whirled up by a gust of forbidden fury. *Should I go flat in the snow?*

"Do what I say!" Running Fox shouted.

Aryuk glimpsed Dzuryan and Seset, how they quailed. Somehow he stood fast, and Tseshu beside him. "What must we do?" he asked in bewilderment.

"You say what is with you and the tall ones. What they want? What they do?"

"Nothing, we know nothing."

Running Fox slanted his spear downward. The stone-edged head sliced across Aryuk's calf. A shallow cut reddened behind it. "Talk!"

The pain was little, the menace bigger than heaven. When at last he meets the lion, a man stops being afraid. Aryuk squared his shoulders. "You can kill me," he said low, "but then this mouth cannot speak. Instead, my ghost will."

Running Fox's eyes widened. Either he knew the word for ghost or he guessed its meaning. He turned to Answerer. They conferred fast and harshly. But always Running Fox stayed mindful of where each of Us was. Aryuk's free hand found Tseshu's.

Answerer's withered face hardened. He barked something. His companion clearly agreed. Aryuk waited to learn the fate of his family.

"You not make *kuyok* against us," Running Fox said. "We take one along. She talk."

He stuck his spear upright in the snow, made a long stride forward, seized Tseshu by the arm. He hauled her from her man's clasp. She wailed.

Daraku!

A wind roared over Aryuk. He himself screamed as he sprang.

Running Fox chopped with his hatchet. Caught off balance, he missed Aryuk's head but struck him on the left shoulder. Aryuk neither saw nor felt the blow. He was in against the Cloud man. His right arm swung. The hand ax crashed on Running Fox's temple. The hunter crumpled.

Aryuk stood above him. Pain smote. He dropped the hand ax and went to his knees, pawing at the hurt shoulder. Dzuryan boiled toward him. A weaponstone of his own, hurled, barely went by Answerer. The old one whirled about and ran off, in among the trees, up the slope. Dzuryan joined Tseshu where Aryuk was. Seset silenced the children.

Aryuk's soul returned as the darkness ebbed from him. Helped by both women, he regained his feet. Blood ran, a red flame amidst the snow, from his shoulder. That arm hung useless. When he tried moving it, the pain was so vast that the night rolled over him again. Tseshu drew his cloak aside to look at the wound. It wasn't deep, the edge had hit bone, but surely that bone was broken.

"Father, shall I catch the other man and kill him?" Dzuryan asked. Did his boy-voice waver, or was that how Aryuk heard it?

"No," said Tseshu. "He is too far ahead of you now. You are too young."

"But he, he will tell the Red Wolf what happened."

Dimly surprised, Aryuk found he could think. "That is best," he muttered. "We must not make this thing worse . . . for all of Us."

He stared downward. Running Fox sprawled limp. The blood that had gushed from the man's nose flowed no more, only trickled, slower and slower as the cold thickened it. The open mouth had gone dry, the open eyes had filmed over, the open bowels had emptied. A snowbank into which he had fallen hid the smashed part of his head.

"I forgot myself," Aryuk whispered at him. "You should not have laid hand on my woman. Not after my daughter. We were both unwise, you and I."

"Come in by the fire," Tseshu said.

He shambled obediently along. The women tended him as best they could, stanching the cut with moss, binding arm to side with thongs. Dzuryan built the fire up and fetched a frozen rabbit from a small cairn nearby. Tseshu laid it in the coals.

Hot meat gave heart, and Aryuk drew more strength from the bodies pressed against his. At last he could tell them: "In the morning I must leave you."

"No!" moaned Tseshu. He knew that she knew what he intended. Nonetheless she protested. "Where can you go?"

"Away," he said. "They will come after their dead man when they hear, and after me. If they found us together, it would go very badly with you. When Barakyn and Oltas return, everybody must go different ways, seeking shelter and help among friends. The Cloud men will know that I and I alone killed him. I think, if they do not see you where he lies, they will be content with my death. Tracking me down will use up most of their anger."

Seset hugged herself, rocked to and fro, wept aloud. Tseshu sat moveless, except for taking her man's good hand in hers.

"Say no more now," Aryuk ordered. "I am weary. I need a night's rest."

He and Tseshu sought their hut. Lying beside her, he found he could sleep—lightly, skimming above pain, dreams flickering like bits of rainbow. *I have lived longer than many*, he thought once, half wakeful. *It must be time for me to go find our children who died. They have been lonely.*

At dawn he ate again, let her clothe him, and went out. The ravine reached shadowy, its alders hunched into their own dreams. A few stars still glimmered overhead. Breath smoked into the chill. From the sea rumbled sounds of waves and of ice grinding ice. His wound throbbed, hot, but if he moved with care the pain seldom bit too hard.

His woman, son, and first son's woman gathered about him. He pointed at the corpse. "Bring this inside and close the entrance before you leave," he told them. "The Mammoth Slayers may feel milder if gulls and foxes have not eaten of their friend. But first—" He tried to stoop. His wound forbade. "Dzuryan, you are the man now, until your brothers come home. Dig those eyeballs out. If I carry them away, his ghost should follow me and leave you alone." The youth hung back, lips fluttering in the twilit blur of his face. "Do it!"

When the things rested safe in his pouch, Aryuk, one-armed, drew Tseshu to him. "Had I grown old and feeble, I must go into the wilderness," he said. "I leave a little sooner, only a little sooner."

From Dzuryan he took a hand ax. He wasn't sure why. He had refused a food ration, and was in no shape to knock down an animal or even make a trap. Well, the stone was something to hold. He nodded, turned, and trudged off, toward the easiest path up the slope and out of sight.

Surely you never wanted this for me, You Who Know Strangeness, he thought. *When you learn of it, will you come help? Better if you help my children and grandchildren. I do not matter any more.* He sent the memory of her elsewhere and gave himself to his wandering.

VII

Throughout winter, the Tulat were as little active as possible, to conserve energy for survival. They collected what food they were able to; by daylight they did what work came to hand; but mainly they stayed in their dens, and for most of that time they slept or sat in a self-induced, daydreamy trance. It was no wonder that so many, especially infants, took fatally sick. Yet what choice had they?

The Paleo-Indians were different, busy the year round, even during the long nights. They had the skills and the means to keep themselves well fed in all seasons. While some animals, such as the caribou, migrated, others, such as the mammoth, did not. That was the reason they settled on the steppe, though their hunters ranged into the northern highlands and the southern woods. Only the sea daunted them. Their descendants would master it. Meanwhile these, the Cloud People, had the Tulat to glean along its shores for them.

Thus Ralph Corwin grew accustomed to movement and noise after dark. An optical pickup secretly planted in the till enabled him to watch on a screen in his dome, magnifying the view at will. If things got interesting, or if he simply felt like it, he would stroll over and mingle. The folk had long since accepted him as human—enigmatic, potentially dangerous, but fascinating and, it seemed, well-disposed. You could enjoy his company, the mystery adding salt to the pleasure. Girls smiled, and some were quite pretty. Too bad that taking advantage would mean a degree of involvement compromising his mission. The Tulat were easygoing but . . . grubby; nor had he time to spare for them. The Patrol didn't want its too few agents spending more lifespan than necessary on any single job.

How grand it would be if Wanda Tamberly, who otherwise fitted what he'd heard about outdoorsy California girls of the later twentieth century, were forthcoming. *No matter*, he often scolded himself.

On this night he forgot about her. Tumult was rising in the village. He dressed warmly and left.

The air lay still, as if wind had congealed in the cold. Passing through his nostrils, it felt liquid. A moon just past the full made his breath a phantom akin to the hills north and south. Snow glistened and crunched underfoot. He had no need of a flashlight, nor did torches flare among the houses ahead. It was an extravagance the Wanayimo could have afforded, thanks to their tributaries. A fire was being built at the cairn of the skulls. Folk milled about, talking, gesticulating, sometimes howling. When the flames were high, they would bring drums and dance.

It would be a dance of mourning and propitiation, Corwin judged. That meant leadership, which meant certain plans and preparations.

He steered wide of the crowd and made his way to the home of Red Wolf's extended family.

His guess proved right. The hingeless door leaned loose between the tusks and light trickled around it. He put his face to the crack. "Aho," he called softly. "Tall Man speaks. May he enter?" Ordinarily that would have been an affront, implying that those inside were not hospitable, but rules changed when demonic forces were abroad, and Corwin also had an idea that Answerer was on hand. Unease had waxed these past few days, after the shaman sequestered himself; and now this abrupt excitement—

After a minute, a form within blocked off the light. "Be welcome," said Red Wolf, and drew the barrier aside. Corwin stepped through. Red Wolf accompanied him back to the middle of the room, where the banked coals had been stoked up. That small, smoking blaze gave about as much illumination as the fat that burned in four soapstone lamps. Beyond hulked darkness. Corwin could barely see a screen, hide stretched over a driftwood frame, propped across the rear end. Behind it must be such of the family as had no business here tonight and were not out among the howlers.

Those who had met were a chosen few. Corwin recognized the hunters Broken Blade and Spearpoint, the respected elder Fireflint, standing. On the floor, arms across drawn-up knees, sat Answerer. Shadows lay doubly deep in the furrows of his visage, the sockets of sunken eyes. His back and neck were bent. *Utter exhaustion*, Corwin realized. *He's been away, but I don't think it was on any spirit journey*.

"Yes, best is that Tall Man be in our council," said Red Wolf. His tone was steely. "Did you summon him, Answerer?"

The shaman made a noncommittal noise.

"I saw what appears to be trouble, and came to see if I might be of use," Corwin told them, not insincerely.

"Trouble indeed," said Red Wolf. "Now Running Fox is dead, the cleverest of men."

"Ill is this." Corwin had found that man valuable—quick on the uptake, talented at explaining things—though apt to ask disconcerting questions. His shrewdness and independence of mind were a distinct loss to the tribe. "How did it happen?" *Some extraordinary way, obviously*.

Gazes through the gloom ransacked the outsider. "The Vole man Aryuk slew him," Red Wolf replied. "That Aryuk for whose sake Sun Hair gave up her knife."

"What? No, can't be!" *They're cowed, the Tulat, they've had it stabbed into them that they're helpless.*

"It is so, Tall Man. Answerer has just arrived with the news. He escaped by a gnat's wing, he, whose person should be inviolable."

"But—" Corwin drew his lungs full of warm, odorous, sooty air. *Stay calm. Stay alert. This situation could get nasty fast.* "I am surprised. I am grieved. I ask that you tell me how the woe came about."

Answerer looked up. Flame glinted in his eyes. Malignancy hissed: "It was because of you and your woman. Running Fox and I went to find out why those Voles are so dear to you."

"Friends, only friends. Sun Hair's from earlier years. Not mine. I hardly know them."

"Aryuk said the same."

"It was true!"

"Aryuk may have cast a spell on her," Fireflint ventured.

"Answerer needed to find out," Red Wolf said. "Running Fox went with him. They spoke for a while, then suddenly Aryuk attacked. He took Running Fox off guard and killed him with a blow of a hand ax. Somebody threw another at Answerer, who fled."

No wonder he's done in, Corwin thought distantly, *an old man—perhaps as old as fifty—going day and night over the snow in terror for his life.* The shaman had slumped again. "But what could make Aryuk do this?"

"It is not clear," Red Wolf replied. "A demon may have seized him, or the evil may long have nested in his heart . . . You truly have no knowledge?"

"None. What will you do now?"

Glance met glance. The silence grew until Red Wolf reached a decision. *He's still leery of me,* Corwin knew, *but he wants to believe Wanda and I are honest. He wants to show his own good will by being candid.*

"I will not dance for Running Fox tonight," Red Wolf said. "With certain hunters I will be bound for the sea. We must bring our friend home."

"Yes, you must," Corwin understood.

It was more than sentiment: "We need him here. His is a strong ghost, like Snowstrider's, to aid us against evil spirits and hostile ghosts."

"Hostile. . . . Tulat?"

"Who else? Although I will see to it that Aryuk's body lies afar with his ghost tightly bound to it. Answerer will give me the tools and words for that."

"Do you mean to kill him?"

Surprise murmured through the crackling of the flames. "What else?" Red Wolf demanded. "We cannot let a Vole man harm a man of the people and go unscathed."

"We should kill many of them," Broken Blade growled.

"No, no," said Red Wolf. "Then how can they bring tribute? They must be quelled, but I think it will be enough to slay Aryuk."

"What if we fail in that?"

"Then, true, we must avenge Running Fox on others. Let us see what happens."

"I wish you would stay your hands," Corwin exclaimed. Immediately he knew what foolishness that was. He'd been thinking how Wanda would feel when she got back from the field.

The faces before him hardened. Answerer looked up again and croaked almost gleefully, "Then you do favor the Vole People! What *is* between you and them? That is what Running Fox and I went to learn, and he died."

"Nothing," Corwin said. "You went there for nothing. It is truth what Sun Hair and I have told you; we are only sojourners here, and in a while we shall leave forever. We only want friendship with . . . with everybody."

"You, maybe. But she?"

"I vouch for her." Corwin saw he'd better put up a brave front. He roughened his tone. "Hear me. Think. If we had ill intentions toward the Cloud People, need we hide it? You have seen a little of what we can do. A little."

Red Wolf moved his hands, a calming gesture. "Well spoken," he said quietly. "Yet I think it best if you, Tall Man, make sure that your wife Sun Hair keeps apart from this matter."

"I will," Corwin promised. "Oh, I will. She must not act. Such is the law of our tribe."

VIII

Young hunters could travel swiftly. With brief stops for rest and a bite of dried meat, Red Wolf and his three companions reached Alder River the night after they left home. The moon was up, its fullness gnawed by the Dark Hare but still casting shimmer and shadow across clouds, snow, ice. The three huts crouched misshapen. Red Wolf breathed deeply and took a magic bone between his teeth before he could make himself crawl into the one whose entrance had been blocked. Inside, sightless, he laid hand on something that felt colder than the air. No stranger to death, he nonetheless jerked the hand back.

Mastering terror, he tried once more. Yes, a face lay stiff beneath his palm. "Running Fox, this is Red Wolf come to give you your honor," he muttered around the bone. Getting hold of the coat, he dragged the dead man forth.

Moonlight grayed skin. Running Fox was frozen as hard as river or sea. Blood clotted black on the left temple and around the chin. Black too were the gaping mouth and the horrible twin emptinesses above.

The hunters squatted around. "They gouged his eyes out," whispered Broken Blade. "*Why?*"

"To blind his ghost, lest it pursue them?" wondered Spearpoint.

"Their ghosts will suffer worse," snarled White Water.

"Enough," said Red Wolf. "These are unlucky things to speak of, worst by dark. We shall know more in the morning. Now let us take him from this ill place, that he may sleep among his comrades."

They carried the body above the ravine, put it into the bag they had brought along for it, and spread their own. Wind whittered. The moon flew between clouds. Wolf-howls afar were homelike when men heard, as well, the mumbling of the sea beyond the ice. Red Wolf drowsed off, but his dreams were jagged.

At dawn his band cast about. The tracks they found in the snow, though days old, told a tale they understood. "Some have gone east, some west," Red Wolf related. "Small footprints are in both sets. Those are surely Aryuk's kin, seeking refuge till our wrath has been slaked. One trail goes inland, and is a grown man's. That is Aryuk's."

"Or somebody else's, like a son's?" asked Spearpoint. "They are sly beasts, those."

Red Wolf signed a no. "Why should a son mislead us, when we would hunt the father down too? If they meant to protect him, they would have gone at his side, ready for a fight. But they knew they would lose. Best that he die alone for what he did." With a grin: "We will do as they wish."

"If he dies before we catch him, Running Fox is cheated of revenge," Broken Blade fretted.

"Then he shall have it tenfold on the other Voles," White Water vowed.

Red Wolf scowled. Punishment was one thing, no different from slaying a dangerous animal. Slaughter of the harmless was something else, like killing animals without need of their skin, flesh, gut, or bone. No good would come of it. "We shall see," he replied. "White Water, do you and Spearpoint carry Running Fox back to his burial. Broken Blade and I will settle with Aryuk." He gave no time for talk about that, but struck out at once. The quarry had a long head start.

Otherwise there was little more to fear than evil spirits and whatever uncanny powers Aryuk possessed. Red Wolf doubted he had any. The hunters were paired only because the trail might grow difficult and because it was seldom wise to travel partnerless.

The tracks led north. As the shore dropped from sight behind him, Red Wolf saw that he followed a man who had already begun to weaken. Answerer's story had been confused, but the shaman thought Aryuk took a blow before felling his enemy. The heart laughed in Red Wolf's breast.

The brief day ended. For a while he and Broken Blade pushed on. If they looked closely they could still trace the spoor by starlight and, later, moonlight. It went slowly, but that did not matter, for they saw how Aryuk had grown slower yet and ever oftener must stop to rest.

Then clouds drew together, smothering sight. Perforce the hunters called a halt. Without fire, they ate of their jerky and rolled up in their sleeping robes. The softest of touches on his face roused Red Wolf. Snowfall. *Father of Wolves, make this cease,* he begged.

It did not. Morning was hushed and gray, skyless, full of white flakes through which men could barely see a spearcast's length. For some time they were able to creep onward, brushing the powdery new snow off the old, but at last that was impossible. "We have lost him," sighed Broken Blade. "Now his tribe must pay."

"Maybe not," responded Red Wolf, who had been thinking. "We cannot be far behind him. He may well be on the other side of the next hill. Let us abide."

The air had warmed sufficiently that they could sit almost in comfort. Lynx-patient, they waited.

About midday the snowfall ended. They went on north. The going was hard, through stuff light but ankle-deep, sometimes knee-deep. *Would that I had magical shoes to walk on top of this,* Red Wolf thought. *Do Tall Man and Sun Hair? They own so much else that is wonderful. . . . Well, Aryuk is hindered too, worse than us.*

From a ridge they saw hugely ahead, across the steppe. Clouds had parted and shadows reached long and blue over purity. Every bush and boulder stood marked. Right, left, forward the men peered, until Broken Blade pointed and cried, "Yonder!"

Red Wolf's heart jumped. "Maybe. Come." They struggled downslope. By the time they reached what they had glimpsed, the sun was gone, but some light remained by which to read the troubled snow.

"Yes, a man," said Red Wolf. "Surely no long way off. See how he floundered and . . . yes, here he stumbled, fell, and picked himself up awkwardly." His mittened hand tensed on the spearshaft. "He is ours."

They went on at an easier pace than before, saving their strength, less for the prey than for the trek home afterward. Night rolled across the world. The sky was mostly clear, the moon still down; stars were soon aswarm, frost-sharp. The trail stayed plain.

Suddenly Broken Blade stopped short. Red Wolf heard his gasp and likewise looked up. Above the northern horizon, the Winter Hunters were kindling their fires.

In billows and rays light shivered aloft, brighter, higher, brighter, higher, until it licked at the roof of heaven. Cold had deepened and all sound lay frozen. Only the sheen of light on snow was alive. Awed beyond terror, the men stared. There danced the mightiest of their forebears, ghosts too strong for earth to hold them.

"Yet you *are* ours," Red Wolf breathed at last. "You remember, do you not? Watch over us. Ward us. Keep horrors and vengeful ghosts from us, your sons. In your name, for you, we make our kill tonight."

"I think they have come for that," said Broken Blade as low.

"We should not keep them waiting." Red Wolf moved onward.

Presently he saw something, a blot on the snow beneath the chill fires. He hastened his stride. The other must have seen him in turn, for a shrill, keening chant reached his ears. What, did Vole men also sing their death songs?

As he neared, he made Aryuk out, seated cross-legged in a hollow he had scooped for himself. "I will do this, Broken Blade," Red Wolf said. "Running Fox was close to my spirit." He went on as if no fresh snow burdened his feet.

Aryuk rose. He moved very slowly, clumsily, his last strength spent. But he never cringed. He finished his song and stood slump-shouldered, left arm lashed to his side below the skin cloak, yet steadfast. Frost whitened his beard. When Red Wolf drew nigh, he smiled.

Smiled.

Red Wolf halted. What was this? What might it portend?

The silent fires burned overhead, commanding him. He took another step, and another.

Here is no animal brought to bay, he knew. *Aryuk is ready for death. Well, he shall have it as easily as I can give it. He has earned that much.*

Two-handed, he thrust the spear. Bone and keen flint went in below the breast and up to find the heart. The blow felt oddly soft, into so worn and wasted a body. Aryuk toppled before it, onto his back. Once he kicked, and his throat rattled. Then he was quiet.

Red Wolf withdrew the spear and leaned on it, staring downward. Broken Blade joined him. The flames leaped and shook in heaven.

"It is done," said Broken Blade finally, tonelessly.

"Not altogether," answered Red Wolf.

He took the graven bone from his pouch and clamped it between his teeth. Kneeling, he opened Aryuk's pouch. Nothing was in it but—yes— He drew out the eyes of Running Fox. "You shall go back to him," he promised. Giving them to Broken Blade: "Wrap these well and sing them the Spirit Song. I have other tasks."

Even for one who knew he was doomed and who was emptied by weariness, Aryuk died calmly. Almost happily, as far as I could tell by this witch-light. What did he know? What did he mean to do . . . later?

Well, he shall not. Answerer has told me how to bind a ghost.

Red Wolf did to the body what had been done to Running Fox's. He crushed the eyeballs between two stones he dug from the snow. He slit the belly and laid more stones among the entrails. He tied wrists and ankles with thongs of wolverine leather. He drove a spear through the chest and out the back, as deeply into the ice beneath as he could. He danced around the corpse while he called on his namesake, the Father of Wolves, to send more wolves—and foxes, weasels, owls, ravens, all manner of carrion eaters—to devour it. "Now it is done," he said. "Come."

He felt exhausted himself; but he would walk as long as he was able before he slept. When morning came, he and Broken Blade ought to spy a landmark, such as a distant mountain, and find their way home.

They set forth across the steppe, beneath the spirit fires.

IX

To Wanda Tamberly, over the months the old rogue mammoth had come to be like a friend. She almost hated to bid him goodbye. But now he'd given her what information he could, which might well include a key to the entire history of Beringia. If she hoped to learn more about other aspects, she'd better get busy on them. "Already" her superiors wanted her elsewhere and elsewhen. It was with difficulty, as messages went to and fro across space-time, that she had persuaded them to let her spend just a bit more lifespan here, finish out the season and observe one last interstadial spring. She suspected that they suspected her real reason was to see, in daily detail, how her Tulat would fare.

Not that genuine science did not remain to be done, man-centuries' worth of it. She had heard that civilian researchers made studies of their own, both pastward and futureward of this period. But they came from civilizations uptime of hers, too alien for her ever to work with them. She was of the Patrol, whose concern was with things impinging directly on human affairs.

There were advantages to that, she often reflected. The real comprehension of an ecology lay in its foundations, geology, meteorology, chemistry, microbes, plants, worms, insects, humble small vertebrates. She got to trail the big glamorous creatures near the top of the food chain. Of course, she too must gather a lot of nitty-gritty data. In a general way, she oversaw the activities of the tiny robots that scuttled beetlelike about, sampling, observing, passing information on to the computer in her dome. But she also followed slot, examined scat, watched from a distance or from a blind, punted around lakes, mingled with herds; and that was fine, fun, real.

I'll be sorry to leave for good. Although—her spine tingled—*next assignment, Crô-Magnon Europe?*

She had made this trip alone. Wanayimo guides were often invaluable, much better than any Tulat before them, but must not be exposed to really high tech. Loaded with camp gear, her timecycle rose on antigravity till it hung high. Instruments gave her a final look around. Their sensitivity and versatility were part of the reason that she, all by herself, could report on an entire region after a couple of years' work. Overleaping miles, piercing mists, amplifying light, they spotted single animals and brought views as magnified as she wanted before her eyes. Musk oxen stood back to the wind, a hare lolloped through drifting snow, a ptarmigan took wing, and yonder wandered and grumbled the old mammoth. . . .

Upon the vast white land, his shagginess was dark as the cliffs rearing northward. His one tusk scuffed snow off moss and his trunk grubbed the fodder. It was sparse, but the best that a solitary male, defeated in fight and driven from his fellows, could find. Sometimes Tamberly had thought that mercy required she shoot him. No, he was providing an important clue; and now that she had it, well, leave him in his gaunt pride. Who knew, he might survive into summer and fill his belly again.

"Thanks, Jumbo," she called across the wind. She believed she had discovered why his kind were growing scarce in Beringia, while continuing common in both Siberia and North America. Though the land bridge was still hundreds of miles wide, rising sea level had shrunk it, even as encroaching birch scrub changed the nature of the steppe. She hadn't known that these elephantines were so dependent on specific conditions. Elsewhere, related species occupied a variety of habitats. But the rogue had not gone south to the seaboard woods and grasslands, he had gone north to scrape out a marginal existence under the mountains.

This in turn bore implications that excited Ralph Corwin. Although the Paleo-Indians hunted game of every sort, mammoth was the prize. In Beringia they'd wipe out the already threatened herds of any given area in the course of a few generations; it is another myth that primitive man lives in harmonious balance with the life around him. The presence of mammoth farther east would then draw adventurous persons onward sooner than would otherwise have been the case, in spite of today's Alaska being for the most part pretty desolate.

Therefore, probably the migration into America went more quickly than he had supposed, and later waves of it had a distinctly different character from their predecessors. . . . However, this couldn't account for the Cloud People moving away as early as next year. . . .

The wind swirled and bit. Vapors blew around her, gray rags. *Let's get back and put our feet up with a nice hot cuppa*. Tamberly set controls and activated.

In her dome she dismounted, shoved the hopper into its place amidst the kipple, and switched off the antigrav. The machine thumped a few inches down onto the floor. She rubbed her bottom. *Hoo boy, the saddle was cold! Next job, if it's Ice Age too, first I put in for heating coils*.

As she stripped, sponge-bathed, donned loose clothes, she wondered what to do about Corwin. Presumably he was elsewhere. Were he in his own place, his timecycle would have registered this arrival of hers and he'd doubtless have popped right over with an invitation to a drink and dinner. It would be hard to decline gracefully when she'd been gone for ten days. So far she'd managed to get him talking about himself, which diverted his attention and was, she admitted, by no means uninteresting. Sooner or later, though, he was pretty sure to make a serious pass, and in that she was posolutely not interested. How to avoid an unpleasant scene?

Too bad Manse isn't an anthropologist. He's comfortable to be with, like an old shoe—a shoe that's hiked a lot of very strange trails, and stayed sturdy. I wouldn't need to worry about him. If perchance he did *make a pass— Hey, I'm not blushing, am I?*

She brewed her tea and settled down. A voice at the entrance broke through: "Hullo, Wanda. How've you done?"

I guess he was just down in the village. Damn. "Okay," she called. "Uh, look, I'm awfully tired, lousy company. Could I rest up till tomorrow?"

"'Fraid not." The solemnity sounded honest. "Bad news."

An icicle stabbed. She got to her feet. "Coming."

"I think you'd best step outside. I'll wait." And only the wind sounded.

She scrambled into wool socks, down-lined pants, boots, parka. When she emerged, the wind cut at her. It drove ice-dust low across the ground. Sinking behind southern hills, the sun ignited a multitudinous hard glitter in the drift. Also dressed for the weather, Corwin and Red Wolf stood side by side. Their countenances were stark.

"Good fortune to you," Tamberly greeted through the whistling.

"Good spirits travel with you," the Cloud man answered as formally and flatly.

"This tale is for Red Wolf to tell," Corwin stated in the same language. "He told me he should. When I knew you had returned, I fetched him."

Tamberly looked into the hunter's eyes. They never wavered. "Your friend Aryuk is dead," he declared. "I slew him. It was necessary."

For a moment the world darkened. Then: *Bear up. This is a stoic culture. Don't lose face.* "Why is this?"

The narration was short and dignified.

"You could not have spared him?" she asked dully. "I would have paid . . . enough to give Running Fox his honor."

"You have told us you will leave in a few more moons, and Tall Man will not stay much longer," Red Wolf answered. "After that, what? Other Vole men would think they could harm others of us and go free too. Also, Aryuk had won power over Running Fox's ghost. Had we not recovered what he took, after death his own ghost would have been twice as strong, and surely full of hatred. I had to make sure he will never walk among us."

"I have gotten a promise that there will be no further revenge on the Tulat," said Corwin, "if they behave themselves."

"That shall be true," Red Wolf affirmed. "We do not wish to grieve you further, Sun Hair." He paused. "I am sorry. I never wished to grieve you at all."

He made a dismissing gesture, turned, and walked slowly off.

I cannot hate him, Tamberly thought. *He did what he saw as his duty. I cannot hate him.*

Oh, Aryuk, Tseshu, everybody who loved you, Aryuk!

"Tragic," Corwin murmured after a minute. "But take comfort."

It flared in Tamberly. "How can I, when he—when his family—I've got to look after them, at least."

"Their own people will." Corwin laid a hand on her shoulder. "My dear, you must control those generous impulses of yours. We may not intervene more than we already have. What could you do for anyone that is not forbidden? Besides, this tribe will soon be gone."

"How much will be left by then? God damn it, we can't just stand idle!"

He donned sternness. "Calm down. You can't bluff the Wanayimo into anything. If you try, it will only complicate my work. Frankly, as matters stand, you have cost me some prestige, by association, when the news obviously stunned you."

She knotted her fists and struggled not to weep.

He smiled. "But there, I didn't mean to play Dutch uncle. You must learn to accept. 'The moving Finger writes, and having writ,' y'know." Gently, he embraced her. "Come, let's go inside and have a drink or three. We'll toast memories and—"

She tore loose. "Leave me alone!" she cried.

"I beg your pardon?" He raised frosted brows. "Really, my dear, you're overwrought. Relax. Listen to an old campaigner."

"You wanna know what the moving Finger should do to you? Leave me alone, I said!" She grabbed at her dome opener. Through the wind, did she hear a resigned girls-will-be-girls sigh?

Sheltered, she flung herself on her bunk and let go. It took a long while.

When at last she sat up, darkness enclosed her. She hiccoughed, trembled, felt as cold as if she were still outside. Her mouth was salt. *I must look a fright,* she thought vaguely.

Her mind sharpened. *Why has this hit me so hard? I liked Aryuk, he was a darling, and it's going to be grim for his folks, at least till they can rearrange their lives, which'll be tough to do with the Cloud People battening on everybody, but—but I'm no Tula, I'm only passing through, these are old, unhappy, far-off things, they happened thousands of years before I was born.*

Corwin's right, the bastard. We in the Patrol, we've got to get case-hardened. As much as we can. I think now I see why Manse sometimes suddenly falls quiet, stares beyond me, then shakes his head as though trying to throw something off and for the next few minutes gets a little overhearty.

She hammered fist on knee. *I'm too new in the game. I've too much rage and sorrow in me. Especially rage, I think. What to do about it? If I want to stay on here any longer, I'd better make up with Corwin, more or less. Yeah, I was overreacting. I am right now. Maybe. Anyhow, before I can straighten things out I've got to straighten me out. Work off this that's in me and tastes like sickness.*

How? A long, long walk, yes. Only it's night. No problem. I'll hop uptime to morning. Only I don't want anybody seeing me stalk off. Unseemly display of emotion, and might give wrong ideas. Okay, I'll hop elsewhere as well as elsewhen, way away to the seashore or out on the steppe or—

Or.

She gasped.

X

Morning stole gray through falling snow. All else lay white and silent. The air had warmed a little. Aryuk sat hunched in his cloak. The snow had partly buried him. Perhaps he would rise and stagger onward, but not yet, and perhaps never. Although he felt hunger no more, his wound was fire-coals and his legs had buckled under him during the night. When the woman descended from unseen heaven, he simply stared in sluggish wonder.

She got off the unalive thing she rode and stood before him. Snow settled on her head covering. Where it touched her face and melted, it ran down like tears. "Aryuk," she whispered.

Twice he could utter nothing but a croak, before he asked, "Have you too come after me?" He raised his heavy head. "Well, here I am."

"Oh, Aryuk."

"Why, you are crying," he said, surprised.

"For you." She swallowed, wiped the eyes that were blue as summer, straightened, looked more steadily down at him.

"Then you are still the friend of Us?"

"I, I always was." She knelt and hugged him. "I always will be." His breath hissed. She let go. "Did that hurt? I'm sorry." She studied bound arm and blood-caked shoulder. "Yes, you've been hurt. Terribly. Let me help you."

Gladness flickered faint. "Will you help Tseshu and the young?"

"If I can— Yes, I will. But you first. Here." She fumbled in a garment and drew forth an object he recognized. "Here is Lovely Sweet."

With his good hand and teeth he stripped off the wrapping. Eagerly, he ate. Meanwhile she got a box from the thing she rode. He knew about boxes, having seen her use them before. She came back, knelt again, bared her hands. "Do not be afraid," she said.

"I am no longer afraid, with you by me." He licked his lips. His fingers followed, to make sure none of the brown stuff was left behind. The ice in his beard crackled to their touch.

She put a small thing against his skin near the wound. "This will take away pain," she said. He felt a slight shoving. On its heels ran a wave of peace, warmth, not-pain.

"A-a-ah," he breathed. "You do beautiful works."

She busied herself, cleaning and treating. "How did this come about?"

He didn't want to remember, but because it was she who asked, he said, "Two Mammoth Slayers came to our place—"

"Yes, I have heard what the one told who escaped. Why did you attack the other one?"

"He laid hands on Tseshu. He said he would take her away. I forgot myself." Aryuk could not pretend to her that he was really sorry for the deed, in spite of the evil it brought. "That was foolish. But I was again a man."

"I see." Her smile mourned. "Now the Cloud People are on your trail."

"I thought they would be."

"They will kill you."

"This snow may break the trail too much for them."

She bit her lip. He heard that it was very hard for her to say, "They *will* kill you. I can do nothing about that."

He shook his head. "Do you truly know? I do not see how it can be certain."

"I am not sure I see either," she whispered, keeping her gaze upon her busy hands. "But it is."

"I hoped I might die alone, and they find my body."

"That would not satisfy them. They think they must kill, because a man of theirs was killed. If it is not you, it will be your kindred."

He took a long breath, watched the tumbling snow for a bit, and chuckled. "So it is good that they kill me. I am ready. You have taken away my pain, you have filled my mouth with Lovely Sweet, you have laid your arms about me."

Her voice came hoarse. "It will be quick. It will not hurt much."

"And it will not be for nothing. Thank you." That was seldom spoken among the Tulat, who took kindnesses for granted. "Wanda," he went on shyly. "Did you not say once that is your real name? Thank you, Wanda."

She let the work go, sat back on her haunches, and made herself look straight at him. "Aryuk," she said low, "I can do . . . something more for you. I can make your death more than a payment for what happened."

Amazed, marveling, he asked, "How? Only tell me."

She doubled a fist. "It will not be easy for you. Just dying would be much easier, I think." Louder: "Though how can I know?"

"You know all things."

"*Oh, God, no.*" She stiffened. "Hear me. Then if you believe you can bear it, I will give you food, a drink that strengthens, and—and my help—" She choked.

His astonishment grew. "You seem afraid, Wanda."

"I am," she sobbed. "I am terrified. Help me, Aryuk."

XI

Red Wolf awoke. Something heavy had moved.

He turned his head right and left. Again the moon was full, small and as cold as the air. From the roof of heaven its light poured down and glistered away over the snow. As far as he could see, the steppe reached empty, save for boulders and bare, stiffened bushes. He thought the noise—a whoosh, a thump, a crack like tiny thunder—had come from behind the big rock near which he, Horsecatcher, Caribou Antler, and Spearpoint had made their hunters' camp.

"Forth and ready!" he called. He slipped free of his bag and took weapons in a single motion. The rest did the same. They had slept half awake too, in this brilliant night.

"Like nothing I ever heard before." Red Wolf beckoned them to take stance at his sides.

Black against the moonlit snow, a man-form trod from around the rock and moved toward them.

Horsecatcher peered. "Why, it is a Vole," he said, laughing in relief.

"This far inland?" wondered Caribou Antler.

The shape walked steadily closer. A badly made skin cloak covered most of it, but the hunters saw that it carried a thing that was not a hand ax. As it drew near they descried features, bushy hair and beard, hollowed-out face.

Spearpoint rocked. "It is he, the one we went after with Running Fox," he wailed.

"But I killed you, Aryuk!" Red Wolf shouted.

Horsecatcher screamed, whirled about, dashed off across the plain.

"Stop!" Red Wolf yelled. "Hold fast!"

Caribou Antler and Spearpoint bolted. Almost, Red Wolf himself did. Horror seized him as a hawk seizes a lemming.

Somehow he overcame it. If he ran, he knew, he was helpless, no longer a man. His left hand raised the hatchet, his right poised the lance for a cast. "I will not flee," rattled from a tongue gone dry. "I killed you before."

Aryuk halted a short way off. Moonlight welled in the eyes that Red Wolf had plucked out and crushed. He spoke in Wanayimo, of which he knew just a few words when he was alive. The voice was high, a ghastly echo underneath it. "You cannot kill a dead man."

"It was, was far from here," Red Wolf stammered. "I bound your ghost down with spells."

"They were not strong enough. No spells will ever be strong enough."

Through the haze of terror, Red Wolf saw that those feet had left tracks behind them like a living man's. That made it the more dreadful. He would have shrieked and run the same as his comrades, but clung to the knowledge that he could surely not outspeed this, and having it at his back would be worse than he dared think about.

"Here I stand," he gasped. "Do what you will."

"What I would do is forever."

I am not asleep. My spirit cannot escape into wakefulness. I can never escape.

"The ghosts of this land are full of winter anger," rang Aryuk's unearthly voice. "They stir in the earth. They walk in the wind. Go before they come after you. Leave their country, you and your people. Go."

Even then, Red Wolf thought of Little Willow, their children, the tribe. "We cannot," he pleaded. "We would die."

"We will abide you until the snow melts, when you can again live in tents," Aryuk said. "Until then, be afraid. Leave our living ones alone. In spring depart and never come back. I have fared a long, chill way to tell you this. I will not tell you twice. Go, as I now go."

He turned and went off the way he had come. Red Wolf went on his belly in the snow. Thus he did not see Aryuk step behind the rock; but he heard the unnatural noise of his passing from the world of men.

XII

The moon was down. The sun was still remote. Stars and Spirit Trail cast a wan glow across whitened earth. In the village, folk slept.

Answerer the shaman woke when someone pulled his windbreak aside. At first he felt puzzlement, vexation, and mostly how his old bones ached. He crawled from beneath the skins and crouched by the hearth. It held ashes. Somebody brought him fresh fire each morning. "Who are you?" he asked the blackness that stood in the doorway athwart the stars. "What do you need?" A sudden illness, an onset of childbirth, a nightmare—

The newcomer entered and spoke. The sound was none that Answerer had ever heard before in life, dream, or vision. "You know me. Behold."

Light glared, icily brilliant, like the light that Tall Man and Sun Hair could make shine from a stick. It streamed upward across a great beard, to gully the face above with shadows. Answerer screamed.

"Your men could kill me," said Aryuk. "They could not bind me. I have come back to tell you that you must go."

Answerer snatched after his wits and found the graven bone that lay always beside him. He pointed it. "No, you begone, ya eya eya illa ya-a!" Tight as his throat was, he could barely force the chant out.

Aryuk interrupted it. "Too long have your folk preyed on mine. Our blood on the land troubles the spirits beneath. Go, all Cloud People, go. Tell them this, shaman, or else come away with me."

"Whence rise you?" whimpered Answerer.

"Would you know? I could a tale unfold whose lightest word would rip your soul, freeze your blood, make your two eyes break free like shooting stars, your hair unbraid and stand on end like quills upon the fretful porcupine. But instead, I go now. If you remain, Cloud People, I shall return. Remember me."

The light snapped off. Once more the doorway was darkened, then the stars shone unmercifully through.

Answerer's shrieks roused families nearby. Two or three men spied him who walked from them. They told themselves they should not pursue but rather see what help their shaman needed. They found him moaning and mumbling. Later he said that a dire vision had sought him. After sunrise, Broken Blade mustered courage to track the stranger. Some distance from the village, footprints ended. The snow was tumbled there. It was as if something had swooped down from the Spirit Trail.

XIII

Far off southeastward, beyond the ice and the open sea, the sky began to lighten. Stars yonder paled. One by one, they went out. Overhead, north, and west, night lingered. Above snow, whitenesses swirled off the hot springs. Nothing broke the silence but an undertone of waves.

A man-shape arrived at Ulungu's kinstead. He moved heavily. When he stopped among the dwellings he stood bent-shouldered. His call rustled faint. "Tseshu, Tseshu."

They stirred within. Men peeked past windbreaks. What they saw flung them back at the bodies crowded behind. "Aryuk, dead Aryuk!"

"Tseshu," It begged, "this is only Aryuk, your man. I have only come to bid you farewell."

"Wait here," said his woman in the fear-stinking darkness. "I will go to him."

"No, that is death." Ulungu fumbled to hold her.

She fended him off. "He wants me," she said, and crawled out. Rising, she stood before the cloaked form. "Here I am," she told It.

"Do not be afraid," said Aryuk—how gently, how wearily. "I bring no harm."

The woman stared at him in wonderment. "You are dead," she whispered. "They killed you. We heard. Men of theirs went among Us, along the whole shore, and gave Us that news."

"Yes. That is how Wan—that is how I learned where you are."

"They said the Red Wolf killed you for what you did and We should all beware."

Aryuk nodded. "Yes, I died."

Care trembled in her voice. "You are thin. You are tired."

"It was a long journey," he sighed.

She reached for him. "Your poor arm—"

He smiled a little. "Soon I shall rest. It will be good to lie down."

"Why have you come back?"

"I am not yet dead."

"You said you are."

"Yes. I died a moon or more ago, beneath the Ghost Birds."

"How is this?" she asked, bewildered.

"I do not understand. What I know, I may not tell you. But when I begged leave, I was given my wish, that I could come see you this last time."

"Aryuk, Aryuk." She went to him and laid her head against his beard and mane. He brought his usable arm around her.

"You shiver, Tseshu," he said. "It is cold and you have nothing on. Get back inside where it is warm. I must go now."

"Take me with you, Aryuk," she faltered through tears. "We were so long together."

"I may not do that," he answered. "Stay. Care for the young ones, for everyone of Us. Go home to our river. You will have peace. The Mammoth Slayers will trouble you no more. In spring when the snow melts, they will go away."

She raised her face. "This . . . is . . . a great thing."

"It is what I give you and Us." He looked past her to the dying stars. "I am glad."

She clung to him and wept.

"Do not cry," he pleaded. "Let me remember you glad."

Light strenghthened. "I must leave," he said. "Let me go, let me go." He had to draw her arms from him before he could depart. She stood gazing after him till he had limped out of sight.

XIV

Tamberly brought her hopper across space-time and down through the snowfall to earth. She dismounted. Aryuk, who had held onto her waist on this as on other quick flights, left the rear saddle. For a span they were mute amidst the flakes and the gray morning.

"Is it done?" he asked finally.

She nodded. Her neck felt stiff. "It is done. As well as I was able."

"That is good." His right hand fumbled about his person. "Here, I give you back your treasures." Piece by piece he returned them—flashlight, audiovisual pickup by which she had seen and heard what he did, earplug receiver through which she instructed him, speaker that enabled her to talk Wanayimo for him, with lowered voice frequency and some spooky feedback resonance at the transmission end. She dropped them in the carrier.

"What shall I do next?" Aryuk inquired.

"Wait. If . . . if only I could wait with you!"

He considered. "You are kind, but I think I would rather be alone. I have remembering to do."

"Yes."

"Also," he went on earnestly, "if I may, I would rather walk than sit still. Your magic gave me some haleness back. It is ebbing, but I would like to use it."

Feel yourself alive while you can. "Yes, do as you wish. Walk onward until—oh, Aryuk!" He stood there so patiently. Already the snow had whitened his head.

"Do not cry," he said, troubled. "You who command life and death should never feel weak or sad."

She covered her eyes. "I can't help it."

"But I am glad." He laughed. "This is good, what I can do for Us. You helped me. Be glad of that. I am. Let me remember you glad."

She kissed him and smiled, smiled, as she remounted her timecycle.

XV

Wind brawled. The dome shuddered. Tamberly blinked into it, got off the vehicle, turned on lights against the gloom.

After a few minutes she heard: "Let me in!"

She hung up her outer garments. "Come on," she replied.

Corwin stalked through. The wind caught at the entry fabric. He had a moment's fight to reseal. Tamberly posed herself at the table. She felt frozenly calm.

He opened his parka as if he disemboweled an enemy and turned about. His mouth was stretched wide and tight. "So you're back at last," he rasped.

"Well, that's what I thought," she said.

"None of your insolence."

"Sorry. None intended." Her gesture at the chair was as indifferent as her tone. "Won't you sit down? I'll make tea."

"No! Why have you been gone all these days?"

"Busy. In the field." *I needed the terrible innocence of the Ice Age and its beasts.* "Wanted to make sure I'd complete the essentials of my research, what with the season drawing to a close."

He quivered. "And what with you due for cashiering—mind block, or even the exile planet—"

She lifted a hand. "Whoa. That's a matter for higher authority than yours, my friend."

"*Friend*? After you betrayed—ruined— Did you imagine I wouldn't know what had to be behind those . . . apparitions? What your purpose was—to destroy my work—"

The blond head shook. "Why, no. You can continue with the Wanayimo if you see fit, as long as you want to. And then there are plenty of later generations waiting."

"Causal vortex—endangerment—"

"Please. You told me yourself, the Cloud People will push on come spring. It is written. 'The moving Finger,' you know. I simply gave it a little boost. And that was written too, wasn't it?"

"No! You dared—you played God." His forefinger jabbed toward her like a spear. "That's why you didn't return here to the moment after you left on your insane jaunt. You hadn't the nerve to face me."

"I knew I'd have to do that. But I figured it'd be smart if the natives didn't see me for a while. They'd have plenty else on their minds. I hope you kept well in the background."

"Perforce. The harm you did was irreparable. *I* wasn't about to make it worse."

"When the fact is that they did decide to leave these parts."

"Because you—"

"Something had to cause it, right? Oh, I know the rules. I've jumped uptime, entered a report, been summoned for a hearing. Tomorrow I'll pack up." *And say goodbye to the land and, yes, the Cloud People, Red Wolf. Wish him well.*

"I'll be at that session," Corwin vowed. "I'll take pleasure in bringing the charges."

"Not your department, I think."

He gaped at her. "You've changed," he mumbled. "You were . . . a promising girl. Now you're a cold, scheming bitch."

"If you've expressed your opinion, goodnight, Dr. Corwin."

His visage contorted. His open hand cracked upon her cheek.

She staggered, caught her footing, blinked from the pain, but was able to speak quietly. "I said, 'Goodnight, Dr. Corwin.'"

He made a noise, wheeled, groped at the entry fastener, got the dome open, and stumbled from her.

I guess I have changed, she thought. *Grown some. Or so I hope. They'll decide at the . . . court-martial . . . the hearing. Maybe they'll break me. Maybe that's the right thing for them to do. All I know is that I did what I must, and be damned if I'm sorry.*

The wind blew harder. A few snowflakes flew upon it, outriders of winter's last great blizzard.

13,210 B.C.

Clouds loomed whiter than the snowbanks that lingered here and there upon moss and shrub. The sun, striding higher every lengthening day, dazzled eyes. Its light flared off pools and meres, above which winged the earliest migratory birds. Flowers were in bud over all. Trodden on, they sent a breath of green into the air.

Just once did Little Willow look back, past the straggling lines of the tribe to the homes they were leaving, the work of their hands. Red Wolf sensed what she felt. He laid an arm about her. "We shall find new and better lands, and those we shall keep, and our children and children's children after us," he said.

So had Sun Hair promised them before she and Tall Man vanished with their tents, as mysteriously as they had come. "A new world." He did not understand, but he believed, and made his people believe.

Little Willow's gaze sought her man again. "No, we could not stay." Her voice wavered. "Those moons of fear, when any night the ghost might return— But today I remember what we had and hoped for."

"It lies ahead of us," he answered.

A child caught her heed, darting recklessly aside. She went after the brat. Red Wolf smiled.

Then he too was grave, he too remembered—a woman whose hair and eyes were summer. He would always remember. Would she?

1990 A.D.

The timecycle appeared in the secret place underground. Everard dismounted, gave Tamberly his hand, helped her off the rear saddle. They went upstairs to a closet-small room. Its door was locked, but the lock knew him and let them into a corridor lined with packing cases which served as overloaded bookshelves. At the front of the store Everard told the proprietor, "Nick, we need your office for a while."

The little man nodded. "Sure. I've been expecting you. Laid in what you hinted you'd want."

"Thanks. You're a good joe. This way, Wanda."

Everard and Tamberly entered the cluttered room. He shut the door. She sank into the chair behind the desk and stared out at a backyard garden. Bees hummed about marigolds and petunias. Nothing except the wall beyond and an undercurrent of traffic bespoke San Francisco in the late twentieth century. The contents of a coffeepot were hot and reasonably fresh. Neither of them cared for milk or sugar. Instead, they found two snifters and a bottle of Calvados. He poured.

"How're you doing by now?" he asked.

"Exhausted," she muttered, still looking through the window.

"Yeah, it was rough. Had to be."

"I know." She took her coffee and drank. Her voice regained some life. "I deserved worse, much worse."

He put bounce into his own words. "Well, it's over with. You go enjoy your furlough, get a good rest, put the nightmare behind you. That's an order." He offered her a brandy glass. "Cheers."

She turned around and touched rims with him. "*Salud.*" He sat down across from her. They tasted. The aroma swirled darkly sweet.

Presently she looked straight at him and said low, "It was you who got me off the hook, wasn't it? I don't mean just your arguing for me at the hearing—though Lordy, if ever a person needed a friend— That was mostly pro forma, wasn't it?"

"Smart girl." He sipped afresh, put the goblet aside, reached for pipe and tobacco pouch. "Yes, of course. I'd done my politicking behind the scenes. There were those who wanted to throw the book at you, but they got, uh, persuaded that a reprimand would suffice."

"No. It didn't." She shuddered. "What they showed me, though, the records—"

He nodded. "Consequences of time gone awry. Bad." He made a production of stuffing the pipe, keeping his glance on it. "Well, frankly, you did need that lesson."

She drew an uneven breath. "Manse, the trouble I've caused you—"

"No, don't feel obligated. Please. I had a duty, after I'd heard what the situation was." He looked up. "You see, in a way this was the Patrol's fault. You'd been meant for a naturalist. Your indoctrination was minimal. Then the outfit allowed you to get involved in something for which you weren't prepared, trained, anything. It's human. It makes its share of mistakes. But it can damn well admit to them afterward."

"I don't want excuses for myself. I knew I was violating the rules." Tamberly squared her shoulders. "And I'm not—not repentant, even now." She drank again.

"Which you had the guts to tell the board." Everard made fire and brought it to the tobacco. He nursed it along till the blue cloud was going well. "That worked in your favor. We need courage, initiative, acceptance of responsibility, more than we need nice, safe routineers. Besides, you didn't actually try to change history. That would have been unforgivable. All you did was take a hand in it. Which, maybe, was in the pattern of events from the first. Or maybe not. Only the Danellians know."

Awed, she wondered, "Do they care, so far in the future?"

He nodded. "I think they must. I suspect this matter got bucked clear up to them."

"Because of you, Manse, you, an Unattached agent."

He shrugged. "Could be. Or maybe they . . . watched. Anyway, I've a hunch that the decision to pardon you came down from them. In which case you're more important, somewhere up the line, than either of us today knows."

Amazement shrilled: "Me?"

"Potentially, anyhow." He wagged the pipestem at her. "Listen, Wanda. I broke the law myself once, early in my service, because it seemed like the single decent thing to do. I was ready for punishment. The Patrol can*not* accommodate self-righteousness. But the upshot was, I got tapped for special training and eventual Unattached status."

She shook her head. "You were you. I'm not that good."

"You mean you're not that kind of good. I do still doubt you have the makings of a cop. Something else, however— For sure, you've got the right stuff." He lifted his glass. "Here's to!"

She drank with him, but silently.

After a while she said, tears on her lashes, "I can never truly thank you, Manse."

"Hm-m." He grinned. "You can try. For openers, how about dinner this evening?"

She drew back. "Oh—" The sound trailed off.

He regarded her. "You don't feel up to it, huh?"

"Manse, you've done so much for me. But—"

He nodded. "Plumb wore out. Absolutely understandable."

She hugged herself, as if a wind off a glacier had touched her. "And, and haunted."

"I can understand that too," he said.

"If I can just be alone for a while, somewhere peaceful."

"And come to terms with what happened." He blew smoke at the ceiling. "Of course. I'm sorry. I should have realized."

"Later—"

He smiled, gently this time. "Later you'll be yourself again. That is certain. You're too healthy not to."

"And then—" She couldn't finish.

"We'll discuss it when the time is right." Everard laid his pipe aside. "Wanda, you're about ready to keel over. Relax. Enjoy your applejack. Doze off if you want. I'll call for a taxi and take you home."

PART FIVE

RIDDLE ME THIS

1990 A.D.

Lightning flickered in darkness, bright enough to pierce through the lamps of New York. Thunder was still too distant to overcome traffic rush; wind and rain would follow.

Everard made himself look squarely at the enigma who sat opposite him in his apartment. "I thought the matter was settled," he declared.

"Considerable dissatisfaction remained," said Guion in his deceptively pedantic English.

"Yeah. I pulled rank and wires, threw my weight around, cashed in favors owing to me. But I *am* an Unattached and it was, it is my judgment that punishing Tamberly for doing what was morally right would accomplish nothing except lose us a good operative."

Guion's tone stayed level. "The morality of taking sides in foreign conflicts is debatable. And you, of all people, should know that we do not amend reality, we defend it."

Everard knotted a fist. "You, of all people, should know that that isn't always exactly true," he snapped. Deciding that he likewise had better keep this peaceable: "I told her I didn't think I could've pulled it off if some kind of word hadn't come down from on high. Was I right?"

Guion evaded that, smiling slightly and saying, "What I came here for is to give you personal reassurance that the case is indeed closed. You will find no more lingering resentments among your colleagues, no unspoken accusations of favoritism. They now agree that you acted properly."

Everard stared. "Huh?" Several heartbeats passed. "How the devil was that done? As independent a bunch as ever bearded any king—"

"Suffice that it was done, and without compromising their independence. Stop fretting. Give that Middle Western conscience of yours a rest."

"Well, uh, well, this is awfully kind of you— Hey, I've been mighty inhospitable, haven't I? Care for a drink?"

"I would not say no to a light Scotch and soda."

Everard scrambled from his chair and sought the bar. "I am grateful, believe me."

"You needn't be. This is more a business trip than an errand of mercy. You see, you have earned a certain amount of special consideration. You have proved too valuable an agent for the Patrol to want you unnecessarily hampered by unwilling and incomplete cooperation."

Everard busied his hands. "Me? No false modesty, but in a million years of recruitment the outfit has got to have found a lot of guys a lot more able than me."

"Or me. Sometimes, however, individuals have a significance far beyond their ostensible worth. Not that you or I count for nothing in ourselves. But as an illustration of the general principle, take, oh, Alfred Dreyfus. He was a competent and conscientious officer, an asset to France. But it was because of what happened to him that great events came about."

Everard scowled. "Do you mean he was . . . an instrument of destiny?"

"You know very well there is no such thing as destiny. There is the structure of the plenum, which we strive to preserve."

I s'pose, Everard thought. *Though that structure isn't just change-*

able in time as well as space. It seems to be subtler and trickier than they see fit to teach us about at the Academy. Coincidences can be more than accidents. Maybe Jung glimpsed a little of the truth, in his notions about synchrony—I dunno. The universe isn't for the likes of me to understand. I only work here. He drew himself a Heineken's, added a shot of akvavit on the side, and brought the refreshments back on a tray.

As he settled down, he murmured, "I suspect the way has also been smoothed for Specialist Tamberly."

"What makes you think that?" replied Guion noncommittally.

"On your last visit you were inquiring about her, and she's mentioned an evening with you while she was a cadet. I doubt that . . . whoever sent you . . . would be so interested in the average recruit."

Guion nodded. "Her world line, like yours, appears to impinge on many others." He paused. "Appears, I say."

Unease stirred afresh. Everard reached for pipe and tobacco pouch. "What the hell is going on, anyway?" he demanded. "What's this all about?"

"We hope it is nothing extraordinary."

"What are you hoping against?"

Guion met Everard's gaze. "I cannot say precisely. It may well be unknowable."

"Tell me *something*, for Christ's sake!"

Guion sighed. "Monitors have observed anomalous variations in reality."

"Aren't they all?" Everard asked. *And few of them matter much. You might say the course of the world has enormous inertia. The effects of most changes made by time travelers soon damp out. Other things happen that compensate. Negative feedback. How many little fluctuations go on, to and fro, hither and yon? How constant, really, is reality? That's a question without any fixed answer and maybe without any meaning.*

But once in a while you do get a nexus, where some key incident decides the whole large-scale future, for better or worse.

The calm voice chilled him. "These have no known cause. That is, we have failed to identify any chronokinetic sources. For example, the *Asinaria* of Plautus is first performed in 213 B.C., and in

1196 A.D. Stefan Nemanya, Grand Zhupan of Serbia, abdicates in favor of his son and retires to a monastery. I could list several other instances in either of those approximate times, some as far away from Europe as China."

Everard tossed off his shot and chased it with a long draught. "Don't bother," he said harshly. "I can't place those two you did. What's strange about them and the rest?"

"The precise dates of their occurrences do not agree with what scholars from their future have recorded. Nor do various other minor details, such as the exact text of that play or the exact objects depicted on a certain scroll by Ma Yuan." Guion sipped. "Minor, mind you. Nothing that changes the general pattern of later events, or even anyone's daily life to a noticeable degree. Nevertheless they indicate instability in those sections of history."

Everard fought down a shudder. "Two-thirteen B.C., did you say?" *My God. The Second Punic War.* He stuffed his pipe with needless force.

Guion nodded again. "You were largely responsible for aborting that catastrophe."

"How many others have there been?" Everard rasped.

The query was absurd, put in English. Before he could go to Temporal, Guion said, "That is a problem inherently insolvable. Think about it."

Everard did.

"The Patrol, existent humankind, the Danellians themselves owe you much because of the Carthaginian episode," Guion continued after a silent while. "If you wish, regard the steps lately taken on your behalf as a small recompense."

"Thanks." Everard struck fire and puffed hard. "Although I wasn't being entirely unselfish, you realize. I wanted my home world back." He tautened. "What have these anomalies you speak of got to do with me?"

"Quite possibly nothing."

"Or with Wanda—Specialist Tamberly? What're you getting at with the pair of us?"

Guion lifted a hand. "Please don't develop resentments of your own. I know of your desire for emotional privacy, your feeling that it is somehow your right."

"Where I come from, it damn well is," Everard grumbled. His cheeks smoldered.

"But if the Patrol is to watch and guard the evolution of the ages, must it not also watch over itself? You have in truth become one of the more important agents operating within the past three millennia. Because of this, whether you know it or not, your influence radiates farther than most. Inevitably, some of the action is through your friends. Tamberly did have a catalytic effect on a milieu she was supposed merely to study. When you protected her from the consequences of her act, you became involved in them. No harm was done in either case, and we do not expect that either of you will ever willingly or wittingly do harm; but you must understand that we want to know about you."

The hairs stood up on Everard's arms. "'We,' you say," he whispered. "Who are you, Guion? What are you?"

"An agent like you, serving the same ends as you, except that my work is within the Patrol."

Everard pushed the attack. "When are you from? The Danellian era?"

Defense broke down. "No!" Guion made a violent fending gesture. "I have never even met one!" He looked away. The aristocratic visage writhed. "You did, once, but I— No, I am nobody."

You mean you are human, like me, Everard thought. *We are both to the Danellians what Homo erectus—or Australopithecus?—is to us. Though you, born in a later and higher civilization, must know more about them than I'd be able to. Enough more to be terrified?*

Guion recovered himself, drank, and said, again quietly, "I serve as I am bidden. That is all."

With a sudden sympathy, an irrational wish to give comfort, that was itself heartening, Everard murmured, "And so at present you're just tying up loose ends, clearing the decks, nothing fancy."

"I hope so. I pray so." Guion drew breath. He smiled. "Your commonplace way of putting it, your workaday attitude—what strength they give."

Tension ebbed out of Everard too. "Okay. We went up a bad street for a minute, didn't we? Actually, I shouldn't worry, on my account or Wanda's."

Beneath his regained coolness, Guion sounded equally relieved.

"That is what I came to assure you. The aftermath of your clash with Agent Corwin and others is no more. You can dismiss it from your mind and go about your business."

"Thanks. Cheers." They raised glasses.

It would take a little ordinary conversation, gossip and shop talk, to achieve genuine relaxation. "I hear you are preparing for a new mission," Guion remarked.

Everard shrugged. "No biggie. Securing the Altamont case. You wouldn't know about that, nor care."

"No, please, you rouse my curiosity."

"Well, why not?" Everard leaned back, puffed his pipe, savored his beer. "It's in 1912. World War One is brewing. The Germans think they've found a spy who can infiltrate the opposition, an Irish-American called Altamont. Actually he's an English agent, and in the end will turn the tables on them very neatly. The trouble from our viewpoint is, he's too observant and smart. He's uncovered certain odd goings-on. They could lead him to our military studies group in those years. A member of the group knows me and asked me to come help work up something to divert the man's attention. Nothing major. Mainly we'll have to do it in such a way that he doesn't deduce something still curiouser is afoot. It should be kind of fun."

"I see. Your life isn't entirely hairbreadth adventure, then."

"It better not be!"

They swapped trivia for an hour, till Guion took his leave. Alone, Everard felt hemmed in. Conditioned air hung lifeless around him. He went to a window and opened it. The lungful that he drew was sharp with the smell of the oncoming thunderstorm. Wind boomed and buffeted.

Foreboding touched him anew. *He's obviously a high-powered type. Would the far future really send him on an errand as trifling as what he described? Might they not, rather, be afraid of what he barely hinted at, a chaos they cannot chart and therefore cannot turn aside? Are they making what desperate provision they can?*

Lightning flared like a banner suddenly flown above the enclosing towers. Everard's mood responded. *Cut that out. You've got the word that all's well, haven't you?* Let him proceed in good spirits with his next job, and afterward seek what pleasure he could hope for.

PART SIX

AMAZEMENT OF THE WORLD

1137α A.D.

The door opened. Sunlight struck bright and bleak into the silk merchant's shop. Autumn air streamed after it, full of chill and street noises. Then the apprentice stumbled through. Seen from the dimness inside, against the day outside, he was almost a shadow. But they heard how he wept. "Master Geoffrey, oh, Master Geoffrey!"

Emil Volstrup left the desk at which he had stood doing accounts. The stares of the other two boys, one Italian and one Greek, followed him, and their hands fell still upon the bolts of fabric. "What is it, Odo?" he called. The Norman French that he used here rang harsh in his ears. "Did you meet trouble on your errand?"

The slender form stumbled into his arms, the face pressed against his robe. He felt the shuddering. "Master," sobbed at him, "the king is dead. I heard—they are crying it from mouth to mouth through the city—"

Volstrup's embrace dropped away. He looked outward. You couldn't see much through the grilles over the arched windows. The door was still agape, though. Cobblestones, an arcaded building opposite, a Saracen passing by in white cloak and turban, sparrows fluttering up from some scrap of food, none of it seemed real any longer. Why should it? Whatever he saw could at any instant cease ever having been. Everything around him could. He himself.

"Our King Roger? No," he denied. "Impossible. A false rumor."

Odo drew back and flailed a wild gesture. "It's true!" His voice cracked across. The shame of that steadied him a little. He swallowed, swiped at tears, tried to straighten. "Messengers from Italy. He fell in battle. His army is broken. They say the prince is dead too."

"But I *know*—" Volstrup's tongue locked in his mouth. Appalled, he realized that he had been about to describe the future until his conditioning stopped him. Had this tale shaken him so badly? "How would people in the street know? Such news would go straight to the palace."

"The m-messengers—they called it out as they passed by—"

A sound broke through the noises of Palermo, overrode them, strode between the city walls and out the harbor to the bay. Volstrup knew that voice. All did. It was the bells of the cathedral. They were tolling.

For a moment he stood motionless. At the edge of vision he saw the apprentices at the workbench cross themselves, the Catholic left to right, the Orthodox right to left. It came to him that he had better do likewise. That broke his paralysis. He turned to the Greek lad, the most levelheaded. "Michael," he ordered, "speed forth, learn what has indeed happened, as nearly as you can in a short time, and come tell me."

"Yes, master," the apprentice replied. "They should be giving out the news publicly soon." He left.

"Back to your work, Cosimo," Volstrup went on. "Join him, Odo. Never mind what I sent you for. I'll not want it today."

As he sought the rear of the shop he heard a racket rising beneath the clang and jangle of the bells. It wasn't talk, song, footfalls, hoofbeats, wheel-creak, the city's pulsebeat. It was shouts, screams, prayers—Latin, Greek, Arabic, Hebrew, a score of vernaculars, dismay that wailed in this neighborhood and everywhere else. *Ja, det er nok sandt*. He noticed that his mind had gone back to Danish.

The story was probably true. If so, he alone understood in full how terrible it was.

Unless the cause of it also did.

He came out into a small garden court with a water basin, cloistered in Moorish style. This house had been built when the Saracens ruled Sicily. After purchasing it, he had adapted it to his business and to the fact that he would maintain no harem, unlike most of those Normans who could afford to. Now the other sides of the enclosure gave on storerooms, kitchen, dormitories for apprentices and servants, and similar utility. A stair led to the upper story, living quarters for himself, his wife, and their three children. He climbed it.

She met him on the gallery, a small, dark woman, gone plump and her hair, black beneath its covering, streaked with gray, nevertheless rather attractive. He had looked at her middle years before returning to her youth and asking for her hand. That skirted the law of the Time Patrol, but he'd spend a long while with her. He needed a wife for appearance's sake, for family connections, to maintain his household and, yes, warm his bed; by temperament he was a benedict, not a womanizer.

"What is it, my lord?" Her question quavered in Greek. Like most Sicilians born, she got along in several languages, but today she fell back to that of her childhood. *Me too*, he thought. "What is happening?"

"Bad news, I fear," he answered. "See that the children and the staff stay calm."

Though she had become a Catholic in order to marry him, she forgot and crossed herself in Eastern wise. Just the same, he admired the steadiness that came upon her. "As my lord bids."

It made him smile, squeeze her arm, and say, "Fear not for us, Zoe. I will see to things."

"I know you will." She hastened off. His gaze followed her a moment. There passed through him: *If only the centuries of Muslim rule hadn't made women of every faith so submissive, what a companion she might be*. But she handled her duties well, her kinfolk remained helpful to his business, and . . . he couldn't have anybody who wanted to share his secrets.

He crossed a couple of rooms still furnished in the austere, airy Islamic style, and reached the one that was his alone. It wasn't kept locked; that might have raised suspicions of witchcraft or worse. However, a merchant naturally required confidential files, strong-boxes, and occasional privacy. Barring the door behind him, he drew up a stool in front of a large ambry, sat down, and pressed the foliate pattern carved into the wood in a certain order.

A rectangle of luminance sprang forth before him. He ran tongue over dry lips and whispered in Temporal, "Give me a synopsis of King Roger's campaign in Italy from, uh, the beginning of last month and onward."

Text flashed. Memory supplied what had gone before. A year ago, Lothair, the old Holy Roman Emperor, had crossed the Alps to aid Pope Innocent II against Roger II, King of Capua, Apulia, and Sicily. High among their allies was Roger's brother-in-law Rainulf, Count of Avellino. They fought their way far down the Italian peninsula until at the end of August, Anno Domini 1137, they reckoned themselves victorious. Rainulf was created Duke of Apulia, to hold the South against the Sicilian. Lothair left him eight hundred knights and, feeling death nigh, started homeward. Innocent entered Rome although his rival claimant to the throne of St. Peter, Anacletus II, occupied the Castel Sant' Angelo.

At the beginning of this October, Roger did return. He landed at Salerno and laid waste the lands that had repudiated their allegiance to him; the savagery of his vengeance was a shock even to this brutal age. At the very end of the month, he met Rainulf's army at Rignano in northern Apulia.

There he suffered defeat. His first charge, under the captaincy of his eldest son and namesake, Duke Roger, carried the enemy before it. The second one, which he himself led, faltered and failed. Duke Rainulf, a gallant and well-beloved leader, threw his whole force against the king's men. Panic seized them and they fled, save for three thousand whom they left slain. Roger took the remnants of them back to Salerno.

The victory availed little. Roger had other forces at his beck. They besieged Naples and regained Benevento and the great abbey on Monte Cassino. Before long, only Apulia remained to its new duke. Innocent, with his famous partisan Bernard of Clairvaux, must needs agree to let Roger mediate the dispute with Anacletus. Although the anti-Pope was on his side, the king shrewdly declared that he found the case too deep for quick decision. Let there be a further conference in Palermo.

It was never held. Emperor Lothair died in December, on his way home. In January 1138, Anacletus also slipped from life. Roger got a new Pope elected, but this one soon ended the schism by laying down his tiara. Triumphant in Rome, Innocent set about destroying the king, whom he had already excommunicated. He did not succeed. His foremost surviving ally, Rainulf, died of a fever in the spring of 1139; shortly afterward, the elder and younger Rogers ambushed the papal army and took Innocent himself prisoner.

So much for the Middle Ages, when all men were devout sons of Mother Church, gibed the Lutheran in Volstrup's past. Immediately, shocked, he recalled: *But I've let the record run on into the future. I sit here in early November, 1137.*

That fits. So much time is just right for word to reach Roger's capital that he did not merely suffer a reversal at Rignano, he was killed.

Then what becomes of that morrow in which he was to play so mighty a role?

He bade the text stop. For a moment he sat chilled and stinking with sweat. Resolution came. He was—he believed—the only time traveler now on the island; but he was not unique on the planet.

His was scarcely a Patrol base. He was an observer, who also gave assistance and guidance to whatever travelers might arrive. Not many did. The glory days of Norman Sicily were yet to come; and after them, events on the mainland would swallow it up. Headquarters for this entire milieu were in Rome, commencing in 1198, when Innocent III took over the Papacy. But all Europe was astir, and beyond Europe all the world. No matter how desperately thinly they were spread, Patrol agents were trying to monitor its history.

Aided occasionally by the databank, Volstrup ran his mind across the globe. At this moment, Lothair was still on his way back to Germany; strife over the succession would follow his death, becoming civil war. Louis VII had just inherited the crown of France and married Eleanor of Aquitaine; his reign would be largely a series of disastrous blunders. In England, the contest between Stephen and

Matilda was growing violent. In Iberia, an ex-monk had been forced against his will to become King of Aragon, but it would lead to union with Catalonia; Alfonso VII of Castile was proclaiming himself Emperor of all Spaniards and proceeding with the *reconquista*. Poor Denmark, under a weakling lord, lay ravaged by pagan raiders from across the Baltic. . . .

John II ruled ably over the East Roman Empire; he was campaigning in Asia Minor, hoping to win Antioch back from the Crusaders. The Frankish Kingdom of Jerusalem was hard pressed by resurgent Muslims. Yet the Caliphate in Egypt was divided against itself, Arabia had split into a welter of petty realms, and Persia was in the throes of dynastic war.

The principalities of Kievan Russia were likewise at odds with each other. Eastward, the Muslim conquest of India had stalled while Mahmud's family fought the Afghan princes. The Kin Tatars were conquering northern China and had established their own imperium there, while the Sung rulers hung on in the South. The feud between Taira and Minamoto clans tore Japan apart. In the Americas—

A knock sounded. Volstrup lurched to his feet and unbarred the door. Michael stood atremble. "It is true, Master Geoffrey," the apprentice said. "King Roger and his son fell in battle at a place called Rignano, in Apulia. The bodies were not recovered. Couriers sped here from what was left of the army. They say that every part of Italy they passed through is falling away again, ready to open itself to Duke Rainulf. Master, are you ill?"

"I am grieved, of course," Volstrup mumbled. "Go back to your work. I will rejoin you presently. We must carry on with our lives."

Can we?

Alone again, he opened a locked coffer. Within it lay a pair of metal cylinders, smoothly tapered, about the length of his forearm. He knelt and ran fingers across the controls of one. His timecycle was concealed outside the city, but these tubes would carry messages to wherever and whenever he commanded.

If that destination exists.

He rasped his news at the recording unit. "Please inform me of the actual situation and of what I should do," he finished. He set the goal for milieu headquarters in Rome, the time somewhat arbitrarily for this same date in 1200. By then, yonder office should be well organized and familiar with its surroundings, while not yet preoccupied with such crises and disasters as the Latin conquest of Constantinople.

He touched a point on the shell. The cylinder vanished. Air popped. *Please come back soon,* he begged. *Please bring comfort.*

It reappeared. His hands were shaking too much for him to activate the displays. "V-v-verbal report," he stammered.

The synthetic voice uttered his nightmare for him. "There was no establishment to receive me. Nothing reached me on any Patrol communication channel. As policy directs, I have returned."

"I see." Volstrup's tone was more flat and small. He rose. *The Time Patrol no longer guards the future,* he knew. *It never did. My parents, brothers, sisters, old friends, youthful sweetheart, homeland, none of what shaped me will ever be. I am a Crusoe in time.*

And then: *No. Whoever else among us was pastward of the fatal hour, they are still there and then, as I am. We must find each other, join together, seek for some way to restore what has been destroyed. How?*

A little resolution stirred within his numbness. He did have his communication devices. He could call around the world of today. Afterward— He couldn't think beyond that, not at once. This wasn't for an ordinary corpsman like him. Nobody less than a Danellian would know what to do. Or if the Danellians were gone, annulled, then maybe an Unattached agent—if any were left—

Emil Volstrup shook himself, like a man come out of surf that has nearly drowned him, and got busy.

1765 B.C.—
15,926 B.C.—1765 B.C.

A breath of autumn went over the foothills. Chill rang in streams hurrying down slopes and before sunrise laid hoarfrost on grass. Here forest had broken apart into stands of timber, large or small; fir remained dark but ash was yellowing and oak showed early touches of brown. Outbound birds passed aloft in huge flocks, swan, goose, lesser fowl. Stag challenged stag. Southward the Caucasus walled heaven with snowpeaks.

The camp of the Bakhri boiled. Folk struck tents, loaded wagons, hitched oxen to those and horses to chariots while youngsters with dogs rounded up the herds. They were on their way to winter in the lowlands. Yet King Thuliash accompanied the wanderer Denesh a little distance, so that they could bid each other a quiet farewell.

"It is not only that there is something secret about you, and surely you have powers not given to most," he said earnestly. He was a tall man, auburn of hair and beard, lighter-skinned than most of his followers. Clad in ordinary wise, fur-trimmed tunic, trousers, leggings, he carried on his shoulder a bronze-headed battle-ax trimmed with gold bands. "It is that I have come to like you, and wish you would stay longer among us."

Denesh smiled. Lean, thin-faced, gray-haired, hazel-eyed, he topped the other by two hands' breadth. Nevertheless he clearly was not of the Aryas, who lifetimes ago made themselves masters of the tribes throughout these parts. Nor had he pretended to be. He related nothing of himself save that he fared in search of wisdom. "They were good months, and I thank you," he replied, "but I have told you and the elders that once more my god beckons me."

Thuliash made sign of respect. "Then I ask Indra the Thunderer that he bid his warrior Maruts watch over you for as far as their range may reach; and I shall cherish the gifts you brought, the tales you told, the songs you sang for us."

Denesh dipped his own ax. "Fare you ever well, O King, and all who spring from your loins."

He stepped up into his chariot, which had jounced slowly along beside them. His driver was already there, a young man who must belong to a native breed—stocky, big-nosed, hairy—but who had been taciturn while he and his master abode with the Bakhri. At a shout, the two horses trotted off, slantwise across the hillside toward the heights.

Thuliash stood watching until the chariot was gone from sight. He did not fear for them. Game was plentiful, highlanders were hospitable, and wild men would not likely attack when the pair went equipped like the northern conquerors. Besides, although Denesh had made no show of powers, he was clearly a wizard. If only he had stayed . . . the Bakhri might well have changed their minds and crossed the mountains. . . . Thuliash sighed, hefted his weapon, returned to camp. There would be fighting enough in years ahead. The tribes owing tribute to him were growing too big for their pasturelands. He would presently lead half of them around the inland sea and thence eastward to win themselves a new country.

—Neither aboard the chariot spoke much. Keeping their balance as it rocked and swayed had become automatic, but they were suddenly overwhelmed by memories, thoughts, hope tinged the least bit with regret. After an hour they came onto a ridge, a realm of wind and loneliness. "This will do," Keith Denison said in English.

Agop Mikelian drew rein. The team snorted wearily. Light though the vehicle was, pulling it on such terrain, long before horse collars were invented, or stirrups and horseshoes for that matter, wore them down fast. "Poor beasts, we should have stopped sooner," he said.

"We had to be sure nobody was watching," Denison reminded him. He sprang to the ground. "Ah, this feels almost as good as homecoming will." He saw the look on Mikelian. "I'm sorry. I forgot."

"That's all right, sir." His assistant came down likewise. "I've got places to go to." The Patrol recruited him in 1908, following the massacre at Van. Helping trace the dim origins of the Armenian people heartened him to live with their history. Resilient, he grinned. "Like California in the 1930s, trading on William Saroyan's publicity."

Denison nodded. "I remember you telling me." They hadn't had much chance to get acquainted, as busy as their job kept them. Personnel—total available lifespans—were so few, to map a field so vast as the migrations of the early Indo-Europeans. Yet the task was vital. Without a record of them, how could the Patrol guard events that had shaken the world and shaped the future? Denison and his new helper went straight to work.

Still, he thought, the fellow had proved steady and intelligent. Having gained experience, he could take a more active part in the next expedition.

"Where'd you say you're bound for, sir?" Mikelian asked.

"Paris, 1980. Got a heavy date with my wife."

"Why just then? I mean, didn't you tell me she's an attached agent in her own birthtime, closer to the middle twentieth century?"

Denison laughed. "You forget the problems longevity brings. Somebody who didn't grow visibly older in the course of several decades would cause her friends and neighbors to wonder about her. Cynthia was winding up our affairs when I left, prior to moving away. She's to begin a new identity—same name, might as well, but different location—in 1981. And me in my persona as her peripatetic anthropologist husband, of course. How better for us to segue into the manners and mores of a later generation than by taking a twelve-month holiday amongst them, and where better to start than Paris?"

And, by God, I've earned it, he thought. *She too, yes, yes. The time between my leaving and my return will have been much shorter for her than it was for me, and she'll have had her clerical duties in the Patrol to keep her mind occupied, as well as making our move away from New York plausible to our acquaintances there. Still, she'll have worried, and chafed at the rule that she mustn't skip ahead those few weeks to make sure I do come back alive. (Even so slight a loop in causality could breed trouble. Not likely, but it could, and we must often take chances as is, without adding needlessly to the hazard. How well I know. Oh, how very well.) But I have roved for more than a quarter year among those herdsmen.*

Sun, stars, and campfire smoke, rain, lightning, and a river in spate, wolves, stampede, and a cattle raid, song, saga, and ancestral epic, birth, death, and blood sacrifice, comradeship, contests, and lovemaking—Cynthia didn't ask about more than he chose to tell. He knew that, beneath her silence, she had guessed there was somebody in an ancient Persia whose history had been subtly altered. He'd been working ever since on putting Cassandane behind him. But months away from home added up, and if he'd declined Thuliash's kindly offer he might never have gained the king's confidence, which it was necessary for him to do, and— And he wished little Ferya all the best in her nomad world, and this second honeymoon in Paris should bring him back closer to Cynthia, whom the Lord knew was a dear and valiant lady—

His exuberance had faded. He lifted the ax that marked him as of warrior class, worthy to speak with chieftains. It was also a communicator. "Specialist Keith Denison calling milieu headquarters, Babylon," he said in Temporal. "Hello, hello. Talk freely; my associate and I are alone."

The air crackled: "Greeting, Agent. Glad to hear from you. We were growing worried."

"Yes, I'd planned to get away a little sooner, but they wanted me to take part in their equinox rite and I couldn't well refuse."

"Equinox? A pastoral society keeping a solar calendar?"

"Well, this particular tribe observes the quarter days—which is a possibly useful datum. Can you fetch us? We have a chariot and two horses, Patrol stock."

"At once, Agent. Only let me get a fix on your location."

Mikelian danced in the grass. "Home!" he caroled.

A carrier appeared, no hopper but a large cylinder that hovered on antigravity a few inches above ground. It hadn't skipped through time, merely across space. Four men in Mesopotamian costume of the period, complete with curled beards, emerged. Quickly, they got team and vehicle aboard. Everybody embarked, the pilot took his seat, the Caucasus Mountains blinked from sight.

What appeared in the viewscreens was a plain where grass billowed to the horizon. Tree-shaded, a set of timber buildings and a corral stood nearby. Two women clad for rough work hastened to greet the newcomers. They took charge of Denison's transportation. The Patrol could safely maintain a ranch in North America before humans arrived. Mikelian patted the horses an affectionate goodbye. Maybe he'd get the same ones on his next trip.

The carrier jumped again. It emerged in a secret vault below the Babylon where Hammurabi still reigned.

The director of the base met the anthropologists and invited them to dine. They'd be here a couple of days, downloading the information they had gathered. Most was of purely scientific interest, but what was the Patrol for if not to serve civilization in every possible way? Too bad that the knowledge couldn't be made public for thousands of years, after time travel had been developed, Denison thought. Meanwhile scholars would exhaust their lives following merely archaeological clues, often onto wholly false trails. . . . It wasn't for nothing. Their labors carved a bridgehead from which Patrol Specialists launched the real quests.

Over the dinner table, he related those of his findings that were operationally significant. "Thuliash and his confederation will not cross the mountains. They'll be migrating east instead. So he won't augment Gandash's forces on this side, and I believe that is why the Kassites don't make any more gains against the Babylonians, nineteen years from now, than history records."

"Which means we have a somewhat less complicated military-political situation to keep track of than I feared," said the director. "Excellent. Great work." Obviously he was thinking of lifespan released to mount guard over other potential trouble spots.

He arranged for his guests to tour the city, properly disguised and under close guidance. It was Mikelian's first time, and Denison always found such a visit interesting. Nevertheless eagerness seethed in them, and release at last was joy.

They got shaves and haircuts at the base. It didn't keep twentieth-century clothes in stock, but their field outfits were durable, comfortable, pungent in a clean outdoor way that evoked a lot of memories. "I'd like to keep mine for a souvenir," Mikelian said.

"You'll probably want it again for use," Denison told him. "Unless our next assignment is to a very different region, and I don't expect that. You would like to join me, wouldn't you?"

"Would I ever, sir!" Tears stood forth in the brown young eyes. Mikelian wrung his hand, leaped aboard a hopper, waved, and vanished.

Denison selected one for himself from among those that waited in the whitely lit garage. "God be with you, Agent," said the attendant. He was a twenty-first-century Iraqi. The Patrol tried to match somatotypes to eras, and race changes far more slowly than language or faith.

"Thank you, Hassan. Likewise."

Having mounted, for a moment Denison sat half adream. He'd arrive in a cavern little different from this, register, obtain garments and money and passport and whatever else he needed, then walk from the office building that fronted for the Patrol yonder, forth onto the Boulevard Voltaire, Saturday morning, the tenth of May, most beautiful of all Parisian months. . . . Traffic would be frantic, but in

1980 the city hadn't yet suffered its full monstrous overgrowth. . . . The hotel where Cynthia was to make a reservation and meet him stood on the Left Bank, a charming, slightly dilapidated anachronism where croissants for breakfast were fresh-baked on the premises and the staff liked guests who were lovers. . . .

He set for his destination and touched the main switch.

1980α A.D.

Daylight flooded him.

Daylight?

Shock froze his hands on the control bars. As if by a lightning flash at night, he saw a narrow street, high-peaked walls, a crowd that howled and recoiled in pandemonium from him, the women all wore dark ankle-length gowns and kept their heads covered, the men had some color to long coats and baggy pants, the air was full of smoke and barnyard smells— As instantaneously he knew that no vault existed and his machine, built not to arrive within solid matter, had brought him to the surface of some place that was not his Paris—

Get out of here!

Untrained for combat missions, he reacted half a second too slowly. A man in blue leaped, tackled him around the waist, dragged him from the saddle. Denison had barely time and drilled-in reflex to hit the emergency go-button. A vehicle must never, under no circumstances whatsoever, fall into outsider possession. His disappeared. He and his assailant tumbled to the pavement.

"God damn it, stop that!" Denison did know martial arts, they were part of his Patrol education. The blue-clad man got fingers on his throat. Denison struck the edge of his palm into the neck, under the angle of the jaw. His attacker gasped and sagged, a dead weight upon him. Denison could breathe anew. The rags of darkness cleared from his eyes. He scrambled free and onto his feet.

Again too late. The civilians stumbled over each other to get clear—through the general yelling he made out "*sorcier!*" and "*juif vengeur!"*—but another man in blue rode a well-trained horse through the midst of them. Denison saw boots, short cape, flat helmet, yes, some kind of trooper or policeman. Mostly he saw a sidearm drawn and pointed at him. He saw, in the clean-shaven face behind, the fear that can kill.

He raised his hands.

The trooper put whistle to mouth and shrilled thrice. Thereafter he shouted for order and silence. Denison followed his words with difficulty and gaps. They weren't any French he knew, different accent and a lot of what seemed to be English, though this wasn't *franglais* either, he thought dazedly: "Calm! Control yourselves! I have him arrested. . . . The saints. . . . Almighty God. . . . His Majesty—"

I'm trapped, hammered in Denison. *Worse than I was in Persia. That was at least rightful history. This—*

Surprisingly fast, the near panic died down. People stood where they were and stared. They crossed themselves repeatedly and muttered prayers. The man whom Denison had hit groaned back into consciousness. More mounties showed up. Two bore some kind of carbines, though no firearm was familiar to the prisoner. They surrounded him. *"Declarezz vos nomm,"* barked one with a silver eagle on his breast. *"Quhat e vo? Faite quick!"*

Sickness closed Denison's gullet. *I am lost, Cynthia is, the world is*. He could only mumble. A trooper unhooked a billy from his belt and stuck him with cruel precision across the spine. He reeled. The officer reached a decision and barked an order.

Turned stiffly silent, they marched him off. It was a walk of about a mile. Shambling at first, he regained a blurred alertness on the way and began to look around him. Hemmed in by the riders, he couldn't get more than glimpses, but they told him something. The streets he went on were constricted and twisting, though smoothly enough paved. No buildings stood higher than six or seven stories and most seemed centuries old, many of them half-timbered and with leaded windowpanes. Pedestrians were numerous, brisk, men often animated as he remembered from his France but women subdued, decorous. Children were few; were they generally in school? Once away from the scene of action, the party drew little more than glances, now and then a sign of the cross; were captives an everyday sight? Horses pulled wagons and an occasional ornate carriage, leaving their droppings behind them. When he reached the bank of the Seine, he saw barges tugged by twenty-oared rowboats.

From there, too, he spied Notre Dame. But it wasn't the cathedral he remembered. It seemed to cover nearly half the island, a mountain of soot-gray stone soaring up and up and up, tier upon tier, tower above tower, like a Christian ziggurat, till the topmost spires raked heaven a thousand feet aloft. What ambition had replaced the lovely Gothic with this?

He forgot it when the squad brought him to another building, massive and fortress-like above the river. A life-size crucifix was carved over the main door. Within were gloom, chill, more guards, and men in hooded black robes, bearing rosaries and pectoral crosses, whom he took for monks or lay clergy of some kind. His awareness continued vague, as stunned and heartsick as he felt. Not until he was alone in a cell did he come fully conscious.

The room was tiny, dark, its concrete walls bedewed. Light straggled in from the corridor, through the locked and iron-barred door. The furniture was a pallet, with a thin blanket, on the floor, and a chamber pot that he found, dimly surprised, was rubber. Well, he could have used a hard one for a weapon. A cross was chiseled into the ceiling.

Christ, I'm thirsty. Can't I even have a cup of water? He clutched the bars, strained against them, called his hoarse appeal. For answer, somebody gibed from another cell somewhere down the passage. "Stop hoping, will ye? Leave me be!" English, by God, though strangely accented. When Denison replied in that language, he got an inarticulate snarl.

He slumped down on the mattress. What he'd just heard boded ill. Well, he did have time to think, try to prepare himself for interrogation. He'd better start. The decision strengthened him. Presently he was upright again, pacing.

Perhaps two hours had passed when a turnkey opened the door to admit a pair of guards, hands on pistol butts, and a cleric. The blackrobe was an old man, wrinkled, blinking, but sharp. "*Loquerisne latine?*" he demanded.

Do I speak Latin? Denison realized. *Sure, that'd still be a universal second language in this world. How I wish I did. Never thought*

I'd need it, in my line of work, and nothing is left from high school but "amo, amas, amat." The image of little old Miss Walsh rose before him. "I told you so," she said. He choked back a hysterical laugh and shook his head. *"Non, monsieur, je le regrette,"* he attempted in French.

"Ah, vo parlezz alorss fransay?"

Denison formed his words slowly, with care: "I seem to speak another French than yours, reverend father. I come from far away." He must repeat himself twice, trying what synonyms occurred to him, before he got his meaning across.

Withered lips quirked humorlessly. "That is clear, if you do not so much as recognize a friar. Know, I am Brother Matiou of the Dominican order and the Holy Inquisition."

When Denison had understood, fear grabbed his guts. He kept it leashed and slogged ahead. "There has been an unfortunate accident. I assure you, I am on a mission peaceful although of the utmost importance. I arrived untimely and in the wrong place. It is understandable if this aroused fears and caused precautions to be taken. But if you will bring me to your highest authority"—king, Pope, what the hell?—"I will explain the situation to him."

Again unraveling was necessary before Matiou snapped, "You will explain here and now. Think not that demonic art can avail you in Christ's own stronghold. Declare your name!"

The Patrolman got the drift. "Keith Denison, your Rev—uh, Brother." Why not? What did it matter? What did anything matter any more?

Matiou was also catching on, quickly interpreting otherwise unintelligible bits from context. "Ah, of England?" He used that word, not *"Angleterre,"* and went on: "We can fetch one who speaks the patois, if that will make you answer more readily."

"No, my home is— Brother, I cannot give the secrets I bear to anyone less than the supremacy."

Matiou glared. "You will speak to me, and speak truth. Must we put you to the full question? Then, believe me, when you go to the stake you will bless him who lights the fire."

He needed three attempts before he conveyed his threat. *The full question? I suppose less extreme torture is routine. This is only a preliminary quiz.* Fear keened in Denison's brain. He was faintly astonished at his firmness: "With respect, Brother, my duty, sworn before God, forbids me to reveal certain things to anyone but the sovereign. It would be catastrophic, did the knowledge become public. Think of small children given fire to play with." He cast a significant look at the guards. The effect was spoiled by the need to repeat.

Response was clear: "The Inquisition knows well how to keep silent."

"I do not doubt that. But neither do I doubt that the master will be most displeased should word intended for him alone be uttered elsewhere."

Matiou scowled. Denison saw hesitation underneath and pressed his advantage. They were catching on to each other's French rather fast. Part of the trick was to talk somewhat like an American who had read but never heard the language.

Confronted with something unprecedented like this, the monk wouldn't be human if he didn't welcome an excuse to pass the buck. After all, Denison argued, the sovereign could always remand him for interrogation.

"What do you mean by the sovereign?" Matiou asked. "The Holy Father? Then why did you not come to Rome?"

"Well, the king—"

"The *king*?"

Denison realized he'd made a mistake. Apparently the monarch, if they had one, was not on top. He hastened on: "The king, I was about to say, would be the natural person to see in certain countries."

"Yes, among the Russian barbarians. Or in those lands of black Mahound where they acknowledge no caliph." Matiou's gnarled forefingers stabbed. "Where were you truly bound, Keith Denison?"

"To Paris, in France. This is Paris, isn't it? Please let me finish. I seek the highest ecclesiastical authority in . . . these domains. Was I wrong? Is he not in the city?"

"The archcardinal?" Matiou breathed, while the expression on the guards shifted from nervous to awed.

Denison nodded vigorously. "Of course, the archcardinal." What kind of rank was that?

Matiou looked away. Beads on his rosary clicked between his fingers. After a while that became very long to the listener, he clipped: "We shall see. Conduct yourself carefully. You will remain under observation." His robe swirled as he swung about and departed.

Denison sank onto his pallet, wrung out. *Well,* he thought faintly, *I've won a little time before they take me to the rack and thumbscrews, or whatever worse they've invented since the Middle Ages. Unless I've somehow landed— No, can't be.*

When a jailer with an armed escort brought him bread, water, and greasy stew, he inquired about the date. "St. Anton's, in the year of Our Lord one thousand nine hundred and eighty" drove the last nail into the coffin for him.

From despair he drew at length a bleak determination. Something might turn up yet, rescue or— No, to think of oblivion was not only useless, it could paralyze him. Better to keep going, always ready to jump at whatever piece of luck chanced by.

Shivering through the night on his inadequate bed, he tried to lay plans. They were inevitably tentative. What he must do was get the protection of the big boss, the dictator, the—whatever an archcardinal was. That meant convincing the man he was not dangerous but, instead, potentially valuable, or at any rate interesting. He could not reveal himself as a time traveler. The Patrol inhibition would freeze his larynx. Anyway, quite probably no one in this world could comprehend the truth. However, he could scarcely deny having appeared out of thin air, though he might claim that witnesses were confused about details. Things Matiou had let fall suggested a belief in magic, even among educated people. But he should proceed most cautiously if he tried an explanation along those lines. They had enough technology here to produce efficient-looking small arms, and doubtless artillery. The rubber pot indicated contact with the New World on a regular basis, which implied a sufficient knowledge of astronomy for navigation if nothing else— *Would you believe a visitor from Mars?*

Denison coughed a chuckle. Nevertheless, that kind of story looked less unpromising than others. He must feel his way forward. "First let me humbly inquire what the savants among your Sanctity's (?) flock assume to be the case. My nation has perhaps made discoveries they have not." Awkward communication, frequent pauses to figure out what a sentence had meant, would be immensely helpful, giving him opportunities to think and to retrieve any *faux pas*. . . .

He fell into uneasy, dream-ridden sleep.

In the morning, a while after he'd received a bowl of gruel, guards accompanied by a priest took him away. What he glimpsed in an adjacent cell chilled his sweat. He was merely brought to a tiled room where a tub of hot water steamed, and told to bathe himself well. Afterward he was issued a dark set of present-day male clothes, his wrists were manacled, and he was led into an office where Brother Matiou sat behind a desk beneath a crucifix.

"Thank God and your patron saint, if you have one, that his Venerability, Albin Archcardinal Fil-Johan, Grand Duke of the Northern Provinces, graciously consents to see you," the friar intoned.

"I do, I do." Denison crossed himself two-handedly. "I will make many thank offerings as soon as I am able."

"Since you are a foreigner, indeed more foreign than a pagan from Tartary or Mexique, first I shall give you some instruction, that you not squander too grossly his Venerability's time."

Hey, a break! Denison paid his closest heed. He sensed how shrewdly Matiou extracted nibbles of information from him in the course of the hour, but that was all right; it was a chance to rehearse and develop his story.

And at last he was brought in a closed carriage to a palace atop that hill called Montmartre in the lost world, and ushered through sumptuous corridors and up a grand staircase and past a gilt bronze door where bas-reliefs showed Biblical scenes; and he found himself in a high white room, where sunlight streamed through stained glass onto an Oriental carpet, and confronting him sat a man on a throne, in a robe of scarlet and gold.

As ordered, Denison prostrated himself. "You may be seated," said a deep voice. The archcardinal was middle-aged but vigorous. The consciousness of power seemed engraved on his countenance. Spectacles diminished his dignity not at all. Just the same, he was clearly intrigued, prepared to question and to listen.

"I thank your Venerability." Denison took the chair, some twenty feet from the throne. They weren't allowing needless risks at this private audience. A bellpull hung by the prelate's right hand.

"You may simply call me 'lord,'"—the English word—Albin told him. "We have much to speak of, you and I." Sternly: "Beware of attempting tricks or subtleties. There are ample grounds already for suspicion. Know, the Chief Inquisitor, the superior of that cleric you have met, urges me to order you to the flames at once, before you wreak harm. He feels a magician such as this can only be an Avenging Jew."

Denison understood enough to breathe, "A . . . a what, lord?" from a throat suddenly going dry.

Albin raised his brows. "You do not know?"

"No, lord. Believe me, I am from a land so remote that—"

"Yet you know something of our language, and claim to bear a message for me."

Yeah, I'm up against a first-class intellect. "A message of goodwill, lord, in hopes of establishing closer relations. Our knowledge of you is slight, from visions vouchsafed prophets ancient and modern. Unhappily, I suffered shipwreck. No, I am certainly not an Avenging Jew, whatever that may be."

Albin too grasped the general intent, if not every word. His mouth tightened. "The Jews are skilled craftsmen and engineers at the very least, and it is quite possible that they also command black arts. They are descendants of those who escaped when our forefathers scoured Europe clean of their kind. They settled among the worshippers of Mahound, and now they lend their help to them. Have you not even heard that Austria has fallen to those paynim? That the heretic legions of the Russian emperor are at the gates of Berlin?"

And the Inquisition busy in western Christendom. God! I believed my *twentieth century was pretty grim.*

18,244 B.C.

I

Later Manse Everard thought the fact that he was chosen, and precisely where and how it happened to him, would be ironic were the coincidence not so absurd. Later yet he remembered his conversations with Guion, and wondered mightily.

But they were more distant than the stars from his mind when the summons came upon him. He and Wanda Tamberly had been sharing a vacation at the lodge the Patrol maintained in the Pleistocene Pyrenees. On this their last day, they left off skiing and climbing, nor did they flit north to seek out the magnificent wildlife of a glacial era, nor call on any of the nearby Crô-Magnon settlements to enjoy picturesque hospitality. They simply went for a long walk on easy trails, looked at mountain scenery, said little, were aware of much.

Sunset washed gold across white peaks and ridges. The lodge stood at no great altitude, but snowline was lower than in the birthtime of these two. Timberline was also; around them reached alpine meadow, intensely green, flecked with small summer flowers. A little way upslope, several ibex lifted horns and watched them, alertly but without fear. The sky, greenish in the west, deepening through azure overhead to purple in the east, was full of homebound wings. Cries drifted down through silence and gathering chill. Human hunters had made scant mark thus far; they were almost in balance with nature, like wolf and cave lion. The air tasted of purity.

The main building loomed ahead, a darkness from which windows glowed. "It's been grand," Everard said in American English. "For me, anyhow."

"Ditto," Tamberly replied. "You've been so kind, taking a rookie like me in hand and getting me to feel easy here."

"Shucks, a pleasure. Besides, you're the naturalist. You introduced me to stuff in the wilderness I'd never heard or dreamed of." Including hunts for mammoth, reindeer, wild horse with camera rather than gun. Born and raised when she was, Wanda disapproved of blood sports. His background had been different.

Not that such details mattered a lot otherwise if you were in the Patrol. Except— *She hasn't added but four or five years to the twenty-one that were hers when first we met. How many have I?* Longevity treatments or no, Everard didn't care, just then, to reckon them up.

"I wish—" She gulped and looked aside. Finally, in a rush: "I wish I weren't leaving."

His pulse stumbled. "You don't have to, you know," he said.

"Yes. I really must. I've such limited lifespan to give my folks," parents, sister, who would never know that she fared through the ages, whose own years above ground would number less than a hundred and all on world lines running straight from conception to dissolution. "And then I should, I want to, call on Steve," her uncle who was also a Patrol agent, in Victorian England. "Before I go back to work." She could have spent years of experienced time on vacation, then reported to her base camp within minutes of the moment she left it; but agents didn't do that sort of thing. You owed the outfit a fair proportion of your existence. Besides, too long away from the job, you'd go stale, and that could prove fatal, to yourself or, worse, a comrade.

"Okay, I understand," Everard sighed. He plunged at the question they had skirted this whole while. "Can we make another date?"

She laughed and caught his hand. How warm hers was. "Why, sure." Her glance turned toward his. In the fading light he couldn't see the blue of her eyes. Strong bones stood forth, though, and page-bobbed hair bore the hue of amber. She was shorter than he by the breadth of his palm, and he was a big man. "To tell the truth, I was hoping. Didn't want to get pushy. Don't tell me you felt shy!"

"M-m, well—" He had never been glib. How could he now explain? It wasn't quite clear to him, anyway. *The gap between our ranks, I guess. I'm afraid of seeming to condescend, or else of seeming to be trying to overwhelm. Her generation of women grew up with a touchy kind of pride built in.* "Old bachelor type. You, you've got a wide field to play if you want." She had frankly enjoyed the attention paid her by other male guests. And they were exotic to her, several of them handsome and vivacious, while he was only another twentieth-century American, slow-spoken, plain in his tastes, war-battered in the face.

"Foof," she snorted. "You've cut a wider swathe than any field I'm ever likely to find myself in. Don't deny it. You wouldn't be normal if you hadn't taken advantage of opportunities."

And you? . . . None of my business.

"Not that you've ever abused your chances," she added hastily. "I know you never would. I was surprised and, and delighted when you stayed in touch after Beringia. For Pete's sake, did you think I didn't want to?"

Almost, he grabbed her. *Would she like me to? By God, I believe she would.* But no. It would be wrong. She was too wholehearted.

Let her first become clear in her mind about this. Yes, and let him decide what his foremost wishes and needs were.

Be grateful for what you've had, this past couple of weeks, son. He knotted the fist she wasn't holding and muttered, "Fine. Fine. Where might you like to go next?" *To get better acquainted*.

She also seemed to take refuge in banality. "Gee, I'd have to think. Suggestions?"

Then they were at the lodge, mounting its veranda, entering the common room. Flames crackled in a huge stone fireplace. A rack of Irish elk antlers curved above it. On the opposite wall, cast in brass, a heraldic shield bore a stylized hourglass. It was the emblem of the Patrol, the insigne on uniforms that were seldom worn. Folk lounged about awaiting supper, with drinks, conversation, a game of chess, a game of go, a few clustered at the grand piano in a corner, from which danced a Chopin scherzo.

Agents of similar backgrounds tended to visit the same decades of the lodge's long existence. However, the pianist tonight was born in the thirty-second century Anno Domini, in orbit around Saturn. Patrol people did feel curious about other eras than their own, and sometimes they got enchanted by some aspect of one.

Everard and Tamberly draped their mackinaws over their arms. She went around saying goodbye. He lingered near the pianist. "Will you stay on here?" she asked him in Temporal.

"A few days, I think," he answered.

"Good. I too." The topaz gaze dropped. The hairless alabaster-white head—not albino; a healthy product of genetic technology—bent again above the keys. "If you desire your heart eased, I have the Gift of Quietness."

"I know. Thanks." He didn't expect he'd want more than some rambles by himself, but the offer was generous.

Tamberly returned to him. He accompanied her to her room. While he waited in the corridor, she changed into clothes she had brought, suitable for the San Francisco area, summer of 1989, and packed her other stuff. They went down to the underground garage. Hoppers stood row on row, like wheelless futuristic motorcycles, beneath bleak white light. At the one assigned her, she stowed her luggage.

Turning about, "Well, *au revoir,* Manse," she said. "New York

HQ, noon, Thursday the tenth of April, 1987, agreed?" They had settled on it in a few awkward words.

"Agreed. I'll, uh, I'll have tickets to *The Phantom of the Opera*. Take care."

"And you, buster." She came to him. The kiss was long and became hungry.

He stepped back. Breathing hard, a little rumpled, she swung into the saddle, smiled, waved, touched controls. She and her vehicle blinked out of sight. He paid no heed to the usual snap of air rushing in where they had been.

A minute or two he stood alone. She'd spoken of a three-month hitch in the field after her trip home, before their intended holiday. He didn't know how long it would be for him. That depended on what he'd be doing. He had no immediate call, but something was certain, when the Patrol must keep order in the traffic across a million years of time, with what was really a bare scattering of agents.

Abruptly he laughed aloud at himself. After—however much lifespan it was—traipsing through the continuum, was he finally over the hill? Second childhood, no, second adolescence. He saw that he'd felt as if he were sixteen again, and it made no sense. He'd fallen in love often enough before. A few times he'd done nothing about it, because to go ahead would have brought more harm than good. This might be such a case. Probably was, God damn it. Maybe not. He'd find out. They would, bit by bit, together, and either get serious and make whatever sacrifices proved necessary or else part as friends. Meanwhile— He started to go.

Another noise, of a different kind, passed softly behind him. He knew that difference. He halted, looked around, and saw a vehicle newly arrived. The person aboard was about seven feet tall and spidery long-limbed but, in a close-fitting leatherlike coverall, clearly female. Her hair, drawn into a crest as if on a helmet, shone Asian blue-black, but no Mongoloid skin was so deep a yellow, and the eyes were enormous and the same faded blue as his, while the face was narrow and hook-nosed. He didn't recognize the race at all. Her origin must be very far futureward.

Temporal fell harsh from incongruously full lips. "Unattached Agent Komozino," she identified herself. "Quick, tell me, are any of my rank at these coordinates?"

It stabbed in him: *Trouble*. She knew more, and probably had a better brain, than he did. Army habits from the Second World War, almost forgotten, brought him half to attention. "Me," he clipped. "Manson Emmert Everard."

"Good." She got off and approached him. Through the tight control in her voice he heard the tension, the dread. "What data I could access indicated you might be. Listen, Manson Emmert Everard. We have had a catastrophe, some kind of temporal upheaval. As nearly as I have been able to ascertain, it occurred approximately on Julian day 2,137,000. Beyond that, events diverge. No Patrol stations appear to exist. We must rally whatever forces we have left."

She stopped and waited. *She knows what a hammerblow she's dealt me*, trickled down the back of his mind. *I'll need a minute to catch my balance.*

The astronomical number she'd spoken— Somewhen during the European Middle Ages? He'd calculate exactly, no, he'd ask her. *Wanda was bound for twentieth-century California. "Now" she won't come out into anything of the kind. And she isn't trained for such a situation. None of us are—our job is to prevent it—but to her it'll be no more than vaguely remembered classroom theory. She'll be stunned worse than I am. My God, what'll she do?*

II

The dining room in the lodge accommodated all guests and staff, though chairs around tables got a bit crowded. Light came silver-gray and uneasy through the windows, for clouds swept low before a wind whose booming went as an undertone, the sound of autumn on its way south. Everard knew he imagined, but he felt as if a breath of the cold outside seeped inward.

More did he feel the gazes upon him. He stood at the far end, beneath a vigorous mural of bison that a local artist had painted some fifty years ago. Komozino was at his side, impassive. She had told him he had better take the lead. He was much closer in birth-time, memories, ways of thinking, to everybody else. Moreover, behind him lay a relevant experience unique among them.

"We spent most of the night talking, when we weren't shuttling message tubes in hopes of more contacts and information," he said into the appalled silence that followed his announcement. "So far, we know very little. There's reason to think the key event is in Italy, mid-twelfth century. At least, the Patrol has a man then at Palermo, island of Sicily. He got word that the king there was killed in battle on the mainland. It was not supposed to happen. His database says the king lived on for nearly twenty years and was important. Like a sensible fellow, our man sent a tube a short way uptime to his milieu headquarters. It returned, informing him that that office was gone, *spurlos versenkt,* never founded. He called other stations contemporary to himself, and they checked their own futures—very cautiously, of course, not venturing more than a couple of decades ahead. No new Patrol agencies anywhere. As you'd expect, otherwise the scenes weren't strange. They wouldn't be—yet—except perhaps in southern Europe. The effects of a change propagate across the world at varying speeds, depending on factors like distance, ease of travel, and closeness of relations between countries. The Far East might begin to be touched, slightly, pretty soon; but the Americas may well go on unaffected for centuries, Australia and Polynesia longer still. Even in Europe, at first the differences are probably mainly political. And . . . that's a whole new political history, about which we here know nothing.

"Anyhow, naturally, our bases in the twelfth century started communicating with those downtime. This led to contact with Unattached Agent Komozino." Everard gestured at her. "She happened to be in Egypt—uh, Eighteenth Dynasty, did you say?—tracking down an expedition from her home millennium that'd gone back in search of cultural inspiration and evidently gotten lost. . . . No, plain to see, whatever became of it, there was no noticeable effect on history. . . . She took charge of the entire emergency operation, pending the availability of more people with the same rank. A data scan suggested me, so she came in person to inform and confer." Everard braced himself. "At the moment, unless a Danellian shows up, we, ladies and gentlemen, are on the edge of the effort to salvage the future."

"Us?" cried a young man. Everard knew him peripherally, French, period of Louis XIV and assigned to that same milieu, as most agents were assigned to their own eras. It meant he was bright. The Patrol got few recruits from before the First Industrial Revolution, and very few from prescientific societies. A person who hadn't been raised in that style of thinking was seldom able to assimilate the concepts. At that, this lad was having difficulties. "But, sir, there must be hundreds, thousands of our kind active before the crisis date. Shall we not gather them all together?"

Everard shook his head. "No. We're in deep enough trouble already. The vortices we could generate—"

"Perhaps I can make it a little clearer," Komozino offered crisply. "Yes, quite probably most Patrol personnel go into the pre-medieval past, if only on vacation, like you. They are present, so to speak, there and then. Often more than once. For example, Agent Everard has been active in settings as diverse as early Phoenicia, Achaemenid Persia, post-Roman Britain, and viking Scandinavia. He has repeatedly come to this lodge for rest and recreation, at various points of its existence, both downtime and uptime of the present moment. Why should we not call on these Everards also? Certainly two Unattached make an insufficient cadre of leaders.

"The fact is, we have not done so. We will not do so. If we did, that would change reality again and again, hopelessly, beyond any possibility of comprehension, let alone control. No, if we survive what is ahead of us and prevail over this misfortune, we will not double back on our world lines and warn ourselves to beware. Never! If you try it, you will find that your conditioning against such antics is as powerful as your conditioning against revealing to any unauthorized person that time travel occurs.

"The mission of the Patrol is precisely to maintain the ordered progression of history, of cause and effect, human will and human action. Often this is tragic, and the temptation to intervene is almost overwhelming. It must be resisted. That way lies chaos.

"And if we are to execute our duty, we must constrain ourselves to operate in as linearly causational a fashion as possible. We must always remember that every paradox is more than mortally dangerous.

"Therefore I have been flitting about, seeing to it that the news does *not* reach most of our remaining personnel. It is best confined to a few indispensables, and to selected off-duty individuals like yourselves. To further disturb the normal pattern of events is to risk obliteration and oblivion."

Her stiff height sagged a little. "It has been hard," she whispered. Everard wondered how much of her lifespan she had spent on that frantic task. It wasn't just a matter of dashing from post to post, passing on the word here and hushing it up there. She had to know what she was doing. Mostly she must have been immersed in records, databases, evaluations of people and periods. The decisions must frequently be agonizing. Had she been at it weeks, months, years? Awed, he knew that such an intellectual achievement was altogether beyond him.

He had his own strengths, though. He took the word: "Remember too, friends, the Patrol does more than guard the integrity of time. That's a job for special officers, and crucial though it is, it doesn't occupy the main part of our activity. Most of us are police, with the traditional tasks of police." *We give advice, we regulate traffic, we arrest evildoers, we help travelers in distress, now and then we provide a shoulder to cry on.* "Our fellow agents are busy. If we took them off their jobs, all hell would break loose." Actually, Temporal lacked an exact equivalent of the homely English phrase in his mind. "So we'll leave them alone, okay?"

"How shall we do that?" asked a twenty-first-century Nubian.

"We need a headquarters," Everard said. "This'll be it. We can seal it off for a certain limited slice of time without affecting anything else too much. That'd be impossible at the Academy, for instance. We'll bring in people and equipment, and operate mainly out of this base. Just what we do—well, first we have to learn exactly what the situation is, then figure out our strategy. Sit tight for a few days."

A smile, if it was a smile, twisted Komozino's lips. "It is either grotesque or it is appropriate that Agent Everard is involved and that he shall commence out of here," she remarked.

"May one request enlightenment as to the significance of the memsahib's statement?" inquired a babu from the British Raj.

Komozino glanced at Everard. He scowled, shrugged, and said heavily, "It might possibly help, now, if you know. I was caught up in something like this earlier along my world line. A friend and I were staying here. Several years later than today, on the resort's calendar. You're aware how complicated the bookings get for as popular a spot as this. No matter. We decided to finish our furlough in my home, twentieth-century New York, and hopped there. It was totally foreign. Eventually we found out that Carthage had beaten Rome in the Punic Wars."

A gasp went around the room. Some persons half rose to their feet, sank down again and shivered. "What happened?" he heard, over and over.

Everard skipped dangers and deeds. The whole thing still hurt too much. "We went back well pastward, organized a force, and mounted an expedition to the critical point, a certain battle. We found a couple of outlaw time travelers, with energy weapons, on the Carthaginian side. Their idea was to make a godlike place for themselves in the ancient world. We nailed them before they could perform the action that counted, and . . . again history went the way it ought to, the way we remembered because we were born in it." *I condemned a world, uncounted billions of perfectly decent human beings, to nullity. They never were. None of what I had experienced ever happened. The scars on my spirit are simply there; nothing caused them.*

"But I haven't heard of this before, me!" protested the Frenchman.

"Certainly not," Everard answered. "We don't advertise stuff like that."

"You saved my life, sir, my existence."

"Thanks, but spare the gratitude. It isn't called for. I did what I had to do."

A Chinese, once a cosmonaut, narrowed his eyes and asked slowly, "Were you and your friend the only travelers who went uptime into that undesired universe?"

"By no means," Everard replied. "Most skited straight back. Some didn't; they never reported in anywhere; we can only guess they got trapped, maybe killed. My friend and I had a stiff time escaping. It happens that, out of those who returned, we were the ones able to take charge and organize the salvage operation—which happened to be a fairly simple one, or we could not have handled it, at least not without calling in more help. When it was complete, why, that post-Carthaginian world had never existed. People returning futureward from the past 'always' found the same world as 'always.'"

"But you remember differently!"

"Like others who'd seen the changed world, and those Patrol folk who hadn't but whom we co-opted. What the bunch of us had experienced, what we had done, couldn't be erased in us, or we'd never have done it."

"You spoke of persons who entered the alternate future but failed to get away from it. What became of them when it was . . . abolished?"

Everard's nails bit into his palms. "They no longer existed either," he said like a machine.

"Apparently only a relative few entered it, including you. Why not many? After all, in the course of the ages—"

"Those were just the ones who happened to cross the crucial moment, bound uptime, in that larger section of time during which there were related events, like the Patrol's salvage work. We've got a longer section now, with a lot more traffic in it, so our problem is correspondingly bigger. I hope you understand what I'm saying. I don't."

"It requires a metalanguage and metalogic accessible to few intellects," Komozino said. Her tone sharpened. "We haven't time to quibble about theory. The span in which we can use this base without seriously perturbing things is limited. So is the number of personnel, therefore the total lifespan at our disposal. We must make optimum use of our resources."

"How?" challenged the woman from Saturn.

"For openers," Everard told them, "I'm going up to the milieu of that king and learn whatever I can. It's the sort of job that wants an Unattached agent."

And meanwhile, except that "meanwhile" is meaningless, Wanda's caught in yonder alien future. She must be. Else why hasn't she come back to me? Where else would she flee to, if she was able?

"Surely that Carthaginian world has not been the sole invasive reality," said the babu.

"I suppose not. I haven't been informed of any more, but—I've no need to know. Why risk an extra change? It might not damp out; it might bring on a new temporal vortex. And as a matter of fact," Everard flung at him, "we're faced with another reality right now."

Again because of deliberate tampering? The Neldorians, the Exaltationists, lesser organizations and individuals, crazed or greedy or—whatever they are— The Patrol's coped with them. Sometimes just barely. How did we fail against this enemy? Who is it? How to lay him low?

The hunter awoke in Everard. A chill tingle passed through his spine, out to scalp and fingertips. For a blessed moment he could set pain aside and think of pursuit, capture, revenge.

1989 A.D. α

Fog banked in the west caught early morning light and dazzled the blue overhead with whiteness. It was beginning to break up in tatters and streamers before a low, cold breeze off the unseen ocean. Leaves rustled on toyon. Not far away, a stand of cypress glowed darkly green. Two ravens croaked and flapped from a solitary live oak.

Wanda Tamberly's first reaction was mere astonishment. *Why, whatever has happened? Where've I come out? How?* She caught a breath, looked around, saw nothing human. Relief washed through her. For half an instant she'd feared that somehow Don Luis— But no, that was absurd, the Patrol had shipped the Conquistador back to his proper century. Besides, this wasn't Perú. Below the timecycle she recognized yerba buena, even sensed a hint of the fragrance crushed from it by the weight. The plant gave its name to that settlement later called San Francisco—

Her pulse went from quickstep to sprint. "Cool it, gal," she whispered, and brought her gaze to the instruments between the handlebars. Their projected displays gave the date, local standard time, latitude, longitude, yes, precisely what she'd set for, down to the fractional second, except that seconds of time flowed from her as she stared. . . . Simulated crosshairs on a simulated map also declared her position. Finger shaking a little, she summoned a full-scale vicinity chart. The center of the street grid was where it ought to be, at that secondhand bookshop in the Cow Hollow district which fronted for the Patrol's station.

And yonder rose Nob Hill and Russian Hill. Or did they? She

knew them covered with buildings, not brush. In the opposite direction, a glimpse of Twin Peaks seemed familiar; but what had become of the television tower? Of everything? She hadn't appeared in a subterranean garage but on the surface, surrounded by solitude.

Instinct stormed awake. She kicked the power pedal and flung her machine aloft. Air brawled by the force-screen. At once she knew she'd panicked. She grabbed self-control, halted, and hovered on antigrav two thousand feet high. Her ears had popped. They hurt. That helped make things real for her, no fever dream but a mess to cope with.

Is this foolish, hanging in sight of God and radar? Well, nobody to see me, is there? Nobody at all, at all.

No San Francisco, no Treasure Island, no Golden Gate or Bay Bridge, no Eastbay cities, no ships or aircraft, nothing save the wind and the world. Across the strait, Marin County hills hulked summer-brown, as did the range behind an Oakland, Berkeley, Albany, Richmond that didn't exist either. Ocean was slivers of silver to west and north on the far side of the shifting blue shadows in the fog. At the inland edge of mist she saw part of the sand dunes where Golden Gate Park ought to be.

Like before the white man came. A few Indian camps here and there, I suppose. Could the temporal part of this hopper have developed a collywobble, and I landed pastward of the twentieth century? Never heard of any such thing, but neither have I ever heard of any high tech that was not highly temperamental. Like a calming hand laid upon her, the knowledge came that the Time Patrol had operatives someplace at every moment of a million years or more.

She activated her communicator. The radio bands were silent. Wind shrilled, stronger at this altitude than below. She felt how cold she was. Her clothing was blouse, slacks, sandals. This vehicle wasn't equipped for the fancier sorts of transmission, like neutrino modulation, but the Patrol used radio freely in eras before Marconi, or was it before Hertz or Clerk Maxwell or who? Maybe nobody happened to be sending. "Hello, hello, Specialist Wanda Tamberly calling. . . . Come in, please come in. . . ." Shouldn't there be a set of beacons for her to home on? Could she be too distant from any to receive? That didn't figure, when even the scientists of her milieu detected signals of a few watts across the Solar System. But she was no transistor tripper.

Jim Erskine was. He could make electrons dance a fandango. They'd gone together for a while, students at Stanford. If Jim were here— But she'd put such people behind her forever when she joined the Patrol. Her folks too, all blood kin except Uncle Steve; oh, she visited, she lied about her wonderful job that kept her so much on the go; nevertheless— Loneliness smote like the wind.

"Better get someplace warm and take stock," she muttered. "Especially if the someplace serves hot buttered rum." However feeble, the jape encouraged her. She sent the machine slanting downward across the Bay.

Pelican and cormorant winged in their thousands. Sea lions basked along island shores. On the eastern side she found shelter in a redwood grove, majesty through whose shade sunlight cast golden spatters, a brook purled, fish swam and leaped. *Desolation is relative*, she thought.

Dismounting, she kicked off her sandals and did a few minutes' stationary jogging on the soft duff. Warmed, she opened the luggage carrier behind the buddy seat to check what her assets were.

Damn skimpy. Standard emergency stuff, helmet, stun pistol, isotopic battery, flashlight, glowlight, water bottle, food bars, small tool kit, small medical kit. A bag holding the few changes of clothes, toothbrush, comb, et cetera that she'd brought with her to the resort; generally she'd worn garments kept in stock for guests. A purse, with the usual late-twentieth-century American female clutter. A couple of books she'd read at odd moments. Like most of those agents who operated away from their birth milieus and didn't maintain lodgings there, she had a locker at the local station where she kept necessary stuff, including money. Her plan had been to pick up what she wanted and taxi to her parents' home, since it chanced they couldn't conveniently meet her at the airport. Had they been able to, a more elaborate deception would have been required.

Oh, Dad, Mother, Susie. Yes, and the cats too.

Slowly, the serenity around her smoothed down despair. The thing to do, she decided, was not to try springing straight back to the Pleistocene—though God damn, wouldn't it be good to see Manse there, big and solid and able?—or flicker blindly through time in this neighborhood. If she couldn't trust the temporal drive, her best bet was to head spatially east. Maybe she'd find European colonies yonder, or maybe she'd have to continue overseas, but eventually she was bound to make a Patrol contact.

She donned her old jacket from backpacking trips that abruptly felt very remote, and laced stout shoes over socks on her feet. Helmet secured to head, pistol to hip, she was as ready for trouble as she'd ever be. Remounting, she steered her hopper out among the huge trunks and into the sky.

Green bordered the Sacramento and San Joaquin Rivers; elsewhere tawniness passed beneath her, no trace of irrigation, agriculture, highways, towns. Impatience prickled. This jet plane speed was too flinking slow. She could go supersonic, but that was still a crawl and would be extravagant of energy reserves she might need later. For several minutes she mustered nerve, then set the space controls and gingerly touched the button.

The Sierra peaks lay below her, the desert beyond, and the sun stood as much higher as she gauged it ought. So she could safely bypass distance. "Yippee!"

Proceed by jumps— An illimitable grassy plain shimmered under the wind. Thunderheads towered in the south. The radio remained mute.

Tamberly bit her lip. This wasn't right. She spent a while skipping above the prairies. Bird life was rich, but the land reached strangely empty. She spied a herd of wild horses before at last she came above some buffalo. Their abundance should have darkened the ground for miles. . . .

Smoke rose from the right bank of the Missouri. She hovered far up, activated her optical, and magnified. Yes, people, and they kept horses, yet this was a village of sod huts, tilled fields outside the stockade. . . .

Shouldn't be! Once they became riders, the plains Indians turned almost overnight into warriors and nomadic hunters, living off the buffalo till white men slaughtered those, also almost overnight. Had she chanced on some such moment of transition as, say, 1880? No, because then she'd have seen spoor of the whites everywhere, railroads, towns, ranches, farms laid out in homesteaders' quarter sections. . . .

Remembrance struck. *The horse barbarians weren't in any balance with nature either. If they'd been left alone, they'd have wiped out the buffalo themselves, slower but just as surely.*

No. Please, no. Don't let this be.

Tamberly fled on eastward.

1137 A.D.

Going from Ice Age France to medieval Sicily by way of Germany earlier that same year did not strike Everard as funny until he chanced to think about it. His chuckle clanked. Time travel was like that, including what it did to people's minds, the stuff they came to take for granted.

The fact was that the contemporary base in Palermo was a one-man operation. Its front was a shop which, with the live-in family and staff, filled its only building. There was no subterranean addition. The likelihood of you and your vehicle popping out of thin air, being seen and exciting comment, was prohibitive. Patrol facilities were to be expanded later, starting in 1140, when Norman Sicily really began to gain importance. But this didn't happen, because King Roger II died in battle and the future that led to the Patrol was aborted.

Mainz had long been a major city of the Holy Roman Empire, and so headquarters for that milieu were there. At the moment the realm was a loose, often turbulent confederation across what a twentieth-century man would regard as, approximately, Germany, the Netherlands, Switzerland, Austria, Czechoslovakia, pieces of northern Italy and the Balkans. Everard recalled Voltaire's wisecrack that it was neither holy, nor Roman, nor an empire. However, in the twelfth century it was perhaps a bit less undeserving of the name.

On the day Everard arrived, Emperor Lothair was in Italy with an army, helping press his claims and those of Pope Innocent against the claims of Roger and Pope Anacletus. Turmoil would follow his death, until Frederick Barbarossa finally won full control. Meanwhile the main action would be in Rome, to which milieu HQ was to shift in 1198—except that it wouldn't, it hadn't, because no Patrol ever existed to establish that office.

Today, though, Mainz could provide what Everard needed.

Upstairs from the garage he found the director. They retired to a private office. It was a room of handsomely carved wainscots, well-furnished by standards of the period; there were actually two chairs, as well as stools and a small table. A leaded window admitted some light. More came in from another, unglazed, its shutters open to the summer day. Through it rumbled, groaned, creaked, clopped, chattered, whistled, buzzed the noises of the city. Through it also drifted the odors of hearths, horse manure, privies, and graveyards. Across a narrow, filthy, bustling street Everard saw a beautiful half-timbered façade; beyond its roof, cathedral towers rose in majesty.

"Welcome, *Herr Freiagent*, welcome." Otto Koch waved at a carafe and beakers on the table. "Would you care for a little wine? A good year." He was German himself—born 1891, studying medieval history when called into the army of the Second Reich in 1914, recruited by the Patrol while adrift in bitterness and bewilderment after that war. The years here-now had given him a comfortable, middle-aged look, a bit paunchy in his fur-trimmed robe. It was deceptive. You didn't keep a post like his without being plenty competent.

"Thanks, but not at once," Everard replied. "Can I sneak a smoke?"

"Tobacco? Oh, yes. Nobody will disturb us." Koch laughed and pointed. "That bowl is my ashtray. People know I burn a rare Oriental wood in it when I want to smother the municipal stinks. A rich merchant can afford such luxuries." From a humidor disguised as a saint's image he took a cigar and lighter.

Everard declined the one he was offered. "I'll stay with my old friend, if you don't mind." He hauled forth briar pipe and pouch. "Uh, I don't suppose you can indulge often."

"No, sir. Difficult enough to handle my proper work. My public persona takes up most of my time, you realize. The requirements of the guild, the Church— Ah, well." Koch lit up and settled happily into his chair. No need to worry about ill effects. Patrol immunizations, which did not employ the vaccine principle, prevented cancer and arteriosclerosis, along with the infectious diseases that came and went through the ages. "What can we do for you?"

Turning grim, Everard explained.

Horror stared at him. "What? This very year a, a cancellation? But that is—unheard of."

"Unheard of by you. And you will keep it strictly secret, understand?"

The habits of disguise took over. Koch crossed himself, again and again. Or maybe he was a sincere Catholic.

"Don't be afraid." Everard spoke deliberately.

The anger he provoked flushed out dismay. "It is natural that one fears for one's workers, comrades, yes, the family I have in this era."

"None of you will disappear at the critical moment. What will happen is that you stop receiving visitors from the future, and no new posts are started up after this year."

The enormity grew and grew before Koch. He sagged back. "The future," he whispered. "My childhood, parents, brothers, everybody I loved at home—I cannot now go see them again? I did. They believe I moved to America but make a few return visits, until Hitler comes to power and I stay away— They did believe." He had fallen into twentieth-century German. No language but Temporal had the grammar to cope with time travel.

"You can help me restore what we've all lost," Everard said.

Koch rallied admirably fast. "Very good. We shall. Forgive my ignorance. It is long ago in my lifespan that I studied the theory at the Academy, and that was only superficially, because this thing is not supposed to happen, is it? The Patrol guards against it. What has gone wrong?"

"That's what I hope to find out."

Provided with appropriate garb, Everard was introduced around as a trader from England. It accounted for any gaucheries. Nobody had seen him come in the door, but this was a large, busy household-shop, and butlers were for royalty. Folk seldom encountered him anyway during his three-day stay. They gathered that he and the master closeted themselves to discuss confidential matters. The growth of cities in size, wealth, and power was providing untold commercial opportunities.

The hidden section of Mainz HQ possessed an ample database and machinery for putting information directly into brains. Everard acquired a thorough knowledge of recent and current events. No human memory could have contained the details of laws and mores, as wildly as they varied from place to place, but he learned enough that he probably wouldn't make disastrous mistakes. He added to his stock of languages. Medieval Latin and Greek he already had. German, French, and Italian were still sets of dialects, not always mutually comprehensible. He gained sufficient to get by. Arabic he decided against; any Saracens with whom he might deal would almost certainly know *lingua franca*, at least.

He also made his plans and preparations. He intended first to seek the Patrolman in Palermo, shortly after the news of Roger's fall, to confer and get a feel for the milieu. There was no substitute for direct experience. That meant he must enter the city inconspicuously and plausibly. Yet he had damn well better have force in reserve.

Besides his own strength and skills, the force consisted of an officer detached from regular duty. Karel Novak found himself on the run from his Czechoslovakian government in 1950. He was mightily glad when an acquaintance hid him, persuaded him to take some curious tests, and turned out to be a Patrol recruiting agent who'd had an eye on this young fellow. Novak served at several different locales "before" being posted to imperial Mainz. He was the straightforward policeman type who dealt directly with time travelers, counselor, helper, now and then restraining somebody from a forbidden action or rescuing somebody from a bad situation. His public persona was a general-purpose servant of Master Otto, gofer, arranger, bodyguard on the road. He was well informed about the environs, of course, but needn't be expert, since he was admittedly from the backwoods of Bohemia. The tale of how he came this far, when most commoners weren't supposed to move around, was plausible, mendacious, and usually good for a drink or two in a tavern. He was a dark-haired, squat, powerful man with narrow eyes in a broad face.

"Are you certain we should not tell others than him what this is all about?" Koch asked when he and Everard said their private goodbye.

The American shook his head. "Not unless a clear need for somebody to know comes up. I tell you, we've got trouble in carload lots without creating unnecessary sub-effects. Those could have consequences of their own that might get out of hand. So you will not drop any hint to your associates, or to any traveler who comes by in the normal course of affairs."

"You say that soon none will."

"Not from the future, most likely. A few may have reason to jump here from somewhere else in the present or the past."

"But you tell me visits will dwindle till we have none. My people are bound to notice and wonder."

"Stall them. Listen, if we resolve this and restore the proper course of history, the hiatus will never have happened. As far as Patrollers stationed here are concerned, everything will always have been normal." *Or what passes for normal along the twisting time lanes.*

"But I will have had quite a different experience."

"Up until the turning-point moment, sometime later this year. Then, if we're lucky, an agent will come and tell you it's all okay. You won't remember anything you did thenceforth, because 'now' you won't do those things. Instead, you'll simply proceed with your life and work as you did before today."

"You mean that while I am in the wrong world, I must know that everything I do and see and think will become nothing?"

"If we succeed. I know, the prospect for you isn't quite pleasant, but it's not really like death. We count on your sense of duty."

"Oh, I will carry on as best I can, but— Brr!"

"We may fail," Everard warned. "In that case, you'll join the other survivors of the Patrol when they meet to decide what to do." *Will I be there myself? Very possibly not. Killed in action. I almost hope so. It'll be a nightmare world for our sort.*

He thrust away memories of his own that no longer referred to anything real. He mustn't think about Wanda, either. "I'm on my way," he said. "Good luck to us both."

"God be with us," Koch replied low. They shook hands.

I'll skip any prayers. I'm too bewildered already.

Everard met Novak in the garage and took the rear saddle of a hopper. The Czech had been studying a geographical display on the control board. He set destination coordinates and activated.

1 1 3 7_{α} A. D.

Immediately the vehicle poised on antigravity, high aloft. Stars gleamed, a brilliant horde such as you rarely saw in the late twentieth century. The circle of the world below was divided between sheening water and a rugged land mass full of darknesses. The air lay cold and quiet, not a motor anywhere on Earth.

Novak set his optical for light amplification and magnification and peered downward. "Quite deserted, sir," he deemed. He had already scouted ahead and found this site.

Everard studied it likewise. It was a ravine in one of the mountains that formed a semicircle behind the narrow plain around the bay on which Palermo stood. Terrain in the vicinity was steep, rocky, nurturing only scrub growth, therefore doubtless left alone by shepherds and hunters. "You'll wait here?" he inquired needlessly.

"Yes, sir, until I get further orders." It was equally needless to say that Novak would duck elsewhere to eat and sleep, returning within minutes, and would disappear should he notice anybody headed his way in spite of the uninviting surroundings. He'd be back as soon as possible.

"Good soldier." *Who does what he's told and keeps any inconvenient questions behind his teeth*. "First bring me to the highway. Fly low. I want to know how to find you in case I have to."

That would be if, for some reason, he couldn't use his communicator. It was housed in what looked like a religious medallion hung around his neck under his clothes. The range ought to be adequate, but you never knew. (You dared not foreknow.) Novak was well-armed, in addition to the stun pistol that every cycle had in its luggage box. Everard, though, couldn't be, without risking trouble with the local authorities. At least, he couldn't overtly be. He did carry a knife like most men, a utensil for eating and odd jobs; a staff; and a variety of martial skills. Anything more might make somebody too curious.

The cycle flitted a couple of yards above the mountainside, presently above goat trails and footpaths, till it reached the flatlands and rose to avoid a peasant village. Dogs might take alarm and wake sleepers. Without artificial light to choke off night vision, people saw astonishingly well after dark. Everard fixed landmarks firmly in his mind. Novak glided back down to hover above the coast road. "Let me advance you to dawn, sir," he suggested. "There is an inn, the Cock and Bull, two kilometers west. Whoever spies you ought to suppose you spent the night there and set off early."

Everard whistled. "That name's too eerily appropriate."

"Sir?"

"Never mind."

Novak touched his controls. The east went pale. Everard sprang to the ground. "Good hunting, sir," Novak bade.

"Thanks. *Auf Wiedersehen*." Machine and rider vanished. Everard set off in the direction of sunrise.

The road was dirt, rough with ruts and holes, but winter rains had not yet turned it into a mire. When day broke, he saw that a hint of green had begun to relieve the dustiness of plowlands, the tawniness of mountains. At a distance, to his left and ahead, shimmered the sea. After a while he made out a few sails, tiny upon it. Mariners generally fared by day, hugging coasts, and eschewed voyages of any length this late in the year. However, along Sicily you were never far from a safe harbor, and the Normans had cleared these waters of pirates.

The countryside appeared prosperous, too. Houses and sheds clustered in the middle of fields cultivated by their tenants, cottages mostly of rammed earth below thatch roofs but well made, gaily decorated upon their whitewash. Orchards were everywhere, olive, fig, citrus, chestnut, apple, even date palms planted by the Saracens when they held this island. He passed a couple of parish churches and glimpsed, afar, massive buildings that must be a monastery, perhaps an abbey.

As time and miles fell behind him, more and more traffic came onto the road. Mainly the people were peasants, men in smock coats and narrow trousers, women in coarse gowns hemmed well above their footgear, children in whatever, burdens on heads or shoulders or diminutive donkeys. They were mostly short, dark, vivacious, descended from aboriginal tribes, Phoenician and Greek colonists, Roman and Moorish conquerors, more recently and casually traders or warriors out of mainland Italy, Normandy, the south of France, Iberia. Doubtless many, perhaps the majority, were serfs, but nobody acted abused. They chattered, gesticulated, laughed, exploded into indignation and profanity, grew as quickly cheerful again. Others mingled, peddlers making their rounds, the occasional priest or monk telling his beads, individuals less identifiable.

News of the king's death had not dampened spirits. Possibly most hadn't yet heard. In any case, such personages and such events were as a rule remote, nearly unreal, to folk who seldom went more than a day's walk from wherever they were born. History was something to be endured, war, piracy, plague, taxes, tribute, forced labor, lives shattered without warning or meaning.

The common man in the twentieth century was more widely, if more shallowly, aware of his world; but did he have any more say in his fate?

Everard strode amidst a bow wave and wake of attention. At home he stood big; here he loomed, and wholly foreign. His garments were of ordinary cut and material for a wayfarer or townsman, tunic falling halfway to the knees above hose, cap trailing a long tail down his back, knife and purse at the belt, stout shoes, colors fairly subdued; but they were not quite of any regional style. In his right hand swung a staff; on his left shoulder hung a bundle of small possessions. He'd skipped shaving, beards being usual, and sported a respectable growth; but his stiff brown hair wouldn't soon reach below his ears.

People stared and commented. Some hailed him. He replied affably, in a thick accent, without slackening his pace. Nobody tried to detain him. That might not be safe. Besides, he seemed legitimate, a stranger who'd landed at Marsala or Trapani and was bound east on some errand, very likely a pilgrimage. One saw quite a few such.

The sun climbed. More and more, farms gave way to estates. Across their walls he glimpsed terraces, gardens, fountains, mansions like those their builders had also raised in North Africa. Servants appeared, many of them black, a number of them eunuchs, attired in flowing robes, often sporting turbans. Real estate might have changed hands, but the new owners, like the Crusaders in the East, had soon fallen into the ways of the old.

Everard stood aside, head uncovered, when a Norman lord went by on a bedizened stallion. The man wore European clothes, but gaudily embroidered, a golden chain around his neck and rings aglitter on both hands. His lady—astride a palfrey, skirts hiked up but leggings preserving modesty—was as flamboyant and as haughty. Behind rode a couple of body servants and four guards. Those were still purely Norman men-at-arms, stocky, tough, noseguards on their conical helmets, chain mail hauberks polished and oiled, straight swords at hips, kite-shaped shields at horses' flanks.

Later a Saracen gentleman passed with his own train. This group wasn't armed, but in a subtler fashion it was at least as sumptuous. Unlike William in England, the Normans here had given generous terms to their defeated opponents. Although rural Muslims became serfs, most in the cities kept their property and paid taxes that were reasonable. They continued to live under their own laws, administered by their own judges. Except that their muezzins could only call publicly to prayer once a year, they were free to practice their religion as well as their trades. Their learning was eagerly sought and several held high positions at court. Others provided the shock troops of the army. Arabic words were permeating the language; "admiral," for instance, traces back to "amir."

The Greek population, Orthodox Christian, enjoyed a similar tolerance. So did the Jews. Townsmen dwelt side by side, swapped goods and ideas, formed partnerships, embarked on ventures in the confidence that any gains would remain theirs. The result was material wealth and cultural brilliance, a Renaissance in miniature, the embryo of a whole new civilization.

It wouldn't last more than half a dozen generations all told, but its legacy would pervade the future. Or so the Patrol's databanks related. However, they also declared that King Roger II would live another two decades, during which Sicily reached its finest flowering. Now Roger lay in whatever grave his enemies had seen fit to give him.

Palermo drew in sight. The most splendid of its buildings did not yet grace it, but already it shone and soared behind its walls. More domes, often gorgeous with mosaic or giltwork, lifted skyward than did Catholic spires. Entering unquestioned through a gate guarded but open, Everard found streets crowded, noisy, kaleidoscopically alive—and cleaner, better smelling, than any he had trod elsewhere in medieval Europe. Though sailing season was over, craft lay close together around that inlet from the bay which in this era was the harbor: high-castled merchantmen, lateen riggers, war galleys, types from end to end of the Mediterranean and from the North. They weren't all idled for the winter. Business went brisk, raucous, in and out of warehouses and chandleries, as it did at booths and shops everywhere.

Following the map he had learned, the Patrolman made his way through the crowds. That wasn't easy. He had the size and strength to force a passage but not the temperament, which most locals did. Besides, he didn't want trouble. But damn, he was hungry and thirsty! The sun had gone low above the western range, shadows welled upward in the lanes, he'd tramped many miles.

A laden camel squeezed between walls. Slaves bore the litters of a man who was presumably a big wheel in his guild and a woman who was presumably an expensive courtesan. Several housewives gossiped, homebound from market, baskets on their heads, small children clinging to their skirts, a baby at one breast. A Jewish rug seller, cross-legged in his stall, ceased crying his wares and made obeisance as a rabbi passed grave and gray-bearded, accompanied by two young scholars who carried books. Greek voices resounded lustily from a hole-in-the-wall tavern. A Saracen potter had stopped the wheel in his little shop and prostrated himself, evidently guessing this was one of the five times for prayer. A burly artisan carried his tools. Before each church, beggars implored the layfolk who went in and out; they didn't pester the clergy. In a square a young man played a harp and sang while half a dozen others listened. They pitched coins at his feet. He wasn't actually a troubadour, Everard supposed, but he sang in the *langue d'oc* of Provence and must have learned his art there, the homeland of his audience. By now French and Italian immigrants outnumbered the original Normans, whose own blood was fast being diluted.

Everard slogged on.

His destination lay in Al-Qasr, near the nine-gated interior wall surrounding that district of markets and *souks*. Passing by the great Friday Mosque, he reached a Moorish house converted to a place of business. As was usual, the owner and his people also lived there. The door stood open on a large chamber. Within, silks were displayed on tables at the front. Many of the bolts and pieces were marvels of needlework. Toward the rear, apprentices trimmed, sewed, folded. They didn't hasten. Medieval man generally worked a long day but at a leisurely pace; and he enjoyed more free time, in the form of frequent holidays, than his twentieth-century descendants.

Eyes lifted toward the huge newcomer. "I seek Master Geoffrey of Jovigny," Everard announced in Norman French.

A short, sandy-haired person who wore a richly decorated robe advanced. "I am he. How may I serve you"—his voice stumbled—"good sir?"

"I have need to speak with you alone," Everard said.

Volstrup caught on at once. He'd received a message from downtime telling him to expect an agent. "Certainly. Follow me, if you please."

Upstairs, in the room with the cabinet that doubled as a computer and communicator, Everard admitted he was ravenous. Volstrup stepped out for a minute and returned promising refreshment. His wife brought it herself, a tray loaded with bread, goat cheese, olive oil, cured fish, dried figs and dates, wine, water to cut it. When she had left, the Patrolman attacked it like a Crusader. Meanwhile he told his host what had been going on.

"I see," murmured Volstrup. "What do you plan to do next?"

"That depends on what I learn here," Everard replied. "I want to spend a little while getting familiar with this period. You're doubtless so used to it that you don't realize how handicapping it is not to know all the nuances that somehow never get into the databases—the jarring little surprises—"

Volstrup smiled. "Oh, but I well remember my early days. No matter how I had studied and trained beforehand, when I entered this country it was shockingly alien."

"You've obviously adapted well."

"I had the backing and help of the Patrol, of course. I could never have established myself solo."

"As I recall, you arrived as a man from Normandy, a younger son of a merchant, who wanted to start up his own business and had some capital from an inheritance. Right?"

Volstrup nodded. "Yes. But the intricacies, the organizations I must deal with, official, ecclesiastical, private—and then the folkways. I thought that from my youth I had known much about the Middle Ages. I was wrong. I had never experienced them."

"That's the usual reaction." Everard was taking his time, getting acquainted, putting the other man at ease. It would expedite operations later. "You're from nineteenth-century Denmark, is that it?"

"Born in Copenhagen in 1864." Everard had already noted, in the half-intuitive way one senses personalities, that Volstrup was not the Epicurean Dane common in the twentieth century. His manner was formal, a bit stiff; he gave an impression of primness. Yet the psych tests must have shown adventure in his blood, or the Patrol would never have invited him in. "I grew restless during my student days and took two years free, roaming about Europe as an itinerant worker. It was an accepted thing to do. Returning, I resumed my studies, which concentrated on the history of the Normans. I had no thought, no hope of anything more than a professorship somewhere. Then, shortly after taking my master's degree, I was recruited." Volstrup shivered. "But I am not important. What has happened, that is."

"How did you get interested in this period?"

Volstrup smiled again while he shrugged. "Romanticism. Mine was the late Romantic era in the North, you know. And the Scandinavians who originally settled in Normandy, they were not Norwegians, as the *Heimskringla* claims. Personal and place names show they came, at least for the most part, from Denmark. After which they proceeded to fight and conquer from the British Isles to the Holy Land."

"I see." For a silent minute, Everard ran the facts through his head.

Robert Guiscard and his brother Roger, together with other kin, reached southern Italy in the previous century. Countrymen of theirs were already on hand, fighters against both Saracens and Byzantines. The land was in turmoil. A leader of warriors, who joined one of the factions, might come to grief when it did, or he might do very well for himself. Robert ended as Count and Duke of Apulia. Roger I became Grand Count of Sicily, with a firmer hold than that on his own territory. It helped that he had obtained a papal bull making him apostolic legate of the island; that gave him considerable power within the Church.

Roger died in 1101. His older legitimate sons were dead before him. Thus he left the title to eight-year-old Simon, child of his last wife, half-Italian Adelaide. She, as regent, crushed a baronial revolt and, when sickness also took Simon off, handed an undiminished authority over to her younger son, Roger II. He took full mastery in 1122, and set about regaining southern Italy for the house of Hauteville. Those conquests had fallen away after Robert Guiscard's death. The claim was resisted by Pope Honorius II, who did not care for a strong, ambitious lord as the immediate neighbor of the papal territories; by Roger's rival relatives, Robert II of Capua and Rainulf of Avellino, Roger's brother-in-law; and by the mainland people, among whom there stirred ideas of city autonomy and republican government.

Pope Honorius actually preached a crusade against Roger. He must needs retract it when the army of Normans, Saracens, and Greeks from Sicily prevailed over the coalition. By the end of 1129, Naples, Capua, and the rest recognized Roger as their duke.

To nail down his position, he needed the name of king. Honorius died early in 1130. Not for the first or last time, the medieval intermingling of religious and secular politics brought about the election of two claimants to the throne of St. Peter. Roger backed Anacletus. Innocent fled to France. Anacletus paid off his debt with a bull proclaiming Roger king of Sicily.

War followed. Innocent's great clerical partisan, Bernard of Clairvaux, whom the future would know as St. Bernard, denounced the "half-heathen king." Louis VI of France, Henry I of England, and Lothair of the Holy Roman Empire supported Innocent. Led by Rainulf, southern Italy revolted anew. Strife went back and forth across that land.

By 1134, Roger seemed to be getting on top. The prospect of a powerful Norman realm alarmed even the Greek emperor in Constantinople, who lent his aid, as did the city-states Pisa and Genoa. In February 1137 Lothair moved south with his Germans and with

Innocent. Rainulf and the rebels joined them. Following a victorious campaign, in August he and the Pope invested Rainulf as Duke of Apulia. The emperor started home.

Indomitable, Roger came back. He sacked Capua and forced Naples to acknowledge him lord. Then, at the end of October, he met Rainulf at Rignano. . . .

"You've settled in pretty well, I see," Everard remarked.

"I have learned to like it here," Volstrup answered quietly. "Not everything, no. Much is gruesome. But then, that is true in every age, not so? Looking uptime after all these years, I see how many were the horrors to which we Victorians smugly closed our eyes. These are wonderful people, in their fashion. I have a good wife, fine children." Pain crossed his face. He could never confide in them. He must in the end watch them grow old and die—at best; something worse might get them first. A Patrolman did not look into his own future or the futures of those he loved. "It is fascinating to watch the development. I will see the golden age of Norman Sicily." He stopped, swallowed, and finished: "If we can correct the disaster."

"Right." Everard guessed that now going straight to business would be kindest. "Have you gotten any word since your first report?"

"Yes. I have not yet passed it on, because it is very incomplete. Better to assemble a coherent picture first, I assume." As a matter of fact, it was not, but Everard didn't press the point. "I never expected an . . . Unattached agent . . . so soon."

Volstrup straightened where he sat and forced firmness into his voice: "A band of Roger's men who escaped from the battlefield made their way to Reggio, got a boat across the strait, and continued here. Their officer has reported at the palace. I have my paid listeners among the servants there, of course. The story is that Rainulf's total victory, the slaying of the king and prince, was due to a young knight from Anagni, one Lorenzo de Conti. But this is mere hearsay, you understand. It is gossip that reached them after the fact, in fragments, as they straggled homeward through a country in upheaval, full of people who hated their kind. It may be worthless."

Everard rubbed his furry chin. "Well, it needs looking into," he said slowly. "Something that specific ought to have some truth behind it. I'll want to sound out the officer. You can fix that up for me, can't you, in a plausible way? And then, if it seems this Lorenzo fellow may be the key to it all—" Again the hunter's tingle went through his skin and along his backbone. "Then I'll try to zero in on him."

1138$_{\alpha}$ A.D.

To Anagni on its high hill, some forty miles from Rome, came a rider one crisp autumn day. Folk stared, for horse and man were uncommonly large; bearing sword and shield though at present unarmored, he was clearly of rank; a baggage mule followed on a tether; yet he fared alone. The guards at the city gate to which he came answered respectfully when he drew up and hailed them in rough Tuscan. Advised by them, he passed through and wound his way to a decent inn. There he got his gear unloaded and his beasts stabled and fed, while he took a pot of ale and a gab with the landlord. He was affable in a gusty German fashion and readily learned whatever he wanted to know. Presently he gave a coin to one of the boys and bade him carry a message to the right place: "Sir Manfred von Einbeck of Saxony sends his respects to Sir Lorenzo de Conti, the hero of Rignano, and would fain call upon him."

They brewed a grand local beer at Einbeck in those nineteenth and twentieth centuries that Manse Everard remembered. He needed a little whimsy to keep him going, keep him from too much silent crying out to his ghosts.

The title he used, Italian "*Signor*," German "*Herr*," bore a less definite meaning than it would later, when the institutions and orders of chivalry had fully developed. However, it bespoke a fighting man of good birth, and that sufficed. Eventually, on the Continent, it would merely signify "Mister"—or would it, in the strange world uptime?

The boy sped back with an invitation to come at once. Outsiders were always welcome for the news they could convey. Everard changed into a robe, which a Patrol technician had judiciously given the wear and tear of travel, and accompanied his guide on foot. The streets were cleaner than most because a recent rain had washed their steepness. Narrow between walls and overhanging upper stories, they were filling with gloom, but in a strip of sky he glimpsed evening light ruddy-gold on the cathedral that reared at the summit of the hill.

His destination was lower down but near where the Palazzo Civico stood forth from the hillside on arches. The Conti and Gaetani were the chief families in Anagni, which had gained importance during the past several generations. This house was large, its limestone little marked as yet by time, which would at last obliterate it. A fine colonnade and glass in the windows relieved its ruggedness. Servants in blue-and-yellow livery, all Italians, all Christian, reminded Everard how far from Sicily he had come, in spirit if not in miles or years. A footman took over, conducting him through halls and chambers rather sparsely outfitted. Lorenzo was a younger son, rich only in honors, still unmarried, staying here because he could not afford Rome. Decayed though the great city was, landowning nobility in the backward, agricultural papal territories preferred to inhabit fortress-like mansions there, visiting their rural properties occasionally.

Lorenzo was in a two-room suite at the back, easier to keep warm than the larger spaces. Everard's first sense when he entered was of vividness. Even quietly seated, the man somehow blazed. He rose from his bench as a panther might. Expression went across his face like sun-flickers on water where a breeze blew. That countenance was sharply, almost classically sculptured, with big eyes whose gold-brown-russet seemed as changeable instant by instant; it appeared older than his twenty-four years, yet also ageless. Wavy black hair fell to his shoulders. Beard and mustaches were trimmed to points. He was tall for the era, slim but broad-shouldered. His garb was not the usual robe of a gentleman indoors, but blouse, tunic, hose, as if he wanted always to be ready for action.

Everard introduced himself. "Welcome, sir, in the name of Christ and this house." Lorenzo's baritone rang. "You honor us."

"The honor is mine, sir, thanks to your graciousness," Everard responded, equally polite.

A smile flashed. Teeth that good were a rarity nowadays. "Let's be frank, shall we? I itch for talk about faring and fighting. Do you not? Come, make yourself easy."

A buxom young woman, who had been holding her hands near the charcoal brazier that somewhat staved off chill, took Everard's cloak and poured wine, undiluted, from a pitcher into goblets on a table. Sweetmeats and shelled nuts had been set forth too. At a gesture from Lorenzo, she genuflected, bobbing her head, and retired to the adjacent room. Everard noticed a crib there. The door closed behind her.

"She must remain," Lorenzo explained. "The infant is not well." Plainly she was his current mistress, no doubt a peasant girl of the neighborhood, and they had had a baby. Everard nodded without expressing hope for its quick recovery. That was a poor bet. Men didn't invest much love in a child till it had survived the first year or two.

They sat down, across the table from each other. Daylight was waning, but three brass lamps served vision. By their shadowful glow, the warriors in a fresco behind Lorenzo—a scene from the *Iliad*, or maybe the *Aeneid*, Everard guessed—came half alive. "You have been on pilgrimage, I see," Lorenzo said. Everard had taken care to display a palmer's cross.

"To the Holy Land, for my sins," the Patrolman told him.

Eagerness leaped: "And how fares the kingdom? We hear ill tidings."

"The Christians hold on." They would for another forty-nine years, till Saladin retook Jerusalem . . . unless that part of history was also gone awry. A torrent of questions rushed over Everard. He'd briefed himself pretty thoroughly, but had trouble with some, as shrewd as they were. In several cases, where he couldn't well admit ignorance, he invented plausible answers.

"Body of Christ, could I be there!" Lorenzo exclaimed. "Well, someday, God willing. I've a mort to do first, nearer home."

"Everywhere I stopped, on my way up through Italy, I heard how mightily you've wrought," Everard said. "Last year—"

Lorenzo's hand chopped air. "God and St. George aid our cause. We've well-nigh finished driving the Sicilians out. This new King Alfonso of theirs is a bold rogue, but lacks his father's cunning and skill. We'll chase him onto his island soon, I vow, and finish the crusade. But for the moment there's scant action. Duke Rainulf wants to make sure of his hold on Apulia, Campania, and what we've won of Calabria before he proceeds farther. So I've returned, and been yawning till my jaws ache. Man, it's good to meet you! Tell me about—"

Perforce, Everard related the adventures of Sir Manfred. The wine, which was excellent, smoothed his tongue, soothed his impatience, and conferred inventiveness as to details. Having duly visited the sacred places, bathed in the Jordan, et cetera, Manfred had gotten in a little fighting against the Saracens, a little boozing and wenching, prior to embarkation for his homeward voyage. The ship landed him at Brindisi, whence he continued on horseback. One servant had succumbed to illness, another in a skirmish with bandits; for King Roger's ruthless warfare, year by year, had left much desolation and desperate men were many.

"Ah, we'll clean them out," Lorenzo said. "I thought of spending the winter in the South, scouring for them, but travelers are few that time of year, the outlaws will withdraw into whatever wretched dens are theirs, and . . . I am not fain to play hangman, however necessary the task be. Go on with your tale, I pray you."

Nobody else had molested Sir Manfred, which was understandable considering his size. He planned to visit the shrines of Rome and there engage new attendants. Anagni was hardly out of his way, and he had longed to meet the illustrious Sir Lorenzo de Conti, whose exploit last year at Rignano—

"Alas, my friend, I fear you will come back to evil," sighed the Italian. "Do not cross the Alps without strong escort."

"I have heard somewhat. Can you give me fuller news?" was natural for Sir Manfred to say.

"I suppose you know that our valiant ally, the Emperor Lothair, died in December while homebound," Lorenzo explained. "Well, the succession is disputed, and factional strife has led to open war. I fear the Empire will be troubled for a long time to come."

Till Frederick Barbarossa at last restores order, Everard knew. *If history runs the same course that far uptime*.

Lorenzo brightened. "Yet as you've seen, the cause of righteousness is prevailing without its help," he went on. "Now that the blasphemous devil Roger is fallen, his realm crumbles before us like a sand castle under a rainstorm. I take it for a sign of God's grace that his eldest son and namesake perished with him. He would have been almost as able an enemy. Alfonso, the successor they got—well, I've spoken of him."

"Ah, that became a famous day," Everard attempted, "and you carried it. How I have thirsted to hear the tale of it from your very lips."

Lorenzo smiled but rushed ahead on the tide of his enthusiasm: "Rainulf, I told you, is making the southern duchies his own; nobody else counts for much any longer in those parts. And Rainulf is a true son of the Church, loyal to the Holy Father. This January—have you heard?—the false Pope Anacletus died, leaving none to dispute Innocent's right." *In my history, Roger II got a new anti-Pope elected, but that one abdicated within a few months. However, Roger had the personal and political strength to keep on defying Innocent, and eventually took him prisoner. In this history, Alfonso was unable to field even a feeble rival.* "The new Sicilian king does continue to claim the apostolic legateship, but Innocent has denounced that mistaken bull and preached a fresh crusade against the house of Hauteville. We'll cast it into the sea and bring the island back to Christ!"

To the Inquisition, when it gets founded. To the persecution of Jews, Muslims, and Orthodox Christians. To the burning of heretics.

And nonetheless Lorenzo came across as a decent sort by the standards of his epoch. Wine had set him aflame. He sprang to his feet, paced to and fro, gestured wildly, spoke in trumpet tones.

"Then we've our brother Christians in Spain to aid, driving the last Moors from their soil. We've the Kingdom of Jerusalem to fortify for eternity. Roger was gaining a foothold in Africa; already those conquests are falling away, but we'll get them back, and more. That too was once a Christian land, you know. It shall be again. There is the heretic emperor in Constantinople to humble, the true Church to restore for his people. Oh, boundless glory to win! I own to it, sinful I, my lust for a name like—let me not dare say Alexander's or Caesar's—like Roland's, the first of Charlemagne's paladins. But of course it's the reward in Heaven we must think of, the infinite reward for faithful service. I know that isn't won merely on the battlefield. All around us are the poor, the afflicted, they who mourn and they who are oppressed. They shall have comfort, justice, peace. Only give me the power to bestow their due on them."

He leaned down, clasped Everard's shoulders, said almost imploringly, "Abide with us, Manfred! I can well judge might in a man. Yours must be the strength of ten. Go not back to your hopeless home. Not yet. You're a Saxon. So you surely hold by your duke, who holds by the cause of the Pope. You can better aid it here. Charlemagne sprang from your country, Manfred. Let us stand ready to be knights of a new Charlemagne!"

As a matter of fact, Everard recalled, *he was a Frank, who massacred the Old Saxons with Stalin-like thoroughness. But the Carolingian myth has taken hold. The* Chanson de Roland *won't be composed for a while yet, the romances not till later still. However, popular stories and ballads are already in circulation. Lorenzo would be bound to seize on them. I'm dealing with a romantic, a dreamer—who's also a warrior as formidable as they come. Dangerous combination. I can almost see a nimbus of destiny around that head.*

The thought hauled the Patrolman back to his purpose. "Well, we can talk about it," he said cautiously. Given his bulk, he felt the wine much less, just a glow in his veins which the tightly trained mind kept channeled. "I do wish to hear of your deeds."

Lorenzo laughed. "Oh, you shall, you shall. My pridefulness is the despair of my confessor." He took another turn around the room. "Stay. Sup with us this eventide." That would be a light repast, soon served. The main meal was at midday, and given the poor illumination, people rarely sat up much past nightfall. "You've no business at a lousy inn. What must you think of my hospitality? A bed here shall you have, for as long as you wish, beginning at once. I'll send boys after your animals and baggage." With his elders at Rome, he was obviously in charge. Flinging himself back onto his bench, he reached for his beaker. "Tomorrow I'll take you hawking. We can talk freely then, out in the wind."

"I look forward, and thank you greatly." A tingle went through Everard. *This looks like the moment to try my luck.* "I have heard extraordinary things. Especially about Rignano. They say a saint appeared to you. They say that only by a miracle could you have charged through the foe as you did."

"Ha, they say whatever comes onto their tongues," Lorenzo snorted. "Commoners' gabble." Quickly: "Not but what God alone gave us our victory, and I've no doubt St. George and my patron watched over me. I've lighted many candles to them, and when I've won the means, I intend to endow an abbey at least."

Everard stiffened. "But nobody saw . . . anything supernatural . . . upon that day?" *That's how medieveal people would look on a time traveler and his works.*

Lorenzo shook his head. "No. Not I, and I've heard no such claims from anyone else who matters. True, it's easy to get confused in a fight, outright delirious; but your own experience must have taught you to discount that."

"Nothing remarkable earlier, either?"

Lorenzo gave Everard a puzzled glance. "No. If Roger's Saracens were attempting witchcraft, the will of God thwarted them. What makes you ask so intently?"

"Rumors," Everard mumbled. "You understand, being a pilgrim, I'm especially interested in any signs from Heaven—or from hell." He rallied himself, tossed off a mouthful, and managed a grin. "Mainly, though, as a soldier, I'm interested in what did happen there. It was no ordinary battle."

"It was not. In truth, I felt the hand of God upon me when first I lowered lance and spurred horse toward the prince's standard." Lorenzo crossed himself. "Otherwise everything was of this world, tumult and turmoil, hardly a moment free for awareness, let alone any real thinking. Tomorrow I'll be glad to relate what my memory keeps of it." He smiled. "Not now. The story has grown stale in our household. Indeed, I myself would rather dwell on what we'll do next."

I'll ask, I'll get every detail I can from him and everybody else, before Sir Manfred regretfully decides that duty calls him back to Saxony after all. Maybe, maybe I'll pick up a clue to somebody who came out of time and disrupted fate. But I doubt it. The knowledge was freezingly cold.

1137 A.D.

30 October (Julian calendar).

Beneath a pale sky, those few cottages that were the village of Rignano huddled by a road running from the mountains in the west to Siponto on the Adriatic coast. Low above stubblefields and in woodlots and orchards going sere, sunrise mists blurred the horizons of North Apulia. The air was cold and still. Banners drooped, pavilions sagged wet, in the opposing camps.

A mile or so of mostly bare earth separated them, divided by the road. Smoke rose straight upward from a few fires, but only a few. Clang and clatter, shout and shriek of readymaking violated silence.

Yesterday King Roger and Duke Rainulf had conferred. None less than Bernard, abbot of Clairvaux, revered by whole nations, strove to avert bloodshed. But Rainulf was vengefully determined on battle and Roger flushed with victories. Moreover, Bernard was of the party of Pope Innocent.

Today they would fight.

The king trod forth, hauberk darkly shining, and smote fist in palm. "Up and at them!" he exulted. His voice was lionlike. Leonine too were the black-bearded features; but the eyes were viking-blue. He glanced at the man who had shared his tent, beguiling with tales those hours after plans had been laid and before sleep would come. "What, still glum on this day of all days?" he asked jovially. "I should think a djinni like you— Are you afraid yon priest will stuff you back into your bottle?"

Manson Everard forced a smile. "At least let it be a Christian bottle, with some wine in it." His jest was harsh of tone.

For a space more Roger regarded him. Big though the king was, his companion hulked over him. That was not the sole thing strange about the fellow, either.

His story sounded straightforward enough. Bastard of an Anglo-Norman knight, Manson Everard left England years ago to seek his fortune. Like many of his countrymen, eventually he joined the Varangian Guard of the emperor in Constantinople, fought the barbarian Pechenegs, but as a Catholic felt reluctant when the Byzantines moved against the Crusader domains. Discharged, with a fair amount of money from pay and spoils, he drifted west till he landed in Bari, not far from here. There he spent a while taking his ease and pleasure, and heard much about King Roger, whose third son, Tancred, had been made prince of the city. When Roger, having subdued the rebels of Campania and Naples, crossed the Apennines, Manson rode to meet the army and offer his sword.

So might any footloose adventurer do. Manson, though, drew the royal notice by more than his size. He had much to tell, notably about the Eastern Empire. Half a century ago, Roger's uncle Robert Guiscard had come near taking Constantinople; barely did the Greeks and their Venetian allies turn that tide. The house of Hauteville, like others in western Europe, still cherished ambitions yonder.

But there were certain curious gaps in what Manson related; and he bore an underlying bleakness, as though some hidden sin or sorrow forever gnawed him—

"No matter," Roger decided. "Let's to our harvest. Will you ride with me?"

"By your leave, sire, I think I could better serve under your son the Duke of Apulia," said the wanderer.

"As you like. Dismissed." The king's attention went elsewhere.

Everard pushed through roaring swarms. Heedless of the papal ban, the host had said its prayers at dawn; now oaths ripped across commands, japes, yells in half a dozen languages. Standard-bearers waved their staffs to mark locations. Men-at-arms brawled their way into formation, pikes and axes bared aloft. Archers and slingers deferred to them; not yet was the bowman the master of infantry. Horses neighed, mail flashed, lances whipped on high like reeds in a storm. These were Normans, native Sicilians, Lombards and other Italians, Frenchmen, miscellaneous bullyboys from across half of Europe. In flowing white above their armor, silent but wildness aquiver in them, waited the dreaded Saracen corps.

Manson and his two attendants, hired in Bari, had set up camp in the open, until the king summoned him yesterday after returning from parley. In the city he had also purchased—or so everybody else believed—mounts, a pack horse, and a charger, the last a great barb that nickered, tossed head, stamped hoofs, ha, ha among the trumpets. "Quick, help me on with my outfit," he ordered.

"Do you really have to go, sir?" asked Jack Hall. "Damn risky, I reckon. Worse'n fightin' Injuns." He looked upward. Invisibly high, riders poised on their cycles and scanned the field through instruments that could count the drops of sweat on a man's face. "Can't they take out that hombre you're after—quiet-like, you know, with a stun beam from above?"

"Get cracking!" Everard snapped. "No, you idiot, we're steering too bloody close to the wind as is."

Hall reddened and Everard realized he had been unfair. You couldn't expect an instant grasp of crisis theory from an ordinary agent in place, hastily co-opted. This man was a cowboy till 1875, when the Patrol recruited him. Like the large majority of personnel, he worked in his own milieu, maintaining his original persona among the people who knew him. His secret self was a contact for such time travelers as came by, informant, guide, policeman, whatever they needed. If anything really untoward happened, he was to send for qualified help. It simply chanced that he'd been taking a vacation in the Pleistocene, hunting game and girls, when Everard had been, and that he was good with horses.

"Sorry," Everard said, "but I am in a hurry. Action starts in less than half an hour." Given the information he brought from Anagni, Patrolmen had "already" charted the fatally wrong course of the battle. Now he would seek to turn it back.

Jean-Louis Broussard got busy. Meanwhile he explained, "You see, my friend, what we do is dangerous enough. An open miracle, that men witnessed, that is not chronicled in either history, ours or this misbegotten one—it would be a new factor, warping events still worse." He was a more scholarly sort, born in the twenty-fourth century but operating in France of the tenth, not as an enforcer but as an observer. So much information perished when nobody at the time recorded it, or recorded it wrong, or when books moldered, burned, were mislaid. If the Patrol was to guard the time-stream, it must know what it guarded. As vital to it as its police agents were its field scientists.

Like Wanda. "Hurry, God damn it!" *Set her aside. Don't remember her, don't think about her, not now.*

Hall occupied himself with the stallion. "Well, but I'd say you're too valuable a guy to throw into that fracas, sir," he persisted. "Like puttin' Robert E. Lee in the front lines."

Everard made no reply, save inside his skull. *I demanded this. I pulled rank. Don't ask me why, because I couldn't quite tell you, but I've got to strike the blow myself.*

"We have our part, you and I," Broussard reminded Hall. "We are the reserves, here on the ground, if things go badly." He left unspoken the fact that in that case the causality vortex would probably have grown unredeemably great.

Everard had slept in his shirt and pants. Over them went a quilted coat, plus a similar coif and spurred boots replacing shoes. The coat of mail slid smoothly down from head and shoulders to hang to his knees, divided from the crotch so he could ride. Supple, it felt less heavy than you might have expected; the weight was well distributed. A noseguarded spangenhelm was secured above. A sword belt, dagger on the right, completed the ensemble, which a Patrol workshop had produced to his specs. He hadn't needed more than a little practice, for he'd long since made a point of acquiring as many combat techniques as possible.

He put foot in stirrup and mounted. Ideally a war-horse was raised to its master from colthood. This, though, was a Patrol animal, more intelligent than is natural among equines. Broussard reached him his shield. He slipped his left arm through its straps before taking the reins in that hand. Heraldry had not yet developed, but individuals sometimes used symbols, and in a fit of forlornness he had painted on his a fabulous bird—a turkey. Hall offered him his lance. It too handled easier than its length suggested. He gave the men a thumbs-up and trotted off.

Commotion was dwindling as squadrons formed. Borne by a squire, the banner of the younger Roger hung gaudy from a crossarm at the head of the army. He was to lead the first charge.

Everard drew nigh, reined in, and lifted his lance in a kind of salute. "Hail, my lord," he called. "The king bade me join you in the vanguard. My thought is that I might best ride on the outside at the left."

The duke nodded impatiently. Battle eagerness flamed in him, for his years numbered but nineteen though already he had won fame as a brilliant and gallant warrior. In the Patrol's history, his death on another field, eleven years hence, without legitimate issue, would in the long run prove evil for the kingdom, because he was the ablest son of Roger II. But in *this* history, today was doomsday for the lithe and lively boy.

"As you will, Manson," he said. With a laugh: "That should keep things quiet there!" Commanders of later military would have been appalled at such sloppiness, but so far nobody in western Europe was long on organization or doctrine. The Norman cavalry was the best you'd find this side of the Byzantine Empire or the two Caliphates.

As a matter of fact, it was the left flank that Lorenzo would hit. Everard cantered into position and studied his surroundings.

Beyond the road, the enemy had likewise marshalled. Iron glinted, color splashed a mass of horses and men. Rainulf's knights were fewer, about fifteen hundred, but close on their tails pressed foot that brought the numbers up to Roger's or a little more—townsmen and peasants of Apulia, pikes and bills a walking forest, come to defend their homes against this invader who had laid other lands waste.

Yeah, his own contemporaries think Roger's too hard on rebels. But he's only being like William the Conqueror, who tamed northern England by making a desert of it; and unlike William, when he's at peace he governs justly, tolerantly, you could almost say mercifully. . . . Never mind fancy excuses. Magnanimous or monstrous, what he did in my history was establish the Regno, the Kingdom of the Two Sicilies, and it outlived his dynasty and nation, in one form or another it lasted till the nineteenth century, when it became the core of the new Italian state, with everything that that was to mean to the world. I am at a pivotal point in time. . . . But I'm glad I didn't need to meet him before he'd crossed the mountains. I wouldn't have slept well after watching him at work in Campania.

As ever on the verge of combat, Everard lost dread. It wasn't that he didn't know fear; he merely grew too busy for it. Sight turned knife-edge keen, he heard each least sound through the racket as though it breathed alone at dead of night, every sense drew taut, but the slugging of his heart and the stench of his sweat faded from an awareness grown almost mathematical.

"We'll start in a minute," he said low. The medallion under his armor, against his chest, picked up the Temporal and transmitted it aloft. Leaving it on continuously would soon exhaust the energy cell, but this day's business wasn't going to take long, whichever way it went. "Do you have Lorenzo in your optical?"

"Two of us do," vibrated through a bone-transference module built into the crystal structure of his helmet.

"Keep locked onto him. I'll want to know exactly where he is as we approach each other. Somebody warn me about anybody else, of course."

"Of course. Good hunting, sir."

Unspoken: May it indeed be good. May we save Roger the elder and the younger, and recall to reality all our loves and loyalties.

Folks. Friends. Country. Career. Sure. But not Wanda.

Duke Roger drew sword. The blade flared aloft. "Haro!" he shouted, and put spurs to horse.

His followers raised a cry of their own. Hoofs drummed, then thundered, as trot went to canter went to gallop. Lances swayed to the rhythm. The distance narrowed and the shafts came down, horns of a single dragon.

Wanda's up in that future we mean to kill. She must be; she hasn't come back. I couldn't go search for her, none of us could, our duty's not to any single human being but to a universe of them. Maybe she died, maybe she got trapped, I'll never know. When yonder future doesn't exist, she won't either. Her bravery and laughter will only be in the twentieth century when she grew up and the far past when she worked, and . . . I mustn't go back to see her, ever again. From that last moment in the Ice Age, her world line will reach uptime and come to an end. It won't unravel into the tracks of single atoms, this isn't natural death and dissolution, it's nothingness.

Everard rammed the knowledge into the far back of his mind. He couldn't afford it. Later, later, when he was alone, he'd let himself grieve, and perhaps weep.

Dust clogged nostrils, stung eyes, blurred vision. He saw Rainulf's ranks ahead as a blur. Muscles surged, saddle rocked.

"Lorenzo is detaching twenty men on the right," said the flat voice in his helmet. "They circle around."

Yes. The knight from Anagni and those few trusty comrades would hit Roger's force on the left, punch through, cut down the duke, break up the assault as a hurled rock shatters glass. Dismay would fall on the Sicilians rearward. Regrouping, Lorenzo would take the lead in Rainulf's countercharge, which would bring down the king.

And no time traveler, no human blunder or madness or vaunting ambition brought this about. The fluctuation was in space-time-energy itself, a quantum leap, a senseless randomness. There was nobody on whom to avenge Wanda.

She's lost anyway. I have to believe that, if we're to retrieve everybody else.

"Beware, Agent Everard. Your size makes you conspicuous. . . . A knight has turned from Lorenzo's band. He seems to be targeting you."

Damn! While I deal with that pest—

I'll just have to deal with him fast.

"He is at ten-thirty o'clock from you."

Everard spied him, horse and lance. "Okay, Blackie, this way, let's get 'im," he growled to his mount. The animal answered his knees and plunged ahead. Everard glanced back, waved and shouted at Roger's riders, couched shaft and braced himself.

This wasn't a tilting field, where gentlemen in plate rode at each other with a barrier between and intended nothing more than knocking the opposition to the ground. Tournaments like that lay centuries futureward. Here the aim was to kill.

I haven't spent my lifetime practicing the art. But I've picked up enough, and I've got the weight and this superb creature under me— Here goes.

His horse veered ever so slightly. The point aimed for his throat shocked against his shield instead and glided off. Everard also missed a lethal strike but caught ringmail and gave the impact all that was in his shoulders. The Italian went over, lost his right stirrup, fell. Foot caught in the left, he bounced behind his steed.

The encounter had yanked at the attention of those Sicilians who rode near Everard. They saw the enemy detachment on its way. As one, they left the main force and followed the Patrolman. Hoofs crunched over the fallen warrior.

Everard dropped his lance and drew sword. In a mixup at close quarters, he could do things he dared not in the open. He kept going, on into the dust toward the foe.

"One o'clock," said the voice. He directed Blackie and after a moment made out Lorenzo's pennon.

He ought to know it. He'd eaten that man's salt, flown his falcons, chased his deer, he'd yarned and sung, laughed and gotten drunk, gone to church and gone to festival with Lorenzo, heard out his dreams, pretended to tell his own, day after day and night after night, a year in the future of this meeting. Lorenzo shed tears when they parted and called him brother.

The knights met.

Men hewed and battered, horses pushed and reared. Men yelled, horses screamed. Iron crashed and rattled. Blood welled and spouted. Bodies went to earth, threshed for a moment, got trampled to red mush and splinters of bone. The melee churned about in dust as thick as smoke. Everard crammed on through it. The watchers above warned him of danger on either side, in time for him to raise shield or parry with blade. Then he'd be past, deeper into the violence.

Lorenzo was before him. The young man had likewise abandoned his lance. He swept sword right and left. Blood drops whirled off the steel. "On, on!" he cried through the din. "St. George for Rainulf—for the Holy Father—"

He saw Everard loom out of clouds and chaos. He didn't know the giant, of course, he'd never met him, but he grinned gamely and urged his mount around to meet this challenger.

Sportsmanship be damned. Everard pointed his weapon and squeezed in a finger-by-finger sequence. Invisibly, a stun beam sprang. Lorenzo's jaw dropped. The sword left his grasp. He sagged forward.

Somehow he didn't fall from the saddle. He sprawled along the neck of his horse, which whinnied and skittered aside. Were the rider's reflexes so good as to keep him there, even unconscious? In that case, he'd soon wake up, none the worse. He'd guess somebody had dealt him a blow from behind, hard enough to knock him out through the mail and quilting on his neck.

Everard hoped so.

No time for sentiment. "C'mon, Blackie, let's get our ass out of here. Also the rest of us." The tongue that croaked it was dry as a block of wood.

The fight was breaking up anyhow. It had been a minor skirmish, unnoticed by most of Duke Roger's and Rainulf's troops. The Sicilians boomed onward, struck the enemy, scattered him, clove a path through the middle of his host.

Everard rode off across a field where corpses sprawled and gaped, wounded men moaned, mutilated horses thrashed and shrieked. Most likely no one paid him any particular heed. Glancing back, he saw how Duke Roger pursued hundreds down the road to Siponto. He also saw how Rainulf rallied and regrouped his army, while King Roger's stayed immobile.

Mostly that vision was in his mind's eye, from his knowledge of history—of how history was supposed to read. The actual sight was confusion, a mob scene, that ultimate absurdity which is war.

A little distance away rose a tree-grown hillock. Once behind it, he was hidden from view. "All right," he ordered through his medallion. "Come fetch me."

The sharpness still thrilled within him. While it lasted, he should go aloft and survey the battle as a whole, make sure that now events unrolled right.

A vehicle blinked into his presence, large enough for the horse as well as its crew. Quickly, they got the animal stalled inboard. Everard praised him, stroked the wet, dirt-streaked mane, patted the velvety nose. "He'd like a sugar cube better," said a short blond woman—she looked Finnish—and offered him one. She trembled in glee barely controlled. This day, she could believe, she had helped restore the world from which she came.

The vehicle flicked into heaven. Sky surrounded it. Earth was dun land and quicksilver sea, far below. Everard sought an optical. He sat down before it, adjusted magnification, studied what happened. Seen thus, the death and pain, anger and glory became unreal, a puppet show, a chronicler's paragraph.

Gifted in many ways, the Norman cloth of him dyed in Oriental subtleties, King Roger was nonetheless no tactical genius. He owed his victories mainly to crack troops, ruthless determination, and frequent disarray among his opponents. At Rignano he waited too long, he lost the advantage that his son's charge had gained him. When he did attack, his wave broke as if on a sea-cliff. Thereupon Rainulf threw his entire force against the Sicilians. The prince's return was of no avail. Panic seized them and they stampeded, each for himself. Rainulf's people hunted them down by ones and twos, without quarter. At day's end, three thousand lay dead on the field. The two Rogers gathered a few survivors, fought their way clear, and escaped into the mountains, back to Salerno.

But that was as it should be, as it had been in the Patrol's world. The triumph would not long endure. Roger would collect fresh forces and win back what he had lost. Rainulf was to die of a fever in April 1139. The mourning was great and futile. In July 1139, the two Rogers bushwhacked a papal army at Galuccio, whose noble leaders fled while thousands drowned trying to flee across the River Garigliano; and Pope Innocent became a prisoner of war.

Oh, King Roger was very respectful. He knelt before the Holy Father and pledged allegiance. In return he received absolution and approval of all his claims. Little remained thereafter but mopping-up operations. In the end, even Abbot Bernard hailed the king as a righteous lord and relations grew downright affectionate. Further storms were to come, Roger's conquests in Africa, the Second Crusade which he more or less sat out, his attempt on Constantinople, fresh conflicts with the Papacy and the Holy Roman Empire—but meanwhile he timbered strongly the Kingdom of the Two Sicilies, as he nurtured the growth of that hybrid civilization which presaged the Renaissance.

Everard slumped in his seat. Weariness rose to overwhelm him. Victory tasted like the dust still in his mouth. Only let him sleep, let him for a little time forget what he had lost.

"Looks okay," he said. "Proceed to base."

1989α A.D.

Beyond the Mississippi, the first signs of white occupation appeared. They were outposts, thinly strewn across wilderness, little more than wooden forts connected by roads that might better be called trails. Trading posts, Tamberly guessed. Or did they mainly support missionaries? No stockade failed to enclose a building with a tower or steeple, usually surmounted by a cross and often the largest. She didn't pause for closer observation. The radio silence hounded her onward.

East of the Alleghenies she found real colonies. They took the form of walled towns surrounded by plowland and pasture laid out in long strips. Villages dotted the hinterlands, rows of cottages very like each other. A few boasted a sort of plaza that was probably a marketplace, centered on a tall crucifix or a structure somewhat like a Breton calvary. All had a chapel, and every town was dominated by its main church. Never did Tamberly see a farmstead by itself. The scenes reminded her of what she'd read and heard about the Middle Ages. Swallowing tears and terror, she leapfrogged on over the miles.

Settlement thickened as she neared the seaboard. A small city occupied lower Manhattan. Its cathedral (?) dwarfed the St. Patrick's she remembered. The style was foreign to her, massive, many-tiered, brutally powerful. "Enough to scare off Billy Graham," she quavered at her mute communicator.

Several ships lay in the harbor, and she got a good look from on high, through her magnifying optical, at one that was standing out the Narrows. A broad-beamed, three-masted square-rigger, it resembled a merchantman of about 1600, according to pictures she had seen, though even to her landlubber's eye the differences of detail were countless. A flag of lilies on a blue field flew on the staff. At the mainmast top another, yellow and white, displayed crossed keys.

Blackness surged over her. She was well out to sea before she fought halfway clear of it.

Go ahead. Scream.

That steadied her more. The trick was not to let it go on and on, feeding hysteria, but to blow off emotion till you could think again. She loosened her painfully tight grip on the handlebars, worked her shoulder blades to free up those muscles, and was into reasoning about the situation before she noticed, with a harsh little laugh, that she'd forgotten to unclench her jaw.

The cycle flew itself ever farther. Ocean heaved immense, empty, a thousand shifting greens, grays, blues. Split air rumbled and whistled. Cold eddied past the force-screen and around her.

No doubt left. The terrible thing has happened. Something has changed the past, and the world I knew—my world, Manse's, Uncle Steve's, everybody's and everything's—is gone. The Time Patrol is gone. No, I'm thinking wrongly. They never were. I exist without parents, grandparents, country, history, without cause, a random thing tossed up by quantum chaos.

She couldn't grasp it. Though she put it into Temporal, which had a grammar made to deal with the paradoxes of time travel, the concept wouldn't come real to her in the way that something as abstract as evolutionary biology was nevertheless real, hand-graspable. This state of affairs set logic at naught and made reality a cloud-shadow.

Oh, sure, they explained the theory to us at the Academy, but as a sketch, like a freshman general science course required of an English major. My class of cadets wasn't being prepared for police work or anything like that. We'd be field scientists, off in prehistory, when humans were few and it was practically impossible to cause any changes that the course of events wouldn't soon compensate for. We'd go on our expeditions in the same straightforward way that Stanley went to explore darkest Africa.

What to do, what to do?

Leap back to the Pleistocene, I guess. It should be safely far downtime. Manse should be there still. (No, "still" is meaningless, isn't it?) He'll take charge. He's hinted at having already ("already") experienced something of this kind. Maybe now I can get him to tell me what it was. (Maybe I should tell him I know he's in love with me, the dear sweet bear. I've been too bashful, or afraid, or unsure of my own feelings. . . . God damn it, woman, will you stop this woolgathering?)

A pod of whale passed below. One spyhopped, a leap right out of the waves, water fountaining and tumbling from the mighty flanks, white under the sun.

Tamberly's blood quickened. "Yeah," she scoffed aloud, "run right off to the big strong man and let him kiss the universe and make it well for itsy-bitsy sweetums." Here she was. The least she could do was get a better idea of this world, bring back a report on it rather than a sob story. Just a few hours' scouting, nothing reckless. Manse had said more than once, "In our job there's no such thing as too much information." What she discovered might give him a clue to the source of the disaster.

"In short," said Tamberly, "we fight back." Resolution hardened; for a moment she imagined the Liberty Bell being cast, and herself ringing it. A minute longer she pondered, then set the space jump for London and touched its button.

The hour was late, local time, but this high latitude remained daylit. The city spread wide along both sides of the Thames, hazed by coal smoke. She guessed the population as about a million. The Tower was there, and Westminster Abbey might be the same though she wasn't sure, and the spires of other ancient churches soared above roofs; but a giant squatted on the hill of St. Paul's. The dreary sprawl of industry and suburbs was absent. Countryside pressed close around, glowing golden-green under the long light. She wished she were in a state to appreciate the beauty.

What next? Where to? Paris, I guess. She reset.

It was larger than yonder London, maybe twice as big. A spiderweb of paved roads radiated from it. Traffic upon them and the river went heavy, walkers, horsemen, carriages, wagons drawn by oxen or mules, barges, sailboats, oared galleys on whose decks cannon gleamed. Several turreted and battlemented stone forts, if that was what they were, reared among lesser buildings. More attractive were half a dozen palaces, not wholly unlike some she had seen in Venice. The Île de la Cité held one, but also a temple dwarfing its English counterpart. Tamberly's heart thudded. *Here's where more of the action is, much more. Let's cruise a bit.*

She flew in slow outward spirals, peering. Whoever glanced upward from those tangled lanes perhaps saw a speck of brightness in the deepening blue of the sunset sky. But she, she beheld no Arc de Triomphe, no Tuileries, no Bois de Boulogne, no cheery little sidewalk cafés. . . .

Versailles. Or thereabouts. A village clustered beside a highway, more variegated and less constricted than the peasant communities, evidently serving the city, and yes, a great dwelling two miles off amidst a parkscape of woods, lawns, and gardens. Tamberly moved in its direction.

The core of it was once a castle, she judged, a stronghold; and fieldpieces rested in the rear courtyard. Over centuries it had been remodeled and wings had been added, large-windowed, spacious and gracious, for modern habitation. However, sentries paced to and fro on every side. They wore scarlet uniforms striped with gold, beneath fancy helmets; but the rifles on their shoulders looked plenty businesslike. From a tall staff in front, a flag rippled on the evening breeze. She recognized the sign of the keys that she had noticed on the ship.

Somebody important lives here. . . . Hold on. From near the western horizon, rays streamed across grass where deer and peacocks strolled, and over a formal garden around which at intervals stood trellised rose bowers. *What's that blink from inside yonder one?*

Tamberly descended. If somebody noticed, what the devil could they do about it? *Well, careful; they've got those shootin' irons.* Fifty feet aloft, she could look slantwise into the arbors opposite. Set for optical amplification— Yes, in each, another soldier. *Why do they keep watch, from hidey-holes, on a garden?*

She space-jumped high, flitted to a position directly overhead, and turned her viewer downward. Vision sprang at her. She jerked back. "Can't be!"

No, it was, it was. "Stop that shivering," she rapped at herself, with scant effect. Alertness, though, grew doubly keen. Her mind sped in lightning chains of reason, guess, hope, horror.

The grounds near the palace were of the general kind she remembered from her Versailles, strictly patterned, with graveled walks among hedges, flower beds, pollarded trees, fountains, statuary. This was the smallest of the plots, about the size of a football field. It must formerly have been like the rest; the stonework was still there. But today the layout formed one big symbol, defined by colored tiles bordering its beds. It was a stylized hourglass on a heraldic shield. A circle surrounded it and a red line slashed across.

The emblem of the Time Patrol.

No. Not quite. That circle and line— Coincidence? Impossible. Here under my eyes is the signal I've strained my ears for.

Tamberly saw her hand positioned over the controls to push for descent. She pulled it back as if the bar had gone white-hot. *No! You whoop and swoop and—why do you think those guards are waiting?*

She shuddered. *What's a circled red stroke on top of a symbol mean? Why, in the twentieth century, at least, it means "Don't." Prohibited.* Verboten. *Danger. No parking. No smoking. No admittance. Get out. Stay out.*

Only I can't, can I? That's the Patrol *emblem.*

Shadow flowed across the world. A gilt weather vane on the palace flashed once and went dark. Also at Tamberly's altitude, the sun slipped from sight. Early stars trembled in dusk. The cold on high deepened. Wind had died and silence crowded inward.

Oh, Lordy, Lordy, I feel so alone. I'd better skite back to my nice Stone Age and report this. Manse can organize a rescue expedition.

She stiffened. "*Nyet,*" she said to the stars. Not till she'd used up all her options. If the world of the Patrol had been destroyed, then the remnants of the Patrol had more to do than bail out one marooned comrade. Or two. *Should I bust in bawling and distract them from their real duty? Or should I do whatever I can on my own?*

She swallowed hard. *I am . . . expendable, I guess.*

And if she did bring Manse a victory—

Blood heat thrust the night chill from her. She crouched in the saddle and thought.

A time traveler, who might or might not be a Patrol agent, had replanted that garden, or gotten it replanted. That could only be as a signal to any other who might come by. The person wouldn't have gone to the trouble if he or she were in possession of a vehicle; its communicator would serve so much better.

Therefore the person—*Let's dub him or her X, for the sake of originality, and use "heesh" for the pronoun*—was stranded. *Up the famous crick with no paddle. Damn it, stop these childish quips!* If X were otherwise a free agent, the insigne alone would be the thing to use, and in fact heesh could have added more: for instance, an arrow pointing to a repository for a written account. Therefore, probably the bar meant, "Danger. Don't land." Those gunmen indicated the same; likewise the estate itself, isolated and defensible. X was a prisoner here. Apparently a prisoner with some freedom, some influence over hiser keepers, since heesh had talked them into planting and bordering those flower beds. Nevertheless, heesh was closely guarded, and any new arrivals would be taken into custody, for whatever use the lord of the manor wanted to make of them.

Will they? We'll see about that.

Over and over, while the stars came forth, Tamberly counted her assets. They were pathetically few. She could fly, or she could spring instantaneously from one spot to another, into and out of the deepest dungeon or the strongest strongpoint—unless and until a bullet dropped her from the saddle—but she didn't know her way around or where X might be or anything. She could knock a man out at short range with a squeeze on her stun pistol, but meanwhile the rest of them might be everywhere around. Maybe her advent would scare them off in a superstitious frenzy, but she doubted that—all those preparations, as well as whatever the big cheese had learned from X—and it was too long a chance to take, a worse bet than a state lottery. How about doubling around in time, getting a disguise somewhere, spying things out? No, that meant leaving her cycle, with the risks that that entailed. And she had no idea of local customs, manners, life. While her Spanish was fluent, her French had long since fallen down in a cloud of rust, and besides, she doubted Spanish or French or English was much like what she'd ever heard before.

No wonder X left a warning. Maybe heesh was telling every Patrolman, "Sheer off. Forget me. Save yourself."

Tamberly pressed her lips together. *I repeat, we'll see about that.*

As if the sun had suddenly risen: *Yes! We'll see.*

The sun did rise, standing at noon one year earlier. Gardeners were at work around the message, raking, pruning, sweeping.

Ten years earlier, brightly clad men and darkly clad women promenaded among beds in a simple geometrical array.

Tamberly flung a laugh at the wind. "Okay, we've got you bracketed."

The skipping, blink-blink-blink, sun and rain, actions and configurations of people, dizzied her. She ought to go slower. No, she was too wired. Of course, she needn't check every month of every year. The emblem. The not-emblem. The emblem again. Okay, they tore out the old stuff in March 1984 and the new was doing well in June—

Toward the end, she proceeded day by day, and knew it would have to become hour by hour, at last minute by minute. Fatigue weighted bones and made eyeballs smolder. She withdrew, found a meadow on a forested Dordogne hillside where nobody else was near, ate and drank of her supplies, soaked up sunshine, finally slept.

Return to the job. She had grown quite steady, coolly watchful.

25 March 1984, 1337 hours. Gray weather, low clouds, wind

noisy across fields and in trees not yet leafed, slight spatters of rain. (Had the weather been the same this day in the destroyed world? Probably not. There, humans had cut down the vast American forests, plowed the plains, filled skies and rivers with chemicals. They also invented liberty, eradicated smallpox, sent spacecraft aloft.) Two men paced over the stripped and trenched garden. One was in a gold-and-scarlet robe, with something halfway between a crown and a miter on his head. The other, at his side, wore the coat and baggy pants Tamberly had seen elsewhere. He was the taller, lean and gray-haired. Behind them stepped six of the liveried soldiers, rifles at port.

For minutes Tamberly watched, till the knowledge crystallized in her: *Yes, they're discussing the exact plan of the new arrangement.*

Here goes. For broke.

She'd met danger before, sometimes purposely. Now was the same. Everything slowed down, the world became a dancing mosaic of details but she plucked forth those she needed, fear scuttled out of her way, she aimed herself and shot.

Cycle and rider appeared six feet before the pair. "Time Patrol!" Tamberly yelled, perhaps needlessly. "To me, quick!" She worked the stun pistol. The robed man crumpled. That gave her a clear field for the soldiers.

The lean man stood stupefied. "Hurry!" she cried. He lurched forward. A guard brought rifle down, aimed, fired. The *crack* went flat through the wind. The lean man staggered.

Tamberly left her vehicle. He fell into her arms. She dragged him back. A buzz passed her head. She lowered him across the front saddle, vaulted into the buddy seat, leaned over his body to the controls. *Now we skite after help*. A third bullet spanged and whined off the metal.

18,244 B.C.

Everard left his hopper in the garage and started for his room. Some who had been at Rignano were appearing too. Most had gone elsewhere, housing being limited at any single post. All would stand by till success had been confirmed. Those who were staying at the Pleistocene lodge made for the common room, exuberant and loud, to celebrate. Everard wasn't in that mood. He wanted merely a long hot shower, a long stiff drink, and sleep. A night's forgetfulness. Tomorrow and its memories would arrive bloody soon enough.

Shouts and laughter pursued him down the hall. He turned a corner, and there she was.

They both jarred to a halt. "I thought I heard—" she began. She sped toward him. "Manse, oh, Manse!"

The collision nearly bowled him over, in his condition. They caught hold of each other. Mouth sought mouth. It was a while before they came up for air.

"I thought you were gone," he groaned against her cheek. Her hair smelled like sunshine. "I thought you must have been trapped in the false world and you'd . . . go out . . . the light turned off . . . when it did."

"I'm sorry," she said as unevenly. "I didn't stop to think you'd worry. Figured, instead, you w-would need time to find out things, get organized, without us underfoot. So I jumped to a m-month after I'd left here. Been waiting two days, so scared about you."

"Like me about you." Understanding broke upon him. Still holding her by the waist, he stepped back a pace and looked into the blue eyes. Slowly, he asked, "What do you mean, 'us'?"

"Why, Keith Denison and me. He's told me you're friends. I hauled him clear and brought him— Manse, what's wrong?"

His hands fell to his sides. "Are you telling me you found yourself in an obviously altered future and *stayed?*"

"What was I supposed to do?"

"What they taught you at the Academy." His voice rose. "Couldn't you be bothered to remember? What every other agent and civilian traveler who arrived in the changed world had the elementary common sense to do, if conditions didn't prevent. Hop straight back to the departure point, keep your mouth shut till you could report it to the nearest Patrol brass, and follow whatever orders you were given. You fluffhead," he raged, "if you'd gotten stuck there, nobody would ever have come after you. That world doesn't exist any more. You wouldn't have! I assumed you'd had bad luck, not that you were an idiot."

Whitening, she clenched her fists. "I m-m-meant to bring you a report. Information. It might have helped you, mightn't it? And I, I did save Keith. Now you can go to hell."

The defiance collapsed. She shivered, sruggled against tears, and stammered, "No, I'm sorry, I guess it was a, a breach of discipline, but my training and experience didn't cover anything like this—" Stiffening: "No. No excuses. Sir, I did wrong."

His own wrath vanished. "Oh, God, Wanda. You're in the right. I shouldn't have barked at you. It's just I'd taken you for lost and—" He managed a smile. "No officer worth his salt farts around about regs when breaking them's led to success. You did save my old pal from becoming nothing? I'm going to put a commendation in your file, Specialist Tamberly, and suggest a raise in rank for you."

"I—I— Let's do something, Manse, before I bawl. Want to see Keith? He's in bed. Took a wound, but it's mending."

"Suppose I get cleaned up first," he said, as anxious as she to find firmer ground. "After that, you tell me what happened."

"And you tell me, okay?" She cocked her head. "You know, we needn't wait. We can talk while you— Manse, I believe you're blushing."

Exhaustion had steamed out of him. Temptation whistled. *No*, he decided. *Better not push my luck. And Keith'd be hurt if I didn't visit him right away*. "If you want, sure."

From people on hand, she had gotten an idea of the situation. Reveling under the water, he shouted through its rush and the open bathroom door that Operation Rignano had apparently gone well. "Details later."

"I'll hold you to that," she called back. "Boy, have we got gossip to swap."

"Starting with your escapades, young lady." While he toweled himself, he listened to her account. His skin prickled at the knowledge of what might easily have resulted.

"Keith was shot before I could snap us out of there," Tamberly finished. "I went randomly, then set for here and now—two days ago, that is—and jumped again. The medic took charge of him immediately. Slug through the left lung. Patrol surgery and healing techniques are quite something, aren't they? He's supposed to stay mostly in bed for another week, but right away he got ornery. Maybe you'll calm him down."

"I'd certainly like to compare notes. You said he was four years in that world?"

"More like nine, originally. He emerged in 1980, I in '89. But I pulled him out in '84, so the rest of those years never happened to him and he has no recollection of them or anything."

He donned the fresh clothes he'd taken into the bathroom. "Tsk-tsk. A time alteration. Violating the Prime Directive."

"Foof! In that universe, who cares?"

"Good question. To be frank, and don't spread this around, the Patrol does occasionally make, uh, adjustments. Keith and I were involved in one such case. Someday I'll be free to give you the story." *The pain in it has left me. She doesn't leave room for that kind of regrets.*

Everard emerged to find Tamberly cross-legged in his armchair, a small neat Scotch from his bottle for company. "You didn't have to spare my modesty," she remarked.

He grinned. "Impudent wench. Give me a shot of the same, and let's go say hello to Keith."

The man lay in his room, propped against the headboard, plucking at the pages of a book. His visage was pale and drawn. It kindled when the pair entered. "Manse!" he exclaimed huskily. "My God, it's great to see you. I've been worried sick."

"About Cynthia, sure," Everard said.

"Of course, but also—"

"I know. Felt the same way. Well, we can turn our fears out to pasture. The mission went like a hush puppy down a hound dog." *Not really. It was misery, danger, the death and maiming of brave men. But in this glow of mine, everything is wonderful.*

"I heard a racket, and wondered— Thanks, Manse, thanks."

Everard and Tamberly took chairs on opposite sides of the bed. "Thank Wanda," Everard said.

Denison nodded. "Who more? She even lopped five years off my sentence, d'you know? Five years I can very well do without. The four were bad enough."

"Were you mistreated?"

"Well, not exactly." Denison described his capture.

"You have a knack for getting caught, don't you?" Everard teased.

He wished he hadn't when Denison's face went bleak and the man whispered, "Yes. Has it been entirely coincidence? I'm no physicist, but I have read and heard something about quantum probability fields, temporal nexuses."

"Don't fret over it," Everard said hastily. *Don't worry whether chance has made you a gun loaded with trouble, always cocked on a hair trigger. I'm not well up on the theory of that myself.* "You came through both affairs smelling like a rose, which is more than I did. Ask Wanda; she met me before I'd showered. Go on."

Encouraged, Denison smiled and obeyed. "The archcardinal was decent in his fashion, though his position didn't give him a lot of scope in that regard. Besides being a prince of the Church, he was a top-drawer nobleman of France, which included the British Isles. He had to order both the burning of heretics and the massacre of peasants who got above themselves. Not that he minded, he considered it his duty, but he didn't enjoy it either, like some characters I met. Anyway. The clerical title was more important than the secular one. Kings were—are—puppets in that Europe, or junior partners at best.

"Albin, the archcardinal, was an intelligent and educated chap. It took me a long while and a lot of sweat to convince him my visitor-from-Mars story *might* be true. He'd ask me the damnedest sharp questions. But, well, I had appeared from nowhere. I told him my chariot flew too fast to see, like a bullet. That was all right, because they didn't know about sonic booms and stuff. They had telescopes and understood the planets are separate globes. Geocentric astronomy was still doctrine, though it was permissible to assume a heliocentric universe as a mathematical fiction, to help calculations. . . . Never mind. Later. There's so much, so many strangenesses I met, even sequestered as I was.

"You see, not only didn't Albin trust me, he wanted to squirrel me away from the zealous Inquisition types, who'd have interrogated me till any more torture would be fatal and then burned alive what was left. Albin realized that with patience he could learn a great deal more, and he didn't share the common terror about sorcery. Yes, he accepted that magic worked, but looked on it as essentially another set of technologies, with its own limitations. So he put me on an estate of his outside Paris. It wasn't too bad, except for—well, you can guess. I had comfortable quarters, good food, leave to walk around the palace and grounds though always under guard. Yes, and access to his library. He owned a lot of books. Printing had been invented. A monopoly of Church and state, death penalty for unlicensed possession of a press, but books were available to the upper classes. They saved my sanity.

"The archcardinal visited whenever he got a chance. We'd talk the sun down and back up again. He was a fascinating conversationalist. I did my best to keep him interested. Gradually I persuaded him to put a sign outside, in the form of a garden plot. I said an ethereal wind had crashed my chariot and swept it away. However, my friends on Mars would search for me. If one of them happened by, he'd see the symbol and land. Albin meant to bag that fellow and his vehicle. I can't really blame him. He didn't intend any harm, if the prisoner cooperated. Martian knowledge or maybe a Martian alliance would mean plenty. Western Europe was in a bad way."

Denison stopped. His voice had gone raspy. "Don't overdo," Everard said. "We can finish tomorrow."

Denison's lips bent upward. "Now that'd be cruelty to dumb animals. You're more curious than the Elephant's Child. Wanda too. I wasn't up to saying much till today. Your news is a tonic, man. If I could just have a glass of water?"

Tamberly went to fetch it. "I gather she read your intention correctly," Everard said. "Your idea was to declare that a Patrolman was present, but whoever came along should be ultra-cautious, and not take risks on your account." Denison nodded. "Well, we can both be glad she did, and not only sprang you free, but canceled those extra five years. I daresay they ground you pretty far down, or would have."

Tamberly brought the water. Denison took it, his hands lingering noticeably over hers. "You're recovering fast," she laughed. He chuckled and drank.

"Wanda remarked you told her you studied a lot of history," Everard said. "Anybody would, I suppose. Especially in hopes of finding where and when it went wrong. Did you?"

Denison shook his head on the pillows. "Not really. The medieval era isn't my field. I know it as well as an average educated person should, but no better. The most I could deduce was that sometime during the later Middle Ages, the Catholic Church came decisively out on top in its rivalry with the kings, the state. Yesterday I did get some explanation about Roger of Sicily, and remembered that a couple of books mentioned him as a particular villain. Maybe you can fill me in on the initial course of might-have-been."

"I'll try. Meanwhile you rest." Everard was mainly aware of Tamberly's gaze upon him. "In the continuum we aborted, Roger and his oldest, ablest son died in battle at Rignano, 1137. The prince who succeeded couldn't cope. Roger's enemy, Pope Innocent's ally, Rainulf took all their mainland possessions away from the Sicilians. Soon they also lost such African conquests as they'd made. Meanwhile anti-Pope Anacletus died and Innocent reigned with a strong hand. When Rainulf died too, the Papacy became the real power in southern Italy as well as in its own states. This encouraged the election of a series of aggressive Popes. Piecemeal they acquired the rest of Italy and, along the way, Sicily.

"Otherwise, for a spell, history proceeded roughly as before. Frederick Barbarossa restored order in the Holy Roman Empire but didn't come off so well in his quarrels with the Curia. However, in the absence of papal schisms and the presence of papal states growing constantly stronger, imperial ambitions southward were checked. They turned west instead.

"Meanwhile, same as in our world, the Fourth Crusade dropped its original objective. It captured and sacked Constantinople, and installed a Latin king. The Orthodox Church was forcibly united with the Catholic.

"The Far East was little affected as yet, the Americas and the Pacific not at all. I don't know what happened next. This—roughly 1250—was as far as we investigated, and that only sketchily. Too much else to do, too few people for the job."

"And you itch for the rest of the story, both of you," Denison said, more vigorously than before. "Okay, I'll give you a synopsis. No more. In due course I may write a book or two."

"We need that," Tamberly replied soberly. "We'll learn things about ourselves we never would otherwise."

She does have her serious side, and a damn good mind to back it up, Everard thought. *Still young. But am I really old?*

Denison cleared his throat. "Here goes. Barbarossa didn't conquer France, but he gave it enough trouble that its unification process was halted, and in the course of the Plantagenet-Capetian Wars—they must correspond roughly to our Hundred Years' War—the English prevailed, till there was an Anglo-French state. In its shadow, Spain and Portugal never amounted to a lot. And early on, the Holy Roman Empire fell apart in a welter of civil wars."

Everard nodded. "I'd've expected that," he said. "Frederick II was never born."

"Hm?"

"Barbarossa's grandson. Remarkable character. Pulled his ramshackle Empire back together and gave the Popes a hell of a time. But his mother was a posthumous daughter of Roger II, who in our history died in 1154."

"I see. That explains quite a bit. . . . In yonder world, the Welf faction, pro-papal, generally got the upper hand, so Germany became more and more another set of papal states, in fact if not in name. Meanwhile the Mongols penetrated far into Europe, I think farther than in our world, because their internal wars left the Germans in no shape to send help against them. When they withdrew, eastern Europe was a wreck, and German colonists gradually took it over. The Italians got control of the Balkans. The French tail wagged the English dog till there wasn't much to show except a funny pronunciation—"

Denison sighed. "No matter details. As almighty as the Catholic Church became, it suppressed all dissent. The Renaissance never happened, the Reformation, the scientific revolution. As the secular states decayed, they fell more and more under the sway of the Church. That began when the Italian city-states started picking clergymen to head their republics. There was a period of religious wars, schismatic more than doctrinal, but Rome prevailed. In the end, the Pope was supreme over all kings in Europe. A sort of Christian Caliphate.

"They were technologically backward by our standards, but did reach America in the eighteenth century. Their spread over there was very slow. The old countries didn't have the kind of society that would support explorers or entrepreneurs on an adequate scale, and they kept their colonists on a tight leash. Also, in the nineteenth century the whole system began breaking down, rebellions and wars and depressions and general misery. When I arrived, the Mexicans and Peruvians were holding out against conquest, though their leaders were half white and half Christian. Muslim adventurers were intervening. You see, Islam was enjoying a rebirth of energy and enterprise. So was Russia. After they got rid of the Mongols, the Tsars looked more west than east, because weakened Europe was such a tempting prize.

"At the time Wanda rescued me, the Russians were close to the Rhine and the Turk-Arab alliance was pushing into the eastern Alps. Men like Archcardinal Albin tried to play one off against another. I guess they had some success for a while, because she found my garden intact in 1989, but I doubt it lasted long beyond that. I'd say the Muslims and Russians overran Europe and afterward went for each other's throats."

Denison sank back, finally exhausted.

"Looks like we've restored what was better," Everard said awkwardly.

Tamberly stared into a corner. Listening, she had grown sober, even somber. "But we've done away with billions of human beings, haven't we?" she murmured. "And their songs and jokes, loves and dreams."

Anger touched Everard. "Together with their serfdoms, diseases, ignorances, and superstitions," he snapped. "That world never got the idea of science, checking logic against fact. Obviously not. So it went on and on in its wretchedness, till— Except it didn't. We prevented. I refuse to feel guilty. We made *our* people real again."

"Oh, yes, oh, yes," Tamberly breathed. "I didn't—"

The hall door opened. They looked about. A woman stood there, seven feet tall, gaunt, long-limbed, golden-skinned, eagle-faced. "Komozino!" Everard cried. He scrambled to his feet. "Unattached agent," he told his friends, toppling or climbing from homely English to precise Temporal.

"Like you," she said. Her stiff courtesy shattered. "Agent Everard, I have been searching for you. We have reports from our scouts uptime. The mission has failed."

He stood numbed.

"True, King Roger continues his days," Komozino went on unmercifully. "He secures the Regno, extends his holdings in Africa, draws to his court some of the greatest intellects of the age, dies in bed 1154, is succeeded by his son William, yes, everything as it should be. But we still have no contact with the farther future. There is still no Patrol post established later than about the mid-twelfth century. A quick reconnaissance uptime found a world still alien to everything we knew. What now has chaos done?"

1989β A.D.

Three timecycles hung at eagle height over the Golden Gate. Morning fog whitened the coast, the great bay shone, earth rolled inland, summer-tawny. Beside the strait, rock masses traced where walls, towers, strongholds had been. Brush grew about them. It had almost wholly reclaimed the crumbled adobe of lesser buildings. A village occupied the site of Sausalito and a few fishing smacks were out on the water.

Tamberly's radio voice came thin beneath the whittering wind: "My guess is that the city never recovered from the 1906 quake. Maybe enemies took advantage of the broken defenses and sacked what was left. And nobody since has had the means or the heart to restore it. Shall we go downtime and see?"

Everard shook his head. "No point in that, and we've no right to take extra risks. Where should we next look?"

"The Central Valley ought to give us clues. In our twentieth century it was one of the world's richest agricultural areas." He heard the slight quaver, like a shivering in the cold.

"Okay. Pick the coordinates," he said.

She did. He and Karel Novak repeated them aloud before they made the jump. Everard saw light flash off the automatic rifle the Czech kept ready in his grasp. *Well, his life, the life of all his forefathers, made wariness a reflex. We Americans were luckier, in the world where there was a United States of America.*

Already Everard felt sure that, given reasonable caution, his scouting party would meet no danger. Even before they left, he'd expected as much. Else he might have refused Tamberly's suggestion that she be the guide, overridden her insistence, and skipped ahead to Denison's full recovery, despite the difficulties that would create.

Or would he have? The sensible thing in any case probably was to suppress his protective instincts and bring her. The idea was to compare this future with the future now averted. Denison had come to know the latter in depth, but vicariously. Tamberly had had an overview, which was all Everard wanted anyway. *And Lord knows the girl has proved she can cope.*

Small strung-out farms huddled along the rivers and what remained of a rather primitive canal network. Mostly, middle California had gone back to arid wilderness. Mud-walled fortresses stood guard at intervals. Afar, through his optical, Everard spied what seemed to be a band of wild horsemen.

Huge holdings occupied the Midwest. Many lay plundered and desolate, survivors or invaders eking out a squalid existence in sod huts on thinly worked fields. Others endured, ranching or raising a diversity of crops. At the middle of each clustered several large buildings, usually stockaded. Cities, which had never been of much size, were shrunk to towns or hamlets amidst abandoned ruins.

"Manorial economy," Everard muttered. "Produce nearly everything you use at home, because damn little trade goes on any more."

Fragments of a higher civilization clung in the East, though here too cities were dwindled and run-down, often laid waste. Everard noticed the gridiron pattern of nearly all streets and the formidable stone structures at every center. What prosperity anybody still enjoyed was evidently founded on slave labor; he saw coffles driven along the roads and field gangs toiling under armed supervision. He thought they included whites as well as blacks, though sunburn, grime, and distance made it hard to tell. He didn't care for a closer view.

Cannon boomed in the Hudson Valley, cavalry charged, men hewed and perished. "I believe an empire has died, and these are its ghosts at war with each other," Novak said.

Surprised, for he'd come to think of the man as dour and down-to-earth, Everard replied, "Yeah. A dark age. Well, let's try the seaboard, and maybe mid-ocean, before Europe."

It made sense thus to retrace Tamberly's course, more or less. Europe must hold the wellspring of this time distortion, as it did of the last. Approach it from the periphery, always ready to skip out at the first sign of menace. Everard's glance never quite left the array of detectors whose readings glimmered between his hands.

Did transatlantic commerce exist yet? Ships were few, but he saw two or three that were obviously capable of ocean crossings. In fact, they looked somewhat more advanced than those Tamberly had described, perhaps roughly equivalent to the Patrol world's eighteenth century. However, like lesser craft, they were only sailing, well gunned, along the coasts; he found none on deep water.

London was a big version of the slums in the New World. Paris resembled it, astonishingly so. A leveling influence had been at work everywhere, to produce the same right-angle intersections and grim central complexes. Various medieval churches abided, but in poor shape; Notre Dame de Paris was half demolished. More recent ones were small, of humble design.

The smoke and thunder of another battle drifted from those grounds on which Versailles had never stood.

"London and Paris were a lot bigger in the other history." Tamberly sounded quite subdued.

"I guess the power in this one, that's now collapsed, lay farther south or east," Everard sighed.

"Shall we go see?"

"No. No reason to, and we've plenty else ahead of us. We've confirmed what I suspected, which was the main purpose of this junket."

Interest livened Tamberly's tone. "What's that?"

"You didn't know? Sorry, I forgot to explain. It seemed obvious to me. But your field is natural history." Everard drew breath. "Before we try again to correct matters, we have to make certain that this, too, hasn't been due to any time travelers, whether by accident or on purpose. Our operatives pastward are working on that, of course, but I figured we could quickly pick up an important piece of the evidence by reconnoitering far uptime. If someone in the twelfth century did have some scheme, today the world would doubtless look very strange. Instead, what we've seen indicates a, uh, a hegemony over Western civilization, an empire that never had any Renaissance or scientific revolution either, and at last fell apart. So I think we can assume no conscious agency acted; and a blunder is extremely unlikely. Once again, what we're up against is quantum chaos, randomness, events gone wild of their own accord."

Novak spoke uneasily: "Sir, does that not make our task still more difficult and dangerous?"

Everard's mouth tightened. "It sure does."

"What can we do?" Tamberly asked low.

"Well," Everard said, "by 'randomness' I don't mean that things have taken this direction without any cause. In human terms, people have done whatever they did for their own reasons. It just happens that what they did was different from what they did in our history. We've got to find that turning point—or fulcrum point—and see if we can't swing the lever back the way we want it to act. Okay, let's return to base."

Tamberly interrupted before he could read off destination coordinates. "What'll we do then?"

"I'll see what the investigators have found out, and on that basis try a little further detective work. You, well, probably you'd best proceed to your naturalist station."

"Huh?"

"Oh, you've done fine, but—"

Indignation flared. "But you mean that now I should sit twiddling my thumbs when I'm not chewing the nails off them. Well, you pull that self-satisfaction out of your ears, Manson Everard, and listen to me."

He did. Never mind if Novak was disconcerted. She had a point or two to make, and they were valid. What knowledge she needed could readily be instilled. The more basic knowledge, of how to deal with people and danger, could not be; but she already had it, in her experience and her genes. Besides, the Patrol's orphans needed every able campaigner they could find.

1137 A.D.

In his private chamber the silk merchant Geoffrey of Jovigny received two visitors. They were a huge man, well clad, and a tall, fair-haired young woman who, though decently quiet in public, looked about her with a boldness well-nigh brazen. The apprentices were astounded when they learned she would sleep with the children.

Otherwise these callers drew less heed than they would ordinarily have done, for Palermo seethed with tidings. Each newcomer brought a new story. At the end of October King Roger met disaster at Rignano and barely, by aid of the saints, escaped the battlefield. At once he rebounded, laid fresh siege to Naples, won back Benevento and Monte Cassino, forced his enemy Abbot Wibald out of Italy, and got a clerical friend elected to head the great abbey. Now only Apulia held out against him, and it seemed he might actually become arbitrator between the rival Popes. Sicily rejoiced.

In the paneled room upstairs, Everard, Tamberly, and Volstrup sat as bleak as the December day outside. "We've come to you," the Unattached agent said, "because what the databases know about you suggests you're the best man available for a certain mission."

Volstrup blinked above his winecup. "I? Sir, with respect, jokes are inappropriate when we have gone immediately from one crisis to a second, equally desperate one." He alone in the city had experienced Everard's previous visit; in the course of that salvage operation he had twice been brought downtime for consultation.

Everard grinned on the left side of his mouth. "No derring-do required, I hope. What I have in mind involves some travel under medieval conditions, but mainly we need a person quick-witted, tactful, and intimately acquainted with this milieu. Before explaining, though—because it may turn out my scheme is impractical—I want to pick your brains, ask a lot of questions, invite your ideas. You have done very well by the Patrol over the years, handling affairs day by day and laying the groundwork for the expansion of this post."—when Sicily entered its golden age and drew many time travelers—out of a future that had again ceased to be. "You did better yet during the last crunch."

"Thank you. Er, Mademoiselle . . . Tamberly?"

"I think I'll mostly sit and listen," the woman said. "I'm still trying to sort out the encyclopedia that's been pumped into me."

"We really have only a handful of people who know the period well," Everard continued. "I mean this part of the Mediterranean world at just this time. Agents in China or Persia or even England don't do us a lot of good, and they have their work cut out for them already, maintaining their stations under present conditions. Of our knowledgeable personnel, some are not qualified to conduct investigations in the field, where anything can happen. For instance, a man could be a fine, reliable traffic control officer but lack the, um, touch of Sherlock Holmes necessary." Volstrup smiled the least bit, showing he caught the reference. "We have to take anyone we think may be suitable, whether formally rated for that kind of task or not. But first, as I said, I'd like to inquire of you."

"By all means," Volstrup replied, barely audible. In the gloom his nutcracker face showed pale. Outside, wind whooped and a dash of rain blew from wolf-gray heaven.

"When word went around about our failure, you got busy on your own initiative, communicating with other agents and making mnemonic arrangements for yourself," Everard stated. "That gives reason to ask much more of you. I take it your aim was to assemble a detailed picture of events, hoping that might help to locate the new trouble point."

Volstrup nodded. "Yes, sir. Not that I deluded myself I could solve the problem. Nor, I confess, was my motive really unselfish. I craved . . . orientation." They saw him shudder beneath his robe. "This, this uprooting of reality, it leaves us so cold and alone."

"It does that," Tamberly whispered.

"Well, you were a medievalist to start with, before the Patrol recruited you," Everard said. He kept his voice and manner methodical, downright stodgy. Nerves were strained thin enough as was. "You must have gotten the original history well into your head."

"Rather well," Volstrup answered. "But although countless snippets of fact had passed before my eyes, most had long since dropped from memory. What reason would there ordinarily be to stay aware that, oh, the battle of Rignano took place on the thirtieth of October 1137 or that the baptismal name of Pope Innocent III was Lotario de

Conti di Segni? Yet any such tiny datum might prove crucial to us, when the databases we have left are limited. I requested a psychotechnician be sent here to give me total recollection." He grimaced; neither the process nor the result were pleasant. It took a while afterward to return to normal. "And I compared notes with various colleagues, exchanging information and ideas. That is all. I was preparing a full report when you arrived."

"We'll take it from you in person," Everard said. "We haven't got lifespans to squander. What you've passed on indicates you've found a better clue than anybody else, but it isn't clear what. Tell me."

Volstrup's hand trembled a little as he sipped from his cup. "It is surely clear to everyone," he replied. "Pope Honorius III was succeeded directly by Celestine IV."

Everard nodded. "That's the big, blatant thing. But I gather you have a notion as to what may have brought it about."

Tamberly stirred on her stool. "Excuse me," she said. "I am still groping around in a jungle of names and dates. If I stop to think, I can put them in order, but what they signify isn't necessarily plain. Would you mind briefing me?"

Everard reached to squeeze her hand—maybe that encouraged him more than her—and himself took a throat-warming drink. "You can do it better," he said to Volstrup.

As he talked, the dry little man gained confidence, vigor. This history was his love, after all.

"Let me begin at the present moment. Events seem to proceed much as they ought, perhaps identically, for decades to come. The Holy Roman Emperor Henry VI acquires Sicily through marriage, the claim being enforced by his army, in 1194. That same year his son and heir Frederick II is born. Innocent III becomes Pope in 1198. He is one of the strongest men ever to sit on the throne of St. Peter—and in many respects, although it isn't entirely his fault, one of the most sinister. It will be written of him that his was the distinction of presiding over the destruction of three distinct civilizations. In his reign, the Fourth Crusade captures Constantinople; and although the Eastern Empire eventually gets back a Greek ruler of Orthodox faith, it is thereafter a shell. He proclaims the Albigensian Crusade, which will put an end to the brilliant culture that has arisen in Provence. His long contest with Frederick II, Church against state, fatally undermines this diverse, tolerant Norman Sicilian society in which we sit talking today.

"He dies in 1216. Honorius III follows, also an energetic and determined man. He prosecutes the war on the Albigenses and plays a role in much politics elsewhere, but does seem to reach a settlement with Frederick. However, that agreement is breaking down when Honorius dies in 1227.

"Gregory IX should have succeeded him, reigning till 1241. Celestine IV should then be elected but die the same year, before he can be consecrated. Innocent IV should thereupon become the next Pope, who carries on the struggle against Frederick.

"Instead, we have no Gregory. Celestine follows Honorius directly. He is weak, leadership falters among the anti-Imperialists, and at last Frederick triumphs. The following Pope is his puppet."

Volstrup moistened his gullet again. The wind sobbed.

"I see," Tamberly murmured. "Yes, that gives me a little perspective on what I've learned. So Pope Gregory is the missing element?"

"Evidently," Everard said. "He didn't finish the feud with Frederick, in our history; but he waged it for fourteen years, never letting up, and that made the difference. A hard old son of a bitch. He founded the Inquisition."

"Regularized it, at least," Volstrup added in his professorish fashion. Habit took over; he likewise fell into the past tense. "The thirteenth century was the century in which medieval society lost its earlier measures of freedom, tolerance, and social mobility. Heretics were burned, Jews were herded into ghettos when they were not massacred or expelled, peasants who dared to claim some rights suffered a similar fate. And yet . . . that is our history."

"Which led to the Renaissance," Everard interjected brusquely. "I doubt we'd prefer the world that's now ahead of us. But you—you've tracked down what's happened—what will happen—to Pope Gregory?"

"I have only some hints and some thoughts," Volstrup demurred.

"Well, spit 'em out!"

Volstrup looked toward Tamberly. *She's a lot more ornamental than I am,* Everard reflected. As much to her as to the man, Volstrup said:

"The chronicles tell us little about his origins. They describe him as already old when he assumed the tiara, and living on to a great age, active until the end. But they give no birth date. Later authorities made estimates differing by some twenty-five years. Hitherto, with all else it had to do, the Patrol saw no reason to ascertain the facts. It probably never occurred to anyone—myself included, of course.

"We have known merely that he was christened Ugolino Conti de Segni and was a nobleman in the city of Anagni, probably a kinsman of Innocent III."

Conti! speared through Everard. *Anagni!*

"What is it, Manse?" asked Tamberly.

"A notion," the Patrolman mumbled. "Go on, please."

Volstrup shrugged. "Well," he said, "my idea was that we might begin by finding his origins, and for that purpose I instituted inquiries. Nobody could identify any such birth. Therefore, in this world, it most likely never took place. I did turn up a fact, buried in an incidental memory of something that one of our agents happened once to have heard. This agent is to be active during Gregory's reign. He chanced to be taking a holiday in the farther past and—At any rate, with the help of mnemotechnics, he retrieved the year of Gregory's birth, and the parentage. It was as far downtime as certain historians later assigned it, in 1147 in Anagni. Therefore this Pope lived well into his nineties. His father's name was Bartolommeo and his mother was Ilaria, of the Gaetano family." He paused. "That is what I have to offer. I fear you have come to me for very little gain."

Everard stared before him, into shadows. Rain hissed down the walls. Chill sneaked beneath clothing. "No," he breathed, "you may have hit on the exact thing we need."

He shook himself. "We have to learn more. Just what went on. That needs an operative or two who can work themselves into the scene. I expected this, and thought of you, though I didn't know till now exactly where and when we'd want to send our scouts. They should be able to carry it off without getting into trouble. They should. I think"—*I'm afraid, Wanda*—"the pair of you are the logical choice."

"I beg your pardon?" choked Volstrup.

Tamberly sprang to her feet. "Manse, you mean it, you really do!" she jubilated.

He rose also, heavily. "I figure two will have a better chance of learning something than one, especially if they go at it from both the male and the female sides."

"But what about you?"

"With luck, you'll find us some necessary evidence, but it won't be sufficient. A negative can't be. Gregory was never born, or he died young, or whatever it was. That's for you to discover. To understand what came of that—whether it was the unique factor—I aim to work uptime of you, when Frederick's breaking the Church to his will."

1146 A.D.

To Anagni came a hired courier from Rome early in September. He bore a letter for Cencio de Conti or, if the gentleman be deceased or absent, whoever now headed that noble house in those parts. Albeit age was telling somewhat upon him, Cencio was there for a cleric to read the message aloud. He followed the Latin readily enough. It was not so very remote from his native dialect; and, besides religious services, men of his family rather frequently listened to recitals of the warlike or lyrical classics.

A Flemish gentleman and his lady, homebound from pilgrimage to the Holy Land, sent respects. They were kinfolk. True, the relationship was distant. Some fifty years ago a knight visiting Rome had become acquainted, asked for the hand of a daughter of the Conti, wedded her and taken her home to Flanders. (The profit was small but mutual. She was a younger child who might well otherwise have gone into a convent, thus her dowry need not be large. On either side there was some prestige in having a connection across a great distance, and there might prove to be some advantage, now when politics and commerce were beginning to move in earnest across Europe. The story went that it had, moreover, been a love match.) Little if any word had since crossed the Alps in either direction.

Chancing to get this opportunity, the travelers felt it behooved them to offer to bring what scanty news they could. They prayed pardon in advance for their unimpressiveness, should they be invited. All their attendants had been lost along the way, to disease, affray, and at last desertion; belike tales of libertine Sicily had lured that rogue from them. Perhaps the Conti could, of their kindness, help them engage reliable servants for the rest of the journey.

Cencio dictated an immediate reply—in vernacular, which the priest Latinized. The strangers would be welcome indeed. They must for their part forgive a certain uproar. His son, Sir Lorenzo, was soon to marry Ilaria di Gaetani, and preparations for the festivities were especially chaotic in these difficult times. Nevertheless he urged them to come at once and remain for the wedding. He dispatched the letter with several lackeys and two men-at-arms, in order that his guests might fare in such style as would shame neither them nor him.

It was quite a natural thing for him to do. About his Flemish cousins, or whatever they were, his curiosity was, at best, idle. However, these persons had just been in the Holy Land. They should have much to tell of the troubles there. Lorenzo, especially, was eager to hear. He would be going on crusade.

And so, a few days later, the strangers appeared at the great house.

Ushered into a brightly frescoed room, Wanda Tamberly forgot surroundings whose foreignness had amazed and bewildered her. Suddenly everything focused on a single face. It did not belong to the elderly man but to the one beside him. *I'd pay attention to looks like that anytime in the universe*, flashed through her—Apollo lineaments, dark-amber eyes—*and this is hung on Lorenzo. Got to be Lorenzo, who'd have changed history nine years ago at Rignano if Manse hadn't— Hey, quite a bod, too.*

Dazedly she heard the majordomo intone: "Signor Cencio, may I present Signor Emilius"—a stumble over the Germanic pronunciations—"van Waterloo?"

Volstrup bowed. The host courteously did likewise. He wasn't really ancient, Tamberly decided. Maybe sixty. The loss of most teeth aged his appearance more than did white hair and beard. The younger man still had a full set of choppers, and his locks and well-trimmed whiskers were crow's-wing black. He'd be in his mid-thirties. "Welcome, sir," Cencio said. "Let me introduce my son Lorenzo, of whom my letter spoke. He has been ardent to meet you."

"When I saw the party coming, I hastened to join my father," said the young man. "But pray pardon our forgetfulness. *In latine*—"

"No need, gracious sir," Volstrup told him. "My wife and I know your language. We hope you will bear with ours." The Lombard version he used was not incomprehensibly different from the local Umbrian.

Both Conti registered relief. Doubtless they spoke Latin less well than they understood it. Lorenzo bowed again, to Tamberly. "Doubly welcome is a lady so fair," he purred. His glance upon her made plain that he meant it. Evidently Italians today had the same weakness for blondes as in the Renaissance and afterward.

"My wife, Walburga," Volstrup said. Everard had supplied the names. She had already noticed that when the going got tough, his sense of humor got extra quirky.

Lorenzo took her hand. She felt as though an electric shock went through her. *Stop that! Yes, this is weird, history once more turning on the same man, but he's mortal. . . . He'd better be.*

She told herself that her emotion was no more than an echo of the explosion in her head when first she read Cencio's letter. Manse had briefed her and Volstrup as thoroughly as possible, but with no idea that Lorenzo was involved. For all he knew, the warrior never left that battlefield. The information the Patrol had was barebones. Ilaria di Gaetani should have married Bartolommeo Conti de Segni, nobleman of this papal state and kinsman of Innocent III. In 1147 she should have given birth to that Ugolino who became Gregory IX. Volstrup and Tamberly were supposed to discover what had gone wrong.

Everard laid a plan for them that called for approaching the Conti first. They'd need some kind of entry into aristocratic society, and he knew a lot about that family from his stay with Lorenzo in 1138—a visit that, now, had never occurred, but nonetheless was engraved on the Patrolman's memory. The two had grown quite friendly and talk had ranged every which way. Thus Everard heard about the tenuous link to Flanders. It seemed to provide an excellent opening.

In addition, his claim to being lately from Jerusalem had worked fine the first time, so why not repeat?

Could there be another Ilaria di Gaetani in town? Emil and I discussed that possibility. No, too improbable. We'll find out for sure, but I know there isn't. Nor can I believe Lorenzo is again the man on whom everything turns, by sheer coincidence. Touch hands with destiny, my girl.

He released hers, in a sliding slowness that she could interpret however she liked except that it wasn't offensive. Not in the least. "A joyful occasion," he said. "I look forward to much pleasure of your company."

Do I feel my cheeks growing hot? This is ridiculous! Tamberly mustered what she had learned of contemporary manners. That was limited, but a certain awkwardness on the part of a Fleming should not surprise anyone. "Come, come, sir," she replied. Smiling at him proved unexpectedly easy. "You have better anticipations, whose nuptial day draws nigh."

"Of course I long for my bride," Lorenzo said. He sounded dutiful. "However—" He shrugged shoulders, spread hands, rolled eyes upward.

"Ever does the poor bridegroom-to-be find himself mostly underfoot," Cencio laughed. "And I, a widower, must do the work of two, striving to make such arrangements for the celebration as will not disgrace us." He paused. "You know that is a labor for Hercules, under circumstances today. Indeed, I must now reluctantly return to it. We are having trouble about the delivery of sufficient flesh of worthwhile quality. I leave you in my son's hands, hoping that at eventide I can share a cup and converse with you." In a flurry of mutual courtesies, he went out.

Lorenzo raised a brow. "Speaking of cups," he said, "is it too early, or are you too wearied? The servants will bring your baggage to your bedchamber and make all ready for you in a few minutes. You can take a rest if you so desire."

This is too good a chance to pass up. "Oh, no, thank you, sir," Tamberly answered. "We overnighted at an inn and slept well. Refreshment and talk would be delightful."

Was he a little taken aback at her forwardness? Tactfully, he directed attention to Volstrup, who told him, "True, if we don't presume on your patience."

"On the contrary," Lorenzo said. "Come, let me show you around. Not that you will see wonders. This is only our rural house. In Rome—" Mercurially, he scowled. "But you have seen Rome."

Volstrup fielded the ball. "We have. Terrible. They actually levy a tax on pilgrims."

Last year, led by the puritanical monk Arnold of Brescia, the city had declared itself a republic, free of all outside authority, Church or Empire. Newly elected Pope Eugenius III had fled, come back briefly to proclaim a new crusade, then been forced out again. Most aristocrats had likewise withdrawn. The republic wouldn't fall, and Arnold burn at the stake, till 1155. (Unless in the mutant history—)

"You landed at Ostia, then?"

"Yes, and proceeded to Rome, where we visited the sacred shrines." And other sights. It was creepy seeing beggars, shacks, kitchen gardens, cattle paddocks among the relics of greatness. They might as well play tourist; those days established their identity, after the Patrol vehicle let them off in the seaport town.

Tamberly's bosom sensed the medallion that doubled as a radio. It gave confidence, knowing that an agent waited hidden and alert. Of course, he didn't listen in; continuous transmission would soon have drained the power. And if they yelled for help he wouldn't pop up at that instant. On no account could he risk affecting events that maybe, maybe had not yet taken their bad turning. But he could probably figure some dodge for springing them loose.

We should be okay, though. These are nice folks. Fascinating. Yes, we are on a vital mission, but why not relax for a while and enjoy?

Lorenzo pointed out the wall paintings. They were naive but vivid representations of Olympian deities, and he showed his appreciation despite adding an assurance that this was acceptable to Christians. *Too bad he wasn't born in the Renaissance. That's when he really belongs.* Murals were a rather new fashion. "In the North we hang tapestries," Volstrup remarked, "but then, we need them against our winters."

"I have heard. Would that I might someday go see for myself—see this whole wonderful world, everything God has created."

Lorenzo sighed. "How did you and your lady come to learn an Italian tongue?"

Well, it was like this. The Time Patrol has a gadget—

"For my part, I have had business with Lombards over the years," Volstrup said. "Although my house is knightly and I certainly not a tradesman, I am a younger son who must earn his keep as best he can; and you see I am ill suited to a military career, while also too restless for the Church. Thus I oversee certain holdings of the family, which include an estate in the Rhaetian highlands." The locale was safely obscure. "As for my wife, on this pilgrimage we traveled overland as far as Bari." Bad and hazardous though roads were, shipboard in this era was worse. "She not desiring to be mute among commoners, with whom we must generally deal, I engaged a Lombard tutor to accompany us; and when abroad, knowing we would return through Italy, we practiced on each other."

"How rare and admirable to find such wit in a woman. Rare, too, that she make a long and arduous journey, the more so when at home doubtless all the youths faint for lovesickness and all the poets sing her praises."

"Alas, we have no children to keep me home; and I am a terrible sinner," Tamberly couldn't refrain from blurting.

Do I catch a glint of hope in his eye? "I cannot believe you are, my lady," Lorenzo said. "Humility is a virtue of yours, among many higher ones." He must realize he was proceeding faster than was discreet, for he turned to Volstrup and let the smile drop from his lips. "A younger son. How well I understand you, sir. I too. Though I did take the sword, and won scant fortune thereby."

"On the way hither, your father's men often spoke of how valiantly you have fought," the Patrolman replied. It was true. "We would fain hear more."

"Ah, in the end it was bootless. Two years ago Roger of Sicily won everything he wanted, under a seven years' truce that I expect will continue longer—as long as yon devil befouls this earth—and now he sits in peace and wealth." Almost physically, Lorenzo thrust bitterness from him. "Well, a greater cause calls, a holy cause. Why should you care to hear stale stories of the wars against Roger? Tell me how matters are this day in Jerusalem!"

They had been strolling as they talked and come to a room where small kegs rested on shelves and several beakers on a table. Lorenzo beamed. "Here we are. Pray be seated, my friends." He made a production of guiding Tamberly to a bench before he stuck his head out the rear door and shouted for a servant. When the boy appeared, he ordered bread, cheese, olives, fruits. Himself he tapped wine into the cups.

"You are too kind, good sir," Tamberly said. *Too kind by half. I know what he has in mind, and him soon to be married.*

"No, it is you who bless me," he insisted. "Two years have I yawned in idleness. You and your tidings arrive like a breeze off the sea."

"Yes, I can imagine that, after as adventurous a life as you had led," Volstrup agreed. "Er, we heard tell of your valor at Rignano, when Duke Rainulf sent the Sicilians in flight. Did not a very miracle save your life that day?"

Lorenzo frowned anew. "The victory proved meaningless, for we failed to lay Roger by the heels. Why wake the memory?"

"Oh, but I have so wished to hear the true story, not mere rumors, and from the champion in person," Tamberly crooned.

Lorenzo brightened. "Indeed? Well, truth to tell, my part was less than glorious. When the enemy first charged, I led a flank attack on his van. Someone must have smitten me from behind in the combat, for the next thing I knew, I was draped across my horse, and our attempt had failed. The most curious matter is that I kept my seat; but a lifetime of riding teaches the body how to take care of itself. Nor can the blow have been severe, for I awakened clear of mind, with no headache, and could immediately re-enter the fray. Now do you gratify me with some account of your travels."

"I daresay you are most interested in the military situation," Volstrup said, "but as I told you, I am not a fighting man. Alas, what I did hear and see was unhappy."

Lorenzo listened intently. His frequent questions showed he was quite well-informed. Meanwhile Tamberly reviewed what she had been taught.

By 1099 the First Crusade had gained its objectives, with a massacre of civilians that would have done Genghis Khan proud, and the conquerors settled in. They founded a string of realms from

Palestine up into what she knew as southern Turkey—the Kingdom of Jerusalem, County of Tripoli, Principality of Antioch, County of Edessa. Gradually they came more and more under the cultural influence of their subjects. It wasn't really like the Normans in Sicily, learning from the more civilized Arabs; it was as though the Crusaders and their children took on the unhealthiest aspects of Muslim society. Weakness followed, until in 1144 the Amir of Mosul captured Edessa and his son Nur-ed-Din advanced upon Jerusalem. That Christian king appealed for help. Bernard of Clairvaux—St. Bernard to be—preached a new crusade and Pope Eugenius proclaimed it. This Easter, 1146, King Louis VII of France had "taken the cross," vowing to lead an expedition.

"I wished from the first to go," Lorenzo explained, "but we Italians have been sluggish in these enterprises and remain thus, to our eternal shame. What use was a single sword, among Frenchmen who distrust us, likely to be? Besides, father arranged my betrothal to the lady Ilaria. It is a good match, better than a well-nigh penniless soldier could reasonably hope for. I cannot leave him without this added prop for his house and one more grandchild, legitimate, to gladden his old age."

But I see the longing in those hawk eyes, Tamberly thought. *He's a kindly man in his way, and honorable about his obligations. And brave, and a gifted tactician, it seems. Uh-huh, I guess his war record persuaded Ilaria's dad to agree. It'd give hope he might win some real booty for himself, off in Palestine. And if Lorenzo'd like to get in a little tomcatting first, well it is a marriage of convenience and I suspect Ilaria is no raving beauty. Besides, my Patrol education tells me that people may be devoutly religious hereabouts, but their sexual mores are pretty free and easy. For women too, if they don't parade it. Even gays, no matter the law says they should be hanged or burned. Sound familiar, California gal?*

"But now the abbot is preaching among the Germans," Lorenzo went on. His voice rang. "I hear that King Conrad hearkens to him. That was a valiant warrior, when he came down with the Emperor Lothair ten years ago to help us against Roger. I feel sure he too will take the cross."

He would, about the end of this year. And, besides its transalpine possessions, the Empire had close ties throughout Italy. (What with the trouble his turbulent nobles gave him, Conrad never would get around to having himself consecrated emperor, but that was a detail.) Lorenzo could find plenty of comrades behind his banner, and probably get put in charge of a unit. Conrad would march south through Hungary in the autumn of 1147. That gave ample time for Lorenzo first to beget a child on Ilaria, a child who would not become Pope Gregory IX. . . .

"Therefore I abide as patiently as I am able to," Lorenzo finished. "In all circumstances, I will go. I have fought for the right and for Holy Church too long to let my blade rust now. But best if I fare with Conrad."

No, not best. Dreadful. The Second Crusade would prove a grisly farce. Disease would take as heavy a toll of the Europeans as fighting did, until, beaten, frustrated, the survivors slunk home. In 1187 Saladin would enter Jerusalem.

But these Crusades, First, Second, et cetera through the Seventh, as well as those against heretics and pagans in Europe itself, they were an artifact of later historians anyway. Sometimes a Pope, or somebody, called for a special effort, and sometimes, not always, this evoked a serious response. Mainly, though, it was a question of whether you—idealist, warlord, freebooter, or oftenest blend of all three—could get yourself dubbed a crusader. It conferred special rights and privileges in this world, remission of sins in the next. That was the legalism. Reality was men who marched, rode, sailed, hungered, thirsted, roistered, fought, raped, burned, looted, slaughtered, tortured, fell sick, took wounds, died nasty deaths or got rich or became captive slaves or eked out a living in a foreign land or perhaps returned, to and fro for centuries. Meanwhile the wily Sicilians, Venetians, Genoese, Pisans raked large profits off the traffic; and Asian rats stowed away in ships bound for Europe, they and their fleas carrying the Black Plague. . . .

Volstrup and Tamberly had had sufficient knowledge implanted that they could handle Lorenzo's questions about the Kingdom of Jerusalem. They had gotten a quick tour of it, too. *Yes, belonging to the Patrol has its rewards. Though golly, how fast you need to case-harden yourself.*

"But I presume on you!" Lorenzo abruptly exclaimed. "Forgive me. I quite forgot the time. You rode for hours today. My lady must certainly be wearied. Come, let me show you to your lodging, that you may rest, cleanse yourselves, and don good clothes before we sup. There will be a number of fellow guests for you to meet, kinfolk arriving from half of Italy, it seems."

As he bowed his way out of the chamber, he made eye contact with Tamberly. She let it continue for several heartbeats. *Manse was right, a woman who knows her way around can be very helpful. She can learn quite a lot about the situation and what we might do. Only . . . do I qualify? Me, a vamp?*

A deferential manservant revealed where things had been stowed, asked if that was all right, and said that hot water could be brought for a copper mini-tub whenever milord and milady desired. People were rather cleanly in this era, and mixed use of public baths was common. They wouldn't start habitually stinking for centuries yet, when deforestation made fuel expensive.

And yonder stood a double bed. The Roman inn and the one along the road to here had separate quarters for men and women, where you slept beside strangers, naked.

Volstrup looked away. He wet his lips. After two or three attempts, he said, "Ah, Mademoiselle Tamberly, I failed to anticipate— Of course I shall take the floor, and when either of us bathes—"

Laughter whooped from her. "Sorry, Emil, old dear," she replied to his bewilderment. "Have no fears for your honor. I'll turn my back if you want. That mattress tick is plenty wide. We'll rest peaceful." A small inward chill: *Will I, when Manse is working in an uncharted world a hundred years uptime?* And then, warmer: *Also, I'd better give Lorenzo a lot of thought.*

1245$_\beta$ A.D.

Westward lay hills rising toward the Apennine Mountains, but everywhere around reached the Apulian plain. Farmlands white-speckled with villages covered most of it, orchards darkly green, fields goldening for harvest. There were, however, broad stretches of meadow, prairie-like with their tall summer-brown grass, and frequent woods. They were used as commons, where children kept watch over herds of cattle and flocks of geese, but their main purpose was to provide space and wildlife for the emperor's hawking.

His party rode through such a preserve toward Foggia, his most beloved city. At their backs the sun cast long yellow beams and blue shadows through air still warm, still full of earth odors. Ahead of them gleamed the walls, turrets, towers, spires of the city; glass and gilt flung light at their eyes. Loud from yonder, faint from chapels strewn across the countryside, bells pealed for vespers.

The peacefulness struck at Everard as he remembered another scene not very far from here. But the dead of Rignano lay a hundred and eight years in the past. None but he and Karel Novak were alive to remember the pain, and they had overleaped the generations between.

He pulled his mind back to the business on hand. Neither Frederick (Friedrich, Fridericus, Federigo . . . depending on where you were in his vast domains) nor his followers were paying the call to prayer any heed. The nobles among them chatted blithely with each other, they and their horses little tired after outdoor hours. Their garb was a rainbow medley. Tiny bells jingled as if in cheerful mockery on the jesses of the falcons that, hooded, perched on their wrists. Masked, too, to preserve fair complexions, were the ladies; it lent itself to an especially piquant style of flirtatiousness. Behind trailed the attendants. Game dangled at saddlebows, partridge, woodcock, heron, hare. Slung across rumps were the hampers and the costly glass bottles that had carried refreshment.

"Well, Munan," said the emperor, "what think you of the sport in Sicily?" Courteous as well as jovial, he spoke in German—Low Franconian, at that—which his guest knew. Otherwise they had only Latin in common, except for what scraps of Italian an Icelander might have acquired along the way.

Everard reminded himself that "Sicily" meant not just the island but the Regno, the southern part of the mainland, which Roger II defined by the sword in the previous century. "It is most impressive, your Grace," he replied with care. That was the current form of address for the mightiest man this side of China. "Of course, as everybody saw today, though they were too well-bred to laugh aloud, we have few chances to fly birds in my unhappy motherland. What little chase I hitherto witnessed on the Continent was after deer."

"Ah, let those for whom it is good enough practice their venery," gibed Frederick. He used the Latinate word so he could add a pun: "I mean the kind where one pursues beasts with horns. The other kind is too good for them, albeit horns are also often seen in that pastime." Turning earnest: "But falconry, now, it is more than amusement, it is high art and science."

"I have heard of your Grace's book on the subject, and hope to read it."

"I will order a copy given you." Frederick glanced at the Greenland falcon he himself bore. "If you could bring me this over sea and land in prime condition, then you have an inborn gift, and such should never be let lie fallow. You shall practice."

"Your Grace honors me beyond my worth. I fear the bird didn't perform as well as some."

"He needs further training, yes. It shall be my pleasure, if time allows." Everard noted that Frederick did not say "God" as a medieval man ordinarily would.

Actually the bird was from the Patrol's ranch in pre-Indian North America. Falcons were an excellent, ice-breaking gift in a number of milieus, provided you didn't present one to somebody whose rank didn't entitle him to that particular kind. Everard had merely needed to nurse it along from that point in the hills where the timecycle let him and Novak off.

Involuntarily, he looked back west. Jack Hall waited yonder, in a dell to which it seemed people rarely strayed. A radioed word would fetch him on the instant. No matter if his appearance was public. This was no longer the history the Patrol sought to guard, it was one to overthrow.

If that could be done. . . . Yes, certainly it could, easily, by a few revelations and actions; but what would come of them was unforeseeable. Better to stay as cautious as possible. Stick with the devil you somewhat knew, till you found out whence he sprang.

Thus Everard made his reconnaissance in 1245. The choice was not entirely arbitrary. It was five years before Frederick's death—in the lost world. In this one, the emperor, less stressed, would not succumb untimely to a gastrointestinal ailment, and thereby bring all Hohenstaufen hopes to the ground. A quick preliminary scouting revealed that he was in Foggia most of that summer and that things were going smoothly for him, his grand designs advancing almost without hindrance.

You could anticipate that he would welcome Munan Eyvindsson. Frederick's curiosity was universal; it had led him to experiments on animals and, rumor said, human vivisection. Icelanders, no matter how remote, obscure, and miserable, possessed a unique heritage. (Everard had gained familiarity with it on a mission to the viking era. Today Scandinavians were long since Christianized, but Iceland preserved lore elsewhere forgotten.) Admittedly, Munan was an outlaw. However, that meant simply that his enemies had maneuvered the Althing into passing sentence on him: for five years anybody who could manage it was free to kill him without legal penalty. The republic was going under in a maelstrom of feuds between its great families; soon it would submit to the Norwegian crown.

Like others in his position who could afford to, Munan went abroad for the term of his outlawry. Landing in Denmark, he bought horses and hired a manservant cum bodyguard—Karel, a Bohemian mercenary on the beach. They fared south leisurely and safely. Frederick's peace lay heavy upon the Empire. Munan's first goal was Rome, but the pilgrimage was not his first interest, and afterward he sought his real dream, to meet the man called *stupor mundi*, "the amazement of the world."

Not just the gift he brought caught the emperor's fancy. Still more did the sagas he could relate, the Eddic and skaldic poems. "You open another whole universe!" Frederick exulted. It was no small compliment from a lord to whose court came scholars of Spain and Damascus, as diverse as the astrologer Michael Scot and the mathematician Leonardo Fibonacci of Pisa, he who introduced Arabic numerals into Europe. "You must abide for a time with us." That was ten days ago.

Spite cut through drifting memories. "Does the bold Sir Munan fear pursuit, this far from home? He must truly have wronged someone if he does."

Piero della Vigna said it, at Frederick's right side. He was middle-aged, defiant of fashion in his grizzled beard and plain garb; but the eyes were luminous with an intellect equal to that of his master.

Humanist, Latin stylist, jurist, counselor, lately chancellor, he was more than the emperor's man Friday, he was his most intimate friend in a court aswarm with sycophants.

Startled, Everard lied, "I thought I heard a noise." Inwardly: *I've noticed this guy glower. What's bugging him? He can't be afraid I'll shove him aside in the imperial favor.*

Piero pounced. "Ha, you understand me remarkably well."

Everard swore at himself. *That bastard used Italian. I forgot I'm a newly arrived foreigner.* He forced a smile. "Why, naturally I've gained some knowledge of the tongues I've heard. That doesn't mean I'd offend his Grace's ears by trying to speak them in his presence." Maliciously: "I pray the signor's pardon. Let me put that into Latin for you."

Piero made a dismissing gesture. "I followed." Of course so active a mind would learn German, hog-language though he doubtless considered it. Vernaculars were steadily gaining both political and cultural importance. "You gave a different impression erenow."

"I am sorry if I was misunderstood."

Piero looked elsewhere and fell silent, brooding. *Does he think I may be a spy? For whom? As far as we've been able to find out, Frederick doesn't have any enemies left worth fussing over. Oh, the French king is surely concerned—*

The emperor laughed. "Do you suppose our visitor means to disarm us, Piero?" he gibed. He could be a little cruel, or more than a little, even to those who stood him closest. "Set your heart at ease. I cannot see how good Munan could be in anyone's pay, yea, not though that anyone be Giacomo de Mora."

Realization sank into Everard. *That's it. Piero's worried sick about Sir Giacomo, who has in fact taken more interest in me than would have been expected. If Giacomo has not actually planted me here, Piero fears, then maybe he's thought of some way to make a tool of me against his rival. Somebody in Piero's position is apt to see shadows in every corner.*

Pity followed. What was this man's fate in this history? Would he "once more" fall a few years hence, accused of conspiracy against his lord, and be blinded, and dash his brains out against a stone wall? Would the future forget him and instead remember Giacomo de Mora, whose name was not in any chronicle known to the Patrol?

Yeah, these intrigues are like dancing on nitroglycerine. Maybe I ought to shy clear of Giacomo, too. And yet . . . how better might I pick up a clue to what went wrong, than from Frederick's brilliant military leader and diplomat? Who's got a wider and shrewder knowledge of this world? If he's chosen to cultivate me when he's not busy and the emperor is, I should accept the honor with due fulsomeness.

Odd that he made some excuse and didn't come along today—

Hoofs clopped. The party had reached a main road. Frederick spurred his horse and, for a moment, drew well ahead of the rest. His hair tossed auburn-gold from beneath a feathered cap. The low sunlight made a halo of it. Yes, he was getting bald, and the trim, medium-sized frame was putting on weight, and lines were deep in the clean-shaven face. (It was a Germanic face, taking more after his grandfather Frederick Barbarossa than his grandfather Roger II.) Nevertheless, for that instant, he looked somewhat like a god.

Peasants still at work in a nearby field bowed clumsily to him. So did a monk trudging toward the city. It was more than awe before power. There had always, also in Everard's history, been an aura of the supernatural about this ruler. Despite his struggle with the Church, many folk—no few Franciscans, especially—saw him as a mystic figure, a redeemer and reformer of the mundane world, Heaven-sent. Many others saw in him the Antichrist. But that seemed past. In this world, the war between him and the Popes was over, and he had prevailed.

At a ringing canter, the falconers neared the city. Its main gate stood open yet, to be closed an hour after sundown. There was no need for that, no threat, but so the emperor commanded, here and throughout his lands. Traffic must move at certain times, commerce proceed according to regulation. The gate had little about it of the grace and exuberance of Palermo, where Frederick spent his boyhood. Like buildings he had ordered raised elsewhere, strongholds and administrative centers, it was massive, starkly foursquare. Above it a banner rippled in the evening breeze, an eagle on a golden field, the emblem of the Hohenstaufen dynasty.

Not for the first time since he came here, Everard wondered how much of this his history had known. Little remained in the twentieth century, his twentieth century, and the survivors of the Patrol had an overwhelming task already without studying architectural developments. Maybe this wasn't very different from the "original" medieval Foggia. Or maybe it was. A lot would depend on how soon events had veered off track.

Strictly speaking, that happened about a hundred years ago, when Pope Gregory IX failed to be born—unless it was later, when he died young or did not take holy orders or whatever went amiss. But changes in time don't spread outward on any simple wave front. They're an infinitely complicated interplay of quantum functions, way over this poor head of mine.

The tiniest alteration could conceivably annul an entire future, if the event concerned was crucial. There should theoretically be countless such; but hardly ever were they felt. It was as if the time-flow protected itself, passed around them without losing its proper direction and shape. Sometimes you did get odd little eddies—and here one of them had grown to monstrousness—

Yet change must needs spread in chains of cause and effect. Who outside the immediate vicinity would ever even hear what went on, or did not go on, in a couple of families of Anagni? It would take a long time for the consequences of that to reach far. Meanwhile the rest of the world moved onward untouched.

So Constance, daughter of King Roger II, was born after her father's death. She was over thirty when she married Barbarossa's younger son, and nine more years went by before she bore to him Frederick, in 1194. Her husband became the Emperor Henry VI, who had gotten the crown of Sicily through the marriage, and who died soon after this birth. Frederick inherited that glamorous hybrid kingdom. He grew up among its plots and tumults, the ward of Pope Innocent III, who arranged his first marriage and maneuvered for a German coalition to hail him supreme king in 1211, because Otto VI had been giving the Church intolerable trouble. By 1220 Frederick was everywhere triumphant and the new Pope, Honorius III, consecrated him Holy Roman Emperor.

Nevertheless, relations with him had long been worsening. He neglected or disowned promise after promise; only in his persecution of heretics did he seem to proceed with any regard to Mother Church. Most conspicuously, time after time he postponed fulfillment of his vow to go on crusade, while he put down revolts and secured his own power. Honorius died in 1227—

Yeah. As far as we can find out, with what skimpy resources we've got left, things went pretty much the same up till then. Frederick, a widower, married Iolande in 1225, daughter of the titular King of Jerusalem, uh-huh, just as he was supposed to. A smart bit of groundwork for the recovery of that real estate from the paynim. Except that he kept putting the job off, he tried instead to assert his authority over Lombardy by force. And then in 1227 Honorius died.

And the next Pope was not Gregory IX, he was Celestine IV, and after that the world became less and less what it ought to have been.

"Hail!" roared the sentries. They lifted their pikes on high. For a moment the bright hues of the falconers dimmed in the tunnellike gateway. Echoes rolled off stone. They came forth onto the lists, the broad, smoothly paved open space under the wall, beyond which reared the buildings of the city. Above roofs Everard glimpsed cathedral towers. Somehow, against the eastern sky, they looked somber, as if night were already drawing down over them.

A well-clad man with an attendant waited beyond the gate. Judging by the restlessness of their horses, they had been there for a considerable time. Everard recognized the courtier, who brought his mount close and made salutation.

"Your Grace, forgive my intrusion," he said. "I believed you would desire to know at once. This day did word come. The ambassador from Baghdad landed yesterday at Bari. He and his train were to start hither at dawn."

"Hellfire!" exclaimed Frederick. "Then they'll arrive tomorrow. I know how Arabs ride." He glanced about. "I regret the festivity planned for eventide must be stricken," he told the party. "I will be too occupied making ready."

Piero della Vigna raised his brows. "Indeed, sire?" he wondered. "Need we show them great honor? Yon Caliphate is but a wretched husk of ancient greatness."

"The more need for me to nurse it back to strength, an ally on that flank," the emperor replied. "Come!" He, his chancellor, and the courtier clattered off.

The disappointed revelers went their separate ways by ones and twos and threes, chattering about what this might portend. Some lived at the palace and followed their sovereign more slowly. Everard would too. However, he dawdled and went roundabout, preferring to ride alone so he could think.

The significance— Hm. Maybe Fred, or his successor, really will get the Near East bulwarked and stop the Mongols when they invade there. Wouldn't that *be a sockdolager?*

The past ran on through the Patrolman's head, but now it was not his world's, it was the course of this world that ought not to be, as inadequately charted by him and his few helpers.

Mild, in frail health, Pope Celestine was no Gregory, to excommunicate the emperor when the crusade was postponed yet again. In Everard's world, Frederick had, at last, sailed regardless, and proceeded actually to regain Jerusalem, not by fighting but by shrewd bargaining. In this present history, he had not then needed to crown himself its king; the Church anointed him, which gave immense leverage that he well knew how to apply. He suppressed and supplanted such enemies as John Ibelin of Cyprus and cemented firm agreements with the Muslim rulers of Egypt, Damascus, and Iconium. Given that network throughout the region, the Byzantines had no prospect of overthrowing their hated Latin overlords—who must more and more fit themselves to the wishes of the Holy Roman Emperor.

Meanwhile, in Germany, Frederick's heir apparent Henry revolted; in this world, too, the father put down the rebellion and confined the son for the rest of a short life. Likewise, in this world poor little Queen Iolande died young, of neglect and heartbreak. However, without a temporarily conciliated Pope Gregory to arrange it, Frederick's third marriage was not to Isabella of England but to a daughter of the Aragonese royal house.

His breach with Celestine occurred when he, freed from other tasks, took his armies into Lombardy and ruthlessly brought it under himself. Thereupon, in contempt of all pledges, he seized Sardinia and married his son Enzio to its queen. Seeing the papal states thus caught in a vise, even Celestine had then no choice but to excommunicate him. Frederick and his merry men ignored the ban. In the course of the next several years they overran central Italy.

Thus he was able to send a mighty force against the Mongols when they struck into Europe, and in 1241 inflict resounding defeats on them. When Celestine died that same year, the "savior of Christendom" easily got a puppet of his elected Pope as Lucius IV.

He had annexed those parts of Poland where his armies met the Mongols. Aided by him, whose tool they had become, the Teutonic Knights were in process of conquering Lithuania. Negotiations for a dynastic marriage were under way in Hungary— *What's next? Who is?*

"I beg your pardon!" Everard reined in his horse, hard. Lost in thought, passing through a narrow lane where gloom gathered thick, he had almost ridden down a man afoot. "I didn't see you. Are you all right?" Here he dared be fluent in the local Italian. He must, for decency's sake.

"It is nothing, sir, nothing." The man pulled his muck-spattered gown close about him and backed meekly off. Everard made out the beard, broad cap, yellow emblem. Yes, a Jew. Frederick had decreed that Jews wear distinct dress, with no man to shave, and a long list of other restrictions.

Since no real harm had been done, Everard could swallow his conscience and ride on, keeping in character. The alley gave on a marketplace. Dusking, it was nearly deserted. People in medieval cities mostly stayed indoors after dark, whether because of a curfew or from choice. Here they needn't fear crime—the emperor's patrols and hangmen kept that well down—but it was no fun stumbling through unlighted streets full of manure and dumped garbage. A charred stake rose at the middle of the square, not yet removed, the ash and debris only roughly cleaned up. Everard had heard about a woman convicted of Manichaeanism. Apparently this had been the day they burned her.

He clenched his teeth and continued riding. *It isn't that Frederick's really malignant, like Hitler. Nor is he some kind of twisted idealist, nor a politician trying to curry favor with the Church. He burns heretics in the same spirit as he burns defiant cities and butchers their inhabitants—the same spirit as he restricts not only Jews and Muslims, but strolling players, whores, every kind of independent operator—they simply are not subservient. He sees to the welfare of those who are.*

Studying up for this mission, more than once I read historians who said he founded the first modern state (in western Europe, at least;

since the fall of Rome, anyhow), bureaucracy, regulation, thought police, all authority concentrated at the top. Damn if I'll ever feel sorry that it went to pieces after his death, in my world!

On this time line, obviously, it did not. Everard had seen what lay seven centuries ahead. *(Hey, Wanda, how're you doing, gal, a hundred years ago?)* The Empire would expand, generation by generation, till it embraced and remade Europe, and surely had profound impact on the Orient. Just how didn't matter. Everard guessed at an Anglo-Imperial alliance that partitioned France, whereafter the Empire ingested the British Isles, the Iberian peninsula, perhaps everything clear to Russia and maybe a part of that too. Its mariners would reach America, though surely much later than 1492; this history also lacked a Renaissance and a scientific revolution. Its colonies would spread vigorously westward. But all the while, the dry rot that arises in every imperium would be eating the heart out of it.

As for the Church, well, it wouldn't die, nor even break up in a Reformation, but it would become a creature of the state, and probably share the death agonies.

Unless a crippled Patrol could uproot this destiny, without sowing something worse.

At the palace stables Everard dismounted and turned his horse over to a groom. Like a walled city within the city, the compound loomed hard by. The mews were inside but he, self-acknowledged (falsely) as inexperienced, had no hawk to care for. The forecourt seemed full of bustle. To avoid it, he walked around to the rear gate. Steel dimly ashine in the waning light, its guards recognized him and let him by with a genial greeting. They were good joes, whatever they'd done in the past. War was war, throughout the ages. Everard had been a soldier too.

The gravel of a path scrunched softly beneath his boots. A formal garden stretched fragrant to right and left. He heard a fountain splash. As clear sounded the strings of a lute. Hidden from Everard by hedges and bowers, a man lifted his voice in song. Most likely a young lady listened, for the words were amorous. The language was southern German. The troubadours were gone with the Provençal civiliation that the Albigensian Crusade destroyed; but no few minnesingers crossed the Alps to seek Frederick's court.

The palace sprawled ahead. Medieval heaviness was a bit relieved by wings added more recently. Many windows shone. They hadn't the brightness of electric lamps behind plate glass—this world might well never know that—but a dull yet warm flame-glow seeped through small leaded panes. When Everard entered, he came into a hallway illuminated down its length by bracketed lamps.

Nobody else was in view. The servants were taking a light supper in their quarters, prior to making things ready for the night. (The main meal was early in the afternoon. Frederick himself, and therefore his entourage, ate once a day.) Everard mounted a staircase. Although the emperor honored him by giving him a room here, naturally it lay offside and he shared it with his man.

He opened the door and went in. The space was small, its furniture hardly more than a double bed, a couple of stools, a clothes chest, and a chamber pot. Novak rose and snapped to attention. "At ease," Everard said in American English. "How often must I tell you, your Middle European *Ordnungsliebe* isn't necessary around me?"

The Czech's stocky frame quivered. "Sir—"

"One moment." Each of them called Jack Hall sometime during every twenty-four hours, so the man at the timecycle would know they were okay. This was Everard's first chance today to do it privately. Novak had mentioned being noticed a couple of times when he believed himself alone, and getting odd glances, though nobody braced him. It should seem a religious observance, of which there were countless sorts. Everard pulled out the medallion that hung from a chain under his tunic, brought it to his mouth, thumbed the switch. "Reporting," he said. "Back in the palace. No developments yet, worse luck. Hang on, old boy." It must be dull, simply waiting yonder, but cowboy life had schooled Hall in patience.

How so small a device could generate a radio wave reaching so far, Everard didn't know. Some quantum effect, he supposed. He turned it off, to save the power cell, and restored it to his bosom. "All right," he said. "If you want to be of service, fix me a sandwich and pour me a drink. I know you keep a stash."

"Yes, sir." Novak was clearly curbing ants in his pants. From the chest he produced a loaf of bread, a cheese, a sausage, and a clay bottle. Thirsty, Everard reached for that, unstoppered it, and swigged.

"*Vino rozzo* indeed," he snorted. "Haven't you any beer?"

"I thought you had found out for yourself, sir," replied Novak. "In this era, too, Italians cannot brew a drinkable beer. Especially since we lack refrigeration." He drew his knife and started slicing, using the chest lid for a table. "How was your day?"

"Fun, in a strained fashion, and educational." Everard scowled. "Except, blast it, I didn't get a single useful hint. More reminiscences, but none of them old enough to suggest where or when the turning point was. I give us one more week, then we'll say to hell with it and hop back to base." He sat down. "I hope you haven't been too bored."

"On the contrary, sir." Novak looked up. The broad face tensed, the voice hoarsened. "I believe I have gotten some important information."

"What? Say on!"

"I spent more than an hour talking with Sir Giacomo de Mora."

Everard whistled. "You—a hireling, damn near a masterless man?"

Novak seemed glad to keep his hands occupied. "I was astounded myself, sir. After all, one of the emperor's chief counselors, his general against the Mongols, his personal ambassador to the king of England, and— Well, he sent for me, received me alone, and was really quite friendly, considering the difference in our ranks. He said he wants to learn everything he can about foreign lands. What you had told, sir, was most interesting, but humble men also see and hear things, often things their superiors don't notice, and since he happened to have today idle—"

Everard gnawed his lip. He felt his pulse accelerate. "I'm not sure I like this."

"Nor I, sir." Savagely, Novak finished his cutting and slapped a sandwich together. "But what could I do? Play simpleminded, as best I was able. I'm afraid playacting isn't a talent of mine." He straightened. Slowly: "I managed to slip in a few questions of my own. I tried to make them sound like normal curiosity. He obliged. He told me something about himself and . . . his ancestry."

He handed the sandwich over. Everard took it automatically. "Go on," he mumbled, while iciness crawled over his scalp.

Again Novak stood at attention. "I had what you call a hunch, sir. I led him to speak of his family. You know how conscious of their backgrounds these aristocrats are. His father was from— Well, but his mother was a Conto of Anagni. When I heard that, I am afraid I lost my stupid mask for a minute. I said I had heard tell of a famous knight, Lorenzo de Conti, about a hundred years ago. Was that any kin of his? And, yes, sir," Novak exploded, "Giacomo is a great-grandson of that man. Lorenzo had one legitimate child. Soon after, he went off on the Second Crusade, fell sick, and died."

Everard stared before him. "Lorenzo again," he whispered.

"I don't understand this. Like some magical spell, isn't it?" Novak shivered. "I don't want that to be so."

"No," Everard answered tonelessly. "It isn't. Nor a coincidence, I think. Blind chance, always underneath that skin we call reality—" He swallowed. "The Patrol's dealt with nexuses, points in spacetime where it's all too easy to change the course of the world. But can't a nexus be, not an event that does or does not happen, but a person? Lorenzo was, is, some kind of a, a lightning rod; and the lightning strikes through him onward beyond his death—what Giacomo's meant to Frederick's career—"

He climbed to his feet. "There's our clue, Karel. You found it for us. Lorenzo can't have died at Rignano. He must be active yet in that same crisis year to which we've sent Wanda."

"Then we must go to her," Novak said unsteadily. Only now, it seemed, did he see the full meaning of the fact he had unearthed.

"Of course—"

The door flew open. Everard's heart banged. Breath hissed between Novak's teeth.

The man who confronted them was in his forties, lean-faced, dark hair graying at the temples. His athletic body was clad for action, leather doublet over the shirt, close-fitting hose, sword naked in hand. Behind him, four men-at-arms grasped falchions and halberds.

Oh, oh, sounded in Everard's head. *School's out.* "Why, Sir Giacomo." He remembered, barely in time, to use German. "To what do we owe this honor?"

"Hold!" commanded the knight. He was fluent in the language. His blade slanted forward, ready for thrust or slash. "Stir not, either of you, or you're dead."

We naturally left our weapons with the palace armorer. We have our table steel. And wits? "What is this, sir?" Everard blustered. "We're guests of his Grace. Have you forgotten?"

"Quiet. Keep your hands before you. Come out in the corridor."

It gave room for shaft weapons. The point of a halberd hovered close to Everard's throat. A jab would kill him as effectively as a pistol shot, and much less noisily. Giacomo stepped back a few paces. "Sinibaldo, Hermann." His voice held soft, nonetheless carried down the stone space. "Go behind them, each taking one. Remove those medallions they wear around their necks, beneath their clothes." To the prisoners: "Resist, and you die."

"Our communicators," Novak whispered in Temporal. "Hall won't know where we are or, or anything."

"None of your secret tongues," Giacomo snapped. With a grin whose stiffness might bespeak tightly controlled fear: "We'll be hearing secrets aplenty from you erelong."

"Those are reliquaries," Everard said desperately. "Would you rob us of our sacred things? Beware God's wrath, sir."

"Sacred to a heresy, or to witchcraft?" Giacomo retorted. "I've had you watched closer than you know. You've been seen muttering at them, not in any way a man would pray to a saint. What were you invoking?"

"It's an Icelandic custom." Everard felt a hand at his neck. He felt the object slide upward across his chest, the chain pass over his head. The guardsman took his knife as well and immediately withdrew.

"We'll find out. Come along, now. Quietly."

"By what right do you violate the emperor's hospitality toward us?" Everard demanded.

"You are spies, belike sorcerers. You lie about whence you came." Giacomo lifted his free hand. "No, silence, I say." He must, though, want to try breaking down resistance at once, by a showdown. "I had my suspicions from the first. Your tale did not quite ring true. I know somewhat about those parts you claim to be from, you who call yourself Munan. You are sly, clever enough to hoodwink Piero della Vigna, unless you are in his pay. So I called your companion to me, and from him coaxed what he knows." A low, triumphant laugh. "What he *claims* he knows. You landed in Denmark, you say, Munan, and found him there, where he had been for some time. Yet he spoke of strife between the king and his brother, the king and the bishops."

"Oh, God, sir," Novak moaned in Temporal, "I didn't know any better, and I tried to play ignorant, but—" Before Giacomo could tell him to shut up, he steadied himself and said in German: "Sir, I'm a plain soldier. What do I know of these things?"

"You would know whether or not there was war in the air."

We're so few left in the Patrol, tumbled through Everard. *We couldn't think of everything. Karel was given a rough knowledge of Danish history in this period, but it was our history, where the sons of Valdemar II fell out with each other, and the king antagonized the bishops by wanting to tax the churches to raise money for the fight. In this world, yeah, I guess Frederick, making Germany into more than an unwieldy, unstable coalition, scared the Danes so they're hanging together.*

Tears stood in Novak's eyes. "I'm sorry, sir," he mumbled.

"Not your fault," Everard answered. *You couldn't help it that a smart, knowledgeable man trapped you. You were never recruited or trained for intelligence-type work.*

"I arrest you at once, lest you work your evil," Giacomo said. "His Grace is busied, I hear, but he shall be informed at the first opportunity, and will surely himself wish to know whom you serve and why . . . and if that be a foreigner."

Piero della Vigna, Everard realized. *This guy's bitter rival. Sure, Giacomo would love to get something incriminating on Piero. And maybe his notions aren't altogether paranoid. In the end, in my world, Frederick did decide that Piero had betrayed him.*

A knowledge more chilling struck home: *Giacomo, Lorenzo's descendant. It's as if this warped continuum were defending its existence—reaching through Lorenzo, who begot it, beyond his grave to us.* He looked into Giacomo's eyes and saw death.

"You've delayed overmuch," the nobleman said. "Move!"

Everard's shoulders slumped. "We're innocent, sir. Let me speak with the emperor." *Fat lot of use that'll be, except to bring on another round of torture. Where'll we go afterward, to the gallows, the block, or the stake?*

Giacomo turned and started for the stairs. Everard shambled behind, next to a more resolutely walking Novak. The two men with falchions flanked them, the halberdiers took the rear.

Everard swung his arm up. He brought the edge of that palm down in a karate chop on his right-hand guard's neck.

At once he whirled. The halberdier at his back shouted and lowered his weapon. Everard's arm parried the shaft. It cost him a bruise, but then he was at close quarters. He drove the heel of his hand under the man's nose. He felt bone splinter, driven into the brain.

Surprise, and martial arts that wouldn't be known even in Asia for a long time to come. They weren't sufficient by themselves. Two men-at-arms sprawled dead, dying, knocked out, whatever. The other two, and Giacomo, had bounded clear. Novak grabbed the dropped falchion. Everard went for the halberd. The second pole arm chopped. It could have taken his hand off. He jerked clear. Sparks flashed where steel hit stone.

"Help!" Giacomo shouted. "Murder! Treason! Help!" Never mind confidentiality any more. These were outlanders, commoners, who had stricken two of the emperor's men. His remaining followers took up the cry.

Everard and Novak pelted toward the landing. Giacomo slipped aside. Along the corridor in either direction, people were emerging from rooms. "We'll never make it like this," Everard got out between breaths.

"You go on," Novak rasped. "I'll keep them busy."

They were at the head of the stairs. He stopped, turned about, brandished his blade. "You'll be killed," Everard protested.

"We'll both be if you don't run while you have the chance, you fool. You know how to end this damned world. I don't." Sweat runneled over Novak's cheeks and made his hair lank, but he grinned.

"Then it'll never have been. You won't exist any more."

"How's that different from the usual death? Run, I tell you!" Novak crouched where he stood. His sword flickered to and fro. Giacomo harangued the men who were appearing. Others must also hear a little, on the lower level. They'd hesitate, uncertain, for a minute or two, no longer.

"God bless," Everard choked, and sprang down the stairs. *I'm not abandoning him,* he pleaded before his heart. *He's right, we've each of us a special duty, me to bring this knowledge to the Patrol and make use of it.*

Knowledge smote: *No! We should've thought of this right away, but the hurry— Once I've gotten to Jack, we should be able to rescue Karel.* If *he stays alive for the next five minutes or so. I can't reappear any sooner, or I'd risk upsetting my own escape, and God damn it, I do have this duty.*

Hang in there, Karel.

Out the rear door, into the garden. Uproar loudened behind him. He passed a young man and woman in the twilight, maybe the minnesinger and his sweetie. "Call the guards," he told them in Italian as he pounded by. "A riot yonder. I'm off for help." Multiply the confusion.

Approaching the gate, he slowed to a halt. The sentries there had not heard anything yet. He hoped they wouldn't notice how he smelled. "Good evening," he said casually and sauntered on, as if bound for a party or an assignation.

When beyond their view, he took to the byways. Dusk deepened. He could reach a city portal before closing time and, if questioned, talk his way through. He wasn't glib by nature, but he'd learned assorted fox-tricks, as Karel never did. By morning the hunt for him would be ranging across the countryside. He'd need his woodcraft, and probably two or three days, to stay free till he reached the dell where Jack Hall waited—by then, worried half loco.

After that, he thought, *things will really get hairy.*

1146 A.D.

I

"Tamberly checking in. Volstrup isn't here, he's with some of the men guests, but I'm alone in our room and taking this chance to call. We're both okay."

"Hi, Wanda."

"Manse! Is that you? How are you? How've you been? Oh, it's good to hear your voice!"

"And yours, honey. I'm here with Agop Mikelian, your contact. Will you have a few uninterrupted minutes?"

"Should. Wait, I'll bar the door to make certain. . . . Manse, listen, we've found out that Lorenzo de Conti is alive and getting set to marry—"

"I know. And I've confirmed uptime that he's the figure on whom everything turns, has been turning and will be, unless we put a stop to it. The information damn near cost Karel Novak his life."

"Oh, no."

"Well, he covered my retreat. Once I'd reached the hopper, Jack and I doubled back downtime and snatched him out of the fracas he was in. That isn't a history we care about preserving."

"Your tone of voice— It was a near thing for you, wasn't it, Manse?"

"Never mind. I'm unhurt, if that's what's fretting you. Tell you all about it later. Have you anything new to report?"

"Well, uh, yesterday Bartolommeo Conti de Segni arrived, as per invitation."

"Huh?"

"You remember, don't you? You're the one who told me about him. He's a cousin or something. Young, bachelor. Seems in a pretty sour mood. My impression is, he'd hoped to marry Ilaria. It'd be a useful alliance for his family."

"That figures. He's got to be the man who did marry her, in our history, and fathered Pope Gregory. What we have to do is clear Lorenzo out of the way. Fast. I hear the wedding's set for next week. —Wanda? Wanda?"

"Yes. I— Manse, you aren't thinking . . . you can't be—to off him?"

"I hate the notion too. Have we any choice, though? It can be instant, painless, not a mark on the body; neural projector, stop his heart, like switching off a light. Everybody will suppose it was natural. They'll grieve, but life will go on. Our people's life, Wanda."

"*No*. Prevent this marriage of his, sure. We must be able to finagle that somehow. But murder him? I, I can't believe that's you talking."

"I wish to God it weren't."

"Then talk different, damn you."

"Wanda, listen. He's too dangerous. It isn't his fault, but I discovered at Frederick's court he's the focus of, of chaos. So many world lines come together with his that—even his great-grandson nearly ruined our mission; would have, except for Karel. Lorenzo's got to go."

"You listen, Manson Everard. Kidnap him or whatever, fine—"

"What kind of trouble might his sudden disappearance bring on? I tell you, the entire future is balanced in Anagni this month. On him. I didn't know any better, so I didn't make sure of him at Rignano, and look what's come of that. We've no right to take any more unnecessary chances. Don't forget, I like him. This hurts like cancer."

"Shut up. Let me finish. I'm in a position to help you pull off a smooth operation. I don't think you can do it without me. And *you* better not think I'll make myself a party to murder. He—we can't—"

"Hey, Wanda, don't cry."

"I'm not! I, I— Okay, Ev-Ev-Everard. Take it or leave it. Haul me up for insubordination if you want. Whatever they do to me, I ought to have a lot of years left to spend despising you."

—

"Manse? Are . . . you there yet?"

"Yeah. Been thinking. Look, I'm not so weak or selfish I can't shoulder guilt if necessary. But will you believe me when I say it'd have been easier to die there with Karel? If we really can find some other way that doesn't spawn still a third monster, why, Wanda, I'll be in your debt to the bounds of infinity and the end of eternity."

"Manse, Manse! I knew you'd agree!"

"Easy, gal. No promises, except to try my damnedest. We'll see what we can figure out. Suggestions?"

"I'll have to think. It, uh, it's a question of what will work on him, isn't it? His psychology. Intuitive stuff. But I have gotten to know him pretty well."

"Really?"

"Yes, he's been giving me quite a play. I've never had my virtue more delightfully threatened."

"Oh?"

"Don't you see, that's why I can't go along with— If he were just a charming rascal, I might. But he's for real. Honest, brave, loyal, no matter how wrongheaded his causes may be; not well educated by our standards, but with as much life between his ears as any man I've ever met."

"Well, let's both consider how we might use these many qualities of his, and get back to each other tomorrow."

"Why, Manse! Did I catch a note of jealousy?"

II

Master Emilius van Waterloo explained that he was indisposed and had best take to his bed. He wished to make certain he would be in condition to attend the wedding mass and feast three days hence. Sir Lorenzo found goodwife Walburga moping in the solarium. "Wherefore so disconsolate, my lady?" he asked. "Surely it's but a slight malady your man suffers."

"God willing." She sighed. "But—forgive my worldliness—I looked forward more than you know to that outing you spoke of."

"I understand." His gaze ranged over her. Flowing garb did not hide litheness and fullness. From beneath the headcovering peeped a lock or two of golden hair. "One such as you, youthful, far-traveled, must come to feel penned between these walls amidst the clucking of lesser women. I too, Walburga, often and often."

She regarded him wistfully. "You see deeper and kindlier than I would ever have thought a great warrior could."

He smiled. "Well, later I'll take you forth, I swear."

"Alas, make no promises you cannot keep. You shall be wedded, with better duties, while we—we must not presume longer on your father. Straightaway after the joyous day, we start homeward." Tamberly dropped her glance. "I will always remember."

"Uhm, uhm!" He cleared his throat. "My lady, if this is improper, tell me, but . . . perhaps you might grant me the pleasure of escorting you, at least, tomorrow?"

"Oh, you— You overwhelm me, sir." *Am I laying it on too thick? How should I know? He doesn't seem to mind.* "Surely your time is more valuable than— No, but I've come to know you somewhat. You say what you mean. Yes, I'll ask my husband, and believe he will be pleased and honored. Though not as much as me."

Lorenzo flourished a bow. "Threefold are the pleasure and honor mine."

They talked on, merrily, till evening. Conversation with him was easy to maintain, despite his curiosity about the lands she claimed to have come from and to have seen. Like practically every man, he could be steered onto discoursing of himself. Unlike most, he made it interesting.

When at length she returned to her quarters, she found Volstrup staring at the ceiling by the light of a single candle. "How goes it?" she asked in Temporal.

"Incredibly tediously," he answered. "I never before appreciated what a blessing printing, an abundance of books, is." Wryly: "Well, needs must. I have thoughts for company." He sat up. Excitement trembled: "What have you to tell?"

She laughed. "Exactly what we hoped. He'll take me out to the woods in the morning. If you give permission, of course."

"I doubt he expects me to object. It's obvious that I've gained a reputation for, m-m, complaisance." The little man wrinkled his brows. "But you, aren't you afraid at all? Do be careful. Matters can too quickly get out of hand."

"No, I am not afraid, unless afraid that they won't."

Did he blush? The light was too dim to be sure. *Shameless hussy, he must be thinking. Poor guy. Suddenly I wonder how easy this sleep-naked-beside-but-don't-touch business has been for him. Well, one way or another, by tomorrow we should be about at the end of it.* Tamberly's skin tingled. Taking forth her communicator, she called Everard. They spoke fast and to the point.

Odd, how readily she fell asleep. It was a light sleep, alive with dreams, but at dawn she woke refreshed. "Loaded for bear!" she exclaimed.

"Pardon me?" asked Volstrup.

"Nothing. Wish me luck." When she was prepared to leave, impulse took hold. She leaned over and brushed lips across his. "Take care, old dear."

Lorenzo waited downstairs, at a table whereon was set the usual meager, coffeeless breakfast. "We will eat better at midday," he promised. Blitheness danced in his voice. Every gesture was full of the Italian extravagance and grace. "A shame, that no eyes but mine shall savor the feast you spread for them; yet am I selfishly glad of it."

"Please, sir, you grow bold." *Would a medieval Flemish woman really talk like a Victorian novel? Well, he doesn't seem to mind.*

"Bold in the cause of truth, my lady."

As a matter of fact, Tamberly had taken some trouble with her riding habit, lacing the bodice tighter than was quite comfortable, arranging the drape of sleeves and skirts just so; and blue was her best color. She didn't look as dashing as Lorenzo—elbow-length red cape over richly embroidered gold-and-green tunic halfway to the knees, sword at bronze-buckled belt of chased leather, russet hose (matching his eyes) cut to bring out the shapeliness of thigh and calf, curly-toed red shoes—but she was no drab little hen to his rooster, either.

A stab of pity: *Poor Ilaria. Quiet, shy, sort of homely, meant for a pledge of alliance, a mother, a chatelaine; and here I come along and take up most of her betrothed's attention. . . . But it's nothing remarkable in this day and age; and maybe I'm kidding myself, but I've gotten a body-language impression that Bartolommeo does care about her as a person, at least a little bit; and—and whatever happens, I am not conniving at an assassination.*

Horses were ready in the street outside. Lorenzo had spoken imprecisely when he implied lunch would be *tête-à-tête*. Even here, that would occasion some scandal. Two attendants, man and wife, were in charge of supplies and of service in general. Sometime during the day, Tamberly needed to be alone with the knight. If he didn't take the initiative about that, she must, and wasn't sure how. Preferring her relationships straightforward, she had never gone in for seductiveness. But she didn't believe it would be required.

Still, when she mounted and settled herself—no prissiness about sidesaddles—it didn't hurt to show a little snugly stockinged leg, did it?

Hoofs clattered on cobbles. As they left the city gates and city smells behind, Tamberly caught her breath. Sunlight torrented from the east. Downhill the land tumbled away in heights and hollows, brightness and shadow, valley where streams threaded with silver a patchwork quilt of fields, orchards, vineyards. Villages nestled white. She glimpsed two distant castles. Above and beyond the farms, wild brown pasture mingled with remnants of forest, among whose greens lay the first faint tints of autumn. Birds winged and cried multitudinous overhead. The air was cool but rapidly warming, overwhelmingly pure.

"How beautiful," Tamberly said. "We have nothing like this in our flat Flanders." *We do in my California.*

"I will show you a glen where a waterfall sings and little fishes play beneath like shooting stars," Lorenzo replied. "The trees are pillars and arches whereunder you will think you spy wood nymphs aflit. Who knows? Perhaps they linger in that place."

Tamberly recalled Everard remarking that people in the Dark Ages had little appreciation of nature. By the high Middle Ages, it was tamed enough for them to enjoy. Maybe Lorenzo was a bit ahead of his time. . . . Everard— She thrust guilt from her. Tension, too. *Be Zen. Take this pleasure you've got around you while it lasts. Let the duty lying ahead do no more than sharpen it. After all, what a challenge!*

Lorenzo whooped. He touched heels to his mount and started off at a reckless canter. Tamberly kept up. She was a pretty good rider herself. Soon they must have mercy on the servants bouncing behind and slow down. They looked at each other and laughed.

Time went, along winding trails, in rhythms of muscle and deep-drawn breath, creak and jingle, tang from leather and sweat and woodland, vistas intimate or enormous, brief words and, from him, longer snatches of song. "In green and in joy did we lie. 'Tilirra!' the nightingale—"

She judged that about two hours had passed when he reined in. The forest path they were following passed a meadow where a brook tinkled. "Here shall we take our repast," he said.

Tamberly's pulse briefly wavered. "But it's early yet."

"I meant not to ride us saddlesore. Rather, I would fain give you close memories of our land to take home."

With a conscious effort, Tamberly fluttered her lashes. "As my guide wishes. You have never chosen ill, sir."

"If I do well, it is because the company inspires me." He swung from his seat and reached a hand to help her dismount. The clasp lingered. "Marco, Bianca," he directed, "prepare things, but you may take your ease about it. I mean first to show my lady the Apollo bower. She may well desire to stay a while."

"Master commands," the man said impassively. The woman bobbed and couldn't quite suppress a giggle. Yes, they knew what Sir Lorenzo intended, and that they'd better keep mouths shut afterward.

He offered Tamberly his arm. They strolled away. She put hesitancy into her tone. "The bower of Apollo, sir? Isn't that . . . heathen?"

"Oh, no doubt it was sacred to some god in olden times, and if that wasn't Apollo it should have been," her companion replied. "Thus young folk name it these days, for the sun and life, beauty and happiness there. We, though, should have it to ourselves. Surely the next who come will find a new magic."

He continued stringing out his line as they walked. She'd heard much worse. He also had the wit to fall silent now and then, letting her savor the unquestionable charm of the path. Narrow, so that they must go close together, it followed the streambed uphill. Trunks soared to a ceiling of yellow and gold. Sunbeams flecked shade. This late in the year, birdsong was ended, but she heard calls, while squirrels darted fiery and once a deer bolted. The morning grew steadily warmer; the trail steepened. He helped her doff her mantle and folded it over his left arm.

A clear, rushing sound grew louder. They came into another opening. Tamberly clapped palms together and cried out in genuine delight. Beyond, the water tumbled and sparkled down a bluff. Woods ringed and partly roofed the glade through which it ran onward. Turf on either side remained green and soft, richly edged with moss. "Well," Lorenzo asked, "have I redeemed my promise?"

"A thousand times over."

"To hear you say that pleases me more than a battlefield victory. Come, drink if you are thirsty, sit down"—Lorenzo spread her cloak on the ground—"and we will thank God for His bounty by taking our pleasure in it."

I think he means that, flitted through her. *He does have his very serious side; yes, real depths in him, which it would be . . . interesting to explore*. She chuckled inwardly, dryly. *However, the observance he has in mind today is not religious, and that cloth isn't laid for purposes of sitting on*.

Tension seized her. *This is the time!*

Lorenzo gave her a close regard. "My lady, are you faint? You've turned pale." He took her hand. "Rest yourself. We need not go back for hours."

Tamberly shook her head. "No, I thank you, I am quite well." She realized she was muttering and raised her voice. "Bear with me a moment. I've vowed a daily devotion to my patron saint while on this journey." Sending a slow look his way: "If I perform it not at once, I fear I might forget later."

"Why, of course." He stood aside and took his plumed cap off.

For this occasion she had been wearing her communicator out in the open. She raised the disc to her lips and thumbed the switch. "Wanda here," she said in American English; Temporal sounded too alien. She heard her heartbeat louder than the words. "I think the situation is set up, just about how we hoped. He and I are alone in the hills and, well, if he isn't pawing the ground it's because his tactics are smoother than that. Get a fix on my location and give me, m-m, let's say fifteen minutes for things to get lively. Okay?" Not that Everard could respond without derailing the plan. "Out." She switched off, lowered the medallion, bowed her head, crossed herself. "Amen."

Lorenzo made the sign likewise. "Was that your native tongue wherein you prayed?" he asked.

Tamberly nodded. "The dialect of my childhood. It feels more, more comfortable thus. Mine is a motherly saint." She laughed. "I feel purified enough to be ready for mischief."

He frowned. "Beware. That edges the Catharist heresy."

"I did but jest, my lord."

He put his doctrines aside and smiled like the sunshine on the water. "Yon's an unusual badge. Has it a relic inside? May I see?"

Taking consent for granted, he laid hold of the chain, his fingers brushing across her breasts, and lifted it over her head. The case bore in low relief a cross on one side, a crozier and flask on the other. "Exquisite work," he murmured. "Almost worthy of the wearer." He hung it from a nearby twig.

Unease touched her. "If you please, sir." She moved to retrieve the thing.

He moved into her way. "You don't want it back immediately, do you?" he purred. "No, you're overdressed for this air, I see perspiration on that white skin; let me help you to freshness."

His palms cradled her cheeks, slid along them, displaced the cloth that covered her head. "What gold blazes forth," he breathed, and drew her to him.

"My lord," she gasped as a proper woman ought, "what is this? Bethink you—" She kept back the martial arts, and strained only slightly against his strength. His body was hard and supple. The musk on his breath, the springiness of mustache and beard, made awareness whirl. He knew how to kiss, he did.

"No," she protested weakly when his mouth strayed down her throat, "this is wrong, it's mortal sin. Let me go, I pray you."

"It is right, natural, my fate and yours," he insisted. "Walburga, Walburga, your beauty has raised me to the gates of Heaven. Cast me not thence into hell."

"But I, I must depart erelong—"

"Cherishing forever the same memories that shall bear me onward through the crusade and the rest of my days on earth. Deny not Cupid, here in his own abode."

How often has he said the same? He's practiced in it, all right. Does he mean it? Well, a little, I suppose. And, and I've got to keep him on the hook till Manse arrives with the gaff. Whatever that takes. I thought fifteen minutes was safe, but golly, this is like shooting rapids.

Before long—though time was a tumult—she didn't beg him to stop. She did try to keep his hands from going quite everywhere. That effort faded fast. Suddenly she noticed they were down on the cloak and he was ruffling her skirts past her knees and *well, if this is how it is, I could make a lot worse sacrifices for the cause.*

Air banged. "Sinner, beware!" roared Everard. "Hell gapes for you!"

Lorenzo rolled clear of Tamberly and bounded to his feet. Her first, confused thought was, *Oh, damn.* She sat up, too shaky and pulse-pounding to rise immediately.

Everard brought his timecycle to earth, got off, and loomed. A white robe covered his burliness. Great wings rose iridescent-feathered from his shoulders. Radiance framed his head. He was almighty homely for an angel, she confessed; but maybe that gave a convincing force to the illusions that a Patrol photon twister generated.

The crucifix in his right hand was solid. Within it, she knew, was embedded a stun gun. He'd told her he probably wouldn't need the weapon. Their badger game ought to work. He and Keith Denison had pulled a similar stunt in ancient Iran, and thereby straightened out a lesser historical mess than this.

"Lorenzo de Conti, most wicked among men," he intoned in Umbrian, "would you besmirch the honor of your guests on the very eve of your wedding to a pure and trusting maiden? Know that you damn far more than your wretched self."

The knight lurched back, aghast. "I meant no harm!" he wailed. "The woman tempted me!"

Tamberly decided that disappointment was an inappropriate reaction.

Lorenzo forced his gaze to Everard's countenance. He had never seen it before, though the Patrolman knew his well, from a time line annulled. He doubled his fists, squared his shoulders, drew a sobbing breath. "No," he said. "I spoke falsely. The fault is none of hers. I lured her here intending sin. Let the punishment be mine alone."

Tears stung Tamberly's eyes. *I'm twice as glad we're letting him live.*

"Well spoken," Everard declared, poker-faced. "It shall be remembered when judgment is passed."

Lorenzo wet his lips. "But, but why us—me?" he croaked. "The thing must happen a thousand times daily around the world. Why does Heaven care so much? Is she—is she a saint?"

"That is a question for God," Everard answered. "You, Lorenzo, have transgressed greatly because His intentions for you were great. The Holy Land is falling to the paynim and in danger of being altogether lost because those Christians who have held it under Him have fallen from righteousness, until their presence profanes the sacred shrines. How can a sinner redeem them?"

The knight staggered where he stood. "Do you mean that I—"

"You are called to the crusade. You could have waited, preparing your soul within the peace of matrimony, until the German king marches. Now your penance is that you renounce this bridal and go to him at once."

"Oh, no—"

A terrible disruption and fuss, especially if he dares not explain why to anybody but his priest. Poor, spurned Ilaria. Poor old Cencio. I wish we could've done this different. Tamberly had proposed taking Lorenzo back in time and making him decline the proffered marriage at the outset. Everard had responded, "Don't you understand yet how precarious the balance of events is? You've talked me into the biggest gamble I can possibly square with my conscience."

To Lorenzo: "You have your orders, soldier. Obey them, and thank God for His mercy."

The man stood still an instant. Something cold stirred along Tamberly's nerves. He was a child of his era, but tough and smart and not naive about human things. "On your knees!" she urged, and rose to hers, hands clasped before her.

"Yes. Yes." He stumbled toward the angelic form. "God show me what is right. Christ strengthen my will and my sword arm."

He knelt before Everard, clasped the Patrolman's legs, laid his head against the shining robe.

"Enough," said Everard awkwardly. "Go and sin no more."

Lorenzo released him, lifted his arms as if to implore. Then in an instant he brought his left hand down, a vicious chop, across Everard's right knuckles. The crucifix spun free of that grasp. Lorenzo well-nigh flew erect, leaped back. His blade hissed from the sheath. Sunlight burned along the steel.

"Angel?" he shouted. "Or demon?"

"What the hell?" Everard moved to regain his stunner.

Lorenzo pounced, blocked the way. "Hold where you are, or I hew," rattled from him. "Say forth . . . your true nature . . . and be gone to your rightful place."

Everard braced himself. "Dare you defy Heaven's messenger?"

"No. If that is what you are. God help me, I must know."

It whirled through Tamberly: *He's alerted. How? I do recall, yes, Manse said there are stories about devils disguising themselves to entrap people, yes, even taking on the appearance of Jesus. If Lorenzo got a suspicion—*

"Merely behold me," Everard said.

"I have felt you," Lorenzo snarled.

Uh-huh, Tamberly realized. *Angels aren't supposed to have geni-*

tals, are they? Oh, we're dealing with somebody brilliant as well as fearless. No wonder the whole future turns on him.

She went to all fours. The stunner lay about ten feet from her. If Everard could hold Lorenzo's attention while she sneaked across to it, maybe they could still save their plan.

"Why should Satan want you to go on crusade?" the Patrolman argued.

"Lest I be of service here? If Roger the wolf decides to rob us of more than Sicily?" Lorenzo looked skyward. "Lord," he appealed, "am I in error? Grant me a sign."

Manse can't so much as flap those wings.

Everard darted for his vehicle. On it he'd be in control of everything. Lorenzo yelled, sprang at him, slashed. Everard barely dodged. Blood welled over the torn robe, from a cut deep in his right shoulder and down the chest.

"There's my sign!" Lorenzo howled. "No demon, you, nor angel. Die, wizard!"

His rush sent Everard in retreat from the cycle, with not a second free to take out his communicator and summon help. Tamberly scrambled for the stunner. She laid hands around it, jumped to her feet, found that she didn't know how to work it in its disguise.

"You too?" screamed Lorenzo. "Witch!"

He bounded at her. The sword flamed on high. Fury writhed inhuman over the face.

Everard attacked. His right arm lamed, he had only time before the blade fell to hit with his left fist. The blow smote under the angle of the jaw, all his muscle and desperation behind it. A *crack* resounded.

The sword arced loose, glittering like water flung down the fall. Lorenzo went a yard, bonelessly tossed, before he crashed.

"Are you okay, Wanda?" jerked out of Everard's throat.

"Yes, I, I'm not hurt, but—him?"

They went to see. Lorenzo lay crumpled, unstirring, eyes wide to the sky. The mouth hung horribly open, tongue protruding above a displaced chin. His head was cocked at a nasty angle.

Everard hunkered down, examined him, rose. "Dead," he told her slowly. "Broken neck. I didn't intend that. But he'd've killed you."

"And you. Oh, Manse." She laid her head on his bloody breast. His left arm embraced her.

After a while he said, "I've got to return to base and have them patch me up before I pass out."

"Can you . . . take him along?"

"And get him revived and repaired? No. Too dangerous in every way. This surprise we've had—it should never have happened. Hardly made sense, did it? But . . . the tide was carrying him . . . trying to preserve its twisted future— Let's hope we've broken the spell at last."

He moved unsteadily toward the cycle. His words came ever more harsh and faint, through lips turning grayish. "If it'll help you any, Wanda—I didn't tell you before, but in . . . the Frederick world . . . when he went crusading, he died of sickness. I suspect . . . he would've . . . again. Fever, vomiting, diarrhea, helplessness. He deserved this way, no?"

Everard let Tamberly assist him into the saddle. A little strength returned to his voice. "You've got to play the game out. Run back screaming. Tell how you were set upon by robbers. The blood— He'll've wounded one or two. Since you escaped, they decided they'd better scram. People will honor his memory in Anagni. He died like a knight, defending a lady."

"Uh-huh." *And Bartolommeo will press his suit, and before long marry the hero's sorrowing bride*. "Just a minute." She scampered to the sword, brought it back, rubbed it over his red-drenched garment. "Bandit blood."

He smiled a bit. "Bright girl," he whispered.

"On your way, boy. Quick." She gave him a hasty kiss and moved backward. Vehicle and man vanished.

She stood alone with the corpse and the sun, the sword yet in her clasp. *I'm sort of gory myself*, she thought in a remote fashion. Setting her teeth, she made a pair of superficial cuts above her left ribs. Nobody would examine or question her closely. Detective methods belonged to the distant morrow, her tomorrow, if it existed. In Cencio's house grief would overwhelm thought, until pride brought its stern consolations.

She knelt, closed Lorenzo's fingers around the hilt, wanted to shut the eyes but decided better not. "Goodbye," she said under her breath. "If there is a God, I hope He makes this up to you."

Rising, she started back toward the meadow and the tasks that still awaited her.

1990 A.D.

He phoned her at her parents' house, where she was spending her furlough. She didn't want him to call for her there. It already hurt, lying as much as she must. They met downtown next morning, in the anachronistic opulence of the St. Francis Hotel lobby. For a moment they stood, hands joined, looking.

"I think you want to get away," he finally said.

"Yes," she admitted. "If we could be somewhere in the open?"

"Good idea." He smiled. "I see you're wearing warm clothes and brought a jacket. Me too."

He had a car in the Union Square garage. They spoke little while they bucked through traffic and crossed the Golden Gate Bridge. "You're fully recovered?" she asked once.

"Yes, yes," he assured her. "Long since. It took me several weeks of lifespan before things were reorganized enough that I could take this leave."

"History is back as it ought to be? Everywhere and everywhen?"

"So I am told, and what I've seen for myself bears it out." Everard glanced from the steering wheel to her. Sharply: "Have you noticed any difference?"

"No, none, and I came here . . . watchful, afraid."

"Like maybe you'd find your father an alcoholic or your sister never born or something? You needn't have worried. The continuum doesn't take long to regain its form, right down to the finest details." That didn't really make sense in English, but by tacit agreement they were avoiding Temporal. "And the crux of what happened—what we kept from happening—lies eight hundred years behind us."

"Yes."

"You don't sound overjoyed."

"I am—I'm glad, grateful, you've come to me this soon on my own lifeline."

"Well, you told me the date you'd arrive. I figured I should allow you a couple of days to be with your folks and unwind. Doesn't seem you have."

"Could we talk later?" Tamberly switched the radio on and tuned in to KDFC. Mozart lilted around them.

Today was a midweek early in January, overcast and chill. When they reached Highway One, theirs was almost the sole car winding north upon it. In Olema they bought a takeout lunch of sandwiches and beer. At Point Reyes Station he turned into the national seashore. Beyond Inverness they had the great sweep of land practically to themselves. He parked at the coast. They made their way down to the beach and walked along it. Her hand found his.

"What's haunting you?" he asked after a while.

"You know, Manse," she said, "you observe a lot more and a lot closer than you let on."

The wind nearly stole her words from him, as low as they were. It shrilled and boomed above rumbling surf, sheathed faces in cold, laid salt on lips, ruffled hair. Gulls took off, soared, mewed. The tide was flowing but had not yet come far in and they walked on the darkened solidity of the wet sand. Occasionally underfoot a shell crunched, a kelp bladder popped. On their right, and immensely ahead and behind, dry dunes lapped the cliffs. On their left the maned waves marched inward from the edge of sight. A single ship yonder looked very alone. The world was all whites and silvery grays.

"Naw, I'm just an old roughneck," Everard said. "You're the sensitive one." He hesitated. "Lorenzo—is that the trouble? The first violent death, maybe the first death of any kind, of a human, that you ever saw?"

She nodded. Her neck felt stiff.

"I thought so," he said. "It's always hideous. You know, that's what's obscene about the violence on the screens these days. They gloat over the messiness, like Romans watching gladiators, but they ignore—maybe the producers are too stupid to imagine, maybe they haven't the balls to imagine—the real meaning. Which is a life, a mind, a whole world of awareness, stamped out, forever."

Tamberly shivered.

"Nevertheless," Everard went on, "I've killed before, and probably I will again. I wish to Christ things were otherwise, but they aren't, and I can't afford to brood over it. Nor can you. Sure, you'd grown fond of Lorenzo. So had I. We wanted to spare his life. We believed we could. Things got away from us. And our first duty was, is, to everybody and everything we really love. Right? Okay, Wanda, you've had a horrible experience, but you came through like a trouper, and you're too healthy not to start putting it behind you."

She stared down the empty miles before her. "I know," she answered. "I'm doing that much."

"But?"

"But we didn't only kill a man—cause his death—get ourselves involved in his death. We destroyed how many hundreds of billions?"

"And restored how many? Wanda, those worlds we saw never existed. We and some others in the Patrol carry memories; a few of us carry scars; a few lost their own lives. Regardless, what we remember has not happened. We didn't actually abort the different futures. That's the wrong word. We kept them from ever being conceived."

She clung to his hand. "That's the horror that won't leave me," she said thinly. "At first it was theory, something they taught at the Academy along with a lot else that was much more understandable. Now I've felt it. If everything is random and causeless—if there is nothing out there, no firm reality, only a mathematical shadow show that for all we can tell keeps changing and changing and changing, with us not even dreams within it—"

Her voice had been rising into the wind. She snapped it off, gulped air, strode hard.

Everard bit his lip. "Not easy," he agreed. "You'll have to learn to accept how little we know and how much less we can ever be sure of."

They jarred to a halt. Where had the stranger been? They should have seen him from the first, he too walking by the shore, slowly, hands folded, gazing out to sea and then down to the small relics of life strewn on the beach.

"Good day," he said.

The greeting was soft, melodious, its English bearing an accent they couldn't identify. Nor were they certain, at second glance, that this was a man. A robe, cowled like a Christian monk's, dull yellow like a Buddhist's, enveloped a medium-sized frame. The face was not epicene—strong-boned, full-lipped, slightly aged—but it might be either male or female, as might the voice. Nor was the race clear; he, if he it was, seemed to blend white, black, Oriental, and more in harmony.

Everard drew a long breath. He let go of Tamberly's hand. For an instant his fists doubled. He opened them and stood not quite at attention. "How do you do," he said tonelessly.

Did the stranger address the woman more than him? "Your pardon." How mild was the smile. "I overheard your conversation. May I suggest a few thoughts?"

"You're of the Patrol," she whispered. "You've got to be, or you wouldn't have heard, nor known what it meant."

A barely perceptible shrug. Quiet, calm: "In these times, as in many elsewhen, moral relativism is the sin that besets folk of good will. They should realize, taking an example familiar today, that the death, maiming, and destruction of the Second World War were evil; so were the new tyrannies it seeded; and yet the breaking of Hitler and his allies was necessary. Humans being what they are, there is always more evil than good, more sorrow than joy; but that makes it the more needful to protect and nourish whatever gives worth to our lives.

"Some evolutions are, on balance, better than others. This is simply a fact, like the fact that some stars shine brighter than others. You have seen a Western civilization in which the Church engulfed the state, and one in which the state engulfed the Church. What you have rescued is that fruitful tension between Church and state out of which, despite every pettiness, blunder, corruption, farce, and tragedy—out of which grew the first real knowledge of the universe and the first strong ideal of liberty. For what you did, be neither arrogant nor guilt-laden; be glad."

The wind cried, the sea growled nearer.

Tamberly had never seen Everard so shaken. Somehow the word he used was right: "Rabbi, was this, this thing we went through, was it truly an accident, a quirk in the flux, that we, we had to straighten out?"

"It was. Komozino explained matters to you correctly, as far as you and she are capable of comprehension." More toward Tamberly: "Think, if you wish, of diffraction, waves reinforcing here and canceling there to make rainbow rings. It is incessant, but normally on the human level it is imperceptible. When it chanced to converge powerfully on Lorenzo de Conti, yes, then that became like a kind of fate. Do not let it overawe you that you, exercising your free will, have overcome doom itself."

She, with her background, though she knew not what she confronted, begged, "Sensei, tell me. Is that the meaning?"

A smile, a gentleness beneath which lay steel and lightning: "Yes. In a reality forever liable to chaos, the Patrol is the stabilizing element, holding time to a single course. Perhaps it is not the best course, but we are no gods to impose anything different when we know that it does at last take us beyond what our animal selves could have imagined. In truth, left untended, events would inevitably move toward the worse. A cosmos of random changes must be senseless, ultimately self-destructive. In it could be no freedom.

"Has the universe therefore brought forth sentience, in order to protect and give purpose to its own existence? That is not an answerable question.

"But take heart. Reality *is*. You are among those who guard it."

A hand lifted. "Blessing."

Everard and Tamberly stood alone.

They knew not whether she crept into his arms or he into hers. For a long time while they were in the salt wind and the warmth of each other. Finally she dared ask, "Was that?" and he answered, "Yes, surely. A Danellian. I've only met one a single time before, and that was only for a minute. You've been honored, Wanda. Never forget."

"I shan't. I have back—what I need to live by and live for."

They separated and were another while silent, moveless, beside the ocean. Then she tossed her head, laughed aloud, and cried, "Hey, boy, let's get down off this high horse. We are mere humans, aren't we? How about we enjoy it?"

His mirth, a little defensive still but not wholly, joined hers. "Yes, right, I'm hungry as a bear." All at once shy: "What'd you like to do after lunch?"

Quite steadily, she told him: "Phone home to say I'll be gone a few days. Buy toothbrushes and stuff. Winter or no, this is a lovely coast, Manse. Let me show you."